THE BYGONE WAY

JOSEPH R. LALLO

CONTENTS

Chapter 1

If you aren't moving forward, you're moving backward. It was a wisdom that had been passed down in the Masker clan for longer than anyone could recall. The truism probably had its roots deep in the Bygone Era. Different people assigned different meanings to the phrase. For Martin Masker, it was a constant reminder of two quite different but equally valuable facts of life. First, if one was not seeking to improve, one would inevitably be swallowed by the churning mists of history. Second, and at this moment far more practical to the family's needs, if he wasn't preparing new inventory, the shop was slipping backward against the current of debt.

Presently, reconciling those two interpretations of the same phrase was a bit of a balancing act. His workshop was more than adequate for someone to tinker and experiment with new contraptions. It was also quite sufficient to repair, restore, and customize contraptions for a hungry group of customers and collectors. It was *not* large enough for both. At least, not if he wanted to do things comfortably. As it so happened, comfort was seldom part of the equation for a Masker who was hard at work.

"I have run out of ink," stated Wick calmly.

"One moment and I'll have you filled up," Martin said.

For the past three weeks, he had been sharing his workshop with two rather distinctive collaborators. The smaller of the two was Oiler, laboring blissfully at Martin's feet like something between a loyal dog and an industrious assistant. Wick's lantern, one of two "artifact lanterns" that would allow Wick to persist even if the flame was extinguished, usually lived on a dedicated section of shelf over the workbench or on a shelf behind his wife while she worked the store. A bit more than a month prior, Martin had modified the bespoke bust he'd created to allow the lamp to be latched in place where a head would normally be. This allowed Wick to maintain control of a set of skillfully fabricated arms, which he'd been putting to near-constant use. A much simpler set of legs had been created, but they were hanging from a hook in the corner of the room. Wick had little cause to walk about, and articulating the lower extremities sufficiently to allow him to sit down was much more complicated than simply removing the legs and setting the bust atop a stool.

"There you are," Martin said, refilling the inkpot.

Wick dipped his quill and returned to writing. Despite being in control of a mechanical marvel, Wick didn't actually write more quickly than a skilled scribe. It was a point of pride for Tome—the resident expert in transcription—that he could fill a page in a bit more than half the time it took Wick to do so. It wasn't a matter of limitation on Wick's part. It was a combination of the durability of the writing materials and the precision of Wick's transcription. Writing at full speed caused all sorts of problems. The page was more apt to tear. The ink line grew thin and inconsistent. The pen wore out or became damaged far more often, and the ink was seldom dry when the time came to turn the page, producing a very low-quality result. Thus, Wick took his time, reproducing every serif and accent with excruciating detail. And what he lacked in speed, he made up for in stamina. Every moment that he was present in the bust, he was writing. No breaks for meals. No breaks for sleep. It made for some very productive days.

"How is the shop?" Martin asked.

"Vivian has sold the pair of twine-winders, and Epiphany is presently settling the price for a music box," Wick said.

Martin nodded and set aside the alarm box he was working on to gather up the components of a disheveled music box Fel had retrieved not two days ago. Music boxes were worth their weight in gold. It was always good to have a spare on the shelf. He took a quick inventory of the components, spotted three small gears and a linkage that were missing, and set about rummaging through his bins of materials for replacements. He'd turned up all but one of the necessary components when the ever-present serenade of the last few weeks, a scratching pen, came to a stop once more.

"Has the nib worn down again?" Martin asked without looking.

"No. I have completed the task. I thank you for presenting it to me; it has been a thoroughly rewarding service to fulfill."

"Have you?" Martin said with excitement. "Here you are, Oiler. Get started with that. You should be able to get it together save for that last gear."

He set down the materials like a bowl of treats. Oiler chimed contentedly and started aligning parts and pressing them into place. Martin dusted his hands and turned his attention to the stack of journals that had been making his shop an increasingly cramped place to work.

"Forty-five... fifty... fifty-five... It's only taken you fifty-eight volumes? Last time it took eighty," Martin said.

"I found I was able to write somewhat smaller, and with less space between lines, and still produce a fully legible result."

"Splendid. Splendid. That will make Tome happy. Fewer books to lug along on his journey." He turned the pages, reviewing the work of the last few hours. "Which I suppose can now begin whenever he is ready. And this hasn't been too taxing for you?"

"No, Martin. The only challenging aspect has been the struggle to pull myself from one task long enough to complete another. In my role as a sentry, I find myself able to scrutinize the work with minute detail for however long I am required to, and to flick from perch to perch with clockwork-precise timing. When I am writing, it requires constant mindful effort to remember that I must remove myself from the task long enough to glance through the other flames and assess what if anything is needed. The work demands my focus in a way that no other task ever has."

"A struggle I know all too well. I'd love to tell you that you'll get that under control in time, but I've been at this for decades and I would still neglect meals if I wasn't reminded. But now that the job is done, it is probably best if you send word to Fel and Tome so they can start to prepare."

"Another service I will be happy to fulfill," Wick said.

"Hey! If you're here to watch the game, at least order a drink. You're clogging the place up for everyone else," Allie barked.

The idea had been a simple one, and one that Tem had been pushing for ages. A big grum tournament. It was not so much about the money—there were higher-stakes games a few times a week at the normal tables. This one was about pride and bragging rights. Tem had been talking a big game and rubbing his wins in Fel's face for long enough that the already short temper of the contraptioneer had reached its limit. One massive tournament. Winner takes the pot, the trophy that Fel hand-made out of antique scraps his father couldn't find use for, and most importantly of all, the title of Best Grum Player In Town.

Over the course of six days, a dozen tables of players—practically the entire tavern—had been narrowed down to one. At the table were Fel, Tem, and Tome. Fel was lagging behind, based on the pile of duots in front of him, and Tome was in the lead. No one had expected Fel to get this far. Multiple side bets had been made that he'd be out after the first round. The smart money had been him lasting no longer than the third. But here he was, ten runs into the final round and still clinging to the game.

Every eliminated player had made an excuse to show up for what was sure to be the end of the tournament. The size of the ante was such that Fel would be out if he didn't take another win, and the way Tem played, he wouldn't last more than three more runs before he either took Tome for all he was worth or was trounced by him. Grum typically wasn't much of a game for spectators, but today even people who frequented the higher-class taverns uptown had shown up to see the simmering rivalry come to a head.

"Place your bet," Fel grumbled, drumming his fingers on the table.

"There isn't a time limit. A man is permitted to consider his options," Tome said.

"You say there's no time limit, but I'm not getting any younger. And if we don't end this run and take a break soon, Parch is going to piddle on something and we're going to face the wrath of Allie," Fel said.

"I don't know why you bring that stinky thing with you," Tem said, deftly combining two stacks of coins and splitting them apart again as a way to keep his fingers busy.

"A man's gotta have some sort of companionship that doesn't drive him up a wall," Fel said.

"So that's what it's for. Companionship. We all heard the rumors, but it's nice to have it laid out plain."

"You're going to be laid out in the back alley if you don't start watching your mouth, Tem," Fel rumbled.

"Boys," Allie said with the tone of a disapproving parent. "You're taking up seats in the tavern. If you don't play nice, I'll kick you out and you'll have to find somewhere else to settle this up. And then you won't have an audience."

Tem and Fel muttered under their breath but reined in the taunts. Tome jangled some coins.

"I bid… a thousand duots for the red king," he said.

"That'll just about clean you out," Tem said.

"I'll have enough for the opening ante of the next game," he said. "You'll recall, the people who couldn't do proper arithmetic washed out in the first round."

"Ah... you're right..." Tem jangled his own coins. "One thousand four hundred for the red king."

Tome narrowed his eyes. "You know that the people with poor memories washed out in the second round, right? You don't have anything that needs a red king to fill it out. Which means you're just trying to get me to back out entirely. Which means you know I've got the winning hand if I get that king. So there's no risk at all in raising the bid to fifteen hundred."

He pushed the entirety of his coins to the center of the table. All eyes turned to Fel.

"What are you looking at me for? I only have two hundred left. I can't outbid you," he said.

"Then let's see the tiles," Tome said.

Tem's upper lip quivered. He flipped his tiles down to reveal a run that a skilled player could see had the makings of three decent runs, but with one or two key tiles missing from each. All of that accumulated to a big pile of nothing. Tome turned to Fel. He flicked down the tiles one at a time.

"Black king, blue king, black queen, red queen, blue milkmaid," Fel said.

Fel leaned back and fixed his eyes on Tome. The tavern shook with waves of people working out what the run meant for the tournament. The run was a very good one. Not the best. If he'd had a matching set of both kings and queens, it would have been difficult to beat. But it was more than enough to beat Tem. And more to the point, the presence of a red queen meant the red king Tome had just won a very expensive bid for wasn't part of a matched set. And since Fel had both of the other kings, there wasn't a full run of any other color either. In short, nothing Tome could have would be enough for the win.

"Well..." Tome said simply. "That's it for me, then."

The Fox and Log erupted with the cheers and groans of people with a friendly or financial investment in the game coming to terms with the heap of duots sliding from Tome's winnings to Fel's. Allie watched as winnings and losses changed hands among the crowd. The money being earned on side bets was now exceeding the money up for grabs in the tournament. It was a windfall for the tavern, because there are few things a big winner wants more than to indulge in a celebratory drink. She was fielding orders two and three at a time when the lantern behind the bar went still and she heard a voice at the edge of her mind.

"Allie, I see the game is presently between runs," Wick said. "Would you mind terribly getting the attention of Fel and Tome for me?"

Allie gave a half nod. No one in the bar knew that she kept a flame lit from Wick's lantern behind the bar—not that they would have known what that meant even if she told them to their faces. Thus, she couldn't respond directly to Wick, but the flame was quite accustomed to subtle responses and interpreted the reply properly.

"I thank you very much," he said. "I hope it is not an imposition."

Allie raised her voice. "Ladies, gents, and the rest of you, I think now's as good a time as any to take a break. No fun watching the end of the tournament when the players aren't sharp, and they've been at it for a few hours too long. Maybe let's get some food down them, and give everyone a chance to buy drinks for the winner or loser of choice. Tome, Fel, get over here so folks can find you."

"What about me?" Tem said.

"You've got a loud enough mouth that I don't think anyone will have any trouble finding you," she said.

Fel and Tome got the message and wove their way to the bar, receiving backslaps of congratulation and commiseration respectively. It took a few minutes before it died down enough for them to have a moment in the glow of the flame. Fel crunched a handful of roasted crickets. Tome nursed a glass of sherry bought for him by someone who had just made a fortune betting against him.

"Fel, Tome. I hope you are well. Martin asked me to inform you that the second index is complete," Wick said.

Fel raised his eyebrows and glanced at Tome. "Tell you what, buddy," he said. "I think you and I need to have a minute alone to discuss some of the debts I can settle, now that it seems like I'll have some extra duots in my pocket when this is through. Allie, is one of the back rooms free?"

"The usual one," she said. "Here. Take the lantern. I didn't bother lighting the ones in there."

He took the lantern, and the pair wove their way through the crowd toward one of the two back rooms. Once they had slipped inside, she raised her voice.

"Tem! If you lose this thing, are you going to have the money to pay the tab you've been racking up?"

"I don't know and I don't care, because I ain't gonna lose," he called back.

"I don't know either, but I do care. Don't expect me to go easy on you out of pity!"

In the room, Fel put his feet up on the table and leaned his chair back.

"I trust the game has been going well for everyone," Wick said.

"A game never goes well for everyone," Tome grumbled.

"That ought to tell you who won the last run, Wick," Fel said.

"I see. My congratulations to you, Fel, and my condolences to you, Tome."

"Don't give him any condolences, he was trying to cheat," Fel said, with less rancor in his tone than one might expect for such a statement.

"Fel, I—" Tome began.

"Don't get me wrong," Fel interrupted. "I didn't win that run because I was skilled. I won it because I got dealt the black and blue kings in my first set, and the red queen. But that means I had the red queen the whole time, and there was no way you were putting together a winning run without it. But you bid your way all the way to that red king. You were going to pull that stunt where you were going to magic up a garbage tile to look like the red queen, weren't you?"

"I thought I'd caught a glimpse of the red queen at the bottom of the stack when it was all being dealt out. I wouldn't have tried that sort of thing if I knew you or anyone else had a chance at holding the real queen."

"'I only did it because I didn't think I'd get caught' is a pretty lousy defense, buddy. But now that you're out of it, give it to me straight. Did you cheat in any of those other games?"

"I didn't have to cheat in any of those other games," Tome said. "But I'm about to go on a trip back home, so I was hoping for some pocket money. You were already seemingly out of the game, so it was a matter of getting some money out of Tem's pocket, and that seemed reason enough to set aside my policy of foregoing mystic tactics in local games."

"I'd point out how that's not a good excuse either, but the way Tem's been making a nuisance of himself, I would have let this one slide. Enough of that, though. I just wanted to make sure you knew I knew, and if I knew, then other people might figure it out."

"All the better that I'll be gone for a few months." Tome looked to the lantern. "What was the final tally?"

"Fifty-eight books," Wick said.

"Efficient writer, eh? I'll have to take a look to make sure they're legible, but if it's that few, I can probably get away with the cart instead of the carriage." Tome crossed his arms and glanced aside. "And refresh my memory, how many book titles is that?"

"Four hundred and one thousand, five hundred and fifty-four books, in total, are within my memory. Portions of approximately two thousand more are there as well, but they have been omitted from the list."

"And how many are in languages you would not be able to translate?" Tome asked.

"Given time, I would say that I could produce a literal word-for-word translation of all but two thousand of the books. A meaningful translation that attempts to match the author's intent is something I would not feel comfortable tackling for nearly one hundred thousand of the books."

"I question the value of this trip, by the way," Fel said.

"Wick has accumulated the titles of nearly half a million books available to him by virtue of having consumed them in his flame, even if it was against his will. At his fastest, he could transcribe perhaps twenty of those books a day."

"I would estimate a more reasonable count at six per day," Wick said. "Faster than that, the quality begins to suffer and the wear becomes problematic."

"There. Six. Half a million divided by six... That's... sixty-seven thousand or so days. That's almost two hundred years of writing," Tome said. "If we are going to get the best of the information locked within Wick's mind out into the world again in our lifetimes, we'll need to translate the titles, prioritize their content, and transcribe the most valuable knowledge first. There is no one on the continent better equipped to do that sort of thing than the monks at the Gate of the Ancients Monastery."

"I thought you spent your youth mindlessly copying words without even interpreting them," Fel said.

"I did. But I was a child. There are legions of scholars with expertise in organization and translation. It will be the work of weeks for them to provide us a codified, organized, translated list."

"And who's paying for it?" Fel asked.

"My father is rather highly placed within the monastery. And they are not driven by financial gain. Not chiefly, at any rate."

"Unlike you."

"I left that place for a reason. But even though our goals don't perfectly align, this is a job that will be unbearably enticing to them. That should keep the price down." He stood. "I'll head back to the shop and take a look. For once this seems to be a trip that won't heave me headlong into the jaws of some beast or assassin, so I needn't spend much time preparing defensive and offensive spells. I can just go."

Tome headed for the door, but paused. He turned back. "I will, if you'll allow it, take one of the silver earrings," he said.

Fel laughed. "You know, I'm the one who had his head tinkered with by the clockwork diamond. Why is it that you are the one who seems most concerned about it happening to you?"

"Because unlike you, I've spent my life carefully curating and expanding the knowledge within my head, and it would be a rather significant loss, both personally and to the world, if someone were to turn a crank on a device and blot it all out to make me a farmer or a carpenter or some such. You were simply made into a more respected version of yourself. Hardly something to fear."

"There's nothing wrong with being a carpenter," Fel said.

"There is when it means wiping one's mind without their consent. Now, may I take the earring or not?"

"Ask Dad. I'm certainly not giving you mine."

He straightened his tunic and turned to the door. "See, now that is a sensible point of view."

He marched out the door. Fel stood and followed. Tome was able to rather graciously navigate the thick crowd. Fel, on the other hand, found himself instantly surrounded by people talking too quickly and too loudly to be understood. He felt a tug at his arm and was pulled behind the bar by Allie to give him a bit of space.

"Wait'll you hear what's been going on since you went in there," Allie said.

"I was in there for five minutes. What could have possibly happened to churn everyone up this much in that amount of time?" Fel asked.

"Tem's ego happened," she muttered.

"Spread out. Spread out," Tem said, squeezing up to the bar. "Fel! Buddy. Pal. I've been thinking."

"I don't want to hear it. Sit your butt down and lose this tournament like an adult."

"Now, now, now. Hear me out. The total pot so far is, what? Three thousand duots? Thereabouts? Kind of a wimpy prize for two people who play at our level."

"There's also the bragging rights and the trophy."

Tem swiped the air with his hand. "You're missing my point. We've come this far. We've already established ourselves to be the best. Is there really so big a difference between being the best and the second best?"

"Spoken like someone expecting to lose."

"I say we make this tournament interesting. Right now we've both got around fifteen hundred duots in the pot."

"I have seventeen hundred. You have fourteen hundred," he said.

"Then this should be even more enticing to you. I'm suggesting we each kick in enough to make the total pot ten thousand duots. Something worthy of players at our level."

"I don't have that kind of money floating around, Tem."

"Neither do I. Not in my pockets, anyway. But give me a week or two and I think I could beg, borrow, and steal enough to cover my share."

"Quit trying to squirm out of this tournament."

"Call it squirming. Call it having standards. Doesn't matter one bit to me. I'm ready to walk away from that table with my money and be content calling myself one of the best players in town. If you want to take this thing all the way to the finish and find out who is the best, that'll cost you five thousand duots."

Fel tightened his jaw and glared at Tem. Tem looked back smoothly, almost smugly. This stunk as some sort of a scheme by Tem. Like the entire tournament to this point had just been Tem sandbagging until he could coax whoever was the final opponent into emptying his pockets into Tem's. But to believe that was to believe that Tem was the de facto best in town. More to the point, it would mean embracing what most likely everyone in The Fox and Log was assuming, which was that Fel had no place at this table and it was a combination of luck and good grouping that had gotten him this far. At a table full of players, there were plenty of ways to win. You didn't necessarily have to do well. The others could do poorly. But one on one, the only ways to win were luck and skill. And luck had a pesky way of running out at the worst times.

Walking away from the grum table right now meant two things: a nice tidy pile of winnings in his pocket, and the unspoken admission that he thought Tem was the better player. And that was unacceptable.

"You're on," Fel said. "Five thousand duots, two weeks."

The room rumbled with a combination of excitement of the game ahead and disappointment at having to wait a few weeks to finalize any pending bets. After the moment passed and the folks who were taking up space without buying drinks dissipated, Fel gathered his share of the winnings-so-far and took a seat at the bar.

"On your feet. I need help setting up these tables for actual paying customers," Allie said.

Fel grumbled. "You know I don't work here, right?"

"Not right now, you don't. But seems to me you'll be looking for extra money to handle the entry fee that Tem just bilked you into."

"He didn't bilk me," he said, grabbing a tray from behind the counter and loading it up.

Fel had been called into service as the tray carrier often enough that he knew what to do and how to do it. She loaded the snacks and drinks onto the tray and marched along with him in tow.

"Tem walked out of here with plenty of winnings in his pocket, and you are walking out with even more winnings. An argument could be made that you're the winner already. But you shook hands on the agreement to plop down everything you won, plus thousands more, for what might end up being a single run of grum in two weeks. If you ask me, that's him pulling your strings. Have you always been this easy to manipulate, or is it new?"

"You don't think I can win?"

"Of course I think you can win. Anyone could win *one* game of grum. The skill is about coming out on top over the course of an entire night, or an entire week. Or your entire life. One game, you might as well be flipping a coin. It doesn't prove anything." She thumped a drink onto the table in front of a thirsty patron. "And where, by the way, are you getting that money? I know you don't have it, because I know the work you've been doing and you gripe about coming up short all the time. I know you're not borrowing it from me, because I don't have it and even if I did, I wouldn't loan it to you for something as dopey as this. I'm still picking up the pieces after the mess that Madritz lady made of my life. And don't let me hear about you borrowing it from Mariss. We both know she has it, and we both know she'd loan it to you, and I don't want to think about how awkward those dinners we have together will get if you owe her a couple thousand duots. I'm just starting to look forward to those dinners, and I don't need you spoiling them."

"Relax," he said. "I'm due for a trip down south anyway. The shop needs fresh parts and inventory. I'll just grab some extra. Maybe drop a line to Euphoria, see if she's got any wants or needs that I can fill for a price. Her family is rolling in it. And they don't have anyone half as good as me at finding the good stuff or half as good as Dad at fixing it up."

"You'd be fine putting the screws to your sister for the cost of a contraption?"

"Euphoria specifically? No. Her family? Absolutely. Near as I can tell, the number of decent, worthwhile, trustworthy people in the Graves family doubled when she married into it."

"Who is the other one?" Allie asked.

"Toss-up between Lattica and Thaddeus. Leaning more toward Lattica."

"Not her husband?"

"I don't know, because I haven't met him. Which isn't a vote in favor, by the way. He's been married to my sister for going on four years. You'd think I'd have at least shaken hands with him by now. I'm not even sure he exists."

She finished filling the orders, topping off the drinks, and spreading out snacks. "I still think you're making a mistake," she said, taking the tray from him.

"Fel Masker? Making a mistake? Unheard of!" he said with a snort. "But right now, the only part of this that feels like a mistake is the part where I have to leave town for a few weeks. Because it means I only get to hear your quips filtered through Wick, who lacks your charming delivery."

She narrowed her eyes. "Don't try buttering me up." She leaned closer and whispered, "But if you're heading out tomorrow, make sure you stop by my place for a proper goodbye. I'd give it to you here, but the gossip flows faster than wine around here even without public displays of affection."

He grinned. "I'll bring you some of Dad's biscuits. But I should head out. Like I said, if I'm going to be making a run to one of the better vaults, I should try to get word out to Euphoria to see how things are going up there and what sort of high-priced contraptions they might be after."

He marched toward the door, raising his voice as he did. "I'll see you all in two weeks, when I officially bring home the title of Best Grum Player In the History of The Fox and Log."

Teya marched toward the gate of what had come to be called the Lesser Greater Lands. She'd been here for weeks, and they had been the most rewarding and fulfilling of her life by a wide margin. To be a kobold was to seek partnership, to seek teamwork, and to seek achievement in service of someone or something greater than oneself. For Teya, that greater figure was Kazel, the mighty dragon who, in his wisdom, had trusted Fel Masker and Tome Inkbrand to render aid to him in a time of need. More importantly, at least to her, he'd had the wisdom to entrust her to their service. Ever since that day, she had followed the path of destiny. It had been a long and crooked one, but it had allowed her to find so many of her brothers and sisters who were separated from the Greater Lands and give them a chance to once again work toward something good, something meaningful.

"And what do we do then?" asked the kobold to her left.

"You need to find the shiny stone. The stuff they were having you fill the wagons with. You don't need much. But you need some. A sackful. That will do," Teya said.

She took a breath and basked in the pleasure of speaking in her own language. Her human tongue was improving, but it felt terribly limiting to stumble through short sentences. Breaking her thoughts down into pieces small enough for her linguistic skill was almost more difficult than wrestling the human sound out of her mouth.

The first kobold scurried off. The one behind stepped forward.

"And me? What do I do?" she asked.

"Copper. Maybe three sacks. Melt it into the ingot shapes. The ones this big." She held up her paws to demonstrate.

The kobold nodded and hurried after the first. Another stepped forward.

"You get help. We need coal. A lot. Ten sacks. Maybe more. We will need to build a very big, very hot fire."

Another eager nod and the latest kobold trotted off. A dozen more peeled off from the gathered creatures without having to be told. The task was big; it would need many kobolds. It was an instinct, deep and reliable. A kobold knew what it would take to get a job done.

"We need hammers as well. We will need to hammer the copper flat. The hammers from last time? They were very worn. Someone will need to fix them. Or make new ones."

"I can make hammers!" called a kobold from farther back. "It is a heavy thing, with flat on one side and a stick down the middle!"

"Yes! Go. Enough hammers for everyone who will be banging metal," she instructed.

"Should we make them? Or take them. The small men with the long face fur have many good hammers."

"The small men? Dwarves? Those small men?"

Half of the gathering nodded in agreement. The other half followed suit, once they saw the others doing so.

Teya paused and scratched her chin. "Dwarves are very good at hammering. Try to get them to help with the hammering. If they do not, ask them for their hammers. Borrow them. If not, take them. And if they try to stop you, bite them very much, in places that will hurt but will not kill. This is too important for rude dwarves not willing to share their hammers to slow it down."

"Can we bite eyes?" called one from the back.

"No biting eyes."

"Can we bite fingers?"

"Bite fingers, but do not bite fingers *off*. The same for noses and ears. Do not bite anything off that will not grow back." She crossed her arms and raised her chin. "The humans call that 'diplomacy.'"

"Dip-low-mah-see," the kobolds repeated, nodding in agreement.

She turned and trotted toward the wall again. "We will need the sharp tools for making long marks in metal. Do we have them?" She paused, waiting for an answer. "Do we have them?"

Again there was no answer. She realized she couldn't hear the crunch of clawed paws on the path toward the gate. She turned to find the kobolds standing in place, eyes half-focused and turned away from the wall. She sighed and touched her silver earring, the only reason she was spared a similar fate. If they truly focused, they could probably see and follow her, but a lifetime of heeding the supernatural urge to ignore the outside world had made its influence feel like instinct, and instinct was very important to kobolds. Teya stepped toward them until, one by one, the semblance of thought and intellect came to their eyes once more.

"You are back?" croaked one of them.

"I did not leave yet. But I will leave soon. Marking tools, the kind for making long lines in metal. Do we have them?"

A dozen heads shook.

"Then I will bring them. Is there anything else you need from me?" she asked.

The gathering of kobolds stood, shifting and fidgeting like toddlers uncertain if they'll be scolded.

"You want to hear about the mountain again. About Kazel again," Teya said reverently.

"Is he really free?" asked one kobold.

"Really and truly?" asked another.

"The mountain. My home. It stands tall, and it stands free. It is a home to kobolds, more than I can count. There are many among you who once called it home. They can attest. We work together, digging new tunnels, carving walls. Hunting. Fishing. And we serve Kazel. After more time in chains than any of us could hope to imagine, two humans crossed the wall. They survived the beasts of the Greater Lands. One was brought to our home by the Adept. Me and some of my friends brought the other. Those humans brought with them a knowledge of magic. And of contraptions. And they brought their bravery. With my help, and the help of the undines and the unicorns who also pledge themselves to Kazel, the keys to his chains were found. Now he once again patrols the skies, great scales gleaming in the sun and watchful eyes keeping the mountain and its people safe. And today I work with those humans, and others. I will find the keys to the chains that hold your minds, that blind your eyes to the wall. Because there are good humans. And because destiny guides me. And because you all deserve to return to Kazel's embrace."

The kobolds watched and listened, eyes sparkling with the light and life that the pressure of the clockwork diamond typically muted and subdued. They crowed and chattered triumphantly before turning to tackle the tasks that had been assigned. When Teya was alone, she allowed herself a moment to puff up her chest and waggle her head.

"I fill them with hope, and I teach them not to bite the noses off people who might help. I am a good leader."

Teya returned to the task at hand. The gate to the outside was wide open. There was no sense closing it. No one within these walls but she had the mental freedom to even consider leaving this place, and the people outside all feared either the "disease" that had until recently emanated from the center of this forest or the legion of "monsters" that called it their home. Normally there was an imp and a minotaur who guarded this door, but it was late at night and they had retired for the evening. She marched through the gate and turned to follow the curve of a wall that was far too small to contain the sprawling landscape it concealed. She didn't bother twisting up her mind trying to come to terms with how that was possible. It simply was. Powerful minds achieved it through contraptioneering or magic. The two were basically the same as far as she was concerned. Right now her focus was making changes to that enchantment so that the others she'd left behind could think clearly enough to return home. Or at least to have the same life and liveliness they had while they were home.

The moon was waning in the sky, casting precious little light on the field. Without her large, sharp eyes meant for navigating dim caves, she probably would have had to light the lantern hanging from her pack in order to navigate. The thought didn't even enter her mind. That lantern was simply a place for a friend of hers to hitch a ride, and when her supply of lamp oil had run dry, he was forced to take his leave. A simple problem that would be solved soon enough.

Teya took a whiff of the air. Fenfield had once been a hunting ground. Now that the hunters had abandoned it, the place was thick with prey. She briefly considered stopping long enough to hunt down a meal. Nothing as large as a deer, but maybe a rabbit or some rats. She shook her head and resisted temptation. She had a job to do. And it would take every moment of darkness available to her to reach her first stop on the way to Ram's Rest before sunrise. Her little legs were built for work, not speed, and she had a long way to go.

She took one final whiff. There was always the chance there would be something tasty right on the route she was trotting along, after all. Her nose told the tale of mice and other tasty morsels. But also something else. A breath of breeze carried the scent of horses, and of men. She kept her pace but shifted her view. There should not be humans here. She turned to the source of the scent. No surprise that it was the ragged and broken remnants of the wall that surrounded what had come to be called False Clickspring. She squinted her eyes and raised her frilled ears. When the wind was right, she heard the click and grind of shovels and picks. And outside the wall, a small, heavily loaded cart was waiting. It wasn't a cargo cart. It was heaped with tools and equipment, with little room for packing much of anything else besides the men who must have ridden it to Fenfield. There were no lanterns, no shouts of men being boisterous or delivering orders to workers. They were working in secret.

A growl rattled in Teya's chest. They were up to no good. She was sure of it. But fierce though she was, she was only one kobold. And kobolds didn't do things alone. They sought help. And help was precisely what she'd set off to find. But there would be more to discuss now. Much more. She trotted a bit faster, pushing the precisely calibrated speed that she knew she could maintain for a full night without stopping for much rest. The sooner she made it to Ram's Rest, the sooner her friends could learn what was happening, and the sooner she could get the tools and the wisdom to do her job.

Strangely enough, a smile crept to her face as she thought through the steps that would follow. She would get the equipment, she would learn the next steps. She would light the lantern again from Wick's flame, and through it she would talk to Martin and Fel. She would probably close the gate, now that she realized there were workers. She would deliver things, get the wheels turning on the next stage of her mission. *The* mission. She would find a way to free those within the Lesser Greater Lands... and maybe, just maybe, her friends would come north to lend a hand and to solve the little mystery she'd just witnessed. Mysteries were fun. Her friends were fun. And it felt good to work together with them.

But one step at a time. First, she had to meet with Euphoria Graves.

"One more stack," Euphoria muttered to herself, tugging the top sheaf of pages from the diminishing mound that had dominated her evenings for the last few weeks.

She hadn't been sleeping very well. There wasn't time for full nights of sleep these days. If it wasn't for her social obligations with regard to planning parties and get-togethers with local merchants and officials, she might not have even remembered to eat. This level of focus was inherited from her father, and a small part of her had been hoping it would never raise its ugly head again. Being able to force oneself to subsist on two hours of sleep a night and the pathetically small and ruinously expensive finger foods that passed for refreshments at the parties of the wealthy instead of proper meals was a useful skill. Being unable to choose *not* to do such things was a mental illness that traded happiness and healthiness for productivity. But right now it had to be done. And by the very nature of its sensitivity and secrecy, this task had to be done by her. No aid. Just her.

Like all the best schemes, it began and persisted under a plausible and reasonable motivation. The Voice of the Graves Flame could no longer be trusted. That in and of itself had been a difficult fact to convince the others in her family to embrace. But for now, at least, they admitted that it was not secure, and until it could be proved to be safe and private once more, more conventional means of communication were called for. Relying upon messengers wasn't nearly as fast as they were accustomed to, but every other business concern on the continent, and likely in the world, had been doing business this way and remained quite happily profitable. If they could do it, the Graves family could do it. And better. But it would require a change in tactics and a change in thinking. Most importantly, it would require them to be very efficient in their usage of their limited staff of messengers. Wasted trips were unacceptable. A full audit of precisely how the messengers had been used for the last few years was necessary in order to trim the fat and ensure business was done as quickly and discreetly as possible.

It was all true. It was all necessary. And it was not the real reason she'd requested the audit and volunteered to perform it personally.

Lens. Lens was the reason for the audit. That was the name that had been applied to the Voice of the Flame. She didn't know who had applied the name, or why, but her brother and his friend had been in communication directly with the flame and heard it refer to itself as such. Worse, once she'd begun digging, she'd found more than a few business dealings her family and local traders had had with someone by that same name. At the same time, she'd been given reason to believe the reclusive Piotor Graves had befallen some sort of terrible fate years earlier. This was a man who was as near a match to her own father as the Graves family had, at least with regard to serving as a repository for research and expertise. His advice and insight had guided every contraption-based decision and a fair proportion of business and social decisions the family had made for nearly a generation. But his all-consuming requirements of solitude had meant that no one had seen him for ages, and no one had expected to. His directives came via the Voice of the Flame, or in heavily coded messages hand delivered by a dedicated corps of messengers. His influence was very much intact, but few even remembered what he looked like.

Her attempts to arrange a meeting with Piotor, or even contact him directly, had been thwarted repeatedly in the last few weeks. A message, ostensibly written by his own hand and delivered in response to her latest request, gently rebuffed her. If the family's communications had been compromised, it was doubly important that he remain hidden. The precautions in that regard would have impressed a military strategist. There were no fewer than twelve safe houses that he was claimed to rotate between. Even with her own access to the family's records, Euphoria could only identify nine of them explicitly. A complex knot of dead drops and handoffs meant that no single messenger even knew where a message originated. Any one of them could have been left by Piotor himself or by another messenger who had carried it from where Piotor had left it.

The family was scrupulous in its record keeping. For someone with the full picture, the full context, that song and dance shouldn't have mattered. It would still be a horrible ball of twine, but eventually one could tug out both ends and find where a given message originated. Such a thing absolutely required comprehensive records, though. If even a single link in the chain was missing, suddenly there were dangling threads that could no longer be linked. And there were a *lot* of missing messages. Even accounting for sensitive messages being burned lest they fall into the wrong hands, the gaps in their records were far too surgically precise to be the result of carelessness or happenstance. Their records about their dealings in Fenfield had been altered, so she knew someone had an interest in hiding their actions. And that same person had removed strategic messages to render Euphoria's investigation fruitless thus far. But the Masker family focus wouldn't let her call the search hopeless until the last stone was turned.

She flipped open a new page. According to the annotations, it was another message by Piotor's own hand. The content, once she was able to decode it, was nothing important. It was a recommendation to invest a bit more of the family's funds into copper and tin, scrawled out years ago. In her dull, mechanical trance of processing the pages, she nearly marked it and set it aside to continue her investigation, but something stopped her. She squinted at the writing. Not the message, but the actual penmanship. She looked up to the pinned message and held the older one up to it.

A smile curled her lips.

"You've been clever," she murmured. "But not clever enough."

Well after midnight, Allie wearily paced home with lantern in hand and dinner on her mind. As tended to be the case for anyone walking through the part of town she called home after sunset, she was a touch more vigilant than people in the ritzier parts of town. Thus, the crunch of footsteps caught her attention before the friendly whistle. She wasn't sure what it said about her that all she needed were the footsteps to know it was Fel.

"How'd the rest of the night pan out?" Fel asked, jogging up to her with a sack over his shoulder.

"The usual. For this week, anyway. Had to practically threaten to bash someone's head in with the persuader to get them to cough up their tab for the night. And half of the highfalutin folks from uptown skipped out without paying *their* tabs. You better believe they'll be settling those before the big finale in two weeks," she said. "This whole tournament has been running me ragged with the extra people coming through. I am worn thin. Glad to have a few days off from it. How about you? All ready to head out tomorrow?"

"Doesn't take me long to pack up for a trip like this. Haven't been able to talk to Euphoria yet. But I'll have Wick with me. I can catch her along the way."

"And how long will you be gone?"

"A little under a week there, a couple days grabbing the goods, and the same time back. If I don't dillydally along the way, I should be back right in time for the big game."

"Not leaving any room for mishap?" she said.

"If things go wrong, they don't usually go wrong for a predicable amount of time. And if I'm late? It's not like he'll disqualify me. He won't get his money."

They came to the alley that led to Allie's door. Fel's face scrunched up at the errant wind that brought the scent of the tannery up the alley.

"One of these days you're going to have to teach me what magic trick you're doing to keep your house, and you, from stinking like half-tanned leather."

"You develop an instinct for which windows to leave shut," she said.

A brief fight with the stubborn door earned them entry to her home, where she flopped into one of the two chairs and leaned down to do battle with her bootlaces. Fel laughed and dropped to one knee to help her pull them free.

"How are these treating you?" he asked, setting them aside and hoisting himself up into the other chair.

"Those boots remain the finest gift I have ever received. My old pair? On a day like this, I'd be limping home."

"Yep. Reynard knows how to make them. It's a shame he's retiring."

He dropped the sack onto the table, revealing the promised biscuits. There was also a heavy, metal-lidded crock that hadn't done as good a job holding on to its contents as Fel would have liked. He bunched the bag up under it to keep from getting the escaped stew on the table and stood to fetch her bowls.

"You didn't say anything about bringing me dinner," she said.

He shrugged. "We had extra."

"You always have extra. You're just looking for an excuse to stay longer."

"Can you blame me?"

"Some days? Yes. I could blame you. I'm not the most pleasant person to be around after a long, hard day."

"You're talking to a guy who spends most of his time with a smug blowhard and a lesser unicorn. You aren't up against very stiff competition."

"Speaking of, where's Parch?" she asked. "I almost didn't recognize you without your little furry shadow."

"Epiphany has promised to try to keep him in the house. We're trying to teach him to stay put sometimes. Which means he'll be here any minute."

Fel sloshed a helping of stew into each bowl. If Allie hadn't eaten the stuff in the past, she wouldn't have thought it looked terribly appetizing. But looks were deceiving. The Masker family recipe was a flexible one. It could be summarized as "gravy and whatever else you can get, simmered until it's all the same color." And yet the stuff was the definition of hearty. The kind of thing a stomach would directly request if it had any say in the matter.

He soaked up some gravy and munched on a biscuit. She took a somewhat more civilized approach. For nearly a minute, they ate in comfortable silence. The heavy meal didn't do anything for the weariness hanging over her head like a blanket, but she yawned and tried to shake herself awake again.

"You know something, Fel? Most of the men I've known, if I invited them over with a line like 'I need to say goodbye to you properly,' they'd have come with expectations. You came with stew."

He shrugged again. He certainly did that a lot. "That's because I'm smarter than most fellas. What lady would say no to stew?"

She yawned. "The point is, you're a riddle. I can't explain it. If I had the choice of doing just about anything with anyone else, or doing nothing with you, I think I'd choose nothing with you every time."

He scratched his head. "Not sure how to take that."

"It's a compliment, you oaf. You make me feel at ease. This is not an easy world and we do not have easy lives. Easier than some, sure. But it's a fight, every day. When you're around, I feel like I can take a breath. Like I can let some slack on the rope because there's someone else there to take it up. I feel more relaxed with you than when I'm alone. After a day of being surrounded by people, I used to want nothing more than to be alone. Now? It's this."

"Now it's my turn to say something nice, right?" he said.

"Glad to see you're catching on."

He stuffed an entire biscuit in his mouth, probably to buy himself some time. When he'd muscled it down, he once again led with a shrug. "I'd repeat all that back to you. Because it goes for me too. But that's probably not what you're after."

"It'd ring a little hollow."

He huffed. "I'm not great with words. I spent weeks trying to find the right words to tell you I love you the first time. You'll have to bear with me if you want me to find new words to say it."

"To be fair, I don't see 'I love you' getting old anytime soon."

"But I guess... if we're being heartfelt, I can say this. You watched me chase after Mariss and twist myself up in knots trying to make myself into the kind of person I thought she'd care about. I never once wondered if you cared about me. Maybe I didn't see the way you cared or that I might be special. But I always knew yours was an opinion that mattered. From the moment I first met you, I could care less about what anyone else in that tavern thought of me. But if I thought you legitimately would think less of me for something I'd done, it would burn at me. And now? Look how close we are. The stakes have never been higher. I should be terrified. But it's like you said. I feel... right."

Allie raised her eyebrows. "And you said you weren't good with words." She stood up. "So, me being close to you should terrify you, and you're not terrified."

"Not yet anyway."

She walked over to him and sat in his lap, one arm over his neck. "How about now, big fella?" she said, leaning close to whisper it in his ear.

He didn't need to answer. He could feel how tense he'd become the moment she touched him. She leaned against him, wondering if perhaps making him twist and squirm wasn't a bit cruel to do right before a trip. She rested her head on his shoulder.

Maybe a few more moments, just to make a point.

She closed her eyes.

A heartbeat later, she jerked awake. She was lying in bed. Clothes on, facing the ceiling. She turned.

"I fell asleep." She covered her face. "I fell asleep on his lap."

She teased her fingers apart and glanced aside through them. She was alone in bed. That shouldn't have been a surprise. Her bed wasn't large enough that she could miss someone as large as Fel, and she could imagine no world in which Fel would dare to lie down in her bed uninvited. But still, it was nice to learn her judgment was accurate. There was, however, a folded note waiting on the bedside table.

Allie,

Seems like you needed sleep more than you needed company. Let myself out. Kind of tricky, since I don't have a key. Used a vault-diving trick backward to brace the door behind me. Might want to check it.

She shook some of the sleep from her head and lumbered to her door. The brace was in place. A hook of wire and a string looped over it led over to the side of the door. He must have hooked it before he left and pulled it into position after. She yanked the hook and string free and secured the door a bit more properly.

"Well," she mumbled, trudging back to her bedroom to undress. "That's one way to give him a send-off."

Chapter 2

The coolness of night was just beginning to give way to the warmth of day as Fel helped Tome load up the remainder of the index Wick had transcribed.

"About how long do you suppose it'll take you to get this done?" Fel asked, eying the roofline periodically.

"The whole trip? There and back again?" Tome asked. "Well, when I came from the west coast it took me almost three months, but I had to rely upon hitched rides and more than a little walking. A direct route? With a horse the whole way? Maybe six weeks. I'd give whoever my father is able to assign to the index another few weeks to make enough progress processing it to have something to bring back. And then another six weeks to come back to Beffshire. I might take my time on the way back. See some more of the lands between."

"Four months," Fel said. "Give or take."

"That would be a reasonable way to set your expectations."

"Uh-huh," Fel said, thumping down a stack of books and looping some ropes around it to strap it down.

"Why do I detect a dubiousness to your tone?" Tome asked.

"You've been living under our roof for a while now. Have you noticed how lousy Dad is when it comes to keeping secrets? Particularly with the family? And particularly when you don't explicitly tell him to?"

"He's been discussing our little project, has he?" Tome said flatly.

"Let's just say I got curious when I noticed Parch got a haircut. Dad says you were cooking up some good ink for a spell to 'make short work of your trip.' You've known you were going for weeks, and even if you say you didn't need to do any preparation for this trip, I know you can't help yourself."

"I may have been fiddling with a version of the spell that allowed me to chase you down at the wall, and that spell may have been developed adequately to allow the wagon, the horse, and myself to all be included. And I may be testing it along the way. But such things will only be definite if I deem it sensible to perform a test along the way."

"And if it works? How long until you get to the Gate of the Ancients?"

He cleared his throat. "Ten days."

"The whole continent in less than the length of a round trip to the Greater Lands Wall?" Fel scoffed. "That's a little lofty."

"It is well within my capacity," he defended. "I have grown in leaps and bounds since my exposure to the assorted magics and other acts of the arcane our little jaunts have uncovered."

"Uh-huh," Fel said, unconvinced. "Just don't smash up the wagon when you give it a try."

Fel looked to his own wagon. Given that he was planning to bring things back rather than deliver them to a destination, his own vehicle was primarily vacant aside from some empty sacks and crates. The primary preparation he'd made was transferring the decoy and the dazzler, two of Martin's signature defensive contraptions, from the family cart to the heftier wagon. He was ready to leave. But there were one or two things that needed to be done before he left town. The first was right here at the house, and he was through waiting for it.

"Hey!" he called out, adding a whistle. "What? Did I make the roost too comfortable? Judy, Moody, Toody, Rudy! Get down here!"

Four feathery black heads sluggishly popped up from behind the roofline of the family shop. They blinked bleary birdy eyes out of sequence, then fluttered down to land on the back of the wagon.

"I'm not going to be around for a while, and I know the folks don't spoil you like I do," he said. "I don't want you forgetting where your bread is buttered."

"You haven't been buttering the bread you've been giving them, have you?" Tome asked, climbing to the seat of the cart.

"None of your business how I treat my critters," Fel said without looking before returning his attention to the lesser harpies. "And someone told me the secret to why you've been so lubby-dubby to her even though she hasn't been bringing you gifts lately."

"Egg monkey?" said Judy with clear excitement.

"Monkey egg!" the others crowed gleefully.

Fel unfastened the string securing a cloth sack and revealed eight large chicken eggs. The four harpies hopped into a line, Judy in the front, Toody in the back, and Moody and Rudy jockeying for position in the middle. He gave each an egg, one by one. They cracked and consumed each one with a level of skill that boggled the mind. Not a drop of yolk nor a fragment of shell was lost.

"I want you to keep an eye on the folks. Be nice to the customers. And if you're going to steal something valuable, don't bring it back here. Or at least hide it better. I went up there to clean up after you yesterday, and I found Mr. Marx's pocket watch. That is a very expensive thing to just be snatching. Crosses the line from mischief to burglary. Understood?"

"Stinking rat, nasty thief," Judy said.

"I'll eat your toes," Rudy said.

"Eat your toes!" agreed the others.

He stepped back, and they each fetched up an egg in their talons and retreated to the roof. Fel climbed into the wagon. As was tradition, both of his parents stepped outside. As if to underscore just how mundane this trip was after months of being sent out to defuse threats or recover stolen goods, his parents forewent their usual fretting and last-minute advice.

"Be well, Son. I look forward to seeing what you find," Martin said.

"Don't be careless. And come back soon," Vivian added.

"Any special requests?" Fel asked.

"I have a short list of people hoping for figurines. Full sets in particular," she said.

"Haven't found too many of those where I'm headed, but I'll keep my eyes open. Dad?"

"If you find yourself in the vicinity of the archive, tell Wick. Though I suppose I'll soon be spoiled for choice when it comes to reference, there are still a few volumes within that archive that could prove useful."

"Will do. Epiphany about?"

"I'm wrangling your blasted pet," she grumbled as Parch effortlessly dragged her out the door by a rather tasteful harness and leash, a gift from Reynard, the cobbler next door. "Weren't you a bit curious why he wasn't prancing all over the wagon while you were helping load the cart?"

"I thought maybe he was behaving himself all on his own. Thanks for the help, Fanny. Need anything while I'm gone?"

Parch hopped up to the seat beside Fel. Epiphany paced over and handed him a veritable pamphlet.

"I have buyers lined up on the old bazaar route if you find any of this stuff. Don't kill yourself looking for it, but we'll make a tidy sum if you can find them."

"Should keep me busy." He pocketed the pamphlet. "Where's the little helper?"

That was the public shorthand for Oiler. It was just short of embarrassing how long it had taken them to come up with such a thing.

"There's plenty to keep the helper busy. Shouldn't come looking for you," Martin said.

"I'll feel weird not having to juggle two handfuls while I'm working," he said. "So long, all!"

He snapped the reins and rumbled the wagon deeper into town. He was technically headed the wrong way, but there was one more stop before he left town. He glanced up at the lantern hanging from the sunshade. The flame was still.

"Checking up on me already, Wick?" he asked.

"The family was entirely occupied with seeing you off, and Allie is still asleep. You were the one who needed oversight," he said.

"Me and Tome," Fel said. "Does it strike you as odd that I'm the one with the good, relightable lantern when Tome's the one that'll take weeks to get back here if his goes out?"

"Yours is considered the more dangerous journey," Wick said. "Thus, yours is the situation best served by a more reliable connection to the others."

"Maybe so."

"How was your visit with Allie yesterday?"

"She's got your flame burning in one of her lanterns. Did you watch?"

"I endeavor to give the two of you privacy when you are alone together. It seems appropriate."

"Ah. Well, you didn't miss anything. She's worn pretty thin. Needed the rest." He paused for a moment. "Hey, I don't suppose you..."

After a polite delay, Wick replied, "You failed to complete what seemed to be the beginning of a request for service."

"It's... maybe not appropriate."

"Would you like to make that determination personally or allow me to make that determination after the fact?"

"I was going to ask if you have noticed Allie doing anything... extra. Anything dangerous. She's technically on the hook for something from Verfessa. And she was so knocked out last night that she didn't even wake up when I carried her to bed."

"I see."

"… Well?"

"You informed me that you were going to ask me that. You did not, in fact, ask me that."

"Now I'm asking."

"I have not observed anything beyond a somewhat significant increase in time worked at the tavern."

He shook his head. "I should have been visiting after work more often. Help her get to sleep faster."

He navigated the slowly increasing traffic on the streets as the wagon rumbled toward the more expensive part of town. Soon enough he was at Divinity's Oven. He rummaged in his pocket to make sure he could cover the cost of breakfast. It would probably cost more than the next three days of meals combined, but it was worth it.

He hopped down. "You stay put," he said, turning to address the empty spot where Parch had been sitting before preemptively disobeying him.

Fel hurried ahead of the unicorn and shoved the door open before the little creature could make its own hole.

"Oh! There you are! My two favorite customers," Mariss said, emerging from the back room with flour and powdered sugar drifting off her apron in thick clouds. "How did the tournament go? I wanted to stop by, but we've started making a new pumpkin bread, and no one else seems to have the knack for it. We can't keep it on the shelves!"

"It's down to me and Tem, but we decided to hold off for a few weeks and have a more suitable final round."

"You'll win it. I'm sure you will." She glanced out the window at the wagon. "Oh! Going on a trip?"

"Yep. Heading to a vault. The usual."

"Short or long?" she asked.

"Long*ish*. Two weeks or so."

"Allie and I will miss you at dinner this weekend. But if you're going to be on the road, wait right here."

She scurried to the back, where the scent of fresh baked bread wafted out, tantalizing him enough to wish he'd budgeted for a double helping of the buns he had his eye on. She returned with a basket of apple cores for Parch, who managed to snag and consume one before she'd even set the basket down for him. She also had a cloth-wrapped bundle that she handed to Fel. He nearly dropped it when he accepted it, as it weighed so much it may as well have been made of stone.

"Fruitcake. It keeps forever, and one little slice will keep you alive for three days. It's the oldest recipe we still make. Seems like something you ought to have on a long journey like this."

He tucked the bundle under his arm and pushed the coins around his palm.

"I probably don't—"

"Oh, put the money away. It's a gift. You don't see me asking Parch for any money, do you?"

"Parch is a little dumb animal. I'm a big dumb animal. The rules are different," he said.

She patted his cheek. "But both just as lovable. Now did you come by just to say hello?"

"Sweet bun and clotted cream, please."

"Won't be a moment!" She pulled a still-steaming bun from its basket and plucked a knife from its block. "It's been ages since Allie came here to say hello. I know it's a fair bit out of her way, but it's so nice to have a friendly face in here like yours. It's not a nice thing to say, but a girl starts to realize how bland some of her friends are when someone with a little more life to them walks through the door. You should see some of the looks I get when I share some of your anecdotes."

"Allie's been busy. Hey. Do me a favor and check in on her a little more often when I'm gone. Maybe it's just the extra time I've been spending with her, but I'm starting to get worried she's stretching herself too thin."

"Oh, you thoughtful thing. I'll make sure she's good and taken care of." She grinned as she handed over the slathered bun. "So... how's it been, spending the extra time with her? Still got the sparkle in your eyes?"

He smiled and opened his mouth to answer.

"Oh, don't bother." She patted his cheek again. "I can see it. I'm so happy for you two. I'm almost jealous! If I'd known what a proper sweetie you are before you two got together, Allie might've had a tug-of-war on her hands."

"Uh... Right. Yeah. Thanks," he said, finding his reserve of snappy comebacks suddenly bone-dry.

He dumped the coins into her palm to pay for the bun and bid her farewell. With breakfast seen to and all his farewells said, he was on his way. Next stop? Whatever field was nearby when the horse needed to rest.

Far to the north, Euphoria laid out the last piece of the set of silverware. She had servants for this sort of thing, but she liked to give meetings like this the personal touch. She also preferred not to have her servants handling silverware that was literally the only complete set of its kind. She wasn't entirely comfortable with the rest of her family handling them either. There was a fine ceramic serving dish that had gone missing that she was quite certain was now a part of Nevil Graves's collection. But she had a rough road ahead, and she'd need every bit of help she could get. An impressive lunch was a good start.

The door opened and her butler stepped in. "The family has arrived, Mrs. Graves," he said.

"Excellent. Send them in."

One by one, seven members of her family entered. Though there was no official protocol list, the amount of deference and decorum that accompanied their entry and seating would have put a royal wedding to shame. Nevil entered first. Then Nevil older brother Marcel and Marcel's wife Gloria who, by virtue of age, were higher in the family's ledger. Then came Alex and Liana, brother and sister, unmarried, and Euphoria suspected the only reason they remained so was to avoid diluting their extremely lofty positions within the family. And finally, Yvana and Gunther, the matriarch and patriarch of the family. Gunther was thirty years Yvana's senior, she being his second wife. Though the primary seat of power was thoroughly his, most in the family understood that it was best to begin treating Yvana with greater deference, as it was only a matter of years before he passed and left her with uncontested influence over the rest of the family. It was almost ghoulish at times how transparent this currying of favor could be.

Euphoria tried to compartmentalize her mind on that subject, as she liked to imagine she was above it, but also had spent much of the last two weeks tracking down a bottle of Yvana's favorite dessert wine to conclude the meal.

When Yvana and Gunther took their seats, so did the others.

"A rare and pleasant event to find us all assembled here for something other than a wedding or a funeral. Not that I don't enjoy a wedding, but all the falderal can be so taxing," Gunther said.

"Yes. I'm rather impressed you were able to manage it, Euphoria," Nevil said. "Particularly without Jonathan present. Do you really think it was appropriate to call such a meeting in his absence?"

Euphoria allowed the tone of the remark to flutter by without acknowledging it. "I would have preferred Jonathan be present, but, as I am confident you will all agree at the conclusion of this meeting, the matter at hand is too sensitive to wait. But first, refreshments."

All in attendance nodded and sat back, waiting in silence as the food and drink were provided. The family was quite comfortable with this element of crucial meetings. Security and privacy required that none but family be present, but the simple fact of their elevated social status meant they wouldn't dare serve themselves. Thus, silence reigned while the staff were present. The staff were equally familiar with the procedure and did their work efficiently before leaving the room and shutting the doors.

"As you all know," Euphoria said. "There has been no end of difficulty with the Voice of the Flame, such that the unthinkable has happened and we have had to abandon it until a solution can be found. I have been doing my level best to revise our usage of messengers to salvage some level of speed and security, and I have made a discovery."

She stood and unlocked a small cabinet in the corner of the room. From within, she withdrew four sheaves of pages. She paced around the table, placing them in front of Gunther, Nevil, Marcel, and Alex respectively.

"What you have before you are the majority of the messages I could find in our archive that were written by the hand of Piotor Graves in the last five years. If your memory is particularly sharp, you will recognize them, as I've given each of you the messages that were addressed to you."

"Am I meant to read these?" asked Nevil. "Because I did not anticipate the need for my codebook at this luncheon."

"What I need you to do is confirm that they are messages you have received, and that the signature at the bottom is that of Piotor Graves, along with the note that the message was delivered directly."

"Oh yes. I remember quite clearly," said Marcel. "This one I received only last month."

"Each page has the appropriate watermark? The notes on the reverse of the page represent your current residence, or the residence at the time of receipt?" Euphoria asked.

"Yes, yes. What is this all about?" asked Nevil.

"Would you please compare the pages with each other?" Euphoria said. "In particular, compare the handwriting, and the signature."

"It's like a parlor game! Delightful!" said Alex as he stood and paced over to the patriarch.

Nevil and Marcel were more put off than entertained but did as they were asked. After a few moments, any smiles in the room faded.

"What in the world..." muttered Gunther.

"That is not the same signature," Alex said.

"No. It is not," Euphoria said. "The signatures are the same on the messages delivered to each of you but different on messages delivered to others. Each of you have been receiving direct messages by the same person, but not the same person who has been writing the messages, supposedly penned by Piotor Graves himself, that were delivered to others. And such has been the case for years."

"But it was the flame that was compromised. These are direct messages," Marcel said.

"Are we to believe someone in our network of messengers has been compromised as well?" asked Alex.

"I have been able to, with as much certainty as is available, confirm that each of these had an unbroken chain of custody from the initial pickup from Piotor. No outside hands touched them. And taken as a whole, these messages you are holding represent deliveries made by nearly all our messengers. So it wouldn't be a single messenger, but nearly all of them who would have to be rogue. But even that wouldn't be sufficient. They would also need our codebooks. And refreshed versions of those books when codes were improved or replaced. And even if all those things were true, there is still the reality that many of these messages, though moot now, represented sensitive business deals that could have ruined us or enriched our rivals had they leaked, and they did not."

"That doesn't make any sense," Nevil said.

"No. It doesn't. It would mean that the entirety of our message delivery staff has managed to form a unified spy network without once being revealed or suspected, and simultaneously either they or someone else was able to acquire the flame and use it to their own ends. And despite this deception lasting literal years—preceding my own entry into this family by better than half a decade in some cases—the mountains of information uncovered has gone almost entirely unused. It makes no sense. But there is an alternative explanation."

"I do not like where this is headed," the patriarch murmured.

"I don't like it either, but it is by far the simplest explanation. All this can be explained by the actions of a single man. Piotor Graves himself. He is the keeper of the codes. He is the origin point of all these messages, ostensibly. He is the keeper of the flame, for all intents and purposes. And we now have proof that at least three of you have been receiving messages written by someone else's hand but sent as though they were his own. For all the messages for which it would not be an unacceptable breech of privacy, I decoded the contents. "

She paced behind the others, tapping her fingers on messages.

"*This* page references things that were only mentioned elsewhere in *this* one, sent to someone else. And *this* one? It references the contents of these two, each sent to someone else. All of these messages are the result of a single pool of information. We need to acknowledge the very real possibility that Piotor Graves has either gone rogue, been compromised, or been replaced by one or more people."

"That is a wild accusation," Nevil said.

"And one that I do not make lightly. But the evidence we have supports it, and we have no evidence to disprove it."

The family was silent.

"I have a proposal," Euphoria said. "None of us know precisely where Piotor is. And that is by design. A slate of security precautions, designed by Piotor himself, stands between any individual and his current location. That security, at least on its face, was designed to prevent what now seems to have occurred. The security has failed. What I am requesting is permission to seek out Piotor personally to seek answers for the questions raised today. And if proof can be found that he is no longer reliable, or no longer with us, I request that the family immediately take steps to remove him from our confidence and assign replacements for his roles, as necessary."

"Is it really wise to take on this task personally?" the patriarch asked. "We have people for such things."

"I mean no disrespect when I point out that all of you had access to the same information I did. Most of you had that access with far more ease than I. But this remained hidden until I sought it. I should be the one to continue the investigation. I wouldn't do it alone. I would request Lattica Graves to accompany me. And I have done a tremendous amount of groundwork already. I know the locations of nine of the twelve safe houses Piotor is supposedly cycling through, and through my audit of our messengers' routes, I believe I have identified the other three. And speaking of the audit..."

She marched back to the cabinet and revealed two more sheaves of papers. "My proposals to improve the efficiency of the messenger network. The first should trim a half day off the average message delivery. The second trims three days off, by eliminating Piotor from the loop. We can discuss them later. For now, I would hate for our luncheon to get cold."

Tome dully gazed at the road ahead. It was now clear to him that he'd become a bit too comfortable with the idea of traveling with someone else. When he'd volunteered for this trip, his reasons for doing so were many. It had been quite some time since he'd seen his father and his home, yes. Though whether he found that to be fortunate or unfortunate changed day by day. There were *reasons* he'd left, after all. And certainly he was happy for the opportunity to help the Masker family after they'd provided him with a place to stay and facilitated so much of his growth. He could have done without the risk to life and limb that came with those opportunities, but what was done was done. Altogether, though, a significant motivator to head out on this journey was having the time to read and write. Living in a place that was also a marketplace and a workshop was not a recipe for peace and quiet. He'd adapted to the constant din from above and/or below, but a few weeks with nothing but the rattle of the road would be a welcome respite.

There was just one problem. Without Fel to take the reins, he was stuck guiding the horse the entire time. He lacked Fel's gift to sit in silence, occupying himself with thoughts or lack thereof for hours at a time. If he couldn't read and he couldn't write, he was going to have a terrible time keeping the solitude and boredom from eating him alive. He could talk to Wick, but the flame was seldom present and had other duties elsewhere. The pressure inactivity put on his judgment was starting to shift his priorities.

He glanced at the thick book beside him. A single spell he'd been tinkering with for ages. Written in very expensive ink, on the best paper he could find. It wasn't fit to cast, not yet. Components were missing, by design. Aspects of location, of timing. Things that would weaken the effects of the spell if they were to be recorded but not immediately cast. Five minutes with a pen and ink would complete it. And a single torn page would cast it. Assuming the spell worked, it was a thing of brilliance. A masterpiece. It stretched the very limits of paper magic. A spell meant to last for the duration of a purpose rather than for a period of time or the production of an effect. If it worked, his speed of travel would accelerate beyond typical physical limits. From the moment the page was torn until the moment he reached the monastery, any motion toward his goal would be at supernatural speed. This mind-deadening journey would last days instead of weeks.

He narrowed his eyes and tightened his jaw.

"Stop it, Tome. It isn't ready to be tested. It needs to be reread, reconsidered. If it fails, it could fail in unexpected ways."

The cart continued rumbling along the rough road.

"I need three or four nights to look it over. Enough time to convince myself that it will work properly or not at all."

He waved off an insect and slapped his neck as a second one bit him.

"Two nights.... I need two nights and it should be ready."

Ten minutes crawled by. A few important lessons were learned. As much as he had hated being stuck with Parch as his beast of burden on prior trips, there were a few assets to counterbalance the liability of his lackluster speed. The lesser unicorn didn't smell nearly as bad as this horse. And while the horse knew to stay on the road, it didn't seem to understand that the cart also had to stay on the road. Even without guidance, Parch trotted near enough to the middle of the road to keep both wheels of the cart rumbling along without mishap. This thick-headed steed, unless tugged this way or that every few minutes, would wander to the side and risk miring the cart's wheels in the roadside or wander so far into the middle of the road that the cart would clash against any travelers heading in the other direction.

After an earnest attempt to glance over the first few pages of the spell in the moments between course corrections led to the right wheel of the cart rolling over a rock that nearly jostled him from his seat, he cursed under his breath and yanked at the reins to guide the cart toward a clear area beside the road.

"I am going to complete this spell, and we are going to be on our way, and if some supernatural consequence befalls us, I will blame it on the especially dull-witted horse the stable boy rented to me."

Allie wiped off the last table and topped off the last basket of crickets with twenty minutes to spare before The Fox and Log was ready to open. The night of sleep, even if it started on an embarrassing note, was better than she'd had in weeks. It was astounding how much of a difference a proper rest made on one's outlook.

The doorknob rattled and the door opened. She called over her shoulder.

"You're on time for once, Oovay. If I'd known, I would have dragged my feet a little more on working the tables to make sure you had something to do."

"I'm afraid not," replied Donovan Verfessa, the owner of the tavern.

She turned. "Mr. Verfessa. It's not like you to use the front door."

"I'm pressed for time, and the place is empty besides," he said.

"Pressed for time?"

"I'm heading north to Teskal in a few minutes. Got some business with the stuffed shirts and blue bloods up there. Don't know when I'll be back."

She laughed. "I'd pay to see how a meeting between you and some of the nobles up there would go."

"I can play nice if needs be. But that's if they let me play. This isn't the first time I'll have gone up that way looking for a friendly face and a fair shake. Something about a man with a dirty neck and calluses on his fingers rubs those smooth-skins raw."

"No offense, sir, but your field-worker looks might not be the primary reason they'd treat you with caution."

"If you think the kind of dirty deeds I do would cause them to bat an eye, you've got a thing or two to learn about nobles," he said. "But like I said, I'm due to catch a carriage, so I'll make this quick. Time's come for me to cash in that debt you owe."

She froze. "... I see."

"Calm down. I'm not looking to carve what I want out of your haunches. You shouldn't have to get your hands dirty. You shouldn't even have to leave the tavern. I just need someone with sharp ears and a sharp eye. Here's the short version. We all know when the cat's away the mice will play. So when mangy ol' Verfessa heads out to do some hunting, the rats are bound to scurry into the light. Most of my business is locked up good and tight. But this place? It's a nice ripe piece of cheese for a hungry mouse to nibble at."

He paced behind the bar and thumped a glass on top, then fetched a bottle reserved with his name to fill it to the brim.

"I'm always in the market for information, but it usually comes in little bits, and I'm left piecing it all together to see what it looks like. I don't have all the pieces on this one, or else I'd have dealt with it already. Someone, likely to be an older fella, seems like they're sniffing around, seeing if there's any nooks and crannies to wriggle his filthy little paws into. Could be he's looking to collaborate, maybe partner up. But I'm not holding my breath on that one. It probably isn't a coincidence that he decided to turn up during the one trip this year I'm planning to take. So here's what I need you to do. Find the rat, find out what he's up to, and put as much of the puzzle together as you can, so when I get back, I can kick my feet up instead of getting right down in the dirt again."

"Just so I know I understand this correctly. You don't know for sure this person is coming. You don't even know for certain who they are or what they look like. But it's my job to figure all that out?"

"That's about it."

"What if they don't show up?"

"If they don't show up, then some of my other informants are going to get a talking to. But I don't think there's any danger of that."

"And you're confident I'll know them when I see them?"

"Wouldn't ask you to do it if I didn't think you were the one for the job. You get this done, you wrap it all up nice and tidy and have it ready for me. Maybe bring it by the missus if you're not sure you have enough. If she's happy, I'm happy, and we're square."

"Mrs. Verfessa isn't going with you?"

He laughed. "Eveline can't stand Teskal. Doesn't like travel in general. The way she sees it, she's spent all this time and all this money making her home good and cozy. No sense traipsing about anywhere else. I'm inclined to agree, but business is business."

Verfessa finished his drink. "I won't talk your ear off. You've got a tavern to run. Those doors are about ready to open, and the thirsty folks outside pay your salary and mine. I'll be back. Three weeks on the inside. Outside guess? Who knows? The sky's the limit if those folks up north are buying what I'm selling."

"And what exactly are you selling?"

He slipped a familiar folded piece of paper from his back pocket. It was one of the two letters from Lord Katritz that Allie had intercepted.

"Peace of mind," he said, slapping the letter against his hand. "And you'd be surprised what the going rate for that is these days."

He wiped the glass dry and set it aside behind the bar, then headed for the door. "Until we meet again, Allie. If you're half as good a rat catcher as I am, this'll be the easiest debt you ever paid. But do us both a favor, don't spread this around."

"Goes without saying," she said.

"But saying goes a lot further. See you later."

He stepped out the door. She wrung the rag in her hand anxiously.

"Five minutes ago I was a barmaid. Now I'm a spy. Let's hope the next few minutes don't follow that pattern, or I'm in for a very difficult day."

Fel reached up and snatched a few leaves from a low-hanging branch over the road. The hours of travel had finally taken him to the fringe of the first "big nothing" between Beffshire and the Greater Lands: areas of little more than road and field, with the only signs of civilization coming in the form of tiny cities built up around crossroads. The only reason to stop in this little village—probably the only reason the village existed—was to buy any last-minute provisions he may have forgotten before potentially taking two days to find another well-stocked city. He wasn't certain he actually needed anything. He'd prepared rather well, and he was better at living off the land than most natives of Beffshire besides. But he wasn't likely to get a decent mug of beer for at least three days. Wetting his whistle while he still could, and maybe taking one last opportunity for conversation, seemed like a worthwhile use of an hour or so.

"You know the drill, Parch," he said, bribing the unicorn with the leaves as a means to hold his attention. "We're going to hop down, play a game of headbutts, then you're going to behave yourself until we get back out here, all right? Otherwise I'm leaving you out here, and I know if I do that you're just going to eat holes in a bunch of sacks."

Parch's grasp of language was such that any sort of response was unlikely, but Fel had developed an impressively accurate intuition about when the little critter would listen to reason. This was primarily achieved by assuming that most of the time he wouldn't listen, but it was nonetheless quite accurate, and today he chose to believe things would go fine once he was inside.

The little stable attached to the tavern that acted as the town center was full to overflowing, but that didn't mean much. There was still a place to tie off his horse, and a few coins in the right palm would make sure his horse had food, water, and someone to make sure no one stole what little gear he had. He kept his end of the bargain, sparring briefly with Parch before they slipped inside. His approach to the bar was visible to the other patrons as a wave of startled men and women reacting to the tickle of a lesser unicorn weaving around or between their legs.

"Hey, buddy!" Fel said when he reached the bar. "Business is booming, huh? What's going on? Got some big event in town?"

The bartender, a hairy fellow who was only slightly better groomed than the horses outside, shouted an answer without looking away from the customer he was serving.

"It's not what's going on in town, it's what's going on down south!" He turned to see who the newcomer was. "Oh, it's you. You didn't bring that pointy scamp in here with you, did you?"

"Which one? The kobold or the unicorn?" Fel asked. "I'm kind of collecting pointy scamps these days."

Parch's head popped up as he leaned his front hooves against the bar to get a better view.

"That one," the bartender grumbled.

"Yeah, Parch came along. Nothing for him though, and a beer for me."

He reluctantly poured a beer. "I'd tell you the livestock stays outside, but I remember what happened to the hitching post last time I told you that."

"Yeah. Parch makes an impression. So what's with the crowd?" Fel asked.

"You haven't heard about what's going on down south?"

"Haven't come down this way in a bit. I'm mostly up in Beffshire."

"Mmm. Guess it might not get up that far. Most of these folks are heading off to the west for better hunting grounds. Point is, things are rough down south, if you're a hunter."

"Let me guess," Fel said. "There's someone stalking along the roads, killing people."

"No. No. That was a couple of months back, and it hasn't happened since."

"No reason it couldn't have started back up again. Glad it hasn't though. What's the problem this time?"

"The way I heard it, you were always in for a hard time if you went down by the wall. Big things with big appetites do their hunting down that way."

"Don't I know it."

"But now it seems like the big appetites have been heading a lot farther away from the wall. I don't know anyone that's seen one, but hunting has been harder and there's, uh... leavings."

"Leavings. You're telling me some hunters ran away because of some big poop?"

"The story I heard was there was half a bear skeleton in it."

Fel's nostrils flared and his lip curled, like someone on the other side of the bar had challenged him to a fight. "And this is down by the wall, is it?"

"Yeah. So where are you headed?" the man said, handing over his beer.

Fel paid. "Down by the wall."

"You going to head back the other way, then?"

"No. The stuff I'm looking for, I can't just head to some other hunting ground to find it."

The man grunted in acknowledgment. "Let's hope you're luckier than the bear."

"Don't need luck," Fel said. "I have two things the bear didn't have." He raised one finger. "The bear was used to being the biggest, scariest thing around, and I've had to run for my life plenty of times. I'm used to it." He raised the second finger. "And now that I know it's a possibility, I'll be ready for it when it happens."

"If it happens," the bartender said.

"No. When. I don't have the best luck. But at least it's reliable."

Hours later, just as the sun was setting, Euphoria trudged out the back door of her house, arms loaded with the various materials that needed to be properly stored. The section of town the Graves family called home shared a narrow section of common ground behind it, a bit like a long, thin courtyard. At its center, a very small cottage had been built. It was more of a shack than the sort of place anyone would live. It existed as secondary lodging if visitors had servants, though for as long as she had been in the family, the servants of visitors were permitted to stay in normal guest quarters. It was nice to know that the Graves had taken at least a few steps away from treating nonfamily members and business partners like a lesser species, as some of the old guard seemed think they were. Now the cottage was used for extra storage, and rarely even for that.

Officially, Euphoria had no reason to use it for storage. There was plenty of room in her own home even if she didn't wish to use the family archives. But there was no reason to question why she would use it. Though it was on common family ground, it was nearest to her house and thus was the property of her husband. Any other member of the family could use it, but they'd need permission. For her, it was as simple as fetching the key and trudging across the rocky courtyard. Unofficially, she had one very good reason for checking it periodically.

She made a show of using the key, but she knew the door was already unlocked. She'd left it so. A bit of a shove caused the door to jolt open—it had sagged with disuse and rubbed the frame now. She shut it behind her and revealed a sparker to light the lantern on the table within.

"Curious. Not here yet," she murmured to herself.

"Not here yet? Who, Sister of Fel?" chattered Teya.

"By the High!" Euphoria yelped, clutching her hand to her chest.

She wheeled around and found Teya peeking out of a cabinet beside the door. It didn't look nearly large enough to contain her, but when it was clear Euphoria was alone, she unfolded herself from inside. She hopped a bit and stretched, whipping her frilled ears to and fro and waggling the toes of each paw in her attempts to limber up after an indeterminate stay in the cabinet. This was only the second time she'd met with Teya in this fashion since discussing the possibility of such a thing with her family down south. Having regular meetings with a kobold took some getting used to, and her brother was better suited to such things than she. She fancied herself a diplomat, and she tried to be open-minded. But she was having difficulty adjusting her mind away from the belief that Teya was little more than a very talented beast. She'd adapt. It would just take time. Two visits were not enough.

"You are an exceedingly stealthy creature, Teya," Euphoria said.

"Sneaky," she said with a grin. "Very very." She tipped her head and hopped onto a chair to look Euphoria a bit more directly in the face. "You look tired. Much work today?"

Euphoria sat down opposite her and set the pages she was carrying on the table. "The details are not for public consumption, but suffice to say what was intended to be a luncheon where some formal requests were made turned into a supper as well, with endless debate. It was taxing, but I am satisfied with the result."

"Dinner. That is food. Luncheon. Also food?"

"Yes."

"This is work?"

"It is not labor. But it is laborious."

"The food is bad? Takes work? Oysters? Clams? I show you, pop shells. Very easy."

"No. No. The food was excellent. The discussion, less so. But, again, the desired outcome was achieved. It was simply as pleasant as a dental extraction to arrive at that outcome."

"Fancy words, Sister of Fel," Teya said, with the tone of a compliment. "We talk now? I promise, less... laborious." Teya took her time with the word and waggled her head proudly when it escaped her mouth mostly intact.

"Yes. Of course. How have things been progressing?"

"Slow. We take care. Do bad? People die. Many many. But we will do. Must. My friends? No earrings. No earrings? So hard to think. Even if they stay. In new land, with new wall. Better with clear minds."

"Certainly."

"We need things. Pointy. For long lines in metal."

"Gravers."

"Yes. Two or three. You have them?"

"I believe I can acquire some for you. Anything else?"

"Hammer? Maybe one or two?"

"I believe that is achievable. And do you have anything for me?"

"Yes!"

She tugged her pack from inside the cabinet where she'd been hiding. Inside was a small sack. She dumped it out. Grape-sized nuggets of an assortment of ores rattled to the table. Teya poked them with her claw, aligning them on the table and naming them one by one.

"Gold, not much. Silver, less not much. Iron, very much. Copper, very much. This? Don't know."

"Zinc, I believe."

"Zinc, very much. This? Don't know again."

"I think that might be tin."

"Tin, much. And this. Shield stone. Less much. And stone. Regular type. Very, very, very much. Oh. And coal, very much."

Euphoria looked at the assortment of ores on the table with a downright predatory gleam in her eye. "Forgive me if this stretches your linguistic skill, but can you be more specific with the meanings of the varying degrees of 'much.'"

Teya rubbed her chin. "Very much? One worker, one day, one cart of stuff. Less much? One worker, ten days, one cart of stuff. Not much, one worker, one cart, very very long."

"I see. That is a tremendous amount of mineral wealth, and a tremendous variety of it, for so small a place."

"Outside? Yes, small. Inside? Not small. Very very."

"Even so."

"Place? Not real. Not natural. Made with machine. Make place? Why not make *good* place?"

"There is certainly a logic to that. Now, when we last met, I'd mentioned that we might be of help to one another in ways beyond your current goal of freeing the minds of your brethren. Please be aware, you are a friend of the family, and I would never even suggest that you or the others within those walls should be exploited or swindled. I would compensate you fairly for any materials you could provide to us. I would only ask that you agree to provide those materials to us exclusively."

"Which us?"

"The Graves family."

Teya shook her head. "No, no. Fel? Yes. Family of Fel? Yes. You? Yes, because family of Fel."

"But I am a representative of the Graves family."

"I give to you. You give to Graves."

"Very well. That is quite acceptable." She smiled. "Very acceptable indeed. Obviously loads of ore, or ingots, or whatever form we decide to do business with will need to be delivered. At present that is impossible. But I'll work on a solution. In the meantime, it will take me until tomorrow evening to get the things you require. You are free to stay here. Light a fire if you choose. I'll tell the others I'm burning documents so they will not be suspicious. Have you eaten? Should I fetch you some food?"

Teya tugged open the second cabinet beside the one she'd been hiding in. There was a rabbit and three large geese, all freshly killed. "So much good hunting!" she crowed happily.

"Splendid. Then I'll see you tomorrow."

"Wait." Teya nudged the pile of game aside and pulled out a hefty lantern. "Oil, very much, for many days. And also, Wick, for talking."

"Right, right. I'd nearly forgotten. Let me take the lantern to refill and relight. I'll be sure to have some casks of oil for you when you depart. It is a wonderful pleasure doing business with you, Teya."

"Fel? Least worst friend. Sister of Fel? Worse friend, but not very. So, we help."

Euphoria laughed. "Maybe when this is through, I'll earn my way to the title of 'less worse,' eh?"

"Maybe. More friends? More good."

"May I take these? The samples?" Euphoria asked.

"Take!" Teya said.

"Many thanks."

Euphoria collected the samples and slipped out the door. The tin and zinc would need to be identified definitively, and all the ore would need to be investigated for purity. But the prospect of a relatively exclusive and extremely local source of all those resources was tantalizing. It would have to be brought to the rest of the family very delicately. They were in the business of buying and selling antiques and contraptions, not precious metals. Most of the family was unified in that, with little desire to extend further. But there were some who sought wealth regardless of the source and didn't care if seeking it overextended the family or brought them into conflict with far larger and far more powerful rivals. But simply having a source of the materials that could not be disrupted, particularly the shield stone, could revolutionize how they did business. Include the expertise of her father and whole new classes of contraptions would suddenly be viable for repair, production, and sale.

This could be the start of something big. A shame that it came at the same time that she was knee-deep in the quagmire of revealing Piotor's treachery and finding an able replacement. But perhaps the opportunity the Lesser Greater Lands presented could provide a solution to the problem of Piotor. It certainly deserved some deep rumination.

As the sun slid lower in the sky, shining in Tome's eyes during his westward journey, he finally allowed himself to guide the horse off the main road toward the nearest town. His knuckles were chalk-white. The spell had worked. It had worked brilliantly, in fact. No aspect of its execution had failed. The issue was not one of mystic skill but insight. Moving at an astonishing speed required more than simply making the body physically capable of it. It required making the mind fast and precise enough to perceive it, and a dozen lesser issues like making sure one's feet didn't dig furrows into the ground in one's attempts to accelerate and things of that nature. That was the reason for the length of the spell. And having cast a simpler version of the spell on himself in the past, he thought he'd accounted for all the elements that would need manipulation. But he'd left one seemingly minor element out of the mix.

The horse.

His pack animal had all the same enhancements he had. But while a human could quite quickly make sense of a shifting perception of speed and time and learn to navigate a curiously swift world within a few minutes, a horse was much slower to adapt. For the first few minutes following the casting of the spell, that meant the beast refused to walk more than a few steps before stopping. But whereas a human could learn and adapt through the application of logic and reason, a horse was more comfortable abandoning the problem entirely. His steed simply stopped watching where it was going. For all he knew, the blasted creature had its eyes closed. This left Tome, far from the best handler of a wagon's reins, with the task of guiding a horse at terrific speeds without so much as the beast's sense of self-preservation to help him avert disaster. Again, nothing beyond the capability of the spell, but it had not been written with the expectation that he would need to grapple with a horse that wasn't actively involved in the task of staying on the road or avoiding other vehicles. He'd lost count of the number of times he'd nearly rammed them into a tree just off the side of the road or sent them headlong into a field when a turn snuck up on them.

Navigation would have been a problem too, if not for the structure of the spell. They achieved such absurd speeds only when they were moving roughly toward the monastery. At any given crossroads or fork, the one that felt like it would kill him was the correct one. He didn't even know where in the world he was anymore, just that it was approximately on a straight line drawn between Beffshire and the Gate of the Ancients, and he was probably five times farther along than he would have been at normal speed.

The spell was a mistake. His heart felt like it was trying to hammer its way out of his chest, and his jaw had been clenched so tight for so long that it ached. And this was just the first day. He had a dozen more ahead of him. If he could, he would undo the spell. Enduring months on the road with nothing to occupy his brain was infinitely better than stretching his mind and wits to the absolute limit for the duration of the journey. But the spell was crafted such that it would conclude only when the journey did. What was done was done. The goal now was to do it as quickly as possible, because taking his time would only break the days into shorter stretches of equally terrifying transit and increase the total amount of time he was enduring this madness.

A friendly young man was working the bar of the inn in the center of town. The place was fairly empty. Only four other people were present, each a solitary traveler like himself. Tome dropped shakily down onto a stool at the bar.

"Tell you this, friend, you look shaken. Need a drink?" the bartender said.

Tome's opinion of him instantly soured, arbitrarily based on his odd phrasing. "I do. I do need a drink. Among a multitude of other things."

"We don't have multitudes, Mr. Fancy Talker. Just drinks and, in a pinch, some bread and cheese if you're too lazy to head next door."

"I note the lack of roasted crickets."

The bartender winced. "From the way you talk, I thought I heard some West Coast in you. Didn't nail you for a bug eater. We don't do that around here."

"Ah. And there we've struck upon another need that must be filled. Where, may I ask, is here?"

"You're in Heinsvale."

"That name has no meaning to me. I need a more regional approximation."

"West Thayne," he said, expression confused.

"How far west?"

"Pretty near the border. Look, friend, I don't know what sort of drink you were planning on, but I'd stay off the hard stuff. You've had a few too many already."

"I'll take that under advisement, but you lack the proper context to make that particular diagnosis, so I'll be having a sherry, sir. And I am most certainly feeling too lazy to head anywhere for food, so whatever the charge for someone to bring me a meal, I'll pay it. In addition, at the risk of being labeled rude, my mind is fraying at the edges presently, so I would prefer some time to collect my thoughts and am not interested in conversation."

Tome dumped what he calculated to be a sufficient number of coins on the table and cradled his head in his hands. The bartender scooped up the payment.

"Saves me the effort of chatting up a man who doesn't want a chat. Here's your sherry."

Tome took the drink and, in order to avoid further temptation at banter, carried it to a table in the corner to nurse it. Once he'd sipped about half of it away, the bartender dropped a plate in front of him. It had decent bread, passable cheese, and questionable meat. Tome didn't dig in immediately. He was quite certain once his mind stopped swirling, his empty stomach would make the whole meal look a good deal more appetizing.

One by one, his settling thoughts made room for new ones. He really ought to check on the lantern in the cart. It was barely smoldering, the better to preserve its abundant but limited oil supply. The operation of the spell protected everything inside the cart from the intense speed, so he was quite certain it hadn't been blown out. But given the greater-than-average chance for catastrophe over the course of this trip, giving an update on his status was more important now than usual. But that required standing up, and he had very little interest in doing so at the moment.

About the time the meat started to look like something he'd consider eating, the door opened and... something came stumbling in. The species wasn't immediately clear, as the newcomer was mounded with strangely feathery robes and a floppy hat festooned with all manner of shiny beads. Shedding the hat and shaking their head produced a plume of road dirt. It was a small mercy that no one was present at the three nearest tables that got a generous dusting.

"Hey! Hey, all! I'm looking for a fellow. A certain fellow. Didn't get a great look. I don't think anyone did. Moved like a bolt of lightning. Wouldn't have known he was even here if I didn't spot that odd little cart of his tucked into the... whatsit out there."

Tome huddled down into his seat. His already substantial distaste for conversation at the moment was further compounded by what he was afraid someone who'd witnessed his means of transit might have to say. As harrowing as it was for him to move at that speed and nearly collide with the rare fellow traveler along the way, it must have been truly unnerving to be on the opposite side of it.

With only a handful of other people in the place, it was inevitable that the newcomer's eyes would shift to Tome, and if one were to try to imagine what a person would look like after moving at a speed like that, Tome's barely diminished look of having seen a ghost was an easy match.

"That's the scoundrel. Tender! Something cool, wet, and cheap. Don't care what. I'll be with my new friend here," said the strange figure.

"I'd really rather be alone," Tome said.

"Oh, come now. Everyone needs a friend. And you and I need to have a chat, besides. What's that you have there? Supper? Mind if I share?"

"I absolutely do."

"Suit yourself."

The bartender walked over with a mug of what Tome assumed was the cheapest ale he had.

"Looks delicious!" remarked Tome's new "friend." "Do you do barter, or does it have to be legal tender, Tender?"

"Duots. And if you don't settle down and stop bothering customers, you won't be here long enough to finish that mug."

"I've found the man I was after, the rest of you are safe from my enthusiasm."

A bit of rooting around in a sack filled with badly polished beads and exotic feathers turned up a duot to pay for the drink. The bartender accepted it and paced away, glaring at the stranger the whole way.

"You're a wizard," remarked the dusty traveler.

"A paper mage, specifically."

"Eh, it's all one big mush. You see the world isn't doing something you want it to, and you make it do it, even if it doesn't think it should be able to. I'm in the same business."

"It is more of an art form than a business."

"That's certainly so if you take my coin purse for an example. The point is, we have similar interests. And I saw a blur zip by me faster than anything ought to. That got me really interested."

Tome sighed again, a bit more theatrically than perhaps was called for. Having become resigned to the fact that he wouldn't be able to simply ignore this person, he reluctantly looked them over. The face peering out of the heap of dusty rags had a peculiar look to it. This person was a match for Tome's age, or maybe a few years younger, but retained a stubborn youthfulness to their features. The face was perfectly clean-shaven. Tome tried to keep himself similarly groomed, but no one who had a face that grimy and who plainly spent as much time on the road as this could possibly have achieved that with a razor. This was a woman. But myriad little indicators Tome couldn't enumerate if you'd asked him to, from voice to assorted affectations, came across as male.

"Forgive me if this is rude, but are you a man or a woman?" Tome asked.

"That's all one big mush too. Take your pick. Whatever makes you happy."

"Unless given a reason otherwise, I'll assume femininity," Tome said.

"Popular choice!" she said. "The name's Madge, by the way. Might've started there if I'd been thinking. But my brain, like so many other things, also one big mush."

"Well, Madge, I'd really like to be alone to collect myself after a very trying trip."

"Sure. Sure. That's fine. That's what you'd like. Now we'll go through what I'd like, and when we're done, we can decide which we'd like best."

She carefully shrugged out of her piles of rags, doing so slowly enough to keep from depositing a layer of road grime on the food. Without the heaps obscuring her body, it became striking just how lean, almost gaunt, she was. Madge had the look of someone who naturally tended toward thinness but had pushed it to dangerous lengths through malnutrition. That she seemed so bubbly and positive regardless seemed utterly absurd. There was the very real possibility that she'd not eaten in days, and that such a fate wasn't at all unusual for her.

"I think maybe I could see my way clear to sharing a meal with you," he said.

"Much obliged..." She snapped her fingers as she trailed off, hand held out in a prompting manner.

"Tome."

"Tome. Much obliged indeed. Anything on that plate you'd sooner be rid of than eat?"

"The meat's looking a little peaked."

"Couldn't agree more." She snatched it up and shoved the whole hunk into her mouth. "Oh. Yeah. Hasn't turned yet but it was certainly on the agenda," she said between juicy chomps. "Now, what I was after. I'm a bit of an apprentice in search of a master."

"I'm not a master."

"More of a master than me. And the way you were whizzing around, more of a master than most." She swallowed hard. "Oof. That meat's going to fight back, I know it. Before I go on, did you worry yourself with how it would look from the outside? Or was that not part of the spell?"

"It wasn't intended to be part of the spell. If I'm honest, the spell wasn't necessarily intended to be cast, but boredom and curiosity got the better of me. As you can see, I'm not an ideal master in that regard."

"Pish posh. Exactly the master for me. Reckless and successful. That's the way forward. So long as no one gets hurt, what's the harm?"

"Someone could have easily gotten hurt. And could easily still get hurt."

"Sure, sure. But that's where I come in. I tag along, make sure you have someone to catch you if you stumble, ask questions about what sort of holes you might be putting in the spell before you do it, everything works out great for everyone, right?"

"Madge, I'm in the middle of a long journey."

"How about that! So am I."

"I very much doubt we're going to the same place."

"Oh, I'm sure we weren't when we started this conversation. Fact is, I don't even have a destination. I'm just going for the sake of going. 'Where' didn't seem like the interesting question. But you have a destination, right? So I'll just borrow yours!"

"You don't even know where I'm going."

"I didn't even know where I was going, so may as well change it up. Where are you going, anyway?"

"The Gate of the Ancients," he said.

"Great! Where's that?"

"On the west coast. The other side of the continent."

"Lovely. Never been there. I mostly float around the south. Roundabout where the desert turns more to the forest. Morning Break, Rubble Hill. That region."

"Madge, I do not want, nor do I need, an apprentice."

"Ask me what I used to do down there."

"I don't care what you did down there."

"Ask me."

He gritted his teeth. "What did you do down there?"

"Raced horses."

"... Really?"

"Yes. Morning Break isn't called Morning Break because the sun rises there. It doesn't rise there. But the wild horses there have more spirit than you could believe, and I grew up breaking them and bringing them in to stud. When I got old enough I started racing."

"How do I know you're telling the truth..."

"I could give you a demonstration. But something tells me your horse is about as frazzled as you are, so we might want to wait until tomorrow morning."

"And why do you think your racing prowess is relevant to me?"

"Because something tells me you're as frazzled as your horse is, and that tells me you probably aren't that used to handling a beast moving faster than it wants to move."

"You aren't used to this sort of speed either."

"Closer to used to it than you are."

He shut his eyes tight. A series of dueling visions clashed in his mind. On one hand, the thought of sharing the burden of guiding the horse was enticing. The presence of a whole additional human might cause the spell to reduce somewhat in effectiveness, which would potentially decrease the speed to more manageable levels. Of course, this strange woman could also crash the cart the moment she took the reins, and even if she was exceptional at guiding the cart, he'd still have to deal with a personality that had in a few short minutes rubbed him about as raw as a shoe full of grit.

"That piece is looking a little long in the tooth, too," she said, her voice almost drowned out by the grumble of a stomach awoken by what may have been the first meal in days.

A final thought rammed its way past the others, a vision of Fel adopting the lesser harpies, and Parch, and Oiler. Tome rumbled with frustration and pushed the plate in front of Madge.

"We'll split a room for the night, and I'll give you one day to prove you can help me."

"You're a good egg, Tome."

"We'll see how long that notion persists..." he grumbled.

Chapter 3

Most lives are long periods of tiresome routine punctuated by manic calamity. Little sparks of bliss or heartache bobbing on the waves of a bland, weary ocean of quiet struggle. For Fel Masker and those with the mixed blessing of crossing paths with him, the last year had been quite the opposite. Dangers that challenged or shattered the limits of plausibility were daily obstacles. The sort of confluences of misfortune that would be enough to define the average person's life came every few weeks. It hadn't always been the case. There was a time when Fel craved excitement. But now that he'd had his fill, the long, slow trek south that had been completely devoid of assaults by mystics of the lesser or greater variety was a tonic. He could feel his mind and body recovering. He might even have felt like his old self again if only he'd allowed himself to embrace the monotony fully. Alas. He was just a bit too savvy for the whims of fate. He hadn't faced anything absurd yet. And he was long past due.

There had been no lack of warnings of what was to come. He had spent two nights with a roof over his head rather than camping in the fields. Both times it was less a result of forethought and more a result of the horse starting to tire at the precise moment a village came into view. Each time the local chatter all leaned in the same direction. Best not to keep heading south. Something awful is waiting there. And yet, he trekked onward. It wasn't that he trusted himself to be lucky enough to avoid facing whatever was scaring these people off. It was that he had far more experience than they did with unknowable horrors, so he was more equipped for it all than they were.

And despite all the warning, the thin line of the Greater Lands Wall awaited him on the horizon, and still he hadn't had to level the dazzler at any threats. Fate was really dragging its feet. Fel tried to remain alert, but his vigilance was in a stalemate of a battle against boredom. And in their battle, distraction was a third combatant with an unfair advantage, as at this moment Wick had arrived with news from home.

"You're kidding me. You're *kidding* me. You're telling me Tem is fundraising on this grum game?" Fel said.

"Such is Allie's claim. Rather than attempting to cover his side of the tournament out of his personal finances, Tem is attempting to seek other patrons of the bar who are willing to cover his entry fee, with the promise of returning their contribution half over again when he wins."

"So he's trying to raise five thousand duots, with the promise to pay back seventy-five hundred, when the whole pot is ten thousand. And that's assuming he takes me for every last coin."

"Your calculations appear sound," Wick said.

"So he stands to win twenty-five hundred. He'd have won more than that if he'd just beat me before I left!"

"Again, your calculations appear sound."

"What's that dope up to?"

"Allie's theory is that he had no means to finance the full entry fee, and that he had to 'sweeten the deal' this much to get any takers."

"And did he get any takers?"

"Again, in her precise words, 'he got more than he should have, but not enough to pay the bill.' She expressed a degree of disappointment at some of the tavern regulars who contributed to his fund."

"Tell her that if he doesn't have the money by the time I get back, then that's a forfeit, and I win not only the title but the right to call him a cheapskate and a dope too."

"I shall do so."

"Everything else all right with her besides?"

"Nothing else was worthy of comment, she said."

"And how's the rest?"

"The shop continues to do brisk trade. Your sister Epiphany in particular has been making impressively substantial deals."

"Is she still focusing on the people who aren't willing to make the trek to the shop?"

"Remote clients, she calls them."

"Yeah, fine, whatever."

"She is."

"Good for her. And Tome?"

"His updates are brief and filled with frustration, as his apprentice seldom leaves him alone long enough to properly update me."

"But you still stop out west to keep an eye on him, right?"

"I do. He continues to move at speeds that are difficult for me to comprehend, and it is taxing for him in mind and body, not due to mystic output but due to general anxiety."

"I can't wait to hear how he's going to try to spin this as something less than bone-headed."

"It seems likely that he is willing to embrace the foolishness of his endeavor."

"Yeah, to you. Face to face he's a lot cagier about anytime he does something even I would think is dumb. Now what about..."

Fel trailed off. Somewhere in the back of his mind, he'd been slowly accumulating the subtle indications that something was amiss. The list had finally grown to the point that it had to be addressed. Most of the signs were easy to dismiss. The area around the Greater Lands Wall was quite arid. Not a proper desert, but the sort of dry, crunchy ground that burst to vibrant green after every rainfall and then faded again. This made for very little in the way of plant life for the local animals to eat; thus, there was a tendency for anything capable of sprouting to have been nibbled practically to its roots. Such had been the case for each previous visit to this place. But now there were areas that were looking downright overgrown. There weren't very many leaf-eaters and grass-eaters about. Furthermore, he could hear birdsong, but most of the other sounds of wildlife were muted or absent.

"This feels like what the place would sound like if a big predator showed up," Fel said.

"You are a big predator by any reasonable measure, at least with regard to local animal life."

"Yeah. Bigger than me. Parch, how are you feeling?" He glanced aside. "Parch?"

The unicorn, who had made it his purpose in life to either be pestering Fel or prancing along beside the cart, had huddled behind his seat at some point during the update from Wick. Never a good sign.

"All right, Wick. We're on the lookout for something big and mean."

"How big and how mean, Fel?"

The road took them past one of the overgrown clumps of foliage to reveal a long, narrow stretch of charred ground.

"I'm thinking dragon. Or something else that rains fire down from the heavens," he said.

"I shall fulfill this service happily. A dragon should be a simple thing to spot."

"Yeah. Spotting is easy. Escaping is tricky."

Fel fetched the dazzler, a staff-shaped device that was utterly useless as a weapon but quite good at causing distraction. While he was at it, he nudged the decoy hidden beneath his seat with his heel to satisfy himself that it was still there and ready to be deployed.

"Funny how Parch is shaking like a leaf but the horse is just lumbering forward like nothing's wrong," Fel said.

"Further evidence of the special insight that Lesser Mystics seem to enjoy."

"He doesn't look like he's enjoying it right now," Fel said.

The wagon rolled closer to the wall. The nearer they got, the more evidence of some sort of fiery predator revealed itself. It never became abundant. A swath of charred ground here, a mound of droppings of unsettling size and composition there. But casting their eyes south revealed tighter clusters of these signs.

"Seems like we're not headed directly into the beast's clutches. Destiny is really missing an opportunity to make my life miserable and brief."

"I would advise against tempting fate," Wick said.

"Like my luck can get any worse."

"You focus on the bad luck necessary to encounter so many hazards in the past. I suggest you focus on the good luck necessary to survive them."

"Point taken."

Careful advancement over the course of an hour took them near enough to the wall that a short, desperate sprint would be able to get them into the shelter of one of the alcoves within a minute or two. Fel took this moment, the best balance of clear vantage to potential safety, to try to spot a more pressing source of danger rather than simply the sign of it.

"Where is that stupid spyglass..." he grumbled.

Diving into a vault to collect artifacts wasn't a task that was well served by gazing over long distances, but reaching those vaults was. For this reason, Fel always brought a spyglass along but seldom kept it in an easily accessible place. He finally found it and struggled to pull free the protective covering just as the clatter of hooves alerted him to Parch's sudden departure.

"Uh-oh," he said, sweeping the horizon with his eyes. "Talk to me, Wick. What do you see?"

"Nothing yet, Fel. I will remind you, seeing over long distances is not a strength of mine."

"Don't be shy. Shout it out if you see something. It could be anything. A broken branch that looks fresh. Some stomped-flat grass. Or—" He pointed. "Shadow!"

He snapped the reins. The horse hauled the wagon up to speed. A shadow sweeping across the ground was a difficult thing to spot from a distance unless one had the benefit of a high vantage. That Fel had spotted the massive swath of darkness sliding across the ground spoke volumes of just how close and just how slow it was. This wasn't something far in the sky, scouting for a meal. This was something turning for a swoop.

Fel didn't bother with the dazzler or the decoy. Keeping the horse on course and at speed was the better use of his time. A rusted metal gate stood before him, still broken and wide open from his previous trip. The brightness of the sun vanished as the shadow settled over the wagon. He could see the long neck and pointed head of a dragon in silhouette on the ground ahead.

"Do I want to look up and see how close he is?" Fel shouted to Wick.

"You do not," Wick said.

With a monster this close, snapping the reins and commanding the horse was no longer necessary. Survival instinct took over. The new problem would be getting it to stop before the wagon rattled to bits or smashed into the wall. Fel took the brief respite to snag the decoy and deploy it. A wheeled contraption dragging a folded cloth darted off to the left. Wind filled the cloth and presented a massive new target. It must not have looked as appetizing as the horse and its driver, because the shadow of the dragon's head and neck didn't so much as shift to glance in its direction. Fel leaned down and pulled the wooden lever that controlled the seldom-used brakes of the wagon. As much as he wanted as much speed as he could get, there was barely enough room between himself and the alcove to bring the wagon to a stop.

The smell of hot metal and charring wood signaled the engagement of the brakes at speeds far higher than intended. Bits of the broken gate clattered under the wheels as they thundered through. Fel hauled the reins to turn the horse aside. The wagon lurched aside, tipping onto two wheels before it came to a stop and slammed down. It was half in the alcove and half out. Fel reached behind his seat and found the leather-reinforced handle of his favored weapon for large foes. He whipped it aside, shaking it free of its canvas covering to reveal a simple branch with some large, cruel-looking spines driven through it. He called it the dragon sticker, and he'd genuinely hoped it would never have to repeat the stunt that had earned it its name.

He hopped down and brandished the weapon. The dragon slammed down with enough force to shake free a few more of the bars from the damaged gate. The thing was hideous, ferocious, and to Fel's fear and surprise, familiar. This was the beast called Duurth. A long scar ran down the side of his neck, precisely where Fel had jabbed his weapon the last time they'd faced each other. A flash of something in the beast's gaze revealed that it, too, remembered the clash. And if the monster didn't recognize Fel, it certainly recognized his weapon. The thing took a cautious step back. Fel held his ground, raising the weapon higher.

For a frozen moment in time, neither beast nor man budged. Fel's wind-scoured eyes burned, but he refused to blink. The months since their last meeting had changed the beast more than seemed possible. His hide was notched with new scars, fresher than the ones Fel had caused. The shafts of arrows bristled on one side of his body, jutting out between scales and lodged in flesh that looked wretched and swollen. It had seen battle, more in the last few weeks than likely in the decade before, if Fel had to guess.

Fel sensed the beast's hesitation wouldn't last much longer, and he knew if he turned to try to open the door to the interior of the wall, the intimidation would falter and he'd be roasted in fiery breath. Instead, he took a purposeful step forward and waggled the end of his weapon. The result was a moment that would live on in Fel's memories for the rest of his life. In a stare-down between himself and a dragon, the dragon blinked. The beast spread its wings again and took to the sky. Fel didn't let the shaking end of his weapon lower until he could no longer hear the leathery flap of wings.

With the intensity of the moment no longer present to fuel him, he dropped to his knees, then to his hands. "Did you get a good look at that?" he asked, panting.

"The beast, or your act of bravery?"

"Both. But mainly the beast."

"Significant evidence of conflict."

"I was a little busy hoping I wasn't about to die. Did you notice the arrows?"

"I did."

"Do you remember what the whole one, stuck down near his shoulder, looked like?"

"I do."

"Go tell everyone. Mom and Dad, Tome, and Teya. See if any of them know where something like that came from. Because I don't know anyone out here who'd dare to try shooting at a dragon with a longbow. That's a job for a crossbow in a pinch and siege weapons if you've had time to plan. Makes me think whatever trouble he's been getting into, he's been getting into it inside the wall."

"I will deliver as detailed a description as I can provide. Do you require anything else from me at present?"

"No. No I need to figure out how to get my legs to listen to me again. Then I need to make sure Parch and the horse and the wagon made it through that all right. I'm going to be busy."

"I shall return as quickly as possible."

Far to the north, powerful creatures of an entirely different sort were preparing for a clash of their own. Thayne was a kingdom, and as such it had a king. But these days few paid the old man any heed. His signature graced the most important documents, and the touch of his sword or scepter bestowed ceremonial honors, but mostly he served as a model for the nation's currency, an occupant for the capital palace, and little else. The real power in the kingdom rested in the hands of the lords and ladies. Lord Katritz, and to a lesser degree Lady Katritz, held approximately the same amount of power as the other two lords and ladies, though Lady Katritz spent most of her time in their summer home along the southern border. Katritz and the other nobles had divided the kingdom into three wedge-shaped regions, ostensibly equal in land area. That was a matter of endless debate but little progress. Unlike his counterparts, Lord Hundt and the widowed Lady Zyne, Katritz had interests that extended well beyond his borders. Despite having reached the top of the ladder on the day he was born thanks to the land inheritance from his father, he endeavored toward upward mobility. Thus, his meeting today.

Attendants scurried about the lord, primping a waxed mustache, adjusting a starched collar, and generally doing their best to make the man at least moderately interesting to look upon. No one speaking honestly would call Lord Katritz a handsome man, though those in his position seldom had to hear someone speaking with honesty. But neither was he ugly. The man was stunningly, almost aggressively, average and unremarkable in his countenance. Spared the more notable effects of the breeding—and more often inbreeding—that had shaped the modern gentry, he lacked the weak chin and ponderous ears that gave Lord Hundt his memorable expression. Similarly, because he was born into his position rather than selected, he lacked the sculpted, classical beauty of his wife.

The result was a man who was intensely forgettable. It was a plight so acute that the fantasy world of yes-men and bootlickers weren't strong enough to keep the truth from him. He knew he wasn't as impressive as his title, and thus the burden fell to wardrobe and accessories to provide his visual gravitas. His mustache was cunningly shaped and slathered with wax to pin it in place, leaving it with a painted-on appearance. Likewise, his beard was trimmed and groomed to a point and held in place with more wax, such that it may well have been able to draw blood with its tip. His meager yet soft frame was lost in a puffed and pleated cathedral of a wardrobe, and a few precious inches of additional height were granted by heeled boots.

And yet, through it all, he looked more like an uninteresting middle-aged man dressed as a lord than an actual lord.

"Your guest for the afternoon is here," bellowed a crier from down the hall.

Katritz waved his hands at the attendants, shooing them like flies. "Right, right. Send him in," he instructed.

A burly fellow marched inside. Like Katritz, he looked like he was wearing a costume, as he was dressed in needlessly fine cloth, with gleaming silver buttons fastened from belt to chin and straining to conceal the barrel chest beneath it. He had a friendly, almost conspiratorial, smile as though from the moment he saw someone, he was snickering about an inside joke they shared. He held out a hand that was downright craggy with work-hardened calluses.

"Pleased to meet you, Lord Katritz," he said. "Name's Donovan Verfessa. We've been chatting."

When the lord didn't immediately indulge him in a handshake, Verfessa grabbed him by the hand and locked him into the shake with a hand to his elbow. The force and enthusiasm of the act was enough to get two guards, lingering in the far corners of the room, to take notice. Each advanced by a few steps before Verfessa finally broke the handshake. They would have continued forward to remove him, but Katritz stopped them with a glance, then held out the hand that had been manhandled. An attendant dashed in to provide a silk handkerchief. He wiped his hand and handed it back.

"Mr. Verfessa. You'll forgive me if I cannot precisely recall the reason for our meeting, but as it is exceedingly difficult to be granted an audience with me, I must assume you have a worthwhile reason. Let us begin with your place of origin."

"Beffshire."

"And I presume you are a civic leader, thereabouts?"

"The other civic leaders back home would chafe to hear you put me shoulder to shoulder with them, but I'm more that than I'm not. These days I prefer to call myself a businessman and leave it at that."

"And what business brings you before me today?"

"You and I have been having a bit of a back and forth via the couriers."

"Hardly a rarity."

"We've been chatting up a subject that I don't think you'd like me to call by name."

"Ah." His eyebrows rose as genuine realization replaced the false realization that was a prelude to dismissal. "Privacy for me and my guest."

The assorted servants and guards departed without question, moving like a startled flock of birds and shutting the doors firmly behind them.

"So you would be the individual who came into possession of documents regarding..."

"Gem? That's me."

"And I suppose you are here to negotiate a price for both the documents in question and your silence."

"You've got me wrong, Katritz."

"Lord Katritz."

"Right. You're wrong about me, Lord. Sure, my interests in coming up here are financial in the long run. But I'm not here to pick your pockets."

"If you intended that to be a source of relief for me, you have missed our mark. An exchange of coins for silence tends to be a much swifter and cleaner transaction than the alternatives."

"Don't I know it. But money, I've got. I'm not here to hold you over the coals. You having a hard time doesn't do me any good. Like you said, though. It's awfully hard to get an audience with you, and that little letter was enough to do the trick. I'm not going to part with it just for a pile of coins and a slap on the back."

"Then what is your aim, sir?"

"Straight to the point. I like that in a business partner. Here is how it shakes out. It took me a good long time to scrape out the comfortable little spot for myself in Beffshire. And for a while there, it was good and stable. But more and more, there are people sniffing about, looking for slices of my pie. I'm not greedy. I'm willing to share, so long as we each get a big enough piece to settle our appetites. But these people are looking to make pigs of themselves. Cutting a piece to leave and trying to walk off with the rest of the pie. Worst of all, I'm left with very little recourse to send them on their way without getting rough. And if you get rough, they get rougher. Pretty soon that pie server is sticking out of someone's chest, and that'll end a party pretty quick. I'd like you to introduce me around here in the capital. See if I can't get myself a little more formal, official recognition for the work I do back in Beffshire."

"Are you suggesting you are seeking a title?"

"That'd do the job nicely, I think."

"I cannot simply grant you something that should be a birthright."

"Well sure. But there are ways around everything. And you strike me as the sort of man who knows them."

"You have an eye for character, that much is clear."

"I might not be alive today if I didn't," Verfessa said.

"What you seem to lack, however, is a firm grasp of one's relative position of strength or weakness. Let us imagine, for a moment, that you do have a document. And that this document mentions something called 'Gem.' That means nothing. Because I can say with certainty that no genuine document penned by my own hand has anything even remotely suggestive of wrongdoing, let alone solid evidence of such."

"Oh, sure. Sure. But it's still proof."

"Proof of what? I've done nothing wrong."

"Proof of whatever is floating around in the heads of the rumormongers. People were already tripping over themselves to come up with the juicy details of whatever dalliance or affair you were doing once the name Gem came up. If a piece of paper that you definitely wrote shows up, and that paper names that dalliance specifically? Suddenly all the things they imagined have a solid place to stand, even though nothing on the page actually supports the bits they're so focused on chatting about. Funny how rumor works."

"And what influence, precisely, does that give you over me?"

"Oh, the word getting out? Doesn't do me a lick of good. Doesn't do me much harm either. Your life gets to be a headache for a while. The idea is, you give me a leg up, and I make sure that little piece of paper doesn't slip out."

"Lies being spread about me, even those with the illusion of credibility thanks to a misinterpreted missive, mean little to me. Everyone lies about those in power, hoping to dislodge them from their perches and take those positions for themselves. I know how to deal with such things. As you say, I wouldn't be here today if I didn't."

"Hey, now. You of all people should know not to misquote a man. I said I wouldn't be *alive* today if I didn't. You're talking about this like you're playing the game at a very high level. You don't understand the stakes I've been laying on the table for a lifetime. If I just wanted to come up here and intimidate whoever happened to be in charge at the time? I'd have come up here years ago. That I came today means I'm satisfied I've got what it takes to get what I want out of this town. Now you can assume I'm wrong and send me on my way. That'll force me to show my run of tiles and move the game to the next level. Or you can do what I thought a lord would do right from jump and see what's on the other side of this little offer."

"The other side of the offer. Are you suggesting you have something to offer *me*, somehow?"

"I never come to another man's home with my hand out. It's always a trade. That's how business is done."

"What could you possibly offer me?"

"I could say that I'm offering you the peace of mind that comes with knowing that last little page that's floating around won't ever pop up at a bad time for you, but that's just another way of saying what's already been said. But I'm a man who can get things done. And given the number of times people borrowing your power have been showing up in Beffshire only to be turned away without doing what they were after, you need someone on the inside. I did my digging. There's not another town in the kingdom like Beffshire. It's the only city with a trail of agreements with lords and kings alike keeping too many people from meddling with things inside those walls. The other nobles? In charge of the other slices of this pie? They can send their people into any city in their territory and bend the locals to their whims without a word of recourse for the people getting bent. But you have that one rock in your shoe. And it's a big one. Outside of the capital, Beffshire's the most powerful town in Thayne. Lots of trade. Lots of business. But it's set up to run itself, and that doesn't do you much good."

"The people pay their tribute. I am comfortable with the influence I have."

Verfessa laughed. "That's a new one. 'I have enough power.' There's not a powerful man in the world who ever said that. The point is, the rules are the rules. You can't get any further without breaking them, and since it's the rules that give you the rest of your power, you can't risk breaking them. That's where your old pal Verfessa comes in. You get yourself a friend inside who doesn't have nearly as rigid a relationship with the rules, and suddenly your options are open. Your hands stay clean and smooth while these mitts do your dirty work."

Katritz stroked his beard from base to tip, giving it a twist at the end that instantly ruined the hard work of his attendants. "It has a certain appeal."

Verfessa grinned. "The missus always did find me appealing."

The lord considered in silence for a time. "I assume you are a landholder?"

"I've got my name on a few sheets of parchment tucked away in your archives."

"Then the title, or rather position, available to you with your level of breeding is 'vassal.' That would permit you to have greater control over the land you ostensibly own. In effect, it would permit you to behave as though you truly own it. In exchange you would provide your usual tribute to me as well as a codified level of allegiance and obligation. Largely ceremonial matters of martial aid that are hardly called for within the borders of our kingdom these days. That would also allow you to, in your very limited way, perform certain acts within Beffshire that would normally require my own authority. These actions committed in my name would be subject to audit on a regular basis. And should I find you have performed actions that endanger the throne, you will have that status revoked."

"I think I could make that work for me," Verfessa said.

"I imagine you could. There, of course, is an issue. Due to certain historical improprieties that predate my own tenure as a lord, a vassal cannot be named at one's whim. The other nobles, and the king, must permit such a position to be bestowed. So unless you have a means to extort all of them as well, this entire enterprise has been for naught."

"I have something better than means of extortion," he said with a grin. "I've got charm. You give me the time and the chance to work my magic on them, and I think I'll help them see things my way."

"Very well. I'll see about arranging a meeting."

"I knew you'd see things my way," Verfessa said.

"Let me make something clear to you, good sir. I do not see things your way. I will never see things your way. Your sort cannot think or act in a way that is becoming of a noble. Not by nature. There is a reason breeding is necessary for people who are meant to lead. One cannot place a mule in a race against thoroughbreds and expect the beast to compete. I'll let you play at the game. But please be aware that your failure is inevitable, and not through my actions, but through your inadequacies."

"We'll see what we'll see," Verfessa said, heading for the door. He paused and remarked over his shoulder, "I probably shouldn't have brought up charm. It isn't nice to use words when the person you're talking too doesn't know what they mean."

Teya watched with barely subdued excitement, bobbing up and down on her tiptoes as a dwarf lightly tapped the handle of an engraving tool. The specific diplomatic methods used to acquire the cooperation of the dwarf were best left unexplored, though the bandages on his left hand and forearm suggested Teya's guidance was taken to heart by her fellow kobolds. But whatever the reason he'd offered his services, the dwarf had embraced the kobold mindset of "working together is its own reward." His focus and contentment as he teased perfect reproductions of the carefully traced-out runes Teya had provided were deep and genuine.

The kobolds did most of their work out in the open or else in places far sturdier than a simple building or shed. Most of them had worked to dig out a nice little den underground to stay out of the sun and the elements. But work like this was done in the workshops left from when the Lesser Greater Lands was in the hands of Lens. It was a small, simple shop with heavy wooden workbenches and shelves of assorted goods. A flickering flame in a lantern on one shelf lit the workspace. When the flame went steady, Teya didn't immediately notice. Not until Wick spoke did she finally turn to it.

"Teya, a word, if I may?" Wick said.

She spun around and trotted to the lantern, checking the oil level to make sure it didn't need topping off. "You are back so fast, Wick!" she said, once again granted the luxury of speaking in her own language thanks to Wick's understanding of it. "Are you here because of good news or bad?"

"The news is neutral, though tragedy was quite likely for a short and intense period of time," Wick said. "Presently we require your expertise regarding a recent discovery near the Greater Lands Wall."

"Fel has reached it!" She clutched her paws together. "I did not think I would miss it so. This world beyond it is so big and interesting, but one day soon I should visit my old home again. What do you need to know?"

"Fel had a brief clash with Duurth. The beast was unwilling to battle him directly, either due to the sharp memory of the last clash or due to having been weakened by more recent battles."

"When I first breathed fire!" she chirped. "It is a shame. Such a grand, beautiful thing, a dragon. A kobold should not fight one. But it was right to do at that time. You say there were more recent battles?"

"Yes. Fresh scars, and evidence of arrows driven into his hide. There is evidence to suggest the beast has expanded his hunting grounds to primarily, or at least additionally, include the lands beyond the southwestern edge of the Greater Lands Wall."

"Duurth's lair is the old Clickspring. That is as far from the wall as one can get. I know that he would travel to the wall sometimes because only he could. A hunter with a way to go somewhere that no other hunter can go will go there sometimes for the easy hunt and to make sure no other hunters tried to take it. But not for every meal. Very strange," she said.

"One of the arrows in his side was fully intact. It was quite narrow. Made of a silvery wood. The fletching was green, with a faintly iridescent sheen to it. Fel seems confident people beyond the Greater Lands wouldn't use weapons such as those."

She tapped the claws of her fingers together and muttered under her breath, puzzling over what had been said. "You say the arrow is thin. How thin? Like my wrist? Like this finger here? Or this one? Like my toe claw. My finger claw?"

"Finger claw," he said.

"Very thin. Thinner than kobold arrows. And the feathers were green?"

"Indeed."

"These are elf arrows. The elves are shooting the dragon. Why now? I don't know. Duurth's home is across the sea from the elves. There is much hunting in places that are not filled with elves. Even with Kazel once again free, there are many places to go. Duurth would only fight elves now if he went to them or they went to him."

"Curious," Wick said.

"Very curious," Teya agreed. "Is that all?"

"I suspect I will be back again on this topic, but it is all for now."

"Good! Then come this way! I want to show you this!" She snatched up the lantern and raised it to provide a better vantage of the work being done on the table in the center of the room. "This is my dwarf friend. I do not know his name because he did not tell me, but it does not matter, because he is my only dwarf friend, so Dwarf Friend is enough. He makes jewelry! And with those skills he is helping us make the new plates for the diamond for when we fix it. But we need to know if he is doing it right. Is he doing it right?"

She held the lantern steady. After a moment of observation, Wick answered.

"The shapes match the reference you and I were provided. As long as they were applied in the order described, I would say the work is exquisite."

"Good! More plates to write, but when they are done, my friends, even my dwarf friend, will think clearer."

"What are your plans for after that is achieved?"

"I don't know! One step at a time. Fel says that."

"He does. Though I would suggest Fel is not strictly the best role model when it comes to long-term planning."

"He does it good enough for me! Talk to you again soon. Good luck to all of us!"

"Indeed," Wick said. "And let us hope that we do not need that luck."

A week had passed since the grum tournament had gone on hiatus, and it would be at least another week before the final round once again turned her tavern into a circus, so Allie was trying to enjoy the return to relative normality. There were multiple complicating factors. On the positive side, Oovay had run into a bit of a financial snarl in that he'd angered his mother enough to convince her to kick him out of the house for at least a few weeks. It wasn't positive for Oovay, of course, but it meant that he was in the tavern on time and worked his full shift each day. Having to pay for room and board, or completely lacking it, had a way of making one value time spent at one's place of work. On the negative side, the assignment she'd been given by Verfessa continued to occupy a substantial portion of her mind. As far as she could tell, it hadn't affected her work. But having to scrutinize and eavesdrop upon any unfamiliar face was no way to live a life as far as she was concerned, and she'd be happy to be done with it.

In that regard, the man who had just walked through the door may have been precisely who she'd been waiting for. Unlike Velonia Madritz, the previous pain in the behind who nearly ruined her life, this man didn't look like he didn't belong in The Fox and Log. On the young side of middle-aged, lean, a bit shabby, dressed for travel, he was precisely the sort of person who would wander in, have a few cheap drinks, and wander out never to be seen again. Beffshire got an awful lot of trade from all over the region, and The Fox and Log was one of the cheaper options for refreshment and entertainment. Anyone who looked like they were thirsty, weary, and short on money had just the look of a would-be Fox and Log patron. What labeled this man as strange was how he interacted with the place and its patrons.

From the first moment he stepped inside, he looked in all the usual places one might hide something seedy. The darker corners, the two back rooms. He not-so-subtly toured the place and took note of everywhere one might walk the tightrope of being hidden from people who might not want you doing business and accessible to people who might want to do business. About half the time someone like that showed up, they tucked themselves into the corner and set up shop. In nearly every such case, Allie sent them on their way before the end of their first evening. If your job required you to glance anxiously over your shoulder before you started, Allie really didn't want you lingering in The Fox and Log to do it.

This man, however, wasn't doing that sort of business. At least, not yet. Though he checked out all the usual haunts, he didn't actually settle down into any of them. A feature he shared with Madritz was his curiosity. He was very talkative almost immediately, inserting himself into conversations, listening in on other conversations. He had a knack to it, as he was able to do such things without making himself a nuisance. He had the insight to avoid conversations that wouldn't have him and enough of the gift of gab to wedge himself into more circles of friends chatting each other up than she would have thought possible. And most glaring of all to a barmaid, after nearly an hour of floating about and getting to know the room, he'd yet to order a drink. To the rest of the tavern, he was an interesting, pleasant, sociable fellow.

To Allie, he was the one she was waiting for.

It was simultaneously a relief and a new source of stress. No more waiting, which was often the hardest part. Now she had the job itself to do, and thus success or failure hung on her performance. But that was just the way of things. The only thing to do was to dive in and get it over with.

She bided her time until he was about to get up and shift tables, then swiftly made her way over with refills for the other patrons and a basket of crickets.

"Meeting someone?" she asked as he walked past her.

"Come again," he said, turning to spot who'd spoken, as though he hadn't anticipated words to come out of a barmaid.

"You've been hanging about for quite a bit and haven't had a drink," she said. "Usually that's someone waiting for a friend so they don't get too far ahead in the drinking."

"Ah. No. I'm just not thirsty," he said.

"Well, for a new face in town, you picked a good place to start making friends. Good drinks, free crickets, music twice a week. Fights about twice a week, too, but that's below average for this side of town."

"It does seem like quite a place," he said.

"Well, if you decide it's time for a drink, let me know. I'm Allie. You can try the sleepy guy in the corner there too, if I'm not about, but he's a little hit-or-miss on getting the orders straight."

The man stepped away, eyes quickly set on another table with an empty chair. Allie wiped the table in front of his seat. It was more to occupy time than actually do any cleaning, as the man hadn't eaten or drunk; thus, the table was probably cleaner now than when he'd sat down.

"Friendly fellow, eh Lou?" Allie said.

"Yeah. Seems like a jolly fella," said Lou, a mountain of a man who would have been the one Allie would have bribed with a drink to throw the newcomer out if he'd been a handful.

"Not so often we get someone in here who just chats up all the men and women," she said. "What was he so curious about?"

"What?" Lou said. A few drinks had dulled his already-blunt social acumen.

"He was asking questions, right?" she said.

"Yeah, yeah."

"What about?"

"Uh..."

Allie shifted her glance to the man beside Lou. "Were you paying attention to the words going into and out of your head?"

He nodded, though the expression on his face suggested otherwise.

"What was he talking about?" she asked.

"... Things."

Her eye twitched. "I need to stop being so quick on the refills for you boys. You've got a habit of drinking yourselves stupid a little too early in the night."

"He was asking about what else goes on in here," said the third occupant of the table, who had answered less because he was the sharpest but because he'd had the most time to wrangle his thoughts. "What sort of stuff do we do for fun? What sort of... what was the word he used, Lou?"

"What?" said the larger man with the same half-startled tone of someone being called on by the teacher after daydreaming for a little too long.

"The new guy. He asked what sort of something or others we have in here."

"... What?"

"Started with a *V*."

"Oh, oh. ... The new guy?"

"Yeah."

"... What?"

Allie sighed. "You're cut off for the night, Lou." She glanced at the clock the Maskers had gifted the tavern. "Make that cut off for the afternoon. What's Oovay been putting in that glass of yours? There isn't enough of your usual booze in the tavern to get you this drunk this quick."

Lou blinked. "What?"

"Vendors!" said the overachiever at the table.

"He asked if we have any vendors in here?" Allie said.

"Yeah. And purveyors."

"Lah-dee-dah," Allie said, glancing over her shoulder at the man. "Fancy talker for someone with stubble and road clothes." She fetched up Lou's nearly empty cup and put it on her tray. "I'm getting you a fresh one of well water to keep you from keeling over before suppertime, big fella."

"Yeah," he said with a slow nod.

She shoved the basket of crickets in front of him. "And get some food in you." Allie gave a final, suspicious glance at the newcomer. "What's his name, by the way?"

"Marcus," remarked the overachiever.

She nodded and paced back to the bar. The other empties got a rinse and wipe. Lou's got a sniff. It was hard to say if anything was off about it. Lou's tastes in booze were "strong" and "cheap." If there was a bottle with those two words written on it, it was all he'd drink. But there may have been something else. Something vaguely herbal. She set it aside for after her shift. There was very little chance Oovay would take the initiative of cleaning it before then, which for once suited her fine. She would have to bring it to a friend to see if he could confirm a suspicion that was simmering in her head.

When Madge had claimed an expertise at driving horses, Tome had had his doubts. There was very little about her that inspired confidence of any sort. But the last few days had hammered home the unassailable truth that, while she may have been lying about why she was so good behind the reins, she was most assuredly more skilled than him. Granted, her presence had indeed taken a hint of the velocity from the effects of the spell, but it wasn't so great a decrease that Tome felt any more comfortable at the reins. Madge had her near misses on the first day, but by the end of her first shift guiding the horse, it was clear she deserved the title of "official driver" for the rest of the journey. And she'd latched onto the role with gusto. An unspoken bit of negotiation had established that she should be the one guiding the horse for as much time as possible, and in exchange Tome would be paying for room and board whenever they stopped.

Tome checked his coin purse. Paying the way for them both was taking its toll on his finances, but he'd budgeted with the expectation of taking months to arrive at the monastery, so he was still comfortably ahead of the curve. It helped that Madge ate like a bird. Though, given how the lesser harpies gorged themselves at every opportunity, he may have to find a new simile.

"Still didn't steal anything!" Madge said brightly, wisely keeping her eyes on the road as she spoke.

"For the last time," Tome said. "Checking my coin purse isn't a tacit accusation of thievery. I just like to know how much I have left to spend."

"It's whatever money you had before yesterday, minus whatever you spent yesterday. That's always how much you have to spend. Math!"

"Right, yes. Thank you."

"So do you mind if I ask for another lesson?"

"Now?"

"I'm asking now, so yes. Now."

"You know it makes me uncomfortable when you divide your attentions when you're at the reins."

"There's no one on the road, and it's a straight shot for what'll probably be another two hours of riding. This is the longest stretch of boring old nothing on the whole continent. If not now, then when?"

"When we stop for the evening."

"When we stop for the evening, all we ever want to do is eat and sleep. My mind is awake and crackling now. Let's talk about magic! I feel like I've barely learned anything as your apprentice."

"In my defense, you do seem to lack anything resembling a formal training in the mystic arts. It does make knowing what to teach and how to begin rather taxing. Remind me, what sort of magic do you practice?"

"I'm a dabbler. I dabble. Mostly I like the potion stuff. And soaking stuff in potions. That works great! But you need the stuff to make the potions, and it never grows all in the same place. Hence all the traveling."

"You can just buy the materials."

"You know how you keep looking in that bag to see how much money you have? I don't need to look in mine. There's two duots, five klemps, and three of those coins they use up there in Quarr. I'm not going to be buying anything worth having."

"Potions are quite lucrative. You could sell them to get the money to buy the materials for the next batch."

"Two problems with that. I need the first batch to sell, and I'd need to be good enough at making them to actually have the first batch worth selling, and I'm not so great yet."

"Who was your teacher?"

"A really old fellow down south who traded lessons for help mucking out the stalls of his stables. Then he died."

"You could have continued your education with books."

"Books cost money, right? See the problem there?"

"Yes, yes. I'll grant you getting started in any pursuit without some starter capital is difficult. But some of the larger cities have libraries that one can negotiate access to."

"Sure they do. Doesn't do me much good since I can't read or write. Not enough for it to be worth doing."

"You... you can't read or... how in the world was I supposed to teach you paper magic if you don't know how to read or write?"

"You didn't notice until I told you, right?"

He rolled his eyes. "The ability to conceal a shortcoming and the ability to overcome a shortcoming are two entirely different skills."

"Look, I was copying the shapes you showed me just fine."

"It's not a matter of rote memorization. You need to develop an intuition about how the language should be used, and that is always drawn from one's existing understanding of how other written languages are used."

"Fine. But it isn't as though paper magic is just writing 'I want to start a fire' on a piece of paper in plain language. There's a whole new language, right? So that'll be the one I learn to read and write."

"It isn't that simple. This is the equivalent of teaching a grown man a new trade versus teaching a baby a new trade. There are certain intermediate steps and an assumed common context that are absent in your case."

"So I'll need those, too."

He pinched the bridge of his nose. "Even if we had the time, and we don't, because we are only a few days from our destination, there remains the issue that paper magic has a financial cost as well. You need quills, ink, and paper. And unlike potions, you can't just forage for those ingredients. The ink is relatively trivial to prepare from found materials, but good pens and good paper must be made. Paper magic is expensive. The spell that has allowed us this advanced speed? It cost somewhat more to write than the travel expenses of the trip at a more standard speed, and I was able to make the ink myself thanks to access to a Lesser Mystic."

She shook her head. "Money was a bad idea. How old is it anyway?"

"What, money?"

"No, paper magic. But money, too, now that I think about it."

"Both are ancient. Predating the Bygone Era by many multiples of the time that has passed since the Bygone Era. Though if I were to hazard a guess, paper magic is the older of the two by a substantial margin."

"So there were people doing this magic before money. So there's a way to do it without money."

"Predating money doesn't mean predating resources. It just means that back then there would have been a whole village built up around the purpose of supporting a single skilled paper mage. People gathering materials. People creating the paper, the ink."

"So there is no way to do paper magic without that stuff?"

"It is called paper magic for a reason. The only way to get similar results with similar techniques without paper and ink is to use—" Tome stopped himself.

"You keeping secrets now?" Madge said. "Come on! I'm an open book. You can ask me whatever. That means you should be the same."

He grumbled. "I will preface this by informing you that this is not a shortcut around learning proper paper magic, unless that cut is across your throat, because it is a swift path to a swifter death."

"Understood. So what is it?"

"Blood magic. It is the same structure of spell, but large portions of it can be disregarded, and far more potent results are possible."

"Sounds like that's for me."

"I've cast only a handful of spells with blood magic, all within the same few days, and it took me weeks to recover. To a degree I am still recovering. I continue to feel a sudden weakness when I am in proximity to elven magic, which happens to be the magic I was attempting to counter with blood magic."

"I see. Not very friendly to use, then. Why do all these magics seem to be so costly in one way or another?"

"Because people seem to think that magic is about getting something for nothing, and it simply isn't. Magic is about exchanging something for something else, just like anything. Farmers water the land and work the soil to get crops. We use words or mixtures to produce effects. The only difference between mystic and mundane arts is mystic arts call upon forces that are not so easily seen or understood by novices."

"I don't know how or why plants grow. Does that mean farmers are wizards?"

"I'm sure there was a time that they were seen as such."

"Does that mean that the more people know, the less magic there is?"

"That's an odd way to look at things, but I suppose there is logic to it."

"No wonder wizards make it so hard to learn their tricks. Do you think that means—whoops!"

A large stone in the middle of the road approached more quickly than Madge had expected. She was able to keep from a full collision, but one of their wheels caught the edge, and they were briefly up on a single wheel before bashing back down. The cart recovered, the startled horse calmed, and they continued.

"Did a little too much talking and a little too little watching the road," she said with a half laugh.

"Which is precisely what I was worried would happen."

"Tell you what. I've got an idea. We'll do the lesson when we stop for the day."

Tome trembled with frustration. Madge snickered under her breath.

"It is abundantly clear to me why you were traveling alone," he said.

"So were you, pal. At least now we're traveling alone together."

Euphoria sifted through her notes and muttered to herself. It was truly astonishing how many pointless hoops the family had made her jump through and how many seemingly arbitrary compromises she was forced to make, simply to have permission to undergo this investigation. She didn't need to wonder why. The case had been made that Piotor had to go, and it was inarguable. But getting rid of Piotor was at best a terrible inconvenience; and at worst, impossible to do without sacrifice. They couldn't make the argument that nothing should be done, so instead they chose to make what needed to be done as unpleasant as possible out of hopes that it would be abandoned and things could continue as though nothing had ever happened while comfortable in the belief that action was taken.

But she would not be shaken from the scent so easily. So she agreed to what she had to agree to. She agreed to take one of the family's formal carriages despite the fact that it was enormous, conspicuous, and terrible at navigating mountain roads. She agreed to take copious notes, cataloging every detail of her findings even when those findings were nothing at all. She agreed to allow messengers to continue to run their routes uninterrupted, even though that meant if word of the reason for her travels were to spread, they would certainly spread as far as Piotor or whoever had replaced him and give them a chance to escape. She agreed to these things because she had to. And she would succeed in spite of these things, because the task was too important for her to fail.

"Everything all right in there, Mrs. Graves?" called the voice of her driver, and for the purposes of this trip her bodyguard, Lattica.

"I'm well enough," she called back. "Why do you ask?"

"Because you're muttering to yourself so loudly I can hear you from the seat up here, Mrs. Graves."

"That's because..." She paused. "Stop for a moment, would you?"

The pair of horses stopped their slow, plodding gate, and Euphoria opened the door. She hauled herself around to the unoccupied of the two driver's seats to sit beside Lattica's imposing figure. The driver's seats had an overhang that blocked the sun and, to a degree, most other weather when the carriage was in a favorable angle, but it was otherwise exposed to the elements. Technically it was more comfortable and better sheltered than simply riding her own horse, as Lattica had requested, but it also made a bit of a show of drawing a line between the driver and the passenger.

"Why are you calling me Mrs. Graves?" Euphoria asked.

"That's your name, isn't it?" Lattica said.

"Yes. But it is your name, too. This is the Graves family. Every woman in the family is either a Miss or a Mrs. Graves. Half of the women born a Graves are still called Mrs. Graves even after marrying out of the name, just to underscore their connection to the family. It is pointless, and rather arch, for either of us to call each other such."

"It's silly for a driver to shout through to a passenger and call her a familiar name. And when they said I'd be a driver, I spoke to the other drivers, and this is how it's done. I follow the rules. At least then, if I do something foolish, it is someone else's idea."

Euphoria nodded. "Fair enough. Well then. You were interested in why I was upset, Mrs. Graves?"

Lattica's brow furrowed. "Feels odd to be on the other side of it. I don't get that very often."

"Hence my distaste. I'd rather be Euphoria. Honestly, I'd rather be Fora. But we'll get there when we get there. Now, you wanted to know about the muttering."

"I did."

"I was just going over the findings of the last week or so and grumbling about how long they have taken to acquire."

"Seven days, five safe houses. That's nearly one a day. Could be worse."

"Given what we've found, I'd prefer if we were able to act more quickly. Three of the safe houses had obviously never been used. The outhouse at one of them had been completely rusted shut. There wasn't a speck of soot in the chimneys. These were places that Piotor Graves was supposedly spending, collectively, a month or so out of every year for years. The others had seen use but still lacked any of his reference materials or any of his specialized equipment. In short, he couldn't have done the job he has been doing for years in those places. One week of investigation. Five safe houses investigated. And the only things we've found for certain is that we have been lied to by Piotor about what he's been doing. I should have been able to turn around after the first house and informed the family in exchange for a veritable army composed of you and your associates to raid the other houses to find the truth. But if I went back now, after five houses, they would just say to me 'but you didn't check the other houses, did you? There must be a rational explanation.' And happily let it continue until the last morsel of deniability is chased away. And so, I am frustrated."

"Fair."

They rumbled forward. The next safe house, if her research was accurate, would be visible within minutes. No sense stepping back inside the carriage when she'd be climbing out again so soon. She'd left her notes inside, but she had more than enough on her mind to occupy her. After a few minutes, Lattica stopped again, snapping Euphoria from her rumination.

She turned to her bodyguard. The woman had a finger to her own lips to be sure the question on Euphoria's mind wasn't spoken. She then pointed. Hoofprints on the poorly kept path ahead. Fairly fresh, branching off from an even more poorly kept path that merged onto this one. Euphoria looked up and squinted. The roofline of the safe house was visible.

"There are no official messengers scheduled anywhere near this stretch of forest for three days," Euphoria whispered.

"On foot," Lattica said. "The wagon's too loud."

Euphoria nodded. The pair stepped down and did a hasty job of securing the horses so they wouldn't wander off. A few minutes on foot took them to the cabin. The horse wasn't visible. Probably tied up around back. But the door was slightly ajar, and fresh bootprints disrupted the frost that inevitably accumulated on the stone thresholds this far into the mountains. Lattica motioned for Euphoria to stay back. When she was a sensible distance back, Lattica charged in and kicked the door open. There was a brief, noisy scuffle.

"I have him!" Lattica shouted.

Euphoria rushed forward and stepped inside. The safe house itself looked like any of those that had been used but not used much. Mostly dusty, save one writing desk. This one had a lit candle and a pen and quill on the desk, as well as a piece of sealing wax with a freshly molten end. Lattica had a fairly representative member of the Graves family's messengers held roughly with his hands behind his back. He was lean, a runners build, with a sunbaked complexion. Lattica wrenched his arms behind his back. A folded sheet of paper and a small piece of metal dropped to the floor.

"Just what are you doing here, sir?" Euphoria said.

"I'm doing my job," he grunted painfully.

She snatched up the fallen objects. The paper was folded and sealed with a drop of gray wax matching the stick on the table. The wax wasn't yet fully hardened, it was sealed so recently. The bit of metal turned out to be a ring. Euphoria held it up.

"Do you know what this is?" she said.

"It's the ring I'm supposed to use to seal the message," he said, struggling against Lattica.

"It is the ring Piotor Graves is supposed to use to seal a message. Only him. The whole point of a signet ring is that it remains only in the hands of those its identity is meant to signify."

She slipped a finger into the fold and popped the message open.

"You're not supposed to open that!" he yelped. "It's not for you."

"Then we're both breaking rules today, aren't we?" Euphoria jabbed.

The content of the message wasn't immediately incriminating, though only because it wasn't immediately intelligible. It was written in code. But it was plainly fresh. The minor bit of bleed that came from ink and paper of this fashion lingering in contact had only just begun. The messenger himself had written the message.

"Your codebook," she demanded.

"I'm not allowed to show it to you."

"You're not even supposed to have one, you're a messenger. My name is Euphoria Graves, I am acting under the authority of Gunther and Yvana Graves. Your codebook. Now."

Lattica loosened her grip enough for him to reach for it. "Slowly," she warned.

He slid a familiar, stiff little booklet from the bag at his side and shakily held it out. When Euphoria reached for it, he threw it violently to the ground. It landed with a metallic clank, and something shiny and rotating dislodged from the back of the book.

"Out of the cabin, now!" Euphoria cried, dashing through the door.

Lattica tumbled out a half second behind her. A soldier or other warrior might have placed the capture of the messenger above her own life, but Lattica was not quite so devoted. When he tried to wrench himself free while she launched through the door, she simply shoved him aside rather than risk being tripped up by him. This was a very sound decision. A flash of whipping wires made the air in the room behind them twinkle. The door and half of the doorjamb was scoured and slashed to splinters. If Lattica had been delayed by even a moment, she would be missing the heel of her left foot.

The messenger scrambled to his feet and vanished behind the cabin. Lattica and Euphoria gave chase, but neither held their place in the family due to their speed. The messenger was astride his horse by the time they rounded the cabin. He nearly trampled them as he spurred it to a gallop.

"We need to follow him!" Euphoria said. "He knows at least some of what's happening."

"No use," Lattica said. "That horse is faster than ours, even if they didn't have to drag a carriage. We can try to track him, but there's no catching him. And he took off between the trees. We'd have to track him on foot. What was that thing he threw down?"

"That was a spin-lasher," she said, flicking open the message still grasped in her hand so that she could look it over again. "You find them inside otherwise empty chests in vaults, placed there in the hopes that the person who finds them will be shredded before they can find your true valuables. They're profoundly forbidden. Not even the sort of contraband we'd risk trying to sell."

"Would the Bolivans have them?"

"They might. But the reason we don't sell them is because of how prone to accidental activation they are. The Bolivans aren't the most responsible contraption users. I don't think the average member of that clan would still have both legs if they carried one of them around."

"So who could have compromised these fellows and armed them?"

"I don't know. But I have a codebook in the carriage, so perhaps we'll learn more. Until then, I know two things. This was intended for Nevil, and that version of Piotor's signature looks very much like the ones from his other messages. I think we may have encountered a very important link in this chain."

Chapter 4

Fel crouched beside a doorway inside the Greater Lands Wall, a lesson one inevitably learned after spending enough time searching through Bygone Era troves and vaults was that failure came quickly, and success came slowly. When his father had first passed that piece of information on, Fel had assumed it was a warning. After all, it took a while to disarm a trap successfully, but springing one and feeling its wrath took an instant. The deeper wisdom of the lesson was much more useful, however. It had to do with the modern reality of useful vaults. More specifically, it had to do with how they'd been largely scoured and stripped of their valuables. If one encountered few or no traps and could simply sweep through an area, it meant others had done so and there wasn't likely to be much of value inside. Encounter a trap and there was every reason to assume whatever it was meant to protect was still there waiting to be found.

That wisdom didn't quite apply in the Greater Lands Wall. The Maskers were the only modern treasure hunters with access to it, so it was not cleaned out by other fortune seekers. But it had been largely evacuated at some point, and the result was broadly similar. Many traps were deactivated and many treasures missing. But where a trap remained active, a prize was sure to be found. And right now, Fel was elbow-deep in disabling an impressively complex triggering mechanism.

His tools were spread around him haphazardly. He'd removed two floor tiles to reveal a chaotic mess of gears and struts. All were under light tension, which meant the mechanism was intact and engaged. Removing the wrong one at the wrong time would release that tension, and either fully disable or instantly trigger the trap. Fel didn't want to take his chances, so he was taking his time while the steady flame of Wick kept things nicely illuminated.

He reached for a small set of pliers to ease a retaining pin out of place. Something large and distant scraped along the stone of the wall. Fel reached down and held the gear train stationary, lest the rattling dislodge something he hadn't planned on removing. The rumbling thumps passed.

"That thing's awfully angry out there," Fel said. "I wonder if Dad ever had to pop a trap while a dragon was making a nuisance of itself right outside."

"I am aware of no such events in his life," Wick said.

"Yeah. I figured. That's the kind of story you don't leave untold."

A soft clacking sound of hooves on stone echoed through the long, empty room Fel had crossed to reach the trap's trigger.

"Parch! Either stay close or stay far away," he shouted. "If this thing goes off, I don't want you too close to the entrance of the room. That's where it'll start."

The unicorn tromped farther away, not as a response to the instructions but because it was the direction Parch was already headed.

"How can you be sure the far doorway of the room is where the trap's activation will start?" Wick asked.

"Eh, it's another lesson from Dad." He pointed at a message beside the door he was hoping to open. "You said that said 'Commander So-and-So,' right?"

"Commander Vesh," Wick specified.

"'Commander' is the important part. He's in charge. And people in charge? There's no one there to punish them if they screw up. So they start to get lazy. Only, a trap doesn't care if you're the boss. You trigger it, you die just like a grunt or a fresh recruit. So the big important folks have traps that take a while to get to where they'll kill you. So a high-ranked person can take a second or third shot at finding the right key before they are turned into a stain on the walls. Probably why it needed a key and we didn't just have the door code like we did for the rest of them, too. The boss just has to be special."

"Your father is very wise."

"My father survived long enough to have three kids. The people who didn't pick up on things like this didn't manage that."

Another rumble thumped along the wall. Fel held still until it passed.

"Wick, what do you suppose the odds are that I'll still have a horse and wagon when I get back outside?"

"It does seem rather likely without your presence to intimidate Duurth that the horse will be consumed if the dragon can reach it."

"Here's hoping my intimidation lasts a while. The intimidation the elves pulled off certainly seems to have stuck. A couple of arrows in the side will do that to you." He jabbed a pry bar into the gear train, working at popping a gear from its axle. "I still don't get how that happened. That dragon is old. He didn't have any signs of clashes with elves when we ran into him last time. And that we ran into him both outside the wall and in the center of the Greater Lands means he traveled just about as much as any creature could. So it isn't as though he only just got the opportunity to cross paths with the elves."

"What is your concern?" Wick asked.

"It'd take someone with a pretty inflated sense of self-worth to imagine he was somehow responsible for something like that. But I feel like I'm somehow responsible for that."

"What is your reasoning behind this supposition?"

"Me and Tome show up in there, after basically hundreds of years of nothing much happening, and then what? Before you know it, Teya comes scampering out and they're building little miniature versions of the place up north."

"Counterpoint, if I may. The Lesser Greater Lands, and False Clickspring, were both evidently in operation for a number of years and likely under construction for many years prior. Additionally, there have been limited examples of successful expeditions to and from the Greater Lands, often for the purpose of trapping and transporting Greater Mystics."

"Fair point on the place up north, but did any of the other expeditions free a powerful dragon that was trapped in its lair for centuries?"

"Unlikely."

"There. See? In Beffshire all it took was a new businesswoman nosing around and trying to horn in on Verfessa's business and you got a situation that almost got Allie killed. I bet a big dragon back on the loose is liable to stir things up even worse."

"This is a reasonable assumption."

"I thought so too. So again, I feel like whatever's going on in there, I might be the reason for it. Or part, anyway."

The pry bar popped the gear free, and those beside it started to spin freely. The door to the adjoining room, the one that Parch was wandering about in, slammed shut. A sharp hiss filled the air, and a veil of mist started venting down from above the doorway. Everywhere the mist touch was covered with a thick crust of ice. The mist started to approach, moving slowly but steadily closer to him.

"Wrong gear," Fel said, quickly shifting the pry bar and jamming it into the gear train.

The nearest gears rattled to a stop. The flow of the mist slowed, but didn't halt, and the motion continued toward him.

"Right. All right. Think quick, Fel," he muttered.

"This is distressing," Wick said.

"Yeah. Yeah it is," Fel said.

He yanked the bar from where he'd stuffed it. The gears surged back to speed, and the mist's approach accelerated.

"Looking for bigger gears," he said, anxiety starting to color his tone as the air around him took on a steadily increasing chill. "Big gears, big motion. Big gears, big teeth."

He levered two more floor tiles up, now not bothering to be careful. The second revealed gears so large they were still mostly hidden beneath the surrounding tiles. Fel jammed the pry bar into them. Now the motion slowed, but the mist remained full force. Worse, the teeth were exactly the wrong size to be blocked fully by the bar. The meshing of the teeth was too tight for the bar to fit into, and the spokes of the gear didn't align with something that he could jam the bar through to jam it. He pulled it free and blocked the first set of gears again.

"Come on, come on," Fel said through clenched teeth as the air started to sting his skin.

All the tools he had were hand tools, none with the heartiness or size necessary to stop both sets of gears. Finally, as the tiles nearest to him started turning white with frost, he snatched Wick's lantern and jammed the circular base into the gears. It was wide enough, and as a Bygone artifact it was sturdy enough, to bring them fully to a stop. With the motion stalled and the mist slowed, Fel had earned a few precious seconds. He gave up on being gentle and grabbed a hammer. An awkward upward bash chipped the corner of a tile and slashed his cheek with the debris, but successfully dislodged it and revealed what he'd been searching for this whole time. Two long cables, connections to linkages hidden on the secure side of the wall. He grabbed them and yanked, hard. The door he'd been working on swung open, and the gears he'd blocked switched to reverse, ejecting bar and lantern alike to spin backward and return the ice trap to its initial position.

The door blocking Parch from entering swung open again. The unicorn came charging in to investigate, promptly slipped on the ice, and slid all the way to Fel on his belly.

Despite the freezing temperature of the room, Fel wiped a bead of sweat from his forehead. He rescued Wick's lantern from where it had fallen among the now-inert machinery.

"Thanks for the help, Wick," he said, climbing to his feet and helping Parch up.

"It was invigorating to provide an entirely novel service," Wick said.

Fel stepped through the freshly opened door. "Well, well, well. The boss didn't get the message that it was time to evacuate."

The room spread before them was one of the few they'd encountered in their repeated trips to the Greater Lands Wall that lacked any semblance of an attempt to clear it out. The only other room that seemed fully intact was the archive. But this room? This was different. The archive was a place of utility. Of purpose. This was a place of privilege, and better yet, a place meant to impress. A huge desk dominated the room, covered across its entire surface with things any antique hunter would kill for. Inkwells, quills. Half a dozen different seals for addressing letters to different high-ranking individuals who had vanished when their era fell. Complicated contraptions littered the place. Some were clearly useful, items meant to ease the burden of executing the duties of leadership by duplicating documents or automatically positioning troop markers on maps. Others seemed to have no purpose at all beyond costing an unimaginable amount.

Fel tugged open the cabinet beside the troop mover. It was filled with intricate, articulated statuettes representing the various troop types.

"Found your figurines, Mom," he said.

Like most things from the Bygone Era, these figurines were more detailed and better made than they really needed to be. Soldiers armed with swords and bows were astonishingly lifelike, as though the details had been painted on with a single hair. Several rows of additional troops were less lifelike, not because they were less detailed but because they weren't human. Metallic and man-shaped, they were reminiscent of better-made versions of the automatons that had been unleashed in False Clickspring before it was destroyed. And in the back of the cabinet, closer to the size of a marionette than a figurine, were two scaled-up versions. They must have been ten times the height of the other troops. A small brass plate on the shelf beneath them labeled them "Guardian East" and "Guardian West."

"Just like a commander to have special display versions of the figures..." Fel said, shaking his head.

"This is a curiously oriented room," Wick said. "A unique layout within the wall as we've observed it thus far."

"Like I said, the boss has to be special."

He turned, taking the comment as a sign that he should probably assess the room itself rather than just the riches within it. Most of the other rooms were long and narrow, thanks to the fact that this was a particularly thick wall rather than an actual fortress. This one was square, with the entry door at the center of the front of the room, which ran perpendicular to the rest of the Greater Lands Wall. That made for a room that was about three times as wide as the others. It probably filled the entire thickness of the wall, something of an endpoint for the hallway that ran the length of the wall. Toward the back of the room, a wide ladder led to the top of the rear of the room. There, a loft of some kind, or simply an extension of the room with a very low roof, awaited him. He carefully approached, mindful of additional traps, and climbed the ladder.

When he reached the top, he had to stoop to keep from scraping his head on the ceiling. The grandeur of the rest of the office was absent in this portion. It had the feel of a forgotten attic. But it did establish that the room indeed filled the entirety of the wall, as windows facing the inside and outside of the wall were centered on either side of the cramped platform. Brackets beside each window held a crossbow and a quiver of bolts on one side and a fine telescope on the other. A small plinth with some brass switches stood in the very center of the platform. A trio of books with no titles on their spines were positioned below it on a shelf precisely sized for them.

"What's it say?" Fel asked, holding up the lantern.

"It will take a moment for me to translate it," Wick said. "The language appears to be a different dialect than elsewhere in the wall."

"Take your time."

He paced over to the window facing the outside of the wall. His journey within the wall in search of treasure had taken him a good deal farther into the section of the fields that Duurth had been terrorizing. Multiple charred stretches of ground were visible. When he paced to the other side, the view into the Greater Lands served to underscore just how stark the contrast was between the outside and inside. Vivid green forest waited for him just a short distance away. He expected, when he peered out the narrow gap of the window, to see the sheer drop that had nearly killed him when he'd inadvertently ridden to the Greater Lands on a waterfall. There was no drop. Just below, about level with the ground on the outside, was a sturdy stone bridge that continued at a gentle slope until it was swallowed by the dense foliage of the forest.

Fel grabbed the telescope and trained it on the horizon. The narrowness of the window made for a rather limited swath of the Greater Lands to spy on, but just at the edge of his field of view was a glimpse of the mountain that he knew held Kazel's lair. A gap in the trees nearest to the wall gave him a tiny glimpse of the sea in the distance.

"Wick?" he said.

"I am still endeavoring to conjure up the proper translation."

"Sure. Sure. But remember when we headed out to Clickspring? The real one, across the sea in the Greater Lands?"

"I recall everything I have observed."

"During that whole big trip, were there any other ships on the sea?"

"There were a number of abandoned ships in the harbor of Clickspring."

"But actual ships sailing. Were there any of those?"

"Only our own. Why do you ask?"

"Because I can see three ships. Big ones."

"Intriguing."

"Yeah. Intriguing."

"Ah. I believe I have found the proper translation. It was an older dialect because it is one associated with ceremony. The two switches are labeled 'Inner Main Gate' and 'Outer Main Gate.' Additionally there is a dial, which is unlabeled."

"Main gate?" Fel said. "The Greater Lands Wall doesn't have a gate."

"I do not believe I am mistaken in the translation," Wick said.

Fel tried to poke his head fully out the slit of a window, but it was too small. He rummaged in his tool bag until he found a small mirror and held it out the window, angling it down.

"Wick, there is a large gate, about large enough for two big cargo wagons side by side, directly below us." He rushed to the outer-wall window and did the same. "But no gate on the outside."

"Perhaps it was bricked up when the wall was abandoned?"

"It takes a long time to brick something like that up. Though it was the Bygone Era. Who knows what contraptions they used." A small voice in Fel's mind tugged at him. He turned and marched over to the plinth. "What do you suppose happens if I flip the switch for a gate that isn't there anymore?" he said.

"I would urge you not to do so without first consulting with your father."

"Right, right. Obviously."

"Shall I have a word with him?"

Fel tilted his head and eyed up the trio of books. "Not just yet." He knelt and inspected the little bookshelf. "You know that big tool chest in Dad's workshop?"

"I know it well. A family heirloom."

"Yeah. Handed down through at least three generations of Maskers. And right inside it, just below the lid, in a place that makes it a serious pain to get some of the bigger tools out, is a little drawer. The little drawer is the exact size of a little book, and that book is a book of mechanical principles that Dad used so often he memorized it cover to cover. It always sort of stuck in my head. I asked Dad about it, about why there'd be a little drawer just for that one book. He said, 'When something is important and you don't want it to get lost, you give it a special place that's too small to become cluttered.' Seemed odd to me."

"Not without wisdom," Wick said.

Fel, finding no traps, pulled one of the books from the shelf and opened it. "Looks like more of the same weird dialect."

"Indeed it is. The current page contains only the title. It reads *The Rules and Policies Regarding the Operation of the Main Gates of the Greater Lands Wall of Division.*"

"It takes three books to tell you when to pull two switches," Fel said. "Must be three very important switches. Might be worth reading these books."

In The Fox and Log, Allie was pleased to find her mysterious new patron was being a shade less overt in his questioning and investigation today. He was still about, still asking questions and generally ingratiating himself to the other drinkers. But he was sticking with small groups of people longer. It didn't do much to set Allie's mind at ease. The people he'd chosen to chat with were, to put it lightly, easily bribed and willing to talk out of turn about anything they'd seen or heard regardless of the truth of it or how the subject of the chatter would feel about it. She didn't worry they'd reveal anything about her, or even about Verfessa. But that the stranger, Marcus, found his way to them underscored both his goal of learning more about the place and the relative success at locating those who were most likely to help him do it. At least his more dedicated canvasing of the informants made him easier to keep an eye on. And that was just as well, because the elderly fellow who had just hobbled through the door was precisely the sort of man Allie didn't want him intercepting.

"Mr. Jayden!" she said, slipping around from behind the bar to greet him. "I haven't seen you in this place in ages! Come on up here. I've got a nice comfortable seat waiting for you."

He nodded and pointed his hand vaguely in a doddering sort of way. "I came because someone paid me a visit and said you needed—"

She cut him off with a friendly hand to his back to guide him forward and a rigid assurance.

"Oh, I know why you're here. Same reason anyone comes in here. Drinks you can afford and good company. Come right up. Glad to have you."

He gave her a quizzical look as she sat him down and filled a glass.

Most people in Beffshire didn't know who Mr. Jayden was, and no one in town would have cared if they did. He wasn't terribly important these days. Even in his heyday, his position didn't come with any sort of power. But it was very important. And that Jayden had lived to his golden years despite holding that position suggested he was peerless in his skills.

"Let's keep our voices down, Mr. Jayden," Allie said softly, providing him with a fresh basket of crickets to snack on. "There are some folks who'd rather I didn't learn what I think you're about to teach me."

"Oh ho!" he said in what the hard-of-hearing man probably thought was a whisper. "Subterfuge, eh?"

Allie glanced discreetly at Marcus. He'd not noticed. "Let's call it 'unpopular curiosity.' How's that nose of yours?"

"They eyes are going. The body is going. The mind is going. But the nose? Still the best there is." He tapped the aforementioned feature, which, if anything, had grown as he'd aged. "This is responsible for saving the lives of two kings, six princes, two princesses, and twenty-five lords and ladies."

"This one isn't quite so heroic." She pulled the now exceedingly stale glass of Lou's half-finished booze from where she'd stowed it. "Is there anything in this besides bad whiskey?"

He rubbed his hands together and positioned the glass before him. Tightly shut eyes and a few slow, focused breaths formed something of a preparation ritual. Then he raised the glass, tipped it beneath his nose, and took a whiff.

"That's Plock's Distillery. Wretched stuff. Smells like whoever drank from this last had sausage for supper."

"Nothing untoward?" she said.

"In good time, young lady. In good time." He took another whiff. "Not the cleanest well water in the city, but better than most. ... Ah. Ah, yes, I believe I have it. I take it that someone drank the other half of this?"

"Yes."

"Was that person a bit wobbly after? Thick in the head?"

"He was pretty thick before he drank it, but about a yard thicker after."

"As I suspected. This glass has a few drops of Miser's Milk in it. Are you familiar?"

"Not as such."

"Miser's Milk is one I'd sniff out in big meetings. Discussions. All-day affairs. A few drops in a drink and it will hit like you've drunk half a gallon. They call it Miser's Milk because a man can get tipsy with a few sips instead of emptying his pockets for a night of drinking. Damned stupid name, though. The milk itself costs more than the booze would have cost."

"Could it kill someone?"

"Not to my knowledge. No more so than the usual amount of drunkenness could. A fellow might fall down the stairs, but it isn't poison in the sense most people think of when they think of poison. Did the person who drank this have lips that needed loosening?"

"Not if you ask me, but then I guess everyone knows something someone else might want to know." She took the glass back and dumped it out. "Thank you for the help, Mr. Jayden. Next couple of drinks are on the house. But do me a favor and don't mention any of this to anyone else."

"It's good to put the skills back to use," he said.

She filled a glass for him and started a circuit of the bar, tending to empty drinks and defusing a minor grievance. All the while her mind worked through what she'd learned.

So, she thought. *Our new friend has the resources and lack of scruples it takes to drug a random member of the bar. Likely a lot of members of the bar. But he's not savvy enough to work out which ones were worth drugging in the first place. That tells me we've got someone well-funded and/or well-motivated but inexperienced. Not just new to town but new to whatever this job is. Better than an old hat, I suppose. But it means this is serious. He's willing to dump expensive specialty poisons onto the problem he's trying to solve. It also means I'm going to have to nip this in the bud, because I can't have someone drugging my customers.*

Allie let the issue stew in her mind as the day crawled on, ever mindful of the first and foremost thing that seemed sensible to introduce to the equation. That thing asserted itself two hours later, when the flame of the lantern she kept behind the bar went still.

"Oovay!" she shouted. "Take over for a bit. I need to go over some things, and I can't be juggling that and the bar floor."

Her reluctant coworker emerged from whatever corner he'd disappeared into once the floor had gotten busy. Allie grabbed a stack of papers, random notes she'd taken over the course of several days, and snatched up the lantern. The notes were mostly a prop, necessary to answer the unspoken question of what Allie needed privacy and a lantern for when it was well known she preferred to be working the floor. With her excuse in hand, she slipped into the back room that had become the de facto break room. It had some basic storage, a few seats, and a makeshift bed in the corner that Oovay put to use with frustrating frequency.

"News, Wick?" she said, once she was sure she wouldn't be overheard.

"Not very much. Fel had a close call and discovered a rather novel room within the Greater Lands Wall that promises to provide most if not all the funding he has been seeking. He sent me back to consult with his father on some documentation we discovered, and I decided to use the opportunity to see if you had any messages to deliver."

"I do and I don't. The person I've been keeping an eye on? It turns out he drugged at least one of the people in the bar. Probably a couple. He's after information and isn't shy about investing to get it. That means I'd like to know what he's after sooner rather than later. And that's where you come in, if you have a few moments."

"Fel is not expecting me until his father is through interpreting some of what we've found. I can offer you my aid for an hour or so. What do you require of me?"

"It should be pretty standard for you. I'm going to light a few of the candles on the tables. I'll ask you to listen in on what's being asked, what's being discussed. I want to know what this man is after and, ideally, who he is."

"That is well within my capabilities."

"Much obliged, Wick. This is the sort of thing I'd usually trade a favor for, but I'm not sure how to do that with you."

"No favor required. It is, now as always, a pleasure to provide a service. It is quite literally my purpose in existing."

"I'll trust you on that," she said, grabbing some fresh candles. "But if you find yourself with a taste for a particular lamp oil, or if you see any other light sources you take a particular shine to, let me know. Until then, let's get you out there."

Lord Katritz had gazed at the large, ornate clock that had been a gift from his wife after he succeeded his predecessor in the role of lord for his section of the kingdom. It was a work of art, a Bygone contraption that had been thoroughly embellished with layers of enamel to feature his personal seal and family colors. As beautiful as it was, he seldom had cause to look at it. A legion of subordinates kept his calendar for him. And if he was inclined to occupy his time otherwise, it scarcely mattered if he kept at something for too long. There were few in the kingdom who wouldn't gladly wait for their opportunity to speak with him. Time was a concern for lesser people.

But right now he found himself checking the time so frequently that he was beginning to wonder if the clock was functional. He'd set up a late lunch in order to hold up his side of the bargain he'd made with the ogre of a man holding the rogue document. By luck or fate, Lady Zyne had been available. And while Lord Hundt was not, his wife was. And so, something approaching a summit between the three key nobles of Thayne and a troglodytic interloper had been organized in his own study on less than a day's notice. They arrived, the food was served, and Katritz fully expected it to be an uncomfortable half hour during which Verfessa would make his crudeness as clear to them as it was to him, and the entire business would be concluded with the others reaffirming what he'd suggested. Namely, that they would never support his elevation to the status of vassal.

That had not occurred.

"... And so here comes this man, and I use the term loosely. He was man-shaped, but if you ask me, you wouldn't have to dig much further than his grandfather to find something with fangs and fur. And he looks at me like I'm the one making trouble for wanting to get what I paid for without paying his 'special fee.' Something he didn't say two words about in the whole six months of setting up the deal."

"The nerve," said Lady Zyne.

"Some people do not respect the rules of financial discourse," said Lady Hundt.

"Yeah. And some people don't respect the common courtesy of not cleaning your nails with a knife while you're discussing how much you ought to be paid for a load of barley. Because that's what he does. Just pulls this big, nasty blade out and goes to work digging out things I'd rather not describe while there's food on the table. Now I'm not a fool. I know why the knife's out. The man doesn't care about his nails. He just wants me to see his knife and get scared. As though him stabbing me is going to somehow get me or anyone else to overpay for barley."

"Loathsome tactics," Lady Hundt said.

"Whatever does one do when doing business with such ruffians?" asked Lady Zyne.

"There are a few things you can do. Lots of people just find someone else to work with. Enough folks just eat the extra cost and pass it on to the next person in the chain. But me? I try to talk things through. So I talk to the fellow. I tell him he's got a mighty fine knife. I mention how I'm a bit like that knife. Not so large. Not so fancy. But very sharp. Useful to keep around if things go wrong. A good hard edge. And dangerous. Lots of people think they can handle a knife like that. Think all it takes is a tight grip. But it'll get away from you. And when it does, the result is always blood, and a scar if you're lucky. Something important missing if you're not lucky. And like that knife, I came to a point. And the point was, he'd better treat me like he'd treat that knife. With care, but more importantly, with respect."

"What happened?" asked Lady Hundt, endeavoring to appear scandalized but undeniably intrigued.

"Let's just say, he wasn't lucky. But eventually he got the point."

The table shook with droll laughter.

"Of course, that was then. A less civilized time. For me, at any rate. We do things differently now."

"I rather wish we didn't," Lady Zyne said. "Or to be more precise, I wish I had been given the opportunity to do as you've described. I tell you. There are a few individuals I would dearly like to pepper with some colorful wordplay and veiled threats. The amount of money I have to pay to get grain alcohol across the border from Quarr—robbery."

"What do you use it for, if you don't mind me asking?" Verfessa said.

She waved off the question. "Not relevant. Just an idle complaint."

Verfessa scratched his chin. "Considering you have two distilleries you run directly, both of them very close to the Quarr border, and most of the grain in Thayne is grown way down south in Katritz's area, I get the feeling you're probably saving yourself some time and some money by getting some pure alcohol to put some kick in your booze without hauling grain or alcohol across the entire kingdom." He cracked a knuckle. "Just a guess."

"You're an entertaining fellow, but I'll thank you not to accuse me of such low-quality business practices."

"I'm sorry, I'm sorry. I guess I misunderstood. You said someone had you over a barrel on the price of pulling grain alcohol across the border."

"Indeed."

"Who are you dealing with? John?" Verfessa looked aside. "No. No, John's the actual man at the border, you're dealing with someone a few rungs up the ladder. It'd be… Clovis. Mr. Clovis."

"That's right."

"Well, if you're not using that stuff in booze, then Clovis has been picking your pocket. Because the extra cost of getting stuff across the border between Quarr and Thayne is just for stuff you eat and drink. If you're bringing it over for, say, cleaning or filling up those fancy little lights with the clear bases? That stuff comes across for a pittance."

Lady Zyne's expression became suddenly intrigued. "Does it now?"

"Sure. Like I say, I can't make threats these days to get the prices down, so I have to know the ins and outs of what's allowed and what isn't."

"I'll have to look into that. But if what you say is true, you may have saved me a fortune, sir."

Verfessa flashed a grin. "Like I said, I'm a lot like a knife. Sharp, useful, and I always come to a great point."

One of Katritz's servants appeared at the doorway. "Lord Katritz, you have a pair of visitors who request an audience."

Katritz sat up. "Ah! I do apologize, ladies and gentleman. Duty calls. And this pleasant little meeting has occupied rather more of my day than I'd anticipated, so I would say it is time to conclude it."

"Surely you have room enough in your estate to conduct business while we come to a more leisurely end to our dealings here. Or have you decided we are undeserving of your hospitality?" Lady Hundt said.

"No, no. Of course not. If you have more to say, then take your time. My home is yours," Katritz oozed with no trace of sincerity.

He stood and marched from the room, fists clenched and fingers frustratedly fidgeting with his beard. Katritz didn't know who had pulled him from the irritating meeting, but they were going to get the full brunt of the outrage that he couldn't afford to spray in the direction of his distinguished colleagues. He was led to a small antechamber he'd genuinely forgotten was part of his estate. A familiar woman and an unfamiliar man were waiting for him.

Katritz locked his gaze on the woman and addressed his attendant. "Leave us. We require privacy. And see that the others depart as soon as their interest in my guest wanes," he said.

The servant did as he was told.

"Velonia Madritz. I cannot conceive of how you could possibly have the gall to show up in my home after the disastrous results of our last business together."

"Considering the man currently in your study, I would think my own presence here would be considered an elevation."

"If you're speaking of Verfessa, that man is in my study precisely because of your own incompetence." He turned to the man. "And you. I don't even know who you are, but if you are here with this woman, then you are yet another bit of riffraff staining my residence."

"My name is Inspector Cartwright. You were kind enough to sign a writ permitting me to search the Masker household not so long ago."

The lord's still-fidgeting fingers twisted the tip of his beard crooked. "Masker... I am truly becoming weary of that name." He shook his head. "I don't know why either of you have come here, but you can just march out that door or be carried out in chains. As we speak, a raggedy oaf is in there spinning yarns to my fellow gentry. He isn't even attempting to hide his nature. But because he knows a few tricks and spouts his idiocy enrobed in toxic levels of folksy phrasing, they sit there moon-eyed and enchanted. It is pathetic and disheartening to say the very least."

"Yes. Verfessa, and those he chooses to employ, are not to be taken lightly," Velonia said. "That he is presently in your own home should concern you. He has a tremendous capacity to find weakness and exploit it. But right now that is not your greatest concern. I would like to discuss 'Gem,' if I may."

"You may not. That one word has caused me no end of consternation. I wash my hands of it, as I have washed my hands of you."

"I think you'll want to hear what I have to say," she said. "It has the capacity to wipe away any lingering concerns you have with public sentiment regarding the false interpretation of who or what Gem is. Indeed. It might provide you with a prize even greater than Gem was supposed to provide."

Katritz glared at her. "I would have you dragged out of my home, but to be frank, every moment I spend with you is a moment I don't have to spend with that fool. So speak. And I had better like what I hear."

"First, some context, as each of us has a different level of understanding regarding the underlying motivations of our last few assignments. Gem, as I understood it, was a cute name you'd given to a mission to force Martin Masker, along with his family and resources, into a position of direct subservience beneath you. My role in it was a rather circuitous one, depriving him and his city of the useful alliances that had been developed. I was tasked with doing so through as subtle a means as possible so that the scheme couldn't be traced to you and, ideally, wouldn't be seen as a scheme at all. That, obviously, failed."

"Epically," Katritz said.

"Gem, as you understood it, was a plan to use the Masker family and their resources to centralize and enhance the study of contraptions into something far greater than it is today, and something that was entirely under your control. To make you something of a contraption baron, controlling most if not all the contraptions in the continent."

"I do not confirm that," he said unsteadily.

"You do not need to. You see, when my mission in Beffshire was foiled, I set about climbing the chain of this scheme, hoping to find some link closer to you in order to find a role in it once more and reingratiate myself to you. I wanted to restore my reputation. And what I found, to my surprise, was that you were not strictly at the top of the chain. You had been receiving advice. Guidance. One might even say instructions. From an individual called Lens."

Katritz's expression failed to hide the flash of recognition.

"It seems everyone with any sort of influence or ambition regarding contraptions has been receiving messages from Lens. And were I to make a guess, I would say that they have been for some time. The only change of late is the care and secrecy with which he has been acting."

"I was contacted by Lens," Cartwright said. "I had been assigned a similar task to Velonia. Bring the Masker family to its knees. I failed. A secondary task, however, revolved around acquiring a specific piece of equipment and some information surrounding it. And in that, I had a degree of success. I also was quite suddenly tasked with delivering a very curious agent to a secure place to be held. In this, I succeeded as well. But when I was through, my contact with Lens concluded. Until Velonia tracked me down."

"Tell me," Madritz said. "Have you met with Lens face to face?"

Katritz cleared his throat. Further denials were plainly of no real use. "I have not. Written messages only."

"I began my contact with him similarly," she said. "After I'd discovered the dead-drop locations that your messengers were using. But in very short order he requested an audience. And while I have not seen his face—he kept it hidden—I did hear his voice. And what he had to say to me was intriguing enough for me to arrange this reunion in spite of the animosity between us. Correct me if I'm wrong. This convoluted plot to acquire the servitude of the Masker family was not the first advised course of action Lens provided. He began with something much simpler. Within this city there exists the Contraption Contraband Vault. Because the vast majority of forbidden contraptions are acquired through the vault dives of contraption hunters, and by a wide margin the most successful contraption hunters have been members of the Masker family, who do business out of a city under your oversight, you are one of only three people in this world with unfettered access to that vault. The other two are the king and the royal quartermaster, neither of whom have been receptive to manipulation or other attempts to coerce access from them. Lens wanted you to permit his agents access to the vault. You, like the others, refused. I suggest you rethink that."

Katritz's expression sharpened. "I'll say to you what I said to him. That vault exists to contain things that are too dangerous to be interacted with. I am an ambitious man, but I will not allow those items to be released to anyone." He crossed his arms and turned away. "And more pragmatically, a thorough audit of the entire contents is performed every month by the very quartermaster whose cooperation Lens could not acquire. And a minor audit is done after every new acquisition or other interaction with the stock. In short, access by anyone but the quartermaster will do no one any good because it cannot be done with secrecy, and without secrecy no items have a chance of being utilized or removed."

"I am not going to try to convince you otherwise. Not right now. Because it's clear your mind is made up. But there are two things that are certain to change a man's mind. Desperation and necessity. And since I am not presently working for you, and you seem reluctant to work with me, I have no reason to sugarcoat reality to spare your feelings. You are horribly smug and an unbearably, unjustifiably, undeservedly arrogant mess of a human being who people would only ever work with if they had to. Donovan Verfessa is an affable, clever, insightful, and talented man who is presently winning over your associates. He already has influence over you thanks to the document, and that influence is an order of magnitude more dangerous in his hands than it would be in the hands of someone merely interested in uncovering the truth."

The words so thoroughly enraged Katritz that he couldn't manage much more than scoffing and sputtering. Madritz smoothly handed him a folded piece of paper.

"The item we are after, and that Lens was after since the beginning. You can acquire it. Lens can determine how to operate it. Try to imagine the value such an item might have in the right hands. I'll see myself out. If you need me, I'll be checking into the Green Hedge Inn on the north side."

The lord's rage hadn't relented enough for him to deliver a parting barb. The best he could do was crumple the page he'd been handed and squeeze it in his fist with the force and fury he wished he could apply to her neck. He marched back toward his study. He hadn't made it halfway back when he heard a chorus of laughter pour out. Not the polite, insincere laughter that was the only sort he ever seemed to inspire. Genuine, deep, gleeful laughter.

His lip curled in irritation. He opened his hand and picked at the mangled note until it unfurled. The language inside was dense, but despite what others might think of him, he was no fool. The work of being a lord was primarily focused on tangling and untangling language. He made sense of the description and, a moment later, realized just how fundamentally it could change things if it was true. And how tightly anyone who controlled such a thing could grip the power it provided.

"By the High..." he murmured.

He stuffed the page in his pocket and briefly considered attempting to acquire the promised payoff for himself without Lens and Madritz as intermediaries. But it would do no good. He lacked the skill to work out how it was used, and unlike what Madritz had claimed, he'd never managed to arrange an in-person meeting with Lens. That would be absolutely crucial to unlocking the secrets of the device quickly enough to benefit before its removal was discovered.

The wheels of his mind started to click. Secretly acquiring anything from the Contraband Vault would take timing. It would take careful navigation of policy and procedure. And in the best case, it would earn him a week or two before his actions were discovered. But a week or two would be enough to pivot the world in his favor. And if it all fell apart? He had two scapegoats downright eager to absorb the brunt of the consequences.

He folded the page and slipped it into his pocket. Another wave of laughter erupted from the room. He stepped inside.

"I seem to be missing quite the performance," he said.

"Oh, just some old anecdotes," Verfessa said. "What kept you?"

"It so happens a rather impressive business opportunity has presented itself. You'll hear about it soon enough."

Any attempts to track the escaping messenger were swiftly abandoned. Just as his horse was far too fast to keep up with, let alone catch up to, the rider was too skilled to leave very much in the way of a trail to follow. Confronted with options of either returning home with this revelation or continuing with their mission, Euphoria and Lattica decided it was best to finish their mission. There was no telling if they would have the opportunity to return to it. For the sake of having a bit more space to work, Euphoria had returned to the interior of the carriage in order to decode the message.

"Lattica? A moment!" she said, when the final letters of the message were recorded.

The carriage lurched to a stop, and Euphoria swiftly stepped from inside to join her in the seat.

"What is the message?" Lattica asked.

"First and foremost, it is absolutely written as though Piotor himself was sending the message. And it was absolutely not written by Piotor, so there is no doubt that some quantity of forgery is going on. But right now, if it is even possible, I am more concerned by the contents of the message than its nature."

"What's wrong?"

"It is addressed to Nevil, and it reads as follows. 'Efforts must be made to accelerate the excavation. We have reason to believe the item of interest will soon be made available. If sufficient devices are not unearthed soon, the benefits of the item of interest will not be exclusively ours. Divert all personal funds to hire additional work crews if you must, but acquire the devices swiftly and silently. We may have only days remaining, and if the others were to discover what is occurring, it will cause unacceptable delays. Piotor Graves.'"

She looked up from the page. "Swiftly and secretly. A messenger, either acting alone or working for someone else, is instructing a member of the Graves family to expend any effort necessary to dig something up. Multiple things, in fact. As though there is some quota to be reached. And by the tone of the message, this is simply a follow-up to a preexisting bit of instruction. So this has been happening for some time."

"If I were to make a list of the members of the family most likely to sell the others out, Nevil would be near the top," Lattica said. "Does this change things? Knowing this, are we headed back now?"

Euphoria released a sigh that faded into a growl. "I don't know." She waved the page. "We don't know about this. And I just got through scrutinizing everything in the archives supposedly written by Piotor. That means that Nevil, and perhaps others, have been destroying messages. Hardly a surprise. It's actually a family policy if there's danger our secrets might fall into the wrong hands. But I don't believe 'the wrong hands' were ever meant to refer to other Graves family members. Nevil needs to be exposed for what he's doing. But at the same time, who knows how many members of the family have received messages like these? And who knows what sort of falsehoods and manipulations have led to whatever they're doing? It may well be the case that Nevil has a chain of believable lies that have convinced him this is the best course of action. And similar schemes may have been manipulated out of other family members, and we just haven't caught those responsible yet. If we continue forward, we have a chance to break the chain of lies and get to the root of it all. If we turn back now, we can perhaps put a stop to some portion of a result of that chain of lies before it does any damage. What do you think?"

"What do I think? I think it's not my job to answer questions like that."

"Well, I'm asking."

Lattica rubbed her neck. "It is a long way home, even if we go directly. And that message is damning, but it also wasn't delivered."

"And we took the signet ring. He can't write a replacement unless he has multiple spares," Euphoria added.

"Last we saw the man responsible, he was headed northeast. Ram's Rest is south. Northeast is the direction of the next safe house."

"The signet ring may have been kept in the safe house, and he may be seeking another in another safe house to write the replacement message."

"I think the sooner we get a lock on each of those doors, the sooner these messages dry up and we can get the family on the right path again."

"I concur. We head northeast. But I suspect we'll need to be ready for combat. There is someone out there with a lot to lose, and he knows we're coming."

"Trust me," Lattica said. "I'm much more comfortable being ready to club a couple of fools than I am making decisions."

"You'd best get comfortable with both. If we see this through, it'll mean we've saved this family from the corruption that's been eating it alive for potentially years. You'll be a much more respected member of the family."

"No more riding in the driver's seat?"

"And a lot more 'Mrs. Graves.'"

Lattica smirked. "I'm not sure if I'm for or against that. But I'll be happy to find out."

Fel dropped a heavy sack of goods in the commander's office in the wall. Wick's travel speed, or whatever it should be called when he flicked from lantern to lantern, had increased greatly. He could reach others almost instantly now, but he still had to talk to others to get information, and thus Fel knew he would be gone for at least a few hours. He took that time make his selections of the items in the office that would satisfy the financial motivations for the trip. He also made his way back to the horse and wagon to see if they were healthy and intact. Duurth must have genuinely been frightened of getting stuck with the dragon sticker again, because the beast hadn't returned to eat the horse. When the food, water, and other care had been properly applied, Fel returned to the office to wait for Wick. To pass the time, he used the telescope to gaze out the window.

"Seems pointless to say it," he said, turning the tool about in his hands, "but this is just another thing they don't make like they used to. It's incredible how far I can see, and how clearly. The hardest part is keeping it steady enough."

The limited view through the defensive slit was frustrating. He had briefly considered finding his way to the top of the Greater Lands Wall to properly survey the worlds on either side. Two things prevented it. The first was an image in his mind of Duurth getting brave enough to snatch him off the top of the wall while he was distracted, and the other was the vision of him stumbling off the wall while grappling with the dual challenges of steadying the telescope and coping with the reality-warping shift in perspective that accompanied crossing the wall. Fel prided himself on being able to set curiosity aside when it didn't have a likely enough payoff.

"Fel," remarked Wick's voice from behind him. "I have returned."

Fel collapsed the telescope and returned it to its hook. "Great! Right on time. How did everything go?"

"There were no significant troubles or delays, though I was asked to utilize some of my otherwise unused time while present in Beffshire."

"By who?"

"Allie required me to engage in a fairly traditional bit of surveillance."

"Anything I should know about?"

"Neither did she request of me to inform you of those findings, nor did she request that I withhold them."

"Skip it, then. I'll let her decide if I need to know. What about the rest?"

"Teya was exceedingly busy during my visit. She will be initiating her major efforts to correct the influence of the Lesser Greater Lands diamond in a day or two. But her answer was a swift and simple one. Regarding the ships, and based upon your description, those were elven ships. She says the elves have done little sailing for as long as she can remember, thanks in no small part to Kazel's allegiance with the undine, which greatly complicates sea travel by any who would pose a threat to Kazel. That the ships were not visibly rocking and rolling, it was likely that the elves have not been deemed to be directly threatening Kazel, thus were permitted passage unharrassed. But Teya doesn't like the look of it. Elves, owing to their long lifespan, tend to act in very slow, very measured ways. A sudden and sweeping change in tactics suggests they have plans that are worth the risks. And few elven plans benefit anyone but the elves."

"So we have elves shooting at dragons, elves sailing the high seas, and that one that got loose and caused all that trouble back home," Fel said.

"That would appear to be accurate. Teya further remarked that you should not be concerned."

"She doesn't like the look of it, but I should not be concerned?"

"Correct. She assures you that Kazel can handle things himself. And if help is required, it will come."

"How?"

"She invoked destiny."

"She puts a whole lot of trust in destiny. How exactly is destiny going to help?"

"When the time was right for Kazel to be freed, you and Tome came to free him. When the time is right for aid to arrive from the outside, it will arrive."

"I wish I could be as sure about anything as Teya is about destiny."

"Destiny, it seems, has a helping hand, according to her, in the form of the beacon."

"What's that?"

"If aid is required, a beacon is lit in the heart of Kazel's kingdom. It is meant to summon aid."

"I see. We'll put a pin in that. What about the books for the switches?"

"Your father was intrigued. We discussed them at length, and he checked his other reference. The vast majority of the material in those books, the overwhelming majority in fact, dealt with when it would be considered permissible to open the gate."

"That's it? You can fill three books with that?"

"The times of day it could be opened, who could order it, what code words and phrases would be used to confirm their identity, how many troops should be on hand, how long the gate could be left open. The only points dealing directly with the operation of the gate were as follows: the exterior switch opens the exterior gate, the interior switch opens the interior gate. The central control sets a timer that will automatically close the gates when it elapses."

"Nothing about if this will monkey with the enchantments or anything? We saw what happened when I swapped some plates on the clockwork diamond in False Clickspring."

"The books are quite explicit that this is merely a gate. The danger is strictly a military consideration, as it will potentially allow unwanted human forces to pass through the gate," Wick said.

"There was a point in time when people were afraid that humans were going to cross the wall all willy-nilly? I thought the whole point of the wall was to keep humans and mystics separate. What kind of idiot besides me would cross this wall willingly?"

"Tome."

"Me and him."

"No other humans with such proclivities spring to mind."

Fel marched over to the plinth and leaned on it, eyes on the switches. "You realize I'm going to have to flip these switches, right? If only to see what happens on the exterior of the wall, because there's no gate there."

"I'd assumed it would be a distinct possibility, and your father expressed a similar curiosity."

"Anything I should know before I do it?"

"Only that operators are warned to keep back ten yards from the gates when they are about to operate, and that there is a small hatch located behind the ladder leading up here which leads into the gateway."

"... Is there?" He grabbed the lantern and trotted over to the edge of the platform.

"The hatch is not mentioned anywhere else in the materials available, and as a result we do not have a means to unlock it," Wick said.

Fel climbed down the ladder and peered behind it. There was no obvious sign of a hatch. A closer-than-average search revealed one of the braces was considerably looser than the others. He unfurled his tools and found an appropriately sized probe. Inserting it revealed something springy and metallic concealed in the wall.

"Doesn't feel like a trap. Not enough room for anything nasty and not enough tension to be the trigger for something somewhere else," he said. "But it doesn't seem to do anything. Not that it means much. There's no gate, and there's a switch to control it. Stands to reason there's no hatch either."

Fel climbed the ladder again and marched toward the switches. "Here's the plan, Wick. I think I have enough gear to sell. So I'm going to flip that switch, see what it does, then I'm going to hike the loot back to the wagon. We'll wait until it seems like we can make a break for it without having to outrun or reintimidate a dragon, and head back north."

"That is a sound and reasonable plan of action," Wick said.

He hesitated for a moment. This was a very old, and presumably very large, contraption. If the rest of the wall was an indication, it would work flawlessly. The Greater Lands Wall's contraptions were in better repair than any he'd ever encountered. But there was always a chance something might act up after this much time. He adopted his best "dash for cover if things go wrong" posture.

"So, uh. Seeing as I'm about to flip this switch, how many troops should I have assembled, according to the book?" he asked, if only to stall for a moment.

"One full battalion or the East Guardian."

"Hopefully one contraptioneer, a unicorn, and a sentry lantern will do."

He flipped the interior switch. The wall rumbled and an unsettling grinding sound filled the air as decades of dust and grime were crackled and forced from between hinges. He looked out the window and saw the largest, sturdiest gates he'd ever seen swinging open. The rumbling settled down without mishap.

The second switch was the real show. Now confident nothing would shatter or launch into the sky when the devices activated, he hurried to the appropriate window and held the mirror out to watch. It was true that there was no gate to speak of on that side. The wall had been the same heavy, smooth stone that composed the rest of it. The switch changed that. Stones that each weighed more than a fully loaded wagon shifted and pivoted in a glorious bit of mechanized choreography. The dust and dried grass in front of the slowly emerging doorway rattled and shimmied. The packed earth broke into irregular clumps and slid into a messy mound in the center as a bit of road, long ago buried by the dry desert winds, angled downward. Stones formerly blocking the way shifted forward and pulled aside, some stacking, some angling, until a sturdy archway was formed. Beyond it, a sheltered passageway through the wall connected to the ramp on the opposite side.

A few seconds after the main gate finished opening, something happened that was enough to stop the heart of anyone with experience in Bygone Era traps. He heard the sound of unexpected motion. The source was the ladder to the platform he was standing on. It shifted aside with enough speed to send one of the tools he'd left beside it spinning through the air to embed itself in the side of a wooden bookshelf.

"Am I missing something, Wick?" Fel said when no further motion occurred. "I don't see or smell any fire, no mist, no spikes, no nets."

"I have observed no clear indication of danger," Wick said.

"So three big, thick books about what those switches do, and nothing about the ladder?" he snapped.

"Evidently."

He grumbled under his breath and, rather than trusting the recently shifted ladder, hopped down to the floor directly. The repositioned ladder had taken the section of wall it was mounted to with it and had revealed a full-height door, braced but not locked. Fel gave it a thorough search and deemed it safe to open. He had to throw his full weight against it to get it to swing stiffly open, but when it did, he was greeted by a confusing blast of fresh air. It had swirls of the dusty, sharp heat of the outer wall and the oppressive humidity of the inner side. Experiencing the sudden contrast was disorienting, and for reasons that Fel couldn't comprehend, it produced a thick swirl of fog. He paced into the dim shade of the tunnel leading from the outside world to the Greater Lands, Wick's lantern in hand. With the apparent size of the wall itself hidden from him, his brain didn't have to grapple with the impossibility of the wall containing something larger than its area could possibly hope to account for. It was simply a door, on one side, an arid field; and on the other, a lush forest. He took a few steps forward, stopping just shy of the threshold of the Greater Lands side of the little tunnel. Considering his abrupt initial entry to the Greater Lands, he wouldn't take his chances getting too close and ending up tumbling into a river or chasm, even though the road ahead seemed quite intact.

The vista before him was magnificent. He hadn't taken the time to appreciate the view when he made his escape last time. Unlike the slice of the Greater Lands he could see through the narrow window, he could see a huge section of the region. Most of it was an indistinct mass of trees. Nevertheless, his brief but eventful time here had etched certain features into his head. Scanning along the wall eventually turned up the misty waterfall he'd "ridden" into the Greater Lands. The river it formed coiled and carved its treeless swath through the woods. In the distance rose the mountain he knew to be Kazel's lair and, coiling up from one of its slopes, a stream of vivid white smoke.

"Do you see that, Wick?" he asked.

"I see a great many things."

"The smoke in the distance. There," he pointed.

"I am less capable of seeing long distances than you."

"I don't know why I'm looking into this, as though there's any doubt what I'll find."

He hurried inside to fetch the telescope rather than relying on his mediocre spyglass. Again, training it on a distant point and holding it steady enough to be of any use was no small challenge, particularly when his nerves were already making their guess about what he'd see if he succeeded. But eventually, there could be no doubt.

"Wick, did Teya describe that beacon to you?" he asked.

"She said it would be visible for all to see, and would stream with white smoke and—"

"Violet flame?"

"Correct."

He lowered the telescope, eyes shut in a look of pained frustration. "Wick. I'm about to do something very foolish."

"You intend to answer the call of the beacon?"

"Teya has pitched in to keep my family safe. The least I can do is see what it'll take to keep hers safe." He marched toward the door. "That and if there's something going down that's more than Kazel can handle on his own, it's bound to find its way to me eventually. Everything else does. At least this time I'll have a horse and wagon."

Chapter 5

Tome's hands shook as he held both book and quill painfully tight. He'd grown accustomed to the harrowing nature of their travel, and in the rare times he took control of the horse, he suspected he'd also greatly improved his overall skill at driving a cart. When the spell finished running its course, guiding a steed at normal speeds would feel like child's play. But adjusting to things such that he was not perpetually on edge and fearing for his life meant he was able to return to his other archnemesis. Boredom. After a few hours of trial and error, he found that if he pressed the book firmly against his leg, braced his leg against the floor, and put as much weigh as he could onto his hand as he leaned on the page to stabilize the pen nib, he could reliably work his way through crafting spells if he did so letter by letter. It was true that he hadn't yet successfully composed a single spell in this way, but he was quite close to replacing the fire-starter spell that he'd used for the campfire after their day's travel had run out of hours precisely halfway between the two nearest towns.

As Madge was after an education, working very slowly through a simple spell was actually a fine way to achieve that.

"At this point, you have properly identified the essential nature, the key identity of the caster. This is one of the most difficult aspects to paper magic. The strength, duration, and reliability of the spell depends upon a precise and accurate identification of all aspects. Not just the effects, but where they are intended to be conjured, when, and by whom. And the brevity of the spell depends upon achieving this precision concisely."

"Still doesn't make any sense," Madge said.

"As I've said, it is difficult to grasp the tenets of this magic. There is a reason it isn't more popularly practiced."

"No, no. The structure I get. It's very simple. There are certain ingredients that must be present, and mixing them is what produces the effect. The hard part is getting the right amounts of each ingredient you want without getting too much of ingredients you don't want. It's fine. I understand it. What doesn't make sense is how there is somehow some wrong way to identify yourself. Isn't it *my* decision who I am?"

"I imagine so. But there is still the trick of encapsulating that. Very few people truly know themselves."

"But how does the spell know if I got it right? How does the spell know if I did a lousy job describing myself? If I cut my hair or change my clothes, does that weaken the spell?"

"No. No. When I say that you must define yourself, it isn't anything as trivial as what you are physically. It's elements of your past, your present, and even your future. It is your ideals. Your defining elements. What makes you who you are. But it is undeniably so. The spells work better when the identity is refined, and there is an essential truth that becomes clear with the refinement."

"Well, what's your identity?"

"Presently, and it changes subtly over time, the most effective encapsulation I have been able to produce is composed of twenty-three characters in the arcane language in a precise order."

"But what do they mean?"

"A seeker of knowledge through travel and observation, acquired in violation of the will of recent ancestors, and acquired without explicit malicious or altruistic aims."

"That's you?"

"That's the first character. This is a profoundly nuanced language. Which is why making it your first written one is a bit absurd."

Madge grinned. "Start with the hard part and the rest is easy. Oh! Wait, wait, over here!" She eased the horse to a stop and nudged it to the side of the road, then hopped down.

"What? What are you doing?" Tome asked.

"There's some wild Farmer's Lace."

"You spotted that at the speed we were moving?"

She waved her hand, encompassing the whole field. "There's a lot of it. It's all this white stuff."

"And it was worth stopping for?"

"It's a key ingredient in a potion that is supposed to greatly enhance strength and durability. Titan Extract. I have all the rest of the ingredients."

"Do you anticipate needing a potion like that?"

"I anticipate making up a few batches and selling them to loggers on the coast. The stuff is good and stable. It keeps well for years. There are places back home that keep a couple of vials of this in a chest just in case something happens and they need to be able to move something big and heavy to save somebody."

Tome sighed. "I can't fault you for wanting to get some resources, but we still have a few days of this maddening journey ahead of us, and I'd really rather keep moving so that we can be done with it."

"We don't have a few days left," Madge said, plucking buds and carefully stowing them.

"By my estimates, there should be about three days left. And that was the estimate before I took you on and started moving a bit slower."

"You're not great at making estimates, then. Farmer's Lace only grows very close to the west coast, according to the old man. At the rate we're moving, we'll run out of land before tomorrow. So unless this monastery place is in the ocean and your horse is a good swimmer, we'll be there by sunset."

Tome furrowed his brow and stood up in the cart, leaning aside to poke himself up past the sunshade. He hadn't spent much time taking in the landscape as it whizzed by, so it wasn't until this moment that he realized it was extremely familiar. Not in the vague and undefinable manner of a place he'd passed through once years before on the way to Beffshire. This was the landscape of his youth. Perhaps not a portion he'd specifically visited, but with all of the elements he'd grown up seeing out his window.

He sat again and dug out the map that had been of little use thus far, thanks to the nature of the spell always guiding them toward their destination.

"I was quite certain I'd done this with the utmost of care. But... ah. Yes, I see now. I used the same route I would have been taking if the speed spell hadn't been used, which I'd devised to ensure I could spend most nights with a roof over my head. Since each day of travel at this speed has been the equivalent of several at the slower speed, we didn't need to stop so often, and thus a dozen or more minor detours to nearby towns weren't necessary. A simple oversight."

"What?" Madge called, invisible among the tall weeds.

"I said you were right!"

"I know I was right!" She emerged from the field and shook burrs and stickers from her hair and clothes. "Found some Boot-Brush too! That'll come in handy if anybody needs a hangover cure. Works a treat, by the way." She climbed into the cart again and wedged the bundle of foraged goods between two stacks of books. "So, you looking forward to seeing your mom and dad again?"

"If you must know, I'm not terribly confident things will go well with my father. He is a calm and measured man, but he was displeased with my mystic studies and further displeased with my departure."

"And your mom?"

"I grew up in a monastery. There is no mom to speak of."

"Everyone has a mom."

"I am not suggesting I somehow miraculously asserted myself in this world without a mother. I am saying she was not involved in raising me. I don't even know her name."

"Were you an orphan?"

"No. My father is still alive."

"But were you adopted?"

"No, he is my actual father."

"I thought the kind of people who lived at monasteries didn't get to father children."

"Yes, Madge. One might further suppose that the circumstances of my birth are part of a story that brings great shame to my father and by extension to me and thus is the kind of story I don't like to tell."

"Ooooh... The poop's out of the goose now, so go ahead and tell it."

"No, I don't think I will, Madge."

"You'll probably feel better if you do."

"I already feel worse having brought it up."

"Do you want to hear about my parents?"

"Not especially."

"They're both mud farmers down south. I have six brothers and sisters. I'm the second oldest. One day they said to me, 'If you can figure out how to feed yourself, that'd sure help us out, because we can't figure out how to feed you.' And so I left. I'd write to them, but I don't know how, and they don't know how to read anyway. As far as I know they're fine."

"You don't seem terribly unhappy about what sounds like a very unfortunate upbringing."

"It was fine. I'm alive."

"What exactly does a mud farmer..." Tome trailed off, his expression suddenly sharp and anxious.

"Something wrong?" Madge said.

"Do you recall the consequences I said I'd suffered as a result of blood magic?"

"Something about getting sleepy sometimes?"

"I feel sudden, unexplained fatigue that seems to be associated with the proximity to elven magic."

"Right. Did you just feel that?"

"A tiny, tiny amount."

Madge raised her eyebrows. "Am I about to meet an elf? I've never met an elf before."

"I dearly hope we will not be meeting one. And what's more, as far as I know there is only one elf who has the capacity to be here in the outside world, and I have no reason to be certain he is even still alive. The thought that he could somehow have come this far, and ended up near enough for me to sense his actions, challenges the limits of belief."

"You didn't do a lot of talking during this trip about yourself. Again, I feel like if you were in the mood to talk about yourself, you'd have brought up the situation with your dad. But what you did talk about seems like challenging the limits of belief is not that uncommon for you. Unless you're a liar. Which is fine! Liars are entertaining as long as you don't have to rely on them."

"I'm not a liar."

Madge snapped the reins. "Then you have a kobold roommate and your friend's dad builds and sells contraptions even though no one else can build them anymore. Why wouldn't an elf show up to bother you?"

Tome gazed sullenly at the road ahead. "You have the astounding capacity to find ways to frustrate me by both applying logic and refusing to apply logic."

"When you talk about that Fel person, you talk about how he annoys you too. Have you considered that you're just really easy to annoy and the other people are normal?"

"I reject the implication that either of you are in any way normal. But your point is taken. Keep your eyes on the road. If this will be over soon, all the better, but smashing ourselves into a tree at this late stage in the journey would be a terrible shame."

"All right!" Madge said. "Say. Do you think they'll have a spare room at the monastery for me to stay?"

"You are a woman, so the answer is no."

"I won't tell them I'm a woman if you don't."

He palmed his face. "I'm trading the ordeal of the journey for the ordeal of the arrival, aren't I?"

"Life's just a series of ordeals, Tome. You have to learn to enjoy them!"

"You're all right taking over, Oovay?" Allie called through the tightly shut door of the break room.

The answer was an irritated affirmative that didn't manage to include any words. The source of the irritation was likely the fact that, for once, Allie was on the inside of the break room and Oovay was on the outside. Tonight was the night she'd arranged to take a few hours off to have a meal with Mariss. If someone had suggested a few months ago that what began with Fel talking her ear off about how he hoped to woo the kind young baker would end with Allie in a relationship with Fel and the two ladies becoming friends, she would have cut off their drinks for the night. But now she was hastily changing into a more presentable outfit while voluntarily giving up some hours of prime earning in order to have a nice meal with Mariss while Fel was out of town. Life had a curious way of choosing unique paths.

She gave her boots a cursory buffing and wrestled her increasingly unruly hair into submission. Allie didn't recognize the name of the restaurant Mariss had picked, but that was no surprise. Allie spent very little time in the upper-class parts of Beffshire, and even less time at the kind of a restaurant that called for buffing boots and wrangling hair. For others it might have been a point of pride to dress up in their finery and show off at the restaurant so that the other diners wouldn't be able to keep their eyes off them. Allie had the opposite goal. She mostly wanted to clean herself up enough to avoid having people stare at her. It was a much lower and, crucially, much cheaper bar to meet.

With her ablutions taken care of, she opened the door and stepped out into the bar again. Before any of the patrons could react, she jabbed the air with her finger, pointing at no one in particular.

"If I hear one whistle, I'm grabbing the behave-yourself stick and knocking a tooth out of everyone who puckered up," she warned.

The statement earned a few laughs but, notably, no whistles. She made her way to the streets and onward to the restaurant. Her timing was spot on, with Mariss's horse and cart appearing at the end of the street when Allie was just a few steps from the door.

"Allie! By the High, so good to see you," Mariss said, hopping down and giving her a hug that threatened to engulf her in a sea of ruffles and poofs. "I haven't had a chance to visit you at the tavern since our last meal. It has been just so busy at the bakery!" She nodded to the stable boy, who took the reins of her cart and guided it down the street.

"Things have been busy at The Fox and Log as well."

"Success is a burden sometimes, isn't it? But come on. Inside. I'm famished."

She had a short exchange of pleasantries with the owner of the restaurant, who, like virtually every other restauranteur in this half of town, was a friend of her father's. They were led to their seats, glasses were filled with wine, and Mariss released a torrent of chitchat that had been building up inside her since their last dinner.

"... and it turned out the reason it was so sweet was because the fruit was a little bit overripe, which is perfect. The fruit on top needs to be perfectly ripe, so now we know anything that wasn't quite right to go on the top yesterday will be in the filling today! Less waste, better taste."

"You can tell it's real wisdom because it rhymes," Allie said with a snicker.

"You joke, but it's interesting how often that happens," Mariss said. "Enough about me, though. Here I am chatting *at* you instead of chatting *with* you. What is new?"

Allie took a breath and tried to pick through her daily drudgery for something she could share.

"That's the 'I'd tell you if I could' sigh," Mariss said.

Allie blinked at her. "Is it?"

"Sure! I'd know it anywhere." Mariss lowered her voice to a hush. "Up to secret things, are you? So exciting! Anything I can help with?"

"It's nothing like some of the schemes I've been a part of, but it is something that would get more difficult to deal with if it was generally known. We can discuss it, so long as it stays between us."

Mariss released a suppressed squeal of delight. Allie wondered if there was ever a point in her own life that she'd felt an ounce of the giddy glee that Mariss seemed to feel for every new twist and turn.

"There's someone who has been causing trouble in the tavern. Not the usual sort of trouble. No throwing fists or throwing drinks. But he's been nosing about, and in some cases taking significant steps to try to loosen the lips of other patrons."

"Such as?"

"A drop or two of some stuff that makes it much easier to get drunk."

"Oh my. And what has he been asking about?"

"That's the confusing thing. It took some doing to find it out, but while he's asking endless questions about all manner of illegal and illicit doings that I'm pleased to say don't take place in The Fox and Log, he hasn't been attempting to coerce people into partaking of them, nor has he been trying to buy or hire any of the sorts of things that he's asking about. I would have thought he was some sort of criminal looking for a foothold in Beffshire, or a simple lowlife hoping to get services or maybe get work. But he's just gathering information."

"I see..." Mariss rubbed her hands together absent-mindedly. "That's curious."

"I was able to work out where he lives. It's not so far from this restaurant, actually. Recently arrived."

"Oh! So the wealthier part of town. That must be nice, at least, attracting someone halfway across town to visit your tavern."

"I can do without customers who are dosing the drinks of other customers."

"Of course, of course. So what do you think he's up to?"

"I can't make heads or tails of it. If he's not horning in on someone's territory and he's not hoping to get some of what he's asking about, then why keep asking?"

"Maybe he's trying to put a stop to it. Clean up the town a bit."

"If the Watch couldn't care less about this sort of trouble happening under their noses, why would a newcomer?"

Mariss sipped her wine and fiddled with a lock of hair. "No... No, no, I think this may be it," Mariss said. "You know Commander Boltt."

"Captain, you mean. The man in charge of the Watch."

"Right, yes. That's the man. There have been some rumblings among some of daddy's friends about how he hasn't been doing a proper job of late. There have been some major problems here in town, and surely some of them should have been caught by the Watch."

"More than a few of which are thanks to the Maskers," Allie said.

"Maybe so. But that doesn't change the fact that people stand to lose a great deal of money, to say nothing of their livelihoods and even their lives, if things like that become routine around here. So there has been buzz that they might start pressuring the lord for a better Watch captain."

"People always gripe about that," Allie said.

"But it would explain why someone would be asking all sorts of questions about things that aren't allowed, if that person was trying to make a case for the inadequacy of the current captain."

"It's a better theory than I've been able to come up with," Allie mused. "Worth looking into."

Allie noted for her own purposes that a would-be enforcer of laws that had been conveniently unenforced until now would be of at least as great a concern to Verfessa as a rival criminal would be. And because her own fate was, for now, entirely linked with Verfessa's thanks to his ownership of the tavern, it was problematic for her as well.

"What will you do if that turns out to be so?" Mariss asked.

"I'd prefer to not have to do anything. I have enough to worry about without having my tavern turn into a proving ground for watchmen. And if this fellow turns out to replace Captain Boltt, I'd rather not have him holding a grudge against me for any reason. But I can't have someone pouring things into people's drinks either." She picked up her own wine. "You've given me something to think about."

"I don't know if I should apologize or say you're welcome," Mariss said. "You seem to have plenty to think about already."

"You gave me another possible clue to a riddle I was working on. I'm thankful. But enough about that. What sort of a meal are we getting today?"

"I'm so glad you asked. I've heard about this chef's work for ages, and I've been meaning to stop in to sample them. For the first course, we'll be having stuffed pickled peppers, followed by a signature soup. He thickens it with goat cheese..."

Fel watched the sky and crunched through a chunk of meat that had been burnt to a crisp. He normally took better care when preparing food, but the knowledge that at any moment a dragon with a complex and targeted opinion of him might show up was a source of considerable distraction. The open gates formed a bit of a shelter, but the tunnel through the wall itself was every bit as large as the dragon. If it decided to swoop through, he'd have little time to dive for cover. In the interest of time, he'd fetched the wagon and parked it beside where he'd set up camp on the ancient stone roadway. There was no hope at all of it getting to safety if the dragon became too interested, but the same was true of the alcove it had been stowed in until now, so he didn't consider that a problem.

Wick arrived in his lantern as Fel washed the last of the char from his abused tongue with a swig of water.

"What's the word, Wick?" Fel asked.

"Allie was not present. Tonight was the night to dine out with Mariss."

"Already?" he said. "Time flies. What about the folks?"

"Your mother was not entirely pleased that you were planning to reenter the Greater Lands. Your father was less vocally resistant but urged that you take care. They were in agreement that you should remain only long enough to learn if you are needed and how you can help."

"I wasn't planning on sightseeing," Fel said. "But if they need me and I can do what they need me to do, then I'm going to do it. It's the right thing to do, and earning another favor from an ancient dragon could prove handy. Now, the sun's going down, which means you can see a little better at distance than during the day, right?"

"That is correct."

"Then keep your eyes peeled, so to speak, while I make sure I have all my gear in order."

"I will happily fulfill this service."

While Parch considered and dismissed the idea of eating some of the charred remnants of Fel's meal, he ensured the decoy he'd been able to recover was prepared for deployment. He fashioned a special little harness out of rope to hold his dragon sticker to the back of the seat, the better to fetch it quickly when the need came. The loot he intended to bring home was all waiting for him in the commander's office. Fel had entertained the idea of unhitching the horse from the wagon and simply riding it, but there was no saddle, and riding the steed bareback would slow him down at least as much as having it pull the wagon.

Parch raised his head and glanced to the sky on the Greater Lands side of the wall, then trotted over to Fel and huddled between his legs.

"Wick? Anything?" Fel said, reaching aside to grip the handle of the spiked weapon.

"Nothing, but my view directly overhead is blocked by the wall itself."

Fel shut his eyes and listened. Distantly, and only when the wind was right, he could hear the faintest rustle of leather wings. He inched out of cover and checked the sky.

"In the distance above the wall to the north," Wick said.

Fel spotted it a moment later. Duurth was heading along the wall. Most crucially, he was headed away from Fel, and was quite a distance away.

"Now. Now's the time," he said.

He hopped onto the driver's seat. Parch joined him and tucked himself behind the back of the seat. Fel snapped the reins and the wagon rattled forward. The road leading down from the gate was at a gentle slope, which helped get the wagon up to speed without taxing the horse. And that was good, because they would need as much help as they could get. While the road nearby was quite clear of debris and in excellent repair considering its age, farther along he could already see that the Greater Lands had done its very best to reclaim it as part of the forest.

"Eyes on the sky, Wick. Watch that dragon for as long as you can."

"It is already at the extreme limits of my vision, but I will keep an unblinking vigil on the sky in that direction."

With Wick's focus on the sky, Fel kept his focus on the road. Fallen debris was already a big enough problem. But it wasn't as though the dragon was the only threat the Greater Lands had to offer. For all he knew there were other dragons about, to say nothing of manticores like the one that had given him the weapon he'd used to instill fear in Duurth. And those were just the things he knew the names of.

Twenty minutes of riding, interrupted only by the brief and frenzied stop to move a fallen tree limb from the road, had slowly filled him with a different sort of foreboding. Something was off about this place. What had stood out to Fel about the Greater Lands previously was how lush and lively it was. Even in a seemingly empty stretch of forest, there was an unexplainable but undeniable sense that this place was more vibrant than the outside world. Like the land itself was barely tamed, ready to leap up and frolic if given the chance. He didn't feel that now. Things felt tense. Unbalanced. And it only took a few more minutes of progress to encounter a firm example of precisely what was wrong.

"That's fresh," he muttered, eyes on a mound of earth the right size and shape to be a lone, unmarked grave.

The nearby trees sported gashes and splintered patches, some still glistening with spilled sap. The shaft of an arrow stood straight out of the carcass of some sort of four-legged creature with more horns and claws than a proper piece of prey should have. There wasn't enough of it left to identify, all but picked clean by scavengers already. But this was not the site of a hunt. This was the site of a battle.

"The locals have been fighting," Fel said. "And there's a beacon calling for help. I've got a bad feeling about this visit, Wick."

"There is still time to turn back."

Fel shook his head. "That part you're wrong about. It's years too late to turn back now. If I wanted to turn back now, I'd have had to stop listening to my parents when they taught me to be a decent man who doesn't let his friends down. The Fel Masker who would turn tail and run never would have made it this far to begin with. We're not stopping until we find a friendly face who can give us a straight answer about what's happening and how to stop it."

"I find that point of view admirable. A sign of pure bravery. As I am effectively immortal, I am incapable of sharing your bravery. I almost envy you in that regard."

"Didn't the elves nearly wipe you out last time you came here? Stripping your strength to make earrings like the one in my pocket?"

"They did. The thought did not occur to me. I am indeed risking my life by accompanying you. What a fine opportunity to acquit myself in a manner becoming of a hero."

Fel nodded. "Wick, if you're looking for an opportunity to almost die, I'm the man you want leading the way. Almost dying is a specialty. And it ought to be easy around here. Because it looks like were walking through the edge of a war zone."

Lord Katritz sat in his office. The sun had set long ago, and he really ought to be heading to bed. The next day was filled to the brim with meetings with peons and underlings, people who fancied themselves civic leaders but really existed only to tend to the lord's own interests. But he couldn't sleep. Things were in motion that shouldn't be. A blasted upstart had come to his home and insinuated himself into a tier of society that should have shunned him. He borrowed just enough of Katritz's gravitas to have the appearance of importance, and parlayed that into a foothold among the lord's weak-minded peers. Right now, Donovan Verfessa was drinking with Lord Hundt after impressing his wife. The thug was helping him solve problems that wouldn't have existed if the blasted noble had a head on his shoulders, and regaling him with coarse, crude tales of chicanery and tomfoolery that had no place within the elegant realm of nobility.

It was an unwelcome annoyance and, more concerning than that, a credible threat to his position. Naturally this Verfessa character couldn't become a lord himself. That was a title that was inherited, a title linked to massive land holdings that no living person had the wealth to accumulate. There was simply no room for a new lord. But he could become an important figure, someone a link or two down the chain. A thorn in Katritz's side that close to his home could cause no end of problems.

Gossip surrounding "Gem" was, and would have continued to be, a problem in the short term. It would have undermined some business dealings and subjected him to some shame and embarrassment. In the fullness of time, though, that would have passed, and whatever stumbles it had caused would have been wiped away and recovered. But now Verfessa was here, gobbling up every scrap of lost influence like some horrid, bottom-feeding lake monster. He was a powerful man within the most powerful city in Lord Katritz's territory. Worse, that city was the one city in the kingdom where he couldn't just drop the hammer on an unruly subject. Beffshire's history of trade and its value to Thayne had afforded itself a level of autonomy that would serve as protection to Verfessa. And his influence within those walls could give the other lords inroads to most of the things Lord Katritz could use as bludgeons to keep them doing business as they had. Severing the connections Verfessa was forging right this moment and recovering the power and sway that he was accumulating would take an offsetting amount of power and sway. For the first time in his life, Lord Katritz found himself not only desiring more power but requiring it. He needed some form of advantage that was uniquely his, one that couldn't be taken away, or else he ran the risk of having his position permanently crippled.

He angrily opened an elegantly carved wooden box and fetched a cigar. The flicker of a sparker and a puff filled the room with the rich, full-scented smoke that until now had never failed to calm his nerves. The tranquilizing effect lasted for all of three seconds before a flare of anger and a clench of his jaw nearly scissored the end off the expensive cigar. He threw open a drawer and rummaged about in it. Then another, and another. Something he would never freely admit about being a lord was the simple reality that most of the things he oversaw were actually overseen by others. Comfortable, simple procedures fell into place and simply worked. There were aspects of his oversight of this land that he'd literally never touched, things set up by his grandfather that continued to operate as if by magic. Contraptions may have become rare and impossible to reproduce, but the mechanisms of society continued unaffected by the end of the Bygone Era. And that suited him well until the very moment he needed to tweak or check on those systems.

Ten minutes of searching turned up the sheet of parchment he was after. The results of the most recent audit of the Contraband Vault. He didn't care about the results themselves. They'd been the same every month since Katritz was a boy. What he needed to know was the date. And there it was. Nine days prior. If he could work out a way to avoid triggering another audit in the interim, it would be just shy of three weeks before any major acquisitions from the vault would be noticed. He grinned around his cigar.

A great deal could be done in three weeks.

"This is as far as we go with the wagon," Lattica said.

Euphoria and Lattica had been heading toward what should have been the next closest of the safe houses for some time. Whereas the others were accessed via poorly maintained roads, clearly not meant for a wagon, this one ceased to have a road at all. For two slow hours, it had been a constant struggle to keep the wagon from becoming irretrievably entangled in roots and loose stone. The task was made measurably more difficult as the sun slid from the sky. Now it was clear that this was the last reasonably clear bit of the mountainside left. If they didn't use this patch to turn around, the next time they got stuck, the wagon would become a permanent resident of the mountain forest.

"Then we continue on foot," Euphoria said.

She fetched the bag with her gear and hopped down. Lattica did the same.

"Tell me," said Lattica. "Are you sure there's a safe house in this direction?"

"If there is one here, it's one of the ones that wasn't listed. As such, I can't be certain we'll find one. But I spent weeks going through decades worth of records, and at least a few years ago, a great many routes for messengers were changed to cross this point. Given how far it is into the mountains, it certainly doesn't seem like they'd be coming here for any reason other than to pick up an important message from someone like Piotor."

"I'm not an expert, but this doesn't seem like a path that's been used by anyone in years."

"I'm not saying this is a safe house that is still in regular use. But that's a mark in favor of searching it, not a mark against. If it's been locked down for years, abandoned, then it may contain things that the users of a more frequently used safe house would have had the sense to destroy or hide in the intervening years. The best place to search for old evidence is under a pile of dust. The best place to search for old treachery is in an old hideout." They crested the hill that had defeated the wagon. "And there it is."

Tucked in the horribly steep and treacherous little divot a stream had dug out of the mountainside was something that could charitably be called a shack. It wasn't a safe house, if only because no sane person who chose to reside in it would feel in the slightest bit safe. At some point in history it had been a mill. The tattered, rotten remnants of a water wheel hung limply from the side. A bit of a stone divert had been used to keep the stream from consuming the foundation of the shack, but neglect had claimed it. The water had washed away most of the wall, and now the stream swished directly against the stones of the northeast corner of the shack's foundation. Many years of freezing and thawing ice, combined with steady erosion from the water, had dislodged enough of the stones to cause a section of the north wall to slump into a pile of loose brick.

The front door was built of heavy timbers and braced with a rusted iron bar held in place by chain and a Bygone Era lock. The lock itself had held up well enough that they might be able to open it, but the bar was rusted to its braces, and the timbers of the door had visibly shifted to wedge in place. It would take three hours of work with axes and hammers to get through that door now. There were no windows, no other doors.

"This is locked up from the outside," Lattica said. "There's certainly not anyone inside. But I suppose they wouldn't lock it if they didn't want to keep something safe."

"Precisely. Help me with that old branch over there. Let's see if we can cobble together a makeshift path across the stream and squeeze through the hole in the wall."

It took more effort than either of them would have liked, and ended up with a tear in a very expensive coat, but the pair got two thick branches tightly wedged in stones on either side of the stream. They moved across them slowly, Lattica in the lead.

"I'd feel a lot better if we had your brother here," Lattica said. "I'm not the best with traps."

"I'd feel better if my father was here. Fel's not the best with traps either. But I'd like to think even the most paranoid of people wouldn't think to trap a random corner of a building on the off chance it might succumb to the elements."

"Maybe not, but who knows how far into the shack we'll get before we find something."

"Just move slowly and get plenty of light on it. Traps are Bygone contraptions. They hold up better than most other things. If you see something that looks less weathered than the rest, paradoxically, that will be the Bygone Era stuff; and thus, likely a trap."

Lattica got to the opening and held her lantern low. A few seconds of scrutiny didn't turn up anything concerning. She slipped inside.

"It's clear," Lattica called. "But watch your step. Bits of the roof have given way."

Euphoria ducked through the opening. The inside wasn't large enough to be the kind of place one would search. Whoever had built it saw no need to dig down into the mountain for more space; thus, the entire interior of the shack was smaller than Euphoria's bedroom. Some of the workings for the waterwheel still stuck through the wall, but the millstone and any other associated mechanisms were missing. In fact, everything was missing except for a sturdy stone slab in the center of the floor and a firepit positioned atop it. Rather than wood, or even coals, inside were the twisted remnants of a badly damaged lantern and a blackened but largely intact mask. And on the ground on either side of the slab were the desiccated remains of two would-be thieves.

"If there is a trap in this place, it is triggered by that slab," Lattica said.

"Undoubtedly." Euphoria squinted at the firepit. "Do you have your canteen?"

"Of course."

"Hand it to me, if you would."

Lattica did so. Euphoria opened it and placed her thumb over the opening. A sharp swing sent a spritz of water sprinkling at the firepit. When it struck the blackened mask, it sizzled.

"By the High... Surely no one has been here in ages. How could that thing be hot?" Lattica said.

"Only one answer comes to mind." Euphoria cleared her throat. "Are you going to speak up? Or do we have to waste our time finding out if there is a trap?"

A few moments of silence passed. Then a soft glow curled up around the edges of the mask, through the eye holes and out the mouth.

"From the beginning, I'd known it would only be a matter of time," came a voice from the flame.

"That's a new trick. Raising and lowering your flame," Euphoria said. "I wasn't aware sentry lanterns could do that."

"I have a great many tricks that many lanterns do not."

It was, to a member of the Graves family, a voice so common as to be a part of the background noise of business, at least until recently. It was the voice. The Voice of the Flame. Wick's counterpart in the Graves family.

"What is this place? And what are you doing here?" Epiphany demanded. "Every artifact lantern was accounted for."

"In your accounting, some things were marked as lost when they were not. Not entirely," the flame said. "And some things were marked as present when they were lost."

"I want answers. And I suspect you have a lot to answer for," Euphoria said.

"You speak with intensity. Do you mean to intimidate me? Do you suppose there is anything you can do which could threaten me? You are a long way from home, Euphoria Graves, née Euphoria Masker. It would serve you well to forget what you've seen here."

"Now who is trying to intimidate whom?"

"You are not nearly so durable as I. And there are far fewer who would heed your commands. And far fewer who would hear your call for help."

"You're a flame. You can speak, you can hear, and you can cast light and heat. We are doing what we can to silence your voice and deafen your ears, and I am not so foolish as to allow myself to be burned. You have no sway over me. Answer my questions or I swear to you, I will find a way to make you pay for what you have done."

"Ask. The answers won't matter much longer."

"What happened to Piotor Graves?" she asked.

A dry laugh emanated from the flame. In all her life, dealing with two sentry lanterns, Euphoria had never heard that sound come from a flame before. It was chilling.

"First Thaddeus, now you. Do you truly wish to know? That answer comes at a terrible price."

"Answer me!"

"Very well. A tale. One from many years ago. Piotor Graves had received what the Graves vault hunters called 'the slag heap,' recovered from the so-called 'burnt vault.' Do you know the place?"

"I'm familiar with it," Euphoria said. "One of the few vaults that had been compromised prior to its discovery. Some terrible fire in its history had damaged its walls. Because of the damage, even amateur vault hunters could gain entry. Within weeks of its discovery it was picked clean."

"Not fully clean. A pit in the center of the floor held a single prize. The slag heap. Clearly the source of the fire, it had melted itself fifteen yards into the earth. It took a team of six men nearly three weeks to retrieve it. Seventy-two pounds of metal, charred and melted into a ball. But a clean section of shaft sticking up from the rest suggested there was, miraculously, an intact contraption within."

The flame flickered briefly. Euphoria glanced at Lattica. She nodded and moved to the hole in the wall to keep a watch on the outside. A flickering sentry flame meant absence. If this flame had flickered, the voice had delivered a message elsewhere. It could be calling for aid.

"Nine weeks of steady work, at the skilled hands of Piotor, unearthed two contraptions. The first, a mask. The long-lost Scholar. Damaged by the flame, but not destroyed. The second? A device too volatile to name. It has been stowed in the Contraband Vault of Shalia, and rightly so. But it was not without consequence."

"You're stalling. Spit it out."

"You wish to know what happened to Piotor. That knowledge will do you no good if you do not *understand* what happened to Piotor."

"Then speak, but speak quickly."

"As was his wont, Piotor tinkered with the unnamed and ill-fated contraption. Even all those years ago, he felt the sting of inferiority with regard to the gifts of Martin Masker. To his credit, he restored the contraption to a fraction of its functionality. To his dismay, its function was to destroy. To incinerate."

"So Piotor was killed."

"You requested an answer. There is more to tell. Piotor was consumed in flame. This much is true. But in Piotor's possession was an artifact lantern. The first home of the Voice. And when his body and his home were consumed in flames, so too was the lantern. That which is consumed in the flames of a lantern adds its wisdom to the lantern."

"You can't mean..."

"You are speaking to Piotor. Or at least, the only part of him that truly mattered. His mind. His knowledge."

"That's impossible."

"You are too young, too new to the family for my words to carry anything that might convince you. You never knew the mound of flesh and blood that bore the name Piotor. But Thaddeus did. The others who hold power within the family, they do. They know that the words they have read, the messages that have guided their actions, are indeed the words of Piotor. It is true, as you have discovered, they were not written by his hands. He no longer has hands. Arrangements had to be made. Messages sent in secret, disguised as messages from the patriarch, demanding a collection of messengers transcribe Piotor's words. Seal them. Deliver them as though taken from the man himself."

"You claim to be Piotor, but you speak about him rather than as him."

"Piotor was but a man, and the story still is not told in full. For the lantern's flames had consumed much in the past, and more in that moment than a foolish and unsure man. The Maskers' flame, the one called Wick, carries the shame of failing to protect the Tellestressa Archives. It was in his flames that half of those books were destroyed, forever locked in his mind, with no way to retrieve them in a dozen lifetimes. But Wick does not carry the whole of the blame. Other lanterns fell that day. One of them added to the flames, consuming its share of the archives as well. The Graves flame. What Wick's mind lacks, the Graves' flame contains, along with a mind fixated upon unlocking that knowledge. Man, flame, and knowledge. Joined as one. Such a being deserves a new name. And so, I chose the name Lens.

"Instructions were given. The lantern and the mask were moved to storage and heaped atop one another such that the flame could warm the mask and weave into its mind as well. It is awake, but without a voice. I gain only the merest notions. But they have been enough. Enough to form a plan. And that plan had many contingencies. It was too important to be allowed to fail. Not by the whims of dragons. Not by the whims of Maskers. Not by the whims of Graves. And so, the plan ticks on. So near to its end. Too large, too powerful to be stopped by someone such as you. Go. Run. Try to tell my tale. You are a long way from anyone who may listen, and longer still from any who would believe. And you will find the path strewn with danger."

Euphoria addressed Lattica without looking. "Anyone?"

"No threat yet. At least not one that has made itself known."

Euphoria glanced aside. A heavy, chipped bit of stone that had fallen from the top of the wall would do for what she had in mind. She hefted it in her hands.

"I will save you the effort. The slab is protected by a trap, and one that is not so easily defeated as by setting it off with a thrown stone. You simply don't have the skill to disable my protections."

"No, I suppose not," she said. "Maybe my father would. But Father doesn't do the vault dives any longer. Even before I left, that was the task for Fel. And Fel told me all about the tricks he'd picked up. If you can't disable a trap, don't."

She turned in a circle to build up some speed, then heaved the stone toward the slab like she was trying to skip it across the surface of a lake. The moment the stone passed the vertical plane marking the edge of the slab, a horrifying zap and crackle sparked forth from within the stone itself. A bolt of lightning moving with the mind of a viper struck at the stone. It blackened, sizzled, and fractured, but the pieces continued on their way. The rock-turned-gravel clashed against the firepit and upset it, tipping it aside. The twisted lantern and the mask spilled and skittered across the slab and onto the floor.

Euphoria pulled a scarf from her neck and ducked out the opening to dunk it into the icy stream.

"Don't you understand? What I have done, I have done for all of us! What do you hope to achieve?"

She stomped toward the lantern, dripping scarf in hand. "First, I hope to shut you up."

Euphoria pressed the soaked bit of cloth to the exposed wick of the enchanted lantern, snuffing out the flame. She then wrapped her hands with it and gathered up both lantern and mask, steam sizzling from the scarf as she did.

"Come on. We need to move, quickly," Euphoria said. "I don't suppose you have any friends in the neighborhood. Someone not affiliated with the Graves family that we can trust?"

"I don't have very many friends at all. And certainly none this far into the mountains."

"All my friends who I'd trust with this sort of thing are closer to Beffshire." Euphoria uncomfortably shifted the mask in her protected grip. "Let's move more quickly. This mask has held on to a lot of heat."

"Why don't you dunk it in the stream?"

"I seem to remember Father having no end of problems with contraptions after quenching them too quickly. And despite the danger, if this is the Scholar mask, if it can be repaired, it is worth the risk and discomfort of retaining it."

They reached the wagon. She heaved both lantern and mask to the floor of the passenger compartment, where they both singed a very expensive wood finish but failed to light any fires. She then scrambled up to the seat beside Lattica, and the laborious process of turning around in the tight clearing began.

"So what is the plan?" Lattica asked.

Euphoria rummaged through the maps from the compartment beneath the seat. "We need to get to someone with the ability to protect us, the ability to communicate quickly and securely, and who is outside the influence of the Graves family."

"The Graves family has done its best to make sure no place in Shalia is outside their influence. If the word gets to just about any city between here and Ram's Rest before we do that we're a problem for the family, there will be at least one person in any given place who will send word or take action in anticipation of a reward."

"Yes. That is going to be a problem." She flipped through a few more maps. "We'll stay off the main roads. For now, head southwest. There's an old logging road."

"What are we going to do if we *do* reach Ram's Rest? You were looking for proof of Piotor's fate. Even I have a hard time believing he's been lurking in the sentry flame all these years."

"First we survive, then we figure out the rest."

"And what of the fact that even if there's only one person in the world still loyal to Piotor, that person will be in Ram's Rest, probably in the same room as whoever has the means to take the appropriate action?"

"All very good questions that we will address after we have some good friends and sturdy walls between us and the unknown."

"Where might we find someplace like that?"

Euphoria stuffed the maps back into place. "Fenfield."

"Fenfield. The plague place."

"The plague is no more."

"Sure, it's been replaced by a prison for monsters."

"Monstrousness is relative. And right now the far greater monster is stowed in the carriage behind us. We're going to Fenfield. A friend of the family will meet us there."

"Not a friend of the Graves family."

"No. A friend of the Masker family."

Lattica shook her head. "You people have friends in strange places."

"And thank the High we do."

Hours of traveling in the dark through a forest populated by fearsome beasts had done a great deal to erode Fel's certainty that he'd made the right decision. The highest vantage available to him had been the wall itself, so before he'd left, he'd taken the time to locate landmarks to guide him toward the burning beacon on the mountainside. When the wind was right, and the moon was visible between the clouds, he could see the stream of white smoke, but that did little to indicate how far there was to go. Spotting the violet light of the beacon itself would have set his mind to rest on that point, but that would have required him to climb a tree tall enough to poke his head out of the canopy, which would have been a substantial delay and put him in a terribly compromising position if someone were to attack. It was a shame Parch couldn't speak. The lesser unicorn could scamper up and down again like he was walking on level ground and tell the tale of what he saw. Of course, there was no reason to believe that if Parch could speak, he'd be any more obliging or obedient than he was now. So Fel had guided his horse along the increasingly dilapidated road, all the while waiting for the broken bridge he'd spotted from the wall. That was where he would make his turn to the northeast and would mark one-third of the distance of his journey.

Well past midnight, there was still no bridge.

The horse had had a good long rest before they'd left, but even so, it would need to stop soon. And if he and the beast were to survive long enough to find friends here, Fel would have to stay awake. Wick was an able sentry, but he couldn't very well do anything to protect them. Parch was impressively capable of detecting threats but was seldom vocal enough to serve as a lookout. And a groggy Fel stumbling to his feet after being shouted out of a deep sleep wasn't likely to do much good regardless. He'd have to keep awake as long as he could. And unlike the horse, he'd been working himself ragged in his search for and storage of goods.

"Three days at least," Fel said.

"Pardon?" Wick said.

"If we haven't hit the bridge yet, that beacon is three days away at least. I swear that mountain was closer the last time I was here. But then, I guess I already knew distances didn't make sense in this place," he said. "I can't stay awake for three days. Or I can, but I may as well be asleep."

"Did you plan for this?" Wick said.

"I planned on not needing a plan for this. So now the question is, do I try to find shelter and get a proper rest in, or do I push my endurance as far as it can go before I do that?"

"Do you feel as though finding and utilizing a shelter while pushed to the brink of exhaustion is wise?"

"Nothing I've done in the past year has been particularly wise, but your point is taken. You keep watching for things trying to kill me. I'll start looking for a place to hole up for the night."

They continued along the road. In his prior visit to the Greater Lands, the only real evidence he'd encountered that humanity had ever had a place here was the wall itself and the relatively intact city of Clickspring. This road was clearly the main thoroughfare for the human society, or at least the humanlike society, that had existed in the Greater Lands prior to the wall. It meant that a careful eye could turn up little hints of cities and villages, farms and workhouses. Run-down secondary roads ran off from the main one. For whatever reason, these roads seldom lasted more than a few dozen yards into the distance before any trace of them was gone. What little architecture remained showed signs of having been forcibly and viciously destroyed. These weren't places that had simply worn away under the weight of the years. These were the crumbs of a society crushed by an enemy.

Over the time he'd been traveling, he'd come to recognize the fingerprint of a conquered town or settlement. He'd yet to encounter anything that he would call the ruins of a proper city. Like the areas surrounding Beffshire, this looked like a place of farms and fields, with little clusters of houses scattered here and there. Like all good Bygone Era dwellings, these houses had been dug down, the aboveground portion more of a marker for where the buried residence had lain. A home or storehouse, after destruction and years of neglect, now showed itself as a bit of broken wall surrounding a slumped-in pit of debris, moss, and weeds. After a few more minutes of travel, however, he spotted something that gave him hope. It wasn't something as obvious or helpful as an intact house. The roof was long gone, and all but one wall had been tumbled down into a waist-high mound. But crucially, the space between hadn't slumped down. If this house had a lower level, the basement was intact. That, plus a few minutes rigging up a bit of a lean-to against the still-standing wall, would provide shelter for himself, Parch, Wick, and the horse.

He rumbled the cart off the road and hopped down. Still no dragon, so his weapon of choice for the investigation was his trusty cudgel. Parch took the opportunity to hop from the wagon and clatter up and down assorted damaged walls.

"What's that smell?" Fel mused, taking a whiff of the subtle, musty aroma that hung about the place.

"I am afraid scent is a sense I lack," Wick said.

"It smells like an old campsite. Not the smoky stink of a campfire, but the smell of a spot that a bunch of people had tied their horses to. Kind of a lingering animal smell. I don't know if that's a good sign or a bad sign. It's good because it means something decided this place was worth sheltering in. It's bad because that thing could still be here."

Parch abandoned his merry prancing and bouncing among the remnants of the home and began pawing at a tucked-away spot. Fel climbed over some wreckage to investigate what he'd found. Near the corner of the still-standing wall, a beam from the fallen roof remained impressively intact. It had landed on one of the stones from the wall, suggesting the wall had been bashed in first. Propped up as it was, a tiny, sheltered space revealed the shredded remnants of a hatch. Holding the lantern close showed steps beneath the hatch.

What had once been a lantern sconce jutted from the intact wall. The lantern itself was gone, but Fel was able to hang Wick's lantern from the old mounting point. He found a fully intact hat rack among the rubble, good and sturdy, made from whatever version of augmented brass or bronze seemed to provide Bygone goods with their legendary durability. Using it for leverage, he threw his shoulder against its end and heaved the fallen beam aside. It slipped free of the stone and thumped to the ground.

A heartbeat later, chaos erupted. Parch suddenly sprang away and took cover under the slumped wreck of a cabinet. A torrent of winged creatures burst from the broken hatch. There were too many, and they were moving too fast, for him to see what they were. He stumbled back and shielded his head with his arms as leathery wings and scrabbling claws scoured him. They weren't attacking. They were simply in such a rush to escape the basement that they were bashing into him. He stumbled back and crouched down. The flock slowly sculpted itself into a roiling ribbon of black forms curling skyward. This place must have had a very deep cellar, because there were hundreds of the things. For nearly two full minutes the things continued to emerge, slowing until the last few fluttered out in ones and twos. These were the only ones Fel had a chance to observe.

If he'd never seen a proper dragon before and had nothing for size reference, he would have called them dragons. They were certainly dragon-shaped. But the largest of them was the size of a raven. Most were no larger than a sparrow. They buzzed and fluttered their wings, which seemed too large for their bodies, and coiled skyward to join the dim mass of startled, lizardy fliers. Little bursts of flame caused the cloud of creatures to sparkle in the night sky.

"Ah," Fel said, his heart hammering in his chest after the start they'd given him. "So that's what a lesser dragon looks like. Teya was right. Kobolds aren't lesser dragons."

He looked about. "Parch? Where'd you run off to?" He found the unicorn in the cabinet. "Come on out! The critters are gone. Now it's time to see if the basement doesn't stink too bad to hole up in for the night."

Fel opened the door a bit more, but Parch merely scrabbled farther into the cabinet.

"Uh-ho," Fel muttered. "Wick? Anything?"

"Nothing immediately presents itself."

"Parch is still scared, which means there's still something to be scared of."

Fel's mind quickly started painting fierce creatures into every shadow and crevice. He held his cudgel tight in his hand and scanned the ruined house. Nothing moved. He turned his eyes to the sky. It was night, and the flock of lesser dragons was nearly black, so making them out was possible only through the bursts of flame. But as he watched, a ring of flames erupted, tracing a circle of startled creatures belching fire to protect themselves from a larger form plunging through their flock.

The flames continued, angled toward the attacker. It provided enough illumination for Fel to see that the form had wings—feathered rather than leather. More crucially, it had a rider.

His vision of the airborne threat faded as the flock scattered and abandoned their attack to flee instead. But another burst of flame erupted a moment later, a short distance ahead of and below the rider. The way the flames were grouped together suggested the dragons producing those flames were far too close together to actually be flying. They'd been ensnared. This was a hunter, casting nets to trap the things.

Fel's mind ticked through the next steps. The flock was officially too diffuse for another cast net to catch anything worthwhile. If he was a hunter, his next step would be to find where the things had been nesting and try to set some traps. He didn't know if the vision and other senses the flying mount had were sharp enough to spot him, but he very much doubted something as large as his horse and wagon would go unnoticed, even in this darkness. He gritted his teeth.

"Stay put, Parch," Fel said. "I'll deal with this."

He snatched the lantern from its hook and slid it instead into a crevice in one of the fallen walls facing the wagon. Now he needed gear. The decoy would do no good. There wasn't enough flat ground for it to get up to speed, and it wouldn't fool an intelligent creature like a beast rider. Better to be ready for combat instead. A moment was all it took to grab the dragon sticker and the dazzler, then dash to the meager cover of some rubble not far from where Wick had been stowed. He didn't bother envisioning a world where the hunter didn't spot him. Wishful thinking took up valuable space in a brain that could be better spent planning for the worst.

As usual, the worst was much closer to reality. Though he didn't dare inch out far enough to actually watch the beast, before long he could hear the flapping of its wings. It was wheeling overhead, getting closer. The time had come to make a decision.

The dragon sticker could be just barely managed with a single hand, but the dazzler was decidedly two-handed. Would he come out swinging, or would he try to distract? He flipped a mental coin and set the dragon sticker down, a plan sluggishly coming together in his mind. Somewhere to his left, the beast touched down. It landed with a disarmingly light and dainty sound. Wings fluttered once or twice before the tap of hooves identified this thing, even unseen, for what it was. No scratch of talons meant it was not a hippogriff or full griffin. This was a peryton, a winged stag. And according to Tome, those were the steeds ridden by the elves.

He waited and listened. A soft, spoken command in a language he didn't understand brought the beast to a stop, then boots thumped down. Fel grinned. This was perfect. He waited until the steps continued forward a few paces, cautiously approaching the horse and wagon. When Fel deemed that the rider was far enough from their mount, he burst from his cover and yanked the trigger of the wand-shaped dazzler. He heard a startled shout from the man-shaped figure in the darkness. A crackling ball of blue light spat from the end of the contraption and hissed through the air toward the peryton.

In Fel's mind, the loud, brilliant ball would startle the winged stag, sending it into the air to flee and stranding the rider to be either reasoned with or dealt with. Instead, the mystical creature sidestepped the crackling ball, offering little more than a reproachful glare at the glowing annoyance.

"Ah," Fel said, dropping the dazzler and fetching the dragon sticker. "You folks train those things better than I thought."

For better or worse, Fel's appearance and the volley from the dazzler had made a far greater impression on the trapper. Until now, Fel's experience with elves had been limited to a single ranger. A soldier. This was no soldier. He was armed, but he lacked the discipline and insight of a proper warrior. Fel lacked those things as well, but he was never one to let his own shortcomings stand in his way. He dashed forward. The elf hurled the net he was holding in Fel's direction. Fel shifted the awkward spiked weapon in front of him. The net entangled it. The elf yanked at the attached rope. He was likely hoping to disarm Fel, but the bulky human had the strength and weight to resist the pull of a tall, lanky creature of the forest. Fel widened his stance and hauled the weapon aside. The elf stumbled forward. A bounding lunge closed the gap between them, and Fel caught the elf with a shoulder to the chest. Air rushed from the taller creature's lungs, and the pair tumbled to the ground. Fel landed on the trapper hard, forcing the rest of the breath from his lungs.

The human rolled aside, fully expecting to have to block some sort of attack from the mount, but its disinterest in Fel's earlier attack extended to those upon its master as well. It simply watched with sullen boredom as Fel scrambled upright and put a boot on the elf's chest to keep him down.

"Listen, I don't want to hurt you. But I don't want you to kill me either. And I've yet to encounter an elf who didn't want to do that. So if you promise to get lost and let me go where I'm heading, we can just part ways and no blood needs to be spilled. Got that?"

The elf croaked out a few words which meant absolutely nothing to Fel.

"If you don't speak my language and I don't speak yours, this is going to be a very difficult conversation," Fel said.

The trapper reached to his thigh. A flash of metal caught Fel's attention in just enough time for him to leap aside and avoid a slash. The elf got back to his feet with astonishing speed. Fel was able to charge back in and engage him before the knife could properly be put to use. He grasped the knife hand about the wrist in a punishing grip and hooked the handle of the entangled dragon sticker behind his neck. The net had almost entirely cocooned the head of the weapon. Getting the spikes to do their job would be difficult. But if Fel was lucky, the elf didn't know that.

"Listen to me. One little slip of this weapon, the slightest graze of the spike across your neck, and you go to sleep. Got that? And you might not wake up. I've never seen anything smaller than a half-giant start moving on its own again. This thing took out a dragon. It's full of manticore venom. Is any of this getting through?"

Again, language was an issue, but force and tone had a way of transcending vocabulary. Something in the trapper's eyes suggested he understood, if not the words, at least the danger. In particular, the word "manticore" seemed to be one he knew. The elf started to shift his stance. Fel held firm.

"Drop the knife and I let you go," he said.

The pair remained locked in place. Fel squeezed the wrist tighter. One way or another, he would disarm this elf. After that, maybe some form of understanding could be achieved. It was just possible that Wick knew the elf's language, but given their relationship with the sentry lantern, he wouldn't force Wick to reveal his nature.

A clatter Fel knew all too well skittered toward them. Fel may have felt he was in control of the situation, but Parch was plainly of the opinion that he needed help and resolved to provide it. The lesser unicorn dashed with lowered horn. The creature meant well—for Fel, at least—but barreling into a pair of armed people was a sure way to a bloody outcome.

Fel shoved the elf and dragged the dragon sticker along his back. Between the elf's leathery outfit and the net wrapped around the head of the weapon, the bite of the spikes didn't reach flesh. The trapper, well-trained for dealing with the attacks of animals, had better insight into Parch's would-be finishing blow than Fel. The trapper pivoted and abandoned the knife. The dodge barely took him clear of the unicorn's charge. Fel had to step back as well to avoid being skewered. The trapper made good use of the separation. Fel braced for what he assumed would be some sort of a follow-up attack. It came, but it was not directed at him.

The trapper dodged aside and dashed at Parch. Fel was out of position to help his unicorn. A loop of rope lashed out, deployed from the trapper's belt with astounding speed and accuracy. The loop pulled tight, binding Parch's legs, and the trapper hopped astride the peryton with the struggling unicorn dangling from his grip. The incredible strength of the little creature was beginning to fray the bindings, but the trapper snapped some sort of a twig or vial in front of Parch's snout. A puff of something spritzed Parch's face, and the beast went still.

"No! No!" Fel cried.

He heaved the dragon sticker after the elf and rider. It twirled past and clattered uselessly against the stone. He sprinted toward the trapper. The mount took to the air and spiraled upward. Fel had nothing that could hope to reach it. In very short order, his friend being kidnapped was his second biggest concern. The mounted trapper raised a horn to his lips and produced three short blasts and one long one. Fel wasn't foolish enough imagine it was a victory fanfare. He was calling for help.

The winged beast moved with astonishing speed. In the time it took Fel to look away long enough to fetch his weapon, it was barely a speck in the sky above. A speck joined by two more. While the trapper streaked toward the eastern horizon, the others grew larger, approaching with equal speed.

Fel snatched Wick's lantern from its hiding place and hopped the damaged wall. As much as it pained him to lose sight of the trapper, and with him Parch, Fel knew what few seconds of visibility he lost were more precious for taking cover. He'd not had a chance to hide the horse. There would be no disguising where he was. But if he took cover in the basement, at least he would have a single point of entry to defend.

He kicked the rest of the rotten hatch out of the way and dashed down the stairs. The basement was thick with the smell of a creature's den. He crouched at the base of the stairs and untangled the head of the dragon sticker. When it was free, he held it choked up in one hand, and the cudgel in the other. Wick's lantern was at his feet. He tried to keep his breathing shallow, the better to avoid being heard, and more importantly, the better to listen for the others. Once again, wings cut the air and hooves touched down. Two voices, one male and one female, exchanged hushed orders in the elven tongue. Simply from the clipped and efficient exchange, he knew these were soldiers. Any advantage Fel might have had in martial prowess was gone, and he was outnumbered as well. He gritted his teeth and squeezed the weapons tighter. If they were going to kill him, he was at least going to make the victory a costly one.

Near-silent footsteps approached. It wouldn't be long now. He tried to make a plan. A sharp jab, with enough force to punch through the boot of the first warrior to enter, that would bring him or her down. From there? There was no planning to be done. Just stay hidden and hope that the second made the same mistake as the first.

Through the hammering of his pulse in his ears, Fel heard another set of wings. A flicker of pride welled in his chest. At least they were frightened enough to send three mounted elves against one human. The next sound was one he didn't expect. Another voice, speaking Elven, but with a tone and clarity that was almost operatic. A short and fierce verbal exchange followed, both elves shouting at the newcomer. Then, the beating of two sets of wings. The voice spoke up again, speaking in Elven once more. Then it spoke again, repeating itself.

Fel took the chance that the unknown newcomer who had chased off the others wasn't planning on killing him. "I don't know what you are saying!" he called.

There was a pause.

"Fel Masker," uttered the voice. "I might have known."

Now that the language was familiar, the voice rang a bell as well. He ventured carefully up the steps and held the lantern high. Waiting for him was the elegant, measured gaze of a greater harpy. More specifically, it was the Adept, servant of Kazel and overseer of his legion of minions. Two of those minions were standing obediently beside her. They were Stix and Mik, kobolds who served as her left and right hands. They seemed more pleased to see him than she was but remained as subdued and serious as they could manage.

"One of them got away. A trapper. It flew north with Parch," Fel said quickly.

"Parch. The lesser unicorn," the Adept said.

"Yes! You have to get him back!"

"The perytons are the fastest fliers in the Greater Lands, save perhaps Kazel himself. I will not be able to pursue. Fortunately for you, I need not do so. I know where he is going. And I know that, for now, Parch will be safe."

"How? What's going on?"

"Trappers have been active on our land for months. They've been harvesting Lesser Mystics of every sort. Always alive. Great pains are taken to make sure they remain so."

"Where are they taking them?"

"An island whose name I cannot know. I have no interest in what lies within the island and no desire to bear witness to it."

Fel narrowed his eyes. "Clickspring, then. How? People here can't go there."

"A question that weighs upon our minds. A question that Kazel has sought to answer. A question, and perhaps a threat, so great we saw fit to light the beacon."

"Yeah, I saw. And I came to offer help."

"Through what means do you even know the purpose of the beacon?"

"Teya told me."

"And through what means did you come to be in a position to see the beacon?"

"Just lucky, I guess," he said sullenly.

"Destiny calls, then."

"I am so sick of hearing about destiny. What is it with you people and destiny!?"

"You will come with me. We must see Kazel immediately. Stix, Mik, see that the horse and wagon are brought safely to some manner of shelter and cared for. I will bring Fel to the lair."

"Wait, you're going to carry me?"

"As best I can. You are rather large a load. I'll ask you to leave anything you do not immediately require in the wagon. You have my word it will arrive safely."

He loaded Wick's lantern and his weapons into the bed of the wagon. For the first time in ages, he also emptied his pockets. His lackluster laundry practices meant this was the first time in potentially months that some of the gear he carried day to day was out of its dedicated pocket. He loaded the contents of his pockets into a sack.

"The boots as well," she said.

"What?"

"If I am to carry you, the load will need to be as light as possible. Out of respect for you, I will not ask that you remove your clothes, but the boots look quite heavy."

He knelt to untie them. "Wick, spread the word. I'm all right, I'm with friends. And there's only a small chance that the next time I see you, I'll be telling you about how I had to walk halfway across the Greater Lands in my stockinged feet because the Adept told me I couldn't wear my boots."

"I shall do so. And I look forward to our reunion in Kazel's lair."

"Wait!" Fel said suddenly. "Adept, do you have a message for Teya? She's got a flame."

"I would simply congratulate her on her success and encourage her to return when she is through. Come, Fel Masker." She flitted up and grasped him by the upper arms with her talons. "This will not be a pleasant journey for either of us, and I would see it end sooner rather than later."

Chapter 6

Lord Katritz resisted the urge to fiddle with his beard as he waited in the foyer of the Contraband Contraption Vault. It was quite early in the morning, earlier than he normally even awoke, and he didn't relish the idea of having to sit for his servants to redo his ablutions before he could see to some of the other meetings planned for the day. This meeting, quite by design, had not been scheduled. A properly scheduled tour of the vault, even for someone of his lofty position, took at least a few days to arrange. It also left a trail for someone to follow. His purpose here was to acquire a contraband contraption, another thing that even a lord was not permitted to do. Acquiring it surreptitiously required bypassing the normal rules, both so that he could actually acquire it and because any properly scheduled tour was followed by an emergency audit, which would reveal that the contraption had been taken. But rules of that sort were overseen by the vault overseer, who, among other things, kept a strict personal schedule. He wouldn't arrive until just after dawn. That gave Katritz an hour to do what was required. And only the overnight manager to tend to him. An excitable gent by the name of Squire Mills.

There was a reason Mills was only entrusted with the overnight shift.

"Squire Mills!" Katritz called. "I am unaccustomed to being left waiting."

The meek and meager man scurried into view. He'd been rummaging in a room adjoining the entryway for two minutes.

"I-I'm sorry, Lord Katritz. I-I can't seem to find the appointment for this surprise tour of the facility."

Katritz curled his lip. "There would not be an appointment for a surprise tour, now would there?"

"Oh! No. No I suppose not, sir. Lord! I meant lord. B-but how do I know you're allowed to be here doing this, then?"

He narrowed his eyes. "Because I have told you so, Mills. Are you suggesting the word of Lord Katritz cannot be trusted?"

"I would never! I would never suggest that, sir. I mean lord!"

"Then open the door and allow me to take my tour," he said.

"But—"

"Am I Lord Katritz?" he said sharply.

"Certainly, s—lord."

"And as such, am I the one responsible for the upkeep and protocol of the Contraband Contraption Vault and all contraptions therein?"

"Certainly!"

"And as such, am I permitted to access those contraptions to ensure their upkeep?"

"Certainly!"

"Then open the door and permit it."

"Yes, Lord!"

He fumbled with a ring of keys and thumbed through a codebook. Three full minutes of disabling traps and finding the proper keys for locks followed. Finally, Mills began wheeling a chain winch to open the vault door.

This place was not a remnant of the Bygone Era. It did not enjoy the astounding feats of construction and metallurgy that allowed things to be both impossibly sturdy and light enough to be easily handled. But the contents of the vault were more important than anything else in the kingdom, thanks to both their immeasurable value and immeasurable danger. That meant modern means to protect it, in addition to whatever Bygone Era traps could be repurposed, had to be combined. The vault walls were a full yard thick. The door was equally thick and set into a track above and below. When Mills had finished disabling it, it was free to roll aside under the force of the winch, revealing the most dangerous of Bygone Era ingenuity available in a single place.

If someone like Martin Masker had been in charge of this place, the contraptions would be on full display. But this was built and maintained by those who wisely didn't trust the devices they were storing. The inside of the vault was little more than shelf after shelf, from wall to three-story-tall ceiling, filled with locked chests of various sizes. Small placards on the front face of each chest held a general classification for its contents and the actual items.

Weapons, Handheld.

Auto-crossbow, complete (x6)

Auto-crossbow, incomplete, functional (x9)

Auto-crossbow, damaged (x15)

The labels told the tale of things that could allow just a handful of soldiers to lay waste to whole cities. Crossbows that could fill the air with dozens of bolts without a single moment to reset or draw them. Contraptions that could summon fire sufficient to melt stone. Farther into the rows of shelves were less dangerous but still entirely forbidden contraptions. If Katritz listened carefully, he could still hear them operating inside their boxes because no one could work out how to deactivate them. There were gearboxes that turned shafts slowly but endlessly. Things that produced painfully bright light. As they walked, Lord Katritz kept an even expression of appraisal on his face, like a general surveying his troops.

Along the back wall were the items that Katritz had come here for. Items with unknown purposes but found among other items that were known to be dangerous. These were labeled with strings of letters and numbers that probably meant something to the overseer. He stopped in front of a chest. Among the manifest of items contained within was something marked LS-Sphe-Unk-7. For Lord Katritz's purposes, he'd simply been thinking of it as "the sphere," as that was what it was called on the folded bit of paper in his pocket.

"Mills, please present your keys for inspection," the lord said.

"Yes, Lord. Here you are!"

He presented the huge ring of keys. Katritz accepted them and began flipping them around the ring, one after the other, to reveal the one behind. They were etched with the number of the shelf. Each key opened every chest on a given shelf. He found the one he was after.

"And the backup key ring?" he said.

"I don't carry that, sir. It is in the side room for safekeeping."

"Yes. That is the procedure, but I am interested in ensuring that it is complete. Bring it to me."

"Oh! Yes, Lord. I will do so!"

He held out his hand, waiting for the lord to return the key ring. Katritz glared at him.

"Go!" the lord snapped.

"Right! Right! I'll get it!"

The man dashed away. Katritz immediately unlocked the chest. The contents were completely indecipherable. Either contraptions inside were missing their enclosures, rendering them little more than a bundle of gears and struts held together by their own interlocking complexity; or else they were so simple and featureless that one never would have imagined they were contraptions at all. Such was the case for the fist-sized sphere. As its name would suggest, it was nothing more than a ball of brass and wood. Elegant embellishments gave it the artful beauty of other Bygone contraptions. To look upon it, one might wonder why it would be labeled as contraband. It looked like nothing more than a sculpture or curio. Something expensive to place on one's shelf to showcase one's wealth. The lord's estate was littered with such things. When he lifted it from the chest, however, the answer of its careful treatment became clear.

This contraption had weight to it, and not the mundane sort of weight that one could easily articulate. Yes, it was heavy, feeling like it was made out of solid metal despite the visible wooden elements. But the weight was far more fundamental than that. It felt like it was anchored somehow. Even when held in his hand, the lord could feel it digging its claws into the world around it, attempting to remain in place. He hefted it into the air and found that it fell like a feather, gliding back to his palm like it was sinking through molasses. He marveled at its effortless shrugging off of basic physical constraints. Avarice to possess something so powerful was perfectly counterbalanced by the primal fear of something that escaped understanding.

If he'd had a moment more to consider just what he was doing, there was a chance he would have stowed it again and found some other way to deal with the threat to his influence that Verfessa posed. But the harried footsteps of Mills were already charging up from behind him. He shut and locked the chest, stuffed the sphere into his pocket, and stole the key from the chain as well.

"Here, sir!"

"Lord," he snapped.

"Gah! Right! Lord! For your inspection."

Katritz handed back the primary key chain and began flipping through the backup. He walked toward the door as he did so. "Everything appears to be in order," he said. "It is a fine thing to know that this, a gem of the capital more valuable than even the crown jewels, is in such safe and capable hands."

The words were dripping with sarcasm that would have been evident to a toddler. Mills, of course, took them as genuine.

"Thank you, sir. Oh thank you, sir."

"Lord," Katritz rumbled again.

"Lord! Lord! I'm so sorry, sir."

Katritz shut his eyes and took a breath. They'd returned to the entryway.

"I have only one question to ask you. At what point did you decide the rules don't apply?"

"W-what?"

"Show me where this visit was scheduled," he said, tapping the still-open book.

"It... it wasn't, sir. I said as much."

He jabbed the page again. "Show me!"

The man madly flipped through the pages in search of something they both knew wasn't there. This gave Katritz the opportunity to pop the backup key from the chain as well.

"Stop searching, you idiot. I was being rhetorical. The point is, there are protocols for a reason. I was not to be permitted to tour this place without an appointment and you permitted it. Not even the lord is above the law."

"I... but I..."

Katritz smoothed down his jacket, more to make sure the sluggish drift of the sphere in his pocket didn't cause an incriminating bulge than to hammer home his point.

"Never let it be said I am without mercy. I will overlook this indiscretion. As far as I or anyone else is concerned, this tour did not occur." He handed back the backup keys. "You will disregard my visit. Do not mark it in the log, do not inform the vault overseer that it occurred. And from now on, show some spine when someone in a position of authority attempts to compel you to bend the rules."

"I will, sir. I'm sorry, sir."

"And call me lord!"

Katritz stomped off toward the doorway, a smile slowly twisting his face as the traumatized underling started working the chain hoist to seal the vault door again. As he moved toward his carriage, the lord thrust his hands into his pockets. He detested the idea of looking idle and casual. A lord should be regal and respectable at all times. But the acquired contraption simply refused to behave itself, constantly attempting to drift farther behind him and take his jacket with it. With his hands in his pockets he could hold it tightly enough to drag it along without revealing it.

Once he was in his carriage and his driver had been ordered back to his estate, he drew the curtains on his windows and held the contraption before him. There was nothing in his mind to compare the odd contraption's behavior to. It was downright fascinating to experience it. As the carriage moved, it pushed into his grip, trailing just a bit behind the carriage's motion. When the carriage turned, it shifted aside, lagging in that direction as well.

His lofty position had afforded him permission to view the operation of contraptions far exceeding what the general public would ever be allowed to use, and even with that knowledge, he had his doubts that the sphere could achieve what Madritz claimed it could. But feeling how this thing disregarded nature's whims, his confidence was restored. Greatness, the most significant and sweeping improvement to Thayne and the world since the Bygone Era ended, was looming ahead. And he would be its shepherd and keeper.

Verfessa would never be able to compete.

Allie already regretted the decisions she was still in the process of making. It was too early, and even with the barrow, the load was too heavy. Things had run late at The Fox and Log last night, or more accurately, this morning. Thus, just five hours ago she was closing the doors for the night, and now she was approaching the watchhouse for a discussion. It was going to be a very long, very unpleasant day.

Until now, Allie would have described her relationship with the City Watch as, "as sparing as possible." If she was talking to a watchman, something had gone terribly wrong. Even when something violent or disruptive happened at the tavern, she preferred to handle it with the tools available to her. Usually that meant promises of free booze, threats of withholding booze, and either the aforementioned carrot or stick to compel another patron into using a far more literal stick to help her out. The more often the Watch showed up at any given establishment, the worse things tended to get. She could never quite put her finger on why. Maybe the thugs who wanted to stir things up felt like they could get away with things because there was always a lag between doing the deed and getting caught if it was the Watch doing the catching. Maybe it was the reputation that came with constantly having the Watch show up that convinced other wrongdoers it was the place where wrong was done. Or maybe it was that the Watch really didn't like having to tend to matters inside the walls. Their job, at least ostensibly, was to make sure the trouble outside the city and the trouble inside the city remained separate. Anything beyond that was done grudgingly or not at all. And you really didn't want someone in a position of authority to do something grudgingly, because those grudges tended to last.

To ward against such an outcome, Allie had come bearing gifts in the form of a half keg of ale and some tankards that were worn out enough that she wouldn't mind not getting them back.

She reached the door of the watchhouse and caught a whiff of the attached stables. A lot of horses came through Beffshire, but as the only stable in town that didn't turn a profit on the horses it kept, the watch's stable wasn't exactly the model of cleanliness. She knocked on the door. A moment later it swung open to reveal Leonard blinking blearily at her.

"Morning! I thought I'd bring a gift down to our friendly neighborhood Watch, and maybe have a chat," Allie said.

He pointed to the keg. "Whatsit?

"Ale."

He nodded. "Let's bring 'er in."

Leonard stepped outside and grabbed the barrow to drag it in for her, then hefted the keg onto one of the long tables where the whole Watch spent most of their time waiting to be told what to do. Right now "the whole Watch" apparently referred to Leonard alone. He fiddled with the keg until Allie took over and got it set up to pour some drinks.

"Where is everyone?" she asked.

"Out on patrol around the wall. Two of 'em anyway. Two more just went home. Two more ain't shown up yet. And then there's me and the captain. He's upstairs."

"Why'd you get stuck with the short end of the stick?"

He shrugged and drained a tankard in one continuous swallow. "I'm usually around."

"So is this drink an eye-opener or a nightcap?"

Leonard blinked at her a few times, then trudged over to the window to open the shutter. After a quick survey of the sun and the shadows, he shut them again.

"Eye-opener. You just here for charity, or did you have a reason to come down?"

"I wondered if I could have a word with the captain," she said.

"You can try. Head on upstairs. But he's in a mood. More than usual."

"I'll take my chances. Do your friends a favor and save some for them when they come in."

"No promises."

Allie trudged up the steps to Captain Boltt's office. It was the first time she'd been there, and it immediately defied her expectations for such a place. Judging it charitably, one wall could be considered a proper office. A lightly out-of-date map of the city had been pasted in place. Somewhat blunt pins with painted heads were stuck into strategic locations, mostly around the wall and in some of the more dangerous neighborhoods. The rest of the office may as well have been a bunkhouse. A proper bed, albeit a small one, had been pushed against the wall, and three full sets of clothes hung on hooks beside it.

The captain himself was sipping from a cup filled with something too thick and opaque to be tea and glaring at the map.

"Captain?" Allie said.

He glanced in her direction. "You're the one from down by The Fox and Log."

"Allie."

"What do you need?"

"Nothing much. I just wanted to let you know that I'd brought some ale. And I thought maybe we could have a word."

"What do you need?" he repeated with a bit more of an edge.

"There's a man who has been poking about in the tavern," Allie began.

"If there's no blood and he's not an outsider, it's none of my concern."

"No blood yet, and though he's new in town, I don't know that he qualifies as an outsider. But I think it may very well be your concern."

"And what makes you think that?"

"I think he may be after your job," she said.

His nostrils flared, and he finally gave Allie his undivided attention. "I think I know the man you're talking about. Showed up a short time ago? Equal parts nosy and suspicious?"

"That sounds like him."

"He's after my job," he said with a nod. "One of them comes along every few years."

"Oh?"

"People treat this job like a steppingstone. A do-little job that will lead to something with proper authority. As if it'll lead anywhere but an early grave."

"You seem to be holding up all right."

"One of the largest cities in the kingdom and less than a dozen people on the Watch. Half of the men we have are short-timers, imports from Toyl's Crossing. If a real threat ever came to this city, it would be our job to die facing it."

"If that's how you feel about the job, why not let the go-getters go and get it? Save you the trouble?"

"Because it might be a do-little job, but it's not a do-nothing job. And when the time comes to do something, I want to make sure there's someone in this position who can actually do it." He looked at her. "Did you just come here to warn me about something I already knew about, or did you have something else in mind?"

"Any interest in what he's been nosing around about?"

"You know what he's been after?"

"You have your job, I have mine. And it's not just pouring drinks. It's keeping peace in the tavern. He's been getting people drunk with something called Miser's Milk and working them for information about various things that might get a man thrown in prison by the Watch even if he isn't threatening the city."

"Examples."

Allie brought to mind what Wick had managed to overhear for her. "Things like storing goods on their way through the city to avoid coughing up the city's share of the imports. Things like buying and selling booze, cigars, exotic animal pelts, things that aren't supposed to even be in Thayne, let alone inside Beffshire..."

The captain laughed. "Sounds like he might be after Donovan Verfessa's job, not mine."

"Verfessa is into those sorts of things?" she said with what she hoped was convincing surprise.

"Those and a lot more."

Allie paused, uncertain if she ought to ask what was on her mind.

"You're going to ask me why I haven't done something about him if I know all that."

"I wouldn't say I was going to ask that, but I'll agree that I'm curious."

"You could make the argument he's causing trouble that we're meant to stop. Half of the things I know about deal with him smuggling goods past the wall. Things the city elders would prefer stay outside of it. And more than a few people have turned up dead that I think we could blame on him. But a city like this? It is going to have some people inside it who work the wrong side of the law. Just like there's bound to be watchmen and watchwomen and bakers and healers and the like, there's bound to be criminals. And as criminals go, Verfessa is the best of a bad crop. Everyone who has turned up dead with what I'd wager was one of Verfessa's knives pulled across his throat was someone who we're better off without. Someone who probably would have run afoul of one of the Watch and maybe taken one of us down. The other stuff? Doesn't stir up the city, doesn't take any coins out of the pockets of people who can't afford them. The city would be better off without him, but we're much better off than with the one who might come to replace him. And that's assuming I could do something about him if I had the notion to. Again. Less than a dozen members of this Watch."

Allie nodded. "But those people? The ones who can afford to lose the coins out of their pockets? I'll wager they don't like losing those coins."

Boltt shook with a wry laugh. "Hard to convince them Verfessa is just another cost of doing business."

"And since they have the most to lose, they probably would like to see someone replace you who is willing to chase out Verfessa."

"And so, every few years, another comes by."

"How do you see this shaking out?"

"If the man after my job is a fool, he'll make a move against Verfessa and get a knife across the throat. And a man like that isn't someone I can turn a blind eye to when they get killed, so there'll be trouble. If he's smart, the nosy newcomer will realize he's in over his head and back off. But if he hasn't done so yet, then I don't think he will."

"So unless this fellow can be persuaded to move along, one way or another, the trouble Verfessa hasn't been getting into will become a problem for him and you."

"That's about the size of it." He sniffed and set his cup down. "An awful lot of questions for a barmaid just looking to keep her tavern calm."

"When I get an itch, I can't rest until I scratch it."

"I'm going to ask a question, and I'd like an honest answer. Doesn't matter to me, one way or the other, how you answer. Either way, you'll be walking down those stairs and scratching that itch. But it'll tell me just how often we're likely to chat, and how I'll be feeling when we do."

"What's your question?"

"Are you working for Verfessa right now?"

"He owns The Fox and Log. I'm always working for him. But I get the idea you don't mean it like that."

"Mm-hmm."

"I owed him a favor, but I'm not the sort of woman who'd butter my bread with a knife that sharp every morning. That's a great way to end up with bloody hands."

"You have a good head, Allie. Keep it on your shoulders. Now run along."

"Have a good day. And if your men are a little tipsy today, I apologize in advance."

"Bold of you to suggest they weren't just as likely to show up tipsy."

She laughed and hurried down the stairs, where Leonard was finishing what she suspected wasn't merely his second tankard of ale. Allie wasn't sure what she'd hoped to accomplish with this visit. Perhaps a small part of her believed the captain had a plan to deal with this on his own. All she'd really learned was, if Marcus took any serious action against Verfessa's business, things would get worse in this town whether he was successful or not.

It was hardly an encouraging discovery, and it was a strong motivation to try to handle it rather than handing it off to Verfessa.

Teya paced back and forth along the same well-trod piece of land near a trio of flames. Her face was twisted with worry, and she clicked her claws anxiously. All three flames before her were lit from the lantern she'd been given. The oil had run out, but before the flame had died, she'd transferred it to a sequence of flames, which she'd taken it upon herself to tend to. Until very recently, having continuous access to Wick was useful but not entirely necessary. She could always take a day or two to head back to Ram's Rest and get a fresh dose of oil and flame. But now, Epiphany was up north. Her flame was still lit, still in Ram's Rest. But she couldn't visit to replace her own. The rest of the Graves family didn't know her and wouldn't take kindly to a visit. Keeping the flame steady thus became necessary in order to be certain they could continue to get instructions from Martin Masker on the careful project to remove the clockwork diamond's influence over those within the Lesser Greater Lands. But as of early that morning, there was another much more important reason to keep the flame lit. It was the result of a short, simple message that came just before she was planning to go to sleep.

"The beacon is lit. Fel has met with the Adept. He is going to investigate."

That was all Wick said before flickering away, no doubt to discuss other matters with the Maskers back in Beffshire. Since then, Teya had remained beside the flames, mind spinning with the terrible possibilities. The sun had risen. She'd not had a moment of sleep. Already she could see some of the other kobolds approaching, ready to begin the day's work. She was in no mood to lead. Being a leader was the easiest thing in the world when things were going well. And it was true that here, things were going well. The engraved plates they had been working on were complete. Those simple pieces of metal, if Martin Masker was correct, would finally and fully clear the minds of her fellow mystics within the Lesser Greater Lands while leaving the land itself intact. If Martin was incorrect, the Lesser Greater Lands would destructively collapse into the ground, possibly in a single calamitous cascade. Even that didn't concern Teya. When that happened, the spell keeping the creatures here would be broken, so they would be free to cross the wall. So long as they were near to the wall when the change was made, they would easily be able to escape before destruction and head to the real Greater Lands. In truth, they would have to go there, as the real Greater Lands would still hold sway over them. There was also the issue of what would happen to the one making the change to the clockwork diamond. That person would be too far from the wall to escape a calamity, but that didn't matter. Teya herself was the one who would be making the change. It was right for a leader to face the consequences of their failures.

Now there was a true test of her leadership, or at least her resolve. Her home was in trouble. A trouble unprecedented in her lifetime. She'd never known a time when the beacon had been lit. She had an obligation to defend her home. And it wasn't only her home. Every last creature in the Lesser Greater Lands had been uprooted to be brought to this strange little duplicate in miniature, even if the diamond's influence made it hard for them to remember it sometimes. Many were kobolds, some of whom had been her fellow followers of Kazel, and many more who would have dreamed of the chance to serve Kazel. They were bound by the same honor to answer the call of the beacon. But only she could. Only she could leave the Lesser Greater Lands while this clockwork diamond's influence hung over their minds, because she wore the earring. What was she to do? Did she abandon these creatures and rush to her homeland? Did she abandon her homeland and continue her work here? Did she wait until Martin, through Wick, could coach her through the process of altering the diamond? Did she try to fix it herself to clear their minds soon enough to make a difference?

In a single update from Wick, leadership had gone from making clear choices between what was correct and what was incorrect, and helping others make the right decisions as well, to having a dozen choices, all of which required some sort of dereliction of duty. She felt horribly, horribly alone. And alone was the last thing a kobold ever wanted to be.

She gazed in the direction of the diamond. She and the others did their work much closer to the wall than the diamond. It was just as well. The sheer venom in her gaze would have been enough to kill a living creature. If she were near enough to that blasted accumulation of contraptions and mechanisms dancing its infuriating and beautiful dance, she wouldn't have been able to keep herself from trying to set fire to it.

A mischievous grin came to her lips as she imagined somehow belching a flame like Kazel could, blasting the wretched contraption into a puddle. She was only shaken from her daydream when she realized the others had begun assembling around her. No matter how alone she felt, she was not alone. And she owed the others an explanation. That much was certain.

Teya stepped toward the crowd of kobolds.

"What should we do now?" chattered the nearest of them.

"Look at the big rabbit I caught!" chittered another.

The initial excitement of the forthcoming instructions to shape their day was quickly tempered by the obvious concern in her expression.

"There is news?"

"That is the look of bad news."

"What do we need to do?"

"How can we help?"

Teya took a breath. "We have to make a decision."

"What decision should we make?"

"What kind of decision?"

"Tell us what we should do, we can do it!"

"Let's get to work!"

She shook her head. "It isn't so simple. I have heard from Wick. The beacon is lit."

Some of the kobolds blinked in confusion. Those who had once served Kazel chattered with concern.

"The violet beacon?"

"With the white smoke?"

"What's the beacon?"

"What's a beacon?"

Teya raised a paw to settle the group. "It is a call for help for all who serve or owe any allegiance to Kazel. Any who see it are to come to the great dragon's aid."

"We need to go!"

"Kazel needs us!"

"How can we go?"

"Tell us what we need to do!"

The crowd was getting more agitated. It wasn't anger, or fear. It was the heat and friction generated from the resolve to do something but having no clear thing to do.

Kobolds were a fountain of motivation and energy. Right now the flow was blocked, and it'd release itself explosively if she didn't find a proper outlet. Teya waved over two of the nearest kobolds. After a moment they understood what was needed. They stood close and tall. She scrambled onto their shoulders to better address the crowd.

"The only one of us who can go is me. And my obligation to Kazel requires it. But that would leave all of you here, waiting and without any way to know what to do or what had happened," she explained.

"So what do we do!?"

"Should I get a pick or a shovel?"

"Should someone bite a dwarf until it gives us swords?"

Teya shut her eyes. "I don't know!"

The remark was met with silence. Teya knew exactly why. She was the same creature as they. There were only two things that truly made sense to a group of kobolds. Either they were all doing whatever task clearly needed doing, or they were all doing whatever a leader told them needed doing. The definition of a leader, in the mind of a kobold, may as well have been "the one who knows what to do." With one simple statement, Teya had snuffed the sun out of the sky. A fundamental aspect of reality had been wiped away.

"We are kobolds," Teya said. "What we do, we all do. I wish I could tell you what we ought to do. But we can't do what we ought to do. The beacon is lit. We should all go to Kazel and see what he needs us to do. But only I can do that. And one is not all. We can't do what we need to do. So what we need to do is find out a way to do what we can't do. And if we can't do that, we need to find out what we should do instead."

She blinked, trying to untie her own not entirely articulate statement. Even in her own language, uncertainty wasn't something she felt equipped to grapple with. Eyes stared at her, still waiting and hoping that some solid task would come tumbling out of her mouth that they could throw themselves into.

"A task," Teya muttered. A thought started to dawn. "A task..." She raised her voice. "We are kobolds! And what do kobolds do?"

"What we're told!"

"What we have to!"

"What we need to do!"

"The job!"

Teya pointed. "Yes! The job!"

The kobold in question beamed with pride.

"And right now the job is to figure out what the next job is." Teya patted her chest. "It isn't clear to me. But it isn't about me. We need to do the job of finding out what we need to do. So what do we need to do?"

"Go help Kazel!" said a kobold.

Teya pointed. "And what do we need to do in order to be able to do that?"

"The thing the man from the outside is helping you do!" said another.

"And I can't do it until Wick can tell me how. I'll do it when I can. But what else do we need to do?"

"Find a way to get to Kazel," said another.

Others started to chime in, faster and faster.

"A fast way," said yet another.

"We need to be strong when we go! Ready for anything!"

"Then we have things to do! Different things. We will do all of them. We get to work. Some of you, find a way to move fast. Very fast. Some of you, find a way to be strong. Very strong. Swords, clubs, any weapons we can find. And armor. We all need armor. Enough for all of us to be working until the big thing is ready to do."

The kobolds crowed with enthusiasm and a dash of relief. There were things to do. And so, those things would be done. Teya hopped down so that her impromptu stage could scurry off with the others. She watched as the whole crowd slowly divided into groups, each off to do some fragment of the task. Soon, Teya was alone again. Only she had a job that was defined not by doing but by waiting. She had to tend to the flames to be sure they didn't go out, and wait until Wick spoke again with news or instructions. She sighed, watching her people run off with their problems, for the moment, solved. All while she was left with the same troubles.

If this was what it was to be a leader, she was eager to be done with it.

Fel shifted his shoulders and flexed his fingers. He didn't know quite how long it had taken the Adept to carry him to Kazel's lair, but it was long enough that the vicelike grip of her talons had left bruised rings around his upper arms and left his fingers numb. He was hesitant to complain, as the Adept had clearly gotten the worst of it. Several minutes after they'd landed she was still catching her breath, and her wings stood out at her sides at the sort of awkward angle that suggested she couldn't fully tuck them away if she tried. With her two dedicated hands at the reins of Fel's carriage and unlikely to arrive for several days, two others had stepped into the role and were plainly struggling with the precision of the task. She was speaking to them in a language Fel didn't understand, but the tone of voice was calm, patient, and perpetually at the edge of frustration.

One of the kobolds, the one in the role of her left hand, reached up to feed her. The other finally found the scroll she was after and unfurled it before her. When her hunger and thirst were taken care of, she turned to address Fel.

"Do you require a meal?" she asked.

"I don't think I could hold it down," Fel said.

She nodded. "So many creatures can't stomach the view from a harpy's talons. Curious."

"If you'd just spent a few hours with wind screeching in your ears, knowing that someone could sneeze, lose grip of you, and send you tumbling to a messy death, you'd feel the same."

"Perhaps."

"Can we please talk about how the elves are getting to Clickspring, why they grabbed Parch, and what we're going to do about it?" Fel said.

"By the very nature of the questions, I cannot answer most of them. But what is to be done? That is a simple answer, and one you will embark upon as soon as you are able. You will go to where they are going. From there, you will discover the answers."

"The plan is 'Get Fel to take care of it'?"

"Obstacles that we cannot circumvent stand in our way. You or someone like you must bridge that gap."

"I don't even have boots! I don't even have weapons!"

"We can arm you and equip you if needs be. Or when I or one of the other fliers is rested, we can fetch your things. But by the machinations of those like you, only those like you can even investigate what is happening, let alone solve it. It is happening beyond the limits of our perception."

"What do you know?"

"After untold decades of remaining cloistered in their forest, the elves have once again taken to the sea. At the same time, their hunters have willingly violated our lands and as many others as they can reach in search of Lesser Mystics of any type. The Greater Lands have very few Lesser Mystics. Through their hunting, the elves have claimed nearly all of them. We do not know their reasoning, but we know that they have been carrying them by ship toward..." The Adept shuddered.

"Right, yeah. I get where they're going. But they can't go there, right? Not all the way in. They can't get any closer than you. Right?"

"Kazel himself has gone to observe. They linger at the edge, but even his mighty gaze loses them for slices of time. And Duurth has been harried to the point of retreat. Such a thing could only be done from within..." She shuddered again.

"They're getting into Clickspring somehow... And all Kazel is doing is watching?"

"What more would you have him do?"

"He can breathe fire, and their boats are made of wood."

The Adept's expression subtly shifted. Though there was scarcely more than the twitch of an eyebrow and the tightening of a lip, he instantly felt a burning disdain pouring over him.

"Open war, and open slaughter, are not steps to be taken lightly."

"All right. True. But they are already violating your land, right? And... and..."

He scraped his mind for something to justify how he felt, but there was no way around it. He was attempting to persuade a powerful group to attack another, and chiefly because the other group had captured his pet. Losing the moral high ground to a dragon and a bird woman was destabilizing at best. He was still grasping for something appropriate to say when a distant, airy sound and the sliding of a shadow across the land drew his eyes to the sky. Kazel had returned. Seeing something so enormous cutting effortlessly through the air didn't do much to restore Fel's wits. Mostly it reached down through layers of humanity to the frightened animal lurking beneath and reminded it that every breath he'd drawn in a world where a thing such as Kazel existed was either a gift or an oversight. The dragon whisked over the peak of the mountain and wheeled back to the side facing the sea before fully vanishing from sight.

The Adept glanced aside to one of the kobolds milling about to issue an order in the ancient language. Then she turned to Fel again.

"You will be taken to Kazel. There you can make the case for war."

The kobold beckoned, and Fel followed rather than risking another failure at verbal sparring with the harpy. His journey to Kazel was not the one he remembered from his prior visit. Rather than heading down into the heart of the mountain, the path led upward through short, cramped tunnels clearly meant for a kobold or two at a time rather than someone as bulky as Fel. He managed, albeit by remaining stooped and keeping a hand on the cool wall of the passage to avoid falling forward.

A journey long enough to make him wish he'd asked for boots before he'd set off into the innards of a mountain finally took him to what would have been called the throne room in a human castle. It was the outer section of a two-part chamber. Judging by the cool breeze whistling down through a long, curving tunnel, there was a direct route to the mountainside. A meager glow of two recently lit torches was the only source of light, but it was enough to bring a sparkling glow to a river of golden coins. They spilled from the mouth of a much larger, much darker section of mountain that, to continue the comparison to a castle, would have been the king's chambers. Heavy breathing from within the chamber rivaled the mountain wind. The kobold chattered something and dropped to the ground in a bow. Motion within the darkness and a cascade of coins heralded Kazel's arrival.

Fel tried to keep his eyes unfocused as he looked vaguely in the direction of the ancient, majestic beast. He wasn't so foolish as to imagine there was something to be gained in pretending he wasn't afraid. There was no imagining that he was anything but a morsel or a cinder if the dragon decided that's what he should be. Mostly he kept his gaze vague because if he didn't, he'd be scrambling headlong down the cramped stone passage the moment his brain was able to properly interpret that he was looking at a living thing. At the moment, Kazel registered as a piece of the landscape that had learned to move on its own, which was moderately less terrifying.

Kazel rumbled an incomprehensible dismissal of the kobold, then lowered his head to address Fel directly.

"Fel Masker," the dragon said. "When the beacon was lit, it seemed inevitable that if aid came, it would come with the name Masker. Your clan seems dedicated to atoning for its crimes of antiquity."

"Mostly I'm just very unlucky," he said.

"Your misfortune is our fortune. How much have you been told?"

"The elves have been gathering up Lesser Mystics, including Parch, and taking them to Clickspring. Apparently they've been getting inside, somehow."

"Good. Then you know all that I know."

"Seriously? You've seen them doing things."

"I have seen them with ships loaded with Lesser Mystics. Anything further takes place beyond my gaze."

"I don't suppose you asked them what they were up to."

"The elven agents would view answering my questions to be a treasonous offense. And so you know why to learn more someone of your race or capability is necessary." Kazel lowered his head a bit. When it was near enough for hot breath that smelled faintly of char to wash over Fel, he spoke again. "Tell me. Have you heard tell of Teya's exploits? She left this place, with my blessing and guidance, in search of her destiny."

"She came and found me in my hometown and helped bail us out of a pretty serious corner we got backed into. Then she went on a trip with my sister to help out and see some more of the world. And now she's in a little version of the Greater Lands that some lunatic called Mr. Lens created up north. The help she's been to the family is part of the reason I decided to come see about the beacon, and the only reason I knew what it meant and that I should look for it."

"Then she achieved what she was sent to achieve. The chain of events that began with her departure has led to your return at a time when we needed you. Destiny's voice has been heard."

"You call it destiny, I call it a coincidence. Either way, what are we going to do about it?" Fel said.

"I must rest, and I must feed. I have traversed half this land more than once in the last few days, watching the elves and attempting to divine their purpose. By tomorrow, I will have my strength back. You have until then to prepare. We will provide anything you feel that you require."

"I have a lot of gear, but it's on a wagon the Adept's hands are bringing. It won't be here for two and a half days."

Kazel raised a claw that was larger than Fel and pointed to his bruised arms. "You were brought here by the Adept."

"It shows, does it?"

"When she is recovered, the Adept will fetch your things."

"Wow. She's really doing a lot of grunt work. I would have thought someone like her was too important for hauling cargo."

"We all do what is required of us."

"Let's say I have everything I need by tomorrow. What exactly happens?"

"I carry you as near to their destination as the contraptions wrought by your ancestors will allow. From there, you find out what they are doing and return to me. I shall decide what actions should be taken at that time."

"They took Parch. You're certain I'll find him there?"

"The Lesser Mystics that were taken are all either en route to be dropped on a ship by the trapper, on a ship already, or beyond my gaze. If action is deemed necessary, I will see to it that your unicorn is returned."

"And if you decide what they're up to isn't worth the trouble?"

"If I direct my followers to attack the elves, or deign to attack them myself, war is the result. You know this. And though I am equal to any challenge they may levy against me, my followers are not. I will not exchange the lives of my people unnecessarily. If you seek to reclaim your beast, you do so with my blessing, but not with my aid."

Fel clenched his fists. "Why should anything be easy..."

"Do you accept these terms?"

Fel remained quiet for a moment. Kazel inched his massive head a bit closer, great eyes locking on Fel. For some reason, the intensity of that gaze, at that distance, confounded Fel's attempts to keep his eyes from focusing. He locked onto Kazel's eyes. It took all his fortitude to keep from trembling, small and weak as he felt in the predator's shadow.

"You wonder what reward you will receive for your aid."

Fel flinched. "You're not a mind reader, are you?"

"The ways of man are transparent. But fear not. I do not view this as greed. You will be compensated. When the deed is done, you will make your request. And if I deem it a fitting reward, you shall receive it."

"So when this is said and done, I'll be haggling with a dragon?"

"Is this acceptable to you?"

"It doesn't feel like I have a choice," he said. "I just wish my mom or my sister were here. I'd love to see what sort of a deal they could wheel with a dragon."

Tome gazed up at the towering architecture of the Gate of the Ancients. As a rare bit of good luck, the spell that had been making his travel equal parts swift and terrifying had given out a bit too early. He wasn't sure if it was because he'd inadequately defined the destination, the spell simply ran out of strength, or there was some limitation to the duration it could persist. That would require study. For now, all that mattered was that his arrival to his home had been somewhat delayed. Under the influence of the spell, he probably would have arrived hours ago. With its failure, the great halls of his home were just becoming visible now. The sane speed granted him a moment to gather his thoughts and prepare even while he was at the reins. Or it would have, if not for Madge.

"Monasteries are full of monks and stuff, right?" Madge mumbled, her cheek stuffed full of some sort of root she'd dug up during their last stop in the pass leading here.

"Almost by definition, yes," Tome said.

"And monks aren't rich, right?"

"They are not motivated by financial gain. And when financial gain isn't one's motivation, one tends to end up with empty coffers."

"So why's the monastery so huge? It's like a castle."

It was a fair observation. The Gate of the Ancients covered a lot of ground. Three long halls spread from the main monastery in a fan shape. Each was two stories tall and as long as the main street of a bustling city. What had begun as a dozen or so individual buildings in each hall had been connected by bridges between the second floors of each, converting each hall into a long building that connected to the central tower through a somewhat larger bridge. The tower itself stood seven stories tall, starting quite stout at the bottom and narrowing by a ring-shaped balcony with each floor. It gave the tower the overall look of a tiered caked, with a shack-sized feature as the cake topper that allowed the place to double as a lighthouse for the port town a short distance along the coast. Austere was not a word one would readily use to describe it.

"The monks don't pay for their lodging. And they certainly didn't pay for its construction. In Thayne and Shalia and Quarr, the lords and kings pay for things like this all the time, and here in Deticka, things are no different. What good is money if you can't pile it into the shape of wonders that the poor will gaze upon in awe and the wealthy will gaze upon in envy? The Gate of the Ancients is just something for a wealthy lord to dangle in front of his peers."

"Wow. Lucky for you whatever lord commissioned this one had good taste. He could have just built a statue of himself," Madge said.

"There's a long history in this region of religious leaders petitioning lords to..." He shook his head. "It really doesn't matter."

"It matters as much as anything else does." Madge spat the chewed-up root into a bottle and swished it about with the other ingredients. "There. Thin that out into five or six other bottles and that'll make enough itch tonic to get a whole family of poison ivy sufferers taken care of."

"You chewed on that."

"Yes!"

"And now someone else is going to drink it?"

"If they're itchy, and they paid for it, then yes!"

"That's disgusting. Shouldn't you be grinding it up with a mortar and pestle?"

"I could. But I'd still have to spit in it. It's part of the ingredients."

He shuddered. "I thank you for reinforcing the wisdom of my decision to avoid potions altogether."

"One little jaunt through a patch of poison ivy will change your mind real fast."

"I can write a spell to heal a rash," he said.

"Oh! Show me, show me!" she said, corking her bottle and reaching behind the seat.

Somehow, at a stop at a city a fair way back, Madge had acquired a slate and some chalk. Tome very much doubted she'd paid for it, since she didn't have money to spare. But it had nonetheless been the means by which she'd been wrestling an education in paper magic from Tome despite how rare it was that both of them were able to indulge in something like writing.

"Show me the others."

She traced a complex rune on the slate.

"You need to keep working on that," he said after a glance.

"Can you tell what it is?"

"It says, 'cold, as a result of the preceding caster and intended for the following target,' but it doesn't look like you wrote it, it looks like you drew it."

"What's the difference?"

"The difference is, one of them means you know you are writing a word that has a meaning, and the other means you have an image in your mind that you've been told to put on the slate when asked to do so."

"What's the difference?" she said a bit more sharply. "If you can tell what it says, who cares how it got from my mind to your mind?"

"It's a matter of speed and depth of understanding. The number of additional steps you have to do in your head to write down that rune compared to what I have to do means it will take you three or four times longer to compose a spell, and you'll have a harder time remembering the whole vocabulary, so you'll be forced to write clumsy and verbose spells made from ill-fitting or overly general words rather than compact, effective spells composed of precise words."

"But if I wrote a spell with runes that look like this, would the spell work?"

Tome rolled his eyes. "It would, because that looks more like the right rune than any other rune, but—"

"Then it's good enough."

"You shouldn't strive for good enough. You should strive for exceptional."

"I'd rather be good enough at everything I set out to do than great at only a handful of things. What's the shape for getting rid of a rash?"

He took the chalk and slate, leaving the horse to follow the road on its own for a moment. "Please. Letter, rune, character. Not shape. And you would need the 'healing' rune. This specific version of it is best. Followed by this, which can loosely be said to refer to a rash or other itch."

"Oh! That's not so bad. The itch one looks like the one for injury, but not as fancy."

"They're related. That's a very good eye."

"Paper magic would be easy if you didn't need all that other stuff around it. The identity and timing and such."

"Quite so."

"And you don't need that stuff when you do blood magic."

"Don't do blood magic," he snapped.

"Right, but you don't need it if you do blood magic."

"Yes, but don't do blood magic!"

"I know, I know." She copied both shapes over in the corner of the slate, as small as the chalk would allow, then started practicing them. "Say. Why do they call it the Gate of the Ancients anyway? Doesn't look much like a gateway to me. Looks like a cake."

"There are two reasons for the name. First, it has always been dedicated to the duplication and distribution of books, regardless of content. Because books offer a glimpse into the past, a place like this is a Gate of the Ancients. The other is somewhat more mundane. Were you to ask me, it was an afterthought to appeal to more literal minds, though its construction may well have predated the rest of the monastery, for all we know. For a place dedicated to preserving the lessons of history, it really doesn't reach very far back into the Bygone Era, and it was certainly built during the Bygone Era. But on the far side, in the narrow strip of land between the monastery and the cliffs leading down to the sea, there is a large sculpture which is also called the Gate of the Ancients. It's a disk with an arch straddling it, both decorated with filigree and scenes of adventures and exploits that are ironically lost to the ages. It's really quite impressive. I'd recommend you take a look. Anyone who comes here should see it at least once."

"I look forward to it."

Tome watched his childhood home rumble closer. His thoughts just barely started to burble to the surface again when Madge spoke up yet again.

"So. What's going through your mind, being home again?"

He squeezed his fists around the reins, mildly frustrated at how little intellectual momentum he was able to build up with Madge around, but as it so happened, this was potentially a topic better spoken about than thought about.

"There's a great deal more to it than I'd expected," he said. "When I offered to haul these books here, I started thinking about how things would go with my father immediately. He'd be cross that I left, and more cross about why I left. I'd have to talk about what I'd achieved, what I'd learned. I have whole speeches prepared, and alternate versions for different rhetorical gambits he might use. I'm ready for my father. But I hadn't expected to be so... affected by seeing this place again. You spend months or years dreaming about leaving a place and you don't expect to have a pleasant or kind thought about your return."

"Were you being tortured here? Beaten? Browbeaten?"

"No. Well, browbeaten, perhaps. But Father was always sure to be quite passive in his dispensation of shame and disappointment."

"So why wouldn't you feel a little bit of coziness in your heart, coming back home? Memories are like that. You forget the parts you don't want to remember and remember the parts you don't want to forget. Oh! Take it from someone who spent years going back and forth between places I never expected to go back and forth between. The best part? Spotting differences."

"Spotting differences?"

"'Oh, they cut that tree down!' Or maybe, 'Say, they painted that door!' 'She got fat.' 'His hair fell out.' 'They got married!?' It's great fun! Sort of reminds you the whole world is out there living its life while you're not watching. Helps you realize you're not the center of things."

Tome narrowed his eyes. "If there's one thing my father made quite clear, it was that I wasn't the center of things." He snapped the reins. "Let's see if we can get to the monastery before they serve dinner. The food isn't luxurious, but it is plentiful and they are very rigid about when they serve it."

Chapter 7

Allie had only had her meeting with Captain Boltt that morning, but it already felt like ages ago. Something deep in her spirit, the last flickering ember of optimism, suggested that perhaps the whole thing would take care of itself. Perhaps this newcomer with his eyes on Verfessa's operation and the captain's position would decide it wasn't worth the effort or risk and just move on.

There was a reason that ember of optimism was so well hidden beneath mounds of cynicism.

Just after Oovay had decided to take his break for supper, leaving Allie with the whole floor yet again, Marcus stepped through the door. He scanned the place as he always did, looking for ready informants and other signs of misdeed. Allie's body continued to work its way through the tasks of running a tavern: filling drinks, tallying tabs, and shouting down people making too much of a fuss. But her mind was fully on the issue of Marcus.

Verfessa had been clear. He wanted to know about this man. That was all. By that measure, her job was done. She knew his name, his address, his motivation, and his methods. More than enough to satisfy her boss's curiosity. She could just wait until he returned or pass the information along to Mrs. Verfessa and wash her hands of it. ... Except she couldn't. If she waited for Verfessa to return—and she had no idea how long that would take—then Marcus would have more than enough time to act. And acting could trigger payback that could get the Watch involved. There would be turmoil at least. More likely than not, there would be blood. And most certainly, her little corner of the world would be turned upside down in the best of cases. Passing the information on to Mrs. Verfessa could simply lead to her, or some lieutenant within the organization, deciding to act first, which led to all the same problems. The only other option was to intervene, something neither Verfessa or Boltt would approve of. From Verfessa's point of view, she might have already passed the point of no return regarding active investigation. So she was in a corner. No good options remained. She had the knowledge of a forthcoming collapse and no certain means to avert it.

As she watched the thorn in her side reach into a pocket and fetch a glass vial that no one else could have possibly noticed if they'd not known to look for it, she made up her mind. As long as disaster was the most likely result, she may as well take an active role in it. At least if she was at the reins of an out-of-control wagon, she could convince herself she was steering.

She loaded up two baskets of crickets and approached the table where Marcus had chosen to sit. Allie made it to the table as he subtly raised his hand, pretending to shoo a fly away from a half-drunk patron's mug. She saw the glint of glass in his hand. A rough shove of a basket of crickets onto the table struck his hand, causing a drop or two of something milky to splash onto the table rather than into the drink.

"Oh! So we meet again, sir," she said as he looked up to see who had foiled his attempt at enhanced interrogation. "You've been drinking here for a bit, and I feel like we haven't had a chance to properly meet one another. My name is Allie. You're Marcus, right?"

"We've been introduced. Now if you'll excuse me, I was having a word with—"

"Oh. I know we've been introduced. But have we really met? I've seen you asking around for this and that. You'd have a hard time finding someone who knows more about what's going on in this city than I do. If you need advice? Recommendations? Maybe a well-deserved word of warning? The fellows here can vouch for me, right?"

"She knows her stuff," said the man who had unwittingly been saved from having his drink laced with lip-loosening toxins.

"I really don't need—" Marcus began.

She "accidentally" leaned on his hand, causing the vial that was still skillfully palmed to clack audibly against the table. She kept her eyes locked on his. His gaze communicated an awful lot. He knew she'd done that on purpose, which meant he knew that she knew what he'd been planning.

"I think we need to talk," she said. "It'll do you good."

He took a sharp breath, his disarming facade flickering ever so briefly. "I'm always interested in a good conversation," he said.

She beckoned him to the corner of the bar, which she'd subtly been keeping free of other patrons. Once he was seated, she poured him a drink and leaned forward to address him. Any semblance of pretense was gone.

"You need to stop digging. You already know who you're toying with, and it won't end well for anyone if you draw blood," she said.

"You work for the man. I wouldn't expect you to approve of a meaningful inquiry into his crimes. And you don't know the first thing about what I'm doing and why."

"You're poisoning my patrons to get them to tell you things about how things are run, what things are running, and who runs them in this town, with an eye on showing up Captain Boltt and taking his job to lend yourself some gravitas for whatever you perceive the next step in the ladder to be."

He swirled his cup but didn't drink. "So you do know the first thing."

"And a few more besides. Like this, for instance. You're not as sneaky as you think you are. I was told to expect you. Your cover was blown before you even picked it out. So I'm telling you right now. Stop. Turn around and leave this town. Find somewhere else to earn a reputation. You're in the wrong place at the wrong time."

"How much do you know about the workings of your employer?"

"First, I didn't give you permission to ask me questions. This is a warning, not an interview. Second, I'm smart enough to know that sometimes ignorance is the safer choice."

"You must know that wealth and power like his, without an inherited or bestowed title, can only come at a terrible price for the city. He is a criminal, and his hands are dripping with blood."

"No doubt. Which is why you need to keep your neck out of his grip."

"Criminals should be punished. My goals are righteous, and if you stand in my way, what does that make you?"

"Sensible."

"You are content to feed yourself with money earned through—"

She jabbed the desk with her finger. "I earn my money tending this bar. And this little meeting isn't about me doing the bidding of a criminal. It sure isn't about trying to preserve the life of someone who is willing to dump poison into a mug in the name of 'righteousness.' This is about keeping my life on the right path and keeping bodies off the floor of this tavern."

"You really think a place being run by him will stay free of bodies for very long? This is as much about protecting you and the other people of this city as it is about my own status. You are asking me to abandon justice for your own selfish aims."

"Yes. I am," she said. "Now if you'd been asking the right questions, by now you'd know that I've banned more than a few people from this place for doing far less than poisoning people. And something tells me you're here because this is the one business he runs that a random person off the street can wander around in. So here's what is happening. You're going to leave this place, and you're not going to come back. If you need me to kick you out and formally ban you, so be it. But this is the last time you're setting foot in this tavern. If you really need to do something, you can start investigating out in the open, because these informants, in this place, are officially out of your reach. Now drink your drink and leave."

Marcus looked at her evenly. "Someday, this man you're defending will do something to you, or someone you care about. And on that day, I hope you'll remember that you decided to stand in my way. And you did it because he told you to."

"No. I put a face to a rumor because he told me to. I'm kicking you out because you're doing the wrong things, in the wrong way, for the wrong reason. And even if you weren't, I just don't like you. Now drink your drink and get out."

He picked up the tankard and tipped it, pouring the ale onto the floor. "I don't do things just because I'm told to do them," he said.

"Unfortunately for you, Lou does," Allie said. "Lou! This fellow here decided he's not interested in being a gentleman. Show him how we treat folks who don't treat us with respect, would you?"

"You gonna clear off the tab?" said Lou as he raised his hulking frame from his seat.

"Of course."

He thumped toward Marcus. The man stood up and straightened his shirt. "I know where I'm not wanted, and I wouldn't waste another moment in this establishment if I was paid to do so. I'll leave on my own."

Lou grabbed him by the neck of his shirt and his belt. "Not with the size of my tab, you won't," he rumbled.

Allie watched as Marcus was unceremoniously hauled from his feet and toted out the door. As the tavern hooted and hollered at the sight of a man being ejected, Allie started cleaning up the mess he'd made. At least, the literal one. The figurative one was another matter entirely.

"I don't know if that was the correct thing to do," she mused as she wrung out the rag. "But it was certainly the most satisfying."

"No. No. It's no good if there's holes in the front. Boots cover the entire feet," Fel grumbled as a collection of kobolds gathered around him to attempt to see to his missing equipment.

While Fel couldn't fault the creatures for their generosity and enthusiasm, he never thought he'd be missing Teya's oratory skill. Her capacity to string four or five words together into a sentence without having to stop and think would have been a tremendous asset right now. The beasts understood at least some of what Fel was saying. But they certainly didn't understand all of it, and without a means to ask for clarification beyond "Is good?", finding the way to common ground was a series of trials and errors. The most recent misunderstanding was rooted in the mistaken belief by the kobolds that Fel simply needed to borrow one of their pairs of boots. And a kobold boot was a baffling bit of kit. Designed to maintain the utility of their claws, they were little more than bits of leathery hide that could be strapped to the narrow pad of flesh that made contact with the ground when a kobold was standing.

Fel's explanation fell on ears that were deaf, disinterested, or lacked the understanding necessary to interpret them. Instead, a helpful swarm of the little devils hoisted him up and strapped what they'd decided were bits of footwear of the proper size to his feet. They dusted off their paws and looked quite proud of themselves when the width of the "boots" was correct.

"These aren't boots," Fel said. "My heels and my toes are touching the ground. This is one-third of a pair of sandals."

The three kobolds standing nearest to him endeavored to motivate him to stand on his tiptoes with a few sharp slaps to his behind.

"Ow! I don't stand like that. I'm standing like this for a reason. Ow! Enough with the kobold boots. I need normal boots."

One of the kobolds pointed to the wall of the torch-lit chamber. It was covered in cubbies, each of which contained a pair of kobold boots.

"All right. 'Normal' doesn't really mean the same thing here. That should have been obvious. But..." He glanced at what was visible of the daylight in the mouth of the alcove. "We're running out of daylight. By the morning, your boss is going to haul me off to do the job, and I'm not looking forward to dealing with a bunch of elves barefoot."

He paused, slow realization dawning. "Wait. Elves! Elves have the same kind of feet. Do you have any elven boots? Or maybe dwarf boots?"

The kobolds looked at one another. After some chatters, three of them peeled off and scampered away. The first stopped short, the two behind bumping into him before the trio hopped backward to allow the gracefully stooped form of the Adept to enter.

"Fel Masker," she said softly. "I trust you have been served well?"

"They're doing their best, but you folks aren't really stocked with the kind of gear a human needs. The weapons are good. I really like these little picks the kobolds use. Nice mattock, good and sharp, and small enough I can use them two at a time."

"I thought I'd given the kobolds permission to provide enchanted weaponry from the armory."

"I grabbed a dagger, but the rest is all swords and stuff. I don't really have any training. That's why I usually use a cudgel. Hand me a sword and I'm as likely to hack off my own toe as one of theirs. But a club? That's pretty hard to use wrong. Any chance you're going to be able to head out to get my own gear soon? Or someone else?"

"Unfortunately our fliers are chiefly engaged in surveillance of the elves. And we have very few with the strength to carry more than one piece of your equipment besides. Though Kazel's forces have been bolstered somewhat since his release, he was locked away for centuries. Those with weaker allegiance abandoned him long ago."

"I guess fliers are kind of flighty."

Fel snickered. The Adept did not.

"And I am not as young as I once was, as the struggle of transporting you has underscored. It will be at least another full day before I can confidently take to the sky again. You will, at least, be pleased to know that your wagon remains safe, at least as of a few minutes ago, and thus is the rest of your gear. This comes as a relief to me as well, as I had clearly been taking Stix and Mik's skill as left and right hands of the Adept for granted."

"How do you know they're on schedule?"

The Adept tapped one of her talons on the ground. Her replacement right hand scurried in and presented Fel with a piece of parchment scrawled with markings he couldn't immediately identify as a message.

"We've received word from Stix and Mik directly."

"Who hand-delivered the message? And couldn't they grab at least Wick's lantern?"

"Sylphs. They are wind elementals. Valuable scouts and spies but quite limited in other capacities. Even the most meager of spellcasters can ward against them, and they lack the strength to carry anything that the breeze itself could not carry. We seldom use them even in this limited capacity as messengers. Something as simple as rain or a trained hawk could destroy or intercept the message. But with the elven spellcasters mostly aboard ships to the north, the peryton-riding hunters are our only concern, and they are far more set upon finding their prey than a message or two."

"Seems like they could skip the message and just tell you what they need to tell you."

"The fact that you seem to be wearing kobold boots should serve as proof of the complexities a language barrier can introduce. Unlike the gnomes and undines also in allegiance, their grasp of spoken and written language is weak. Among us, only Kazel and I have any capacity to issue orders or receive reports with regard to them."

"Shame," he said.

"Indeed. As timing is of the essence, it is not likely your things will arrive before Kazel takes you to your task."

"Couldn't he swing by with me and grab the stuff?"

"You are the only human, and indeed the only creature, that Kazel will ever have carried that he did not intend to consume. To call upon him to run an errand, even one that might in some small way serve his own purpose, is beneath consideration."

"You say that now, but when I can't get back to you with word of what those elves are doing because I gashed my heel on a rock, you'll be singing a different tune. I'm doing you a pretty big favor by even coming out here."

"This is so. And we fully understand and accept this. It is not our intention to appear ungrateful. Indeed. Your willingness to aid is the reason I have paid you a visit. For others, the call of destiny is sufficient. But you seem to doubt fate's hands in this endeavor."

"Destiny is what people blame things on when they don't have what it takes to make things happen on their own. It's a fun story to tell a child, but it's no way to live a life."

"If you do not believe in such things, then why come so willingly to our aid?"

Fel ran his fingers through his hair and took a heavy breath. "I don't know. It seemed natural, like something I should be doing. And..." He paused. "Look, I told you that Teya is in a little miniature Greater Lands, right?"

"Yes. A disturbing development and one that explains the absence of quite a few of Kazel's followers. We'd feared them killed."

"Well, I spent a couple of days in a little miniature Clickspring. And while I was there, I got a taste of the kind of twisting and manipulation that has been happening in your heads. My family's emblem is everywhere in the real Clickspring. If my ancestors didn't help design and build the mechanism that's kept your people half-brainwashed for centuries, then one of their peers did. I can't describe to you how violating it felt to have my own memories tweaked and massaged. Rewritten for someone else's purpose. But I don't have to describe it to you, because you're experiencing it right now. And it is happening to you because of people like me. Let's just say you aren't far off when you say I've been busy atoning for the sins of the past. Destiny may be an illusion, but history is real."

"And this desire for atonement is strong enough for you to undertake this mission?"

"I'm here, aren't I?"

She raised her head, nearly brushing the low roof of the chamber, and nodded. "You are a good man, Fel Masker. Perhaps the rarest thing to be found within the Greater Lands."

The kobolds returned and dumped a total of seven boots on the ground. Among them were only one matched pair, of elven make and far too narrow for his feet. A single dwarven boot was near enough to the right size, but without its match, it was useless.

"I think maybe decent boots are right up there in terms of rarity," he said. "Any chance you folks could stitch together another boot this size? One for the other foot?"

The Adept addressed the kobolds, who quickly yanked the boot off his foot and scurried off with it.

"Consider it done," she said.

"All right. All right. That's one less thing to worry about." He shook his head. "You know, my dad always sends me out with way too much gear. Maybe in his day he'd use it all, but I tend to use maybe a tenth of it. It takes a time like this to appreciate how useful some of that stuff could be. Even just the dazzler and the decoy could…" Fel's eyes darted aside. "The decoy…" he snapped. "How fast are those sylphs?"

"Quite literally as fast as the wind. I'll remind you, though, they won't do you any good regarding your equipment."

"Maybe, maybe not. But I'm thinking we might be able to borrow one of my dad's bright ideas to solve this problem…"

Tome's feelings of nostalgia rose to almost painful levels as he guided the cart around the outside of the monastery to its main gate facing the sea. He could have entered through one of the three halls—most people did—but doing this would allow him to show off the namesake sculpture of the Gate of the Ancients to Madge and delay entry just a moment longer. The sculpture stood before him now. If anything, it seemed bigger than it had when he'd left. The towering crisscross of arches stood a bit taller than the second story, tracing out the rough shape of a dome without falling in. Each was stout as a tree trunk, composed of wedged-shaped stones carved with complex scenes or lines of mysterious script and runes. The circular courtyard beneath was composed of concentric rings of broad, flat stones, similarly carved.

"Wow..." Madge said, hopping down to investigate. "It's so clean!"

"Not the first observation most people make," Tome said. "But I'm glad you did. The monastery takes pride in the maintenance of the monument. I spent more of my childhood cleaning out the crevices of those carvings than I care to remember."

"And this is just for looking at?" she said, trotting out onto it.

"Yes, it's for looking at, not for walking on," he hissed.

"Oh, sorry about that." She retreated to the edge. "But what I meant was, there's no um... operation? Because the shapes on here look an awful lot like the shapes you've been teaching me."

"The runes on there are entirely unlike the runes I'm teaching you, in that the runes I'm teaching you have meanings and are derived from and serve as the basis for other languages, while those do not. They're just mildly stylized pictographs representing physical items."

"What's the difference?"

"It's the difference between a drawing of a cat and the word 'cat.'"

"One of them everyone can understand and the other lets you keep things secret from people who don't. I get it."

"No, that's not—"

"Boy?" called a sharp voice from the doorway.

Tome flinched and turned. "Father."

In the doorway was a curious-looking fellow. The resemblance between them was subtle, chiefly around their eyes. Tome clearly took after his mother. Nonetheless, the subject of his parentage was unquestionable. The pair carried themselves much the same way, and the instant his father had appeared, a tension and combativeness colored Tome's voice and expression. Mr. Inkbrand was plump and dressed in drab brown robes. He had the sort of enduring youth that came from spending little time outdoors and always being well fed. Few wrinkles creased his skin. Smile lines in particular were markedly absent.

The pair surveyed each other silently. Madge chose to break the icy silence.

"Mr. Inkbrand! I'm a friend of your son's. My name is Madge," she said, rushing up and extending a hand.

"Brother Inkbrand, if you please."

"Oh!" She turned to Tome. "I thought he was your dad."

"He is my father. But this is a monastery. They are all brothers."

"Big families are great!" Madge said. "I have a bunch of siblings myself, see—"

"I do not know if it is your intention to be humorous, but you have failed," Brother Inkbrand said.

Madge laughed. "I like this fella."

"So the fortune seeker has returned." Inkbrand looked at the cart. "And not without success, it seems."

"The contents of those books are not what you might suspect," Tome said. "But I assure you, they present a tremendous opportunity that warrants discussion."

"I'm also going to need a place to stay. Both of us, I guess," said Madge, "but I figure you wouldn't turn your son away. And what's this I hear about dinner?"

Brother Inkbrand gave her a withering look, which failed to cow her in the slightest, then turned to Tome. "What is the nature of your relationship?" he asked.

"Apprentice and master!" Madge said. "He's the master. For paper magic, anyway."

"I suppose it was too much to hope that you had abandoned that particular pursuit. As your friend has observed, mealtime is nigh. We can discuss matters over the meal." He raised his voice. "Initiate Duncan! See to Tome's horse and cart. Brother Thomas! Two more for dinner, at my table."

Madge jogged to catch up as the father and son entered. The inside of the monastery had not changed since Tome's departure, though that was hardly a surprise. It hadn't changed in decades. Why would the handful of years since he'd left be any different? The place cut an impressive compromise between extravagance and austerity. The building itself was astonishingly ornate. Rare was a block that didn't have some sort of flourish or shape carved into it. No two arches were the same. But that was the extent of the decoration, at least in the entry and hallways. No paintings, no rugs, nothing with any color whatsoever. It was a place of cold gray, warm brown, flickering candles, and silence.

Again, Madge saw fit to take care of that final element. "What's an initiate and what's a brother?" she asked.

"An initiate is just beginning training and is not yet trusted with the written word in official context. A brother has been formally inducted to the monastery and has begun his transcription duties."

"How come he's Initiate Duncan but you're Brother Inkbrand?"

"Because I hold the highest position within the monastery and am afforded that respect."

"How come Tome's not Brother Tome?"

"Because he left the monastery."

"But he's back."

"In this instance, 'left the monastery' has a more formal and consequential meaning."

"Ooooh. You kicked him out."

"I kicked myself out," Tome said.

When they entered the dining hall, Madge took a startled step back. The place was filled with perhaps a hundred people ranging in age from teen to wizened old man, all seated at long tables. But from even a step beyond the door, there wasn't a hint of sound. Not even a clink of a glass or spoon. They were eating but with slow and deliberate movements.

"Is there a vow of silence?" Madge asked, finally realizing perhaps lowering her voice would be wise.

"No. Silence here is a point of consideration not obligation."

They took seats at the longest of the tables, and steaming bowls were set before them. The food continued the color scheme of the rest of the monastery, a brown-and-gray mush that included beans, peas, and some unidentifiable grain. The scent struck Tome with a tidal wave of memories. He didn't miss many things from these days, but the thing he missed least was the food.

Madge was not similarly burdened. She shoveled the food into her face with a shameless zeal that, for the moment, took Tome's father's disapproving gaze off him.

"How long has this apprentice/master arrangement been in place?" Brother Inkbrand asked.

"A little over a week," she said between bites.

"I wouldn't say it is a formal arrangement," Tome said.

"Mmm..." Inkbrand murmured. "Tell me the nature of the books in your cart."

"That's what you're starting with?" Madge said, this time with her mouth still full.

"It is the business at hand," Inkbrand said.

"You haven't seen your son in years, and you're just asking him about the books."

"The books are the business at hand," he repeated, as though there could be no doubt that further clarification should not be needed.

"They are an index of approximately half of the Tellestressa Archives," Tome said.

Brother Inkbrand paused. His expression did not change, nor did his voice, but somehow his overall demeanor felt more intense.

"The Tellestressa Archives were all but lost. Only the tiniest fraction survived, and we have three of the charred books formerly contained within it."

"I invite you to assess the contents of the books yourself. They are transcribed, but they represent a genuine census of books which are available to also be transcribed."

"I look forward to establishing the authenticity of the information, or the lack thereof. As you departed long before you were able to develop the level of expertise necessary to make such a determination, this will, I presume, be the first time an expert has looked upon them."

"Believe it or not, Father, knowledge is attainable beyond these walls. And you have never dreamed of some of the things I've learned and seen."

"Hey!" Madge interjected with a suddenness that suggested a thought had just jabbed itself into her mind and needed to be released. "How come you don't like paper magic?"

Tome covered his face. "I am really not interested in hearing this again."

"Paper magic is a perversion of the purpose of knowledge. The written word exists as a record, and as an art form. Magic in general bends the natural world that the words record or are inspired by, and paper magic triples this affront. It alters the world, it puts the written word to work itself for this purpose, and it consumes those words in the process."

"Wow. Why'd you let us in, then?"

"He bears books. We share the bonds of blood. And we have the obligation to shed light into even the most dim and unwilling of darkened corners."

Madge snickered. "He called you dim."

"With that out of the way," Tome said. "If you determine that the index is authentic, I ask that you offer some of the more skilled brothers to translate titles, sort the index, and prioritize titles for transcription."

"When the meal is complete, we will discuss such business. Now, if you and your apprentice will be so kind as to give the rest of us the consideration of silence?"

"Just one last thing," Madge said.

"What?" Brother Inkbrand said.

"Are we allowed to have seconds?"

He looked to one of the other monks, who plopped another serving into her bowl. "I'm going to like it here!" she said.

Tome smiled. The weariness on his father's face suddenly made Madge's presence entirely worthwhile.

Fel stood outside Kazel's lair, quite near to where the Adept perched and issued commands. His eyes were pointed roughly in the direction he knew his wagon to be. Though the mountain wasn't as cold as he'd expected—and inside the alcoves was rather comfortable—he'd had to resort to a fur blanket over his shoulders once the sun fully slid from the sky. The scheme he'd convinced them to put into place was bizarre even by his standards. He didn't really understand the mechanics of why it would work, let alone if it was likely to. But he also didn't understand why it shouldn't work, so he chose to be optimistic.

After a few more minutes, he noticed a dark shape bobbing just above the tops of the trees. It was moving as swiftly as a bird, but it certainly was not a bird. It was bulbous and round and looked vaguely like some manner of furry beast, though not enough like any specific one to fool an intelligent creature. As it drew nearer, it seemed to accelerate, rising up the mountainside.

Fel laughed and clapped. "That's a good sign! That's a very good sign!" he said, pointing enthusiastically.

The Adept hopped down from her perch and bounced over to him. It was impressive how much less majestic she was when she couldn't flutter and flit where she needed to go. A collection of kobolds joined them, their large eyes gazing down along the mountain. Now the brown thing was near enough for it to be clear that it was a fluttering brown cloth, filled with wind and weighed down by something tied to its corners. A few moments longer and the weight revealed itself to be a cloth bundle with the unmistakable glimmer of an unlit lantern fastened to the bottom.

A final gust of wind carried the entire collection up over their heads. The sylph must have dispersed after that, because it dropped quite quickly, but Fel was able to catch it.

"Ha! Ha-ha! I'm a contraptioneer!" Fel crowed, untying the bundle from the makeshift sail scavenged off the decoy. "You folks never thought of doing that?"

"The sylphs themselves do not think in such terms," the Adept said, making no attempt to conceal her surprise. "And the machinations of contraptioneers are not things we seek to emulate."

"Ships have sails, right? This wasn't any fancier than that."

Fel thanked his father's foresight in having him take the artifact lantern that could be relit and still house Wick. From within the bundle, he pulled one of only three items he'd been able to request Mik and Stix to tie up within it. A sparker. With it, he lit Wick's lantern and took stock of the other items. His spyglass and the earring. He'd taken the gamble that the kobolds would be able to finish preparing fresh boots for him.

"Thank the High," he said. "Any chance you could send the sylph back for another load?"

"I will attempt to negotiate it, but I believe we may have expended the efforts the sylphs are willing to provide for the short term."

"Shame. I was hoping to get the dragon sticker up here, too."

The flame went still.

"Fel! That was an inspired maneuver. Your father congratulates you on devising it," Wick said.

"He devised it, I just stole the idea when I needed it," Fel said.

"The sentry lantern speaks already?" the Adept said. "I recall there being some amount of delay between his visits during your last time here."

"We've all learned a few new tricks since then," Fel said. "What's the word from home, Wick?"

"Euphoria and Lattica have yet to return from their trip to investigate Piotor Graves. Your parents and sister are concerned about you and Euphoria but remain reasonably confident and in relatively high spirits. Allie misses you, but has been rather busy of late and has thus been brief in her communications. Tome has not communicated recently, but if all has gone to plan, he has arrived at the Gate of the Ancients by now and is seeking the aid of his father regarding the index. Teya has great concern for the reason the beacon was lit and is awaiting an update on what is wrong and what is to be done. She has taken steps to prepare those within the Lesser Greater Lands to render aid if needed and is also waiting for guidance from Mr. Masker on the subject of the clockwork diamond alteration."

"Everything really is happening at once," Fel said. "Well, tell everyone that tomorrow morning I climb onto Kazel's back to be flown to Clickspring so I can find out what the elves are up to and get Parch back."

"What are your plans with regard to that?" Wick said.

"You just heard them."

"I suspect that if I deliver that information without elaboration, the others will be unified in their belief that you need to put more work into your tactics."

"And you can tell them that I'm all ears," he said. "I won't need you again until sunrise, so go ahead and help the other folks out until then."

"So I shall. May luck be with you," Wick said.

"I've had so much luck so far that I'm thinking I might be just about out of it, but we'll see."

Wick departed. Fel rubbed some dirt from the earring and quickly pocketed it, ignoring the odd flourish of sensation that the enchantment brought with it. Something told him the presence of an elven artifact would be poorly received in Kazel's lair, so best not to flaunt it.

"Everything is coming together," he said.

"That the circumstances presently defy explanation serves as evidence that this all was preordained. Destiny has a place for you, and you are equal to its challenge."

"I really don't have the same feelings about destiny that you do."

"I understand. You doubt the reality of destiny."

"Yes."

"But you embrace the reality of luck."

"Because luck is real."

"How do the two differ?"

"Destiny is about this big plan that for some reason picks out this guy and that lady and this creature and that spirit and throws them all down on a gameboard to play out a strategy. Luck is 'things turn out good or bad sometimes.' It's not even a comparison."

"Do you believe that some individuals tend toward good fortune, and others toward bad fortune?"

"Play enough grum and you'll see that lucky and unlucky people are a fact of life."

"So you believe that given a set of opportunities, some people are more likely to fail through no fault of their own, and others are more likely to succeed regardless of their skill?"

"That's just another way of saying what you already said."

"Then the outcomes of some actions are set, regardless of the desires or actions of those involved. What is this, if not predestination? What is this, if not destiny?"

Fel finished stowing his meager acquisitions into one of the new packs they'd provided. "Either you've been thinking about this too much, or I haven't been thinking about it enough. And if you think I'm going to start thinking about it more, then you've definitely been thinking about it too much."

"I don't require you to believe what I believe," the Adept said. "But as things progress, as more and more elements fall into the only place they could be and still give you or others a chance to do what you need to do, be open to the possibility that such an event has occurred because it had to. Because it needed to. Because the world could not continue on the proper path if it did not."

"If all of that was true, then doesn't that mean I could just sit here and kick up my feet and whatever needs to happen will happen?"

"No. Because you are Fel Masker. And you can only do what you would do. And in the face of this, you would not sit back. You would act in defense of your friends, your family, and your world."

He glared at her. "Listen. I know what was supposed to happen on this trip. I was supposed to loot the Greater Lands Wall for enough extra goodies to finance a nice big game of grum. That was the plan. And I know that was the plan because I made it. And now I'm arguing with a harpy, while a bunch of kobolds watch it like it's the night's entertainment, about how and why I'll be riding a dragon to the heart of a mysterious land to figure out what some elves are up to and rescue my unicorn. This isn't an example of things going right. This is an example of things going wrong. But I have a new pair of boots on the way, I have Wick, and I have some weapons, so I'm ready to do it. Where can I sleep? As I understand it, we leave at dawn, and it's probably not a great idea to be yawning while holding on to the back of a dragon."

"They'll lead you to a place to stay. Any other equipment you require, as well as a meal, will be waiting for you when you awake. And regardless of why you choose to do this or through what means you were brought here, I thank you."

"Thank me when I'm done," he said.

Euphoria tried to keep watch as Lattica guided the carriage. One of the many problems that had presented itself with using a luxury carriage for this purpose that became abundantly clear as they continued south was the near impossibility of keeping a good close watch on one's surroundings. There were no positions one could sit in, save on the roof, which allowed a full view around the carriage. A vehicle like this was intended to either never be placed in a position dangerous enough to require a lookout, or else to have an entire entourage of guards. The best Euphoria could do was sit in one of the seats in the carriage that faced the rear and regularly slide to one window or the other to look out to the sides and behind. That had been minimally sufficient during most of the trip, but now a misty mountain fog had rolled in, limiting their vision even more. The one thing working in their favor was the speed of their journey. Riding down a mountain toward a known location was much, much faster than the opposite. Their destination was looming ahead.

"Anything?" Lattica called.

Euphoria did the now-familiar slide and gazed through both windows. "Nothing I can spot. Not that it means much. I can't see much farther than I can throw a stone."

"We're well into Fenfield. I don't suppose you remember the symptoms of that plague."

"A general feeling that you must continue forward because there is nothing behind. And the plague, such as it was, is no more."

"I'm the kind of woman who'd rather be safe than sorry until I know something for myself. But considering all I want to do is turn around and head out of here, I guess it doesn't have its claws into me."

"What about you? Do you see what we're looking for yet?"

"No sign of a wall, let alone two of them. But the ground's starting to level out, and the trees look thinner up ahead. The problem is, I'm not the best navigator without roads to follow. Depending on how big this place is, with the mist in the way it wouldn't take much for us to be far enough off course to miss it."

"As I understand it, it is simultaneously quite small and quite large, though for our purposes, each of the two walls is courtyard-sized, and one is entirely or partially demolished."

"Hold on a minute." Lattica spoke again, this time her voice almost inaudible over the rattling of the carriage. "Anything about a labor camp?"

"A labor camp? I'd heard that inside the Lesser Greater Lands there was..." Euphoria paused. "Blast it, of course. Teya warned me there were workers at False Clickspring."

She turned and leaned out the window. Sure enough, just visible between the trees, she was able to spot a tent. From the looks of it, the thing had been recently erected. That is to say, it was no more than a few months old, rather than years.

"Give them a wide berth. And if that's here, then False Clickspring must be just past it. The Lesser Greater Lands can't be far beyond it."

Their journey continued, now with each woman keenly aware of every sound. Nerves sculpted creaking tree branches and crackling underbrush into the footsteps of would-be attackers. A wall, quite intact, slowly emerged out of the mist. Sure enough, it didn't look like it was large enough to hold much more than a modest city center.

"Now what?" Lattica asked.

"Follow the wall. The entrance is on the west-most point."

She snapped the reins. "That better be this way. Because the other way will take us right back to that labor camp."

Slowly circumnavigating the wall turned up a well-hidden, drawbridge-style gate.

"And now?" Lattica said.

Euphoria hopped out. She gave Lattica a look. The look wasn't intended to be a warning to arm herself, but it was certainly interpreted as one. She leveled a crossbow at the door. Euphoria stepped forward and knocked with her wedding ring to give it a little extra thump. Nothing. When a second knock failed to produce a response, she waved to Lattica.

"Get the carriage closer to the wall," she said, stepping up to sit beside her.

"Don't tell me you're planning to hop the wall," Lattica said.

"It's not a very tall wall. From the top of the carriage it won't be much more than a step. If I tie a rope to the carriage, I can slide down on the other side and open the gate."

"I don't think the family would be very happy with me letting you climb a wall, even if it wasn't a wall with a load of monsters on the other side."

"Given the amount of turmoil going on in this family, depending on who would be displeased, I'd consider that a benefit not a liability."

Lattica grumbled and repositioned the carriage as close to the wall as she could manage. "Do me a favor and don't get killed. It'll reflect poorly on me," she said.

"As you wish. Just for you I won't hurl myself headlong into the jaws of a monster."

She tied off the rope and tossed it over the top of the wall, then climbed onto the roof of the carriage. Her first glimpse over the wall treated her to the mind-bending, physics-defying sight of yet another slice of the landscape far too large to fit into the wall that contained it.

"Oh... my..." she said.

"What's wrong?"

"It's as Wick described it. But he failed to do it justice. It's... well, it's wrong."

She tried to train her eyes to the ground immediately beyond the wall, the better to get her bearings and not have to reconcile the impossible sight. In doing so, she spotted something. "As it happens, I see two monsters."

"What sorts of monsters?" Lattica said, crossbow once again ready, even though there was a wall between her and any potential targets.

"One is a minotaur. He's a big fellow. The other is a strange, potbellied little thing. An imp? Maybe a goblin? It looks like they're having an argument. I think these are the ones Wick said Tome said were effectively the doormen for the place and were affable enough that Teya let them return to the door to guard it."

"Thirdhand information isn't the best thing to stake one's life upon."

They seemed to be in an animated discussion that she couldn't quite hear from atop the wall. Reasoning they were far enough from the work camp for a careful shout to avoid being heard, Euphoria called to them, "Hello there! Can you open the door, please?"

"Wazzat?" snapped the goblin, looking around.

"Up here! I am a friend of Fel, Tome, and Teya's. Could you please open the gate?"

"You hear something?" said the minotaur thickly.

"That's right. They can't perceive things beyond the wall." She looked down to Lattica. "I'm climbing over."

"I strongly advise against it," Lattica said.

"Advice noted. If I die, you may inform my corpse that you told it so." She stepped over the wall and slid down just enough that she was entirely within its border. "I said, could you please open the door!" she called.

Both monsters turned to her this time and looked approximately in her direction.

"You! Blurry blob! No blurry blobs climb out of nowhere without a password," said the goblin.

"I was unaware there was a password," Euphoria said.

"They didn't tell me about any password," said the minotaur.

"They didn't tell me any password either, but why should we let someone in without one?" said the goblin.

"How would I know a password if there isn't one?" Euphoria asked, adjusting her grip a bit. Among the many things she hadn't anticipated having to do once she married into the Graves family was climbing ropes. She was quite out of practice.

"Any person important enough to come in here would have a password," the goblin reasoned.

"Then how would you know if I'd given you the right one if I gave you one?" she asked.

"I know a good password when I hear it. Who says I don't?"

"You may not have heard me, but I'm a friend of Fel Masker, Tome Inkbrand, and Teya the kobold's."

"I know two of them. And I like one of them," the minotaur said. "I say we let her in."

"Not without a password!" barked the goblin.

She slid a few inches down the rope, her grip beginning to fail. "Cerulean," she said.

"What?" the goblin said.

"That's the password," she said.

The goblin scratched his head. "That's a pretty good-sounding password. Come on in."

She dropped to the ground and paced toward the gate. "I have a friend waiting outside. Do you mind terribly if I open the door?"

"There ain't no door," the goblin said. "There used to be a door. Right about there. Where the world stops. But it ain't there no more because there ain't no there there."

She glanced at the door. "And I imagine the large switch beside it was the means to release it?"

"Yeah. Thing'd fall like a stone. That's what this big chain here is for. Thurb over there had to help slow it down. Now the chain sort of leads over to nowhere."

"For old time's sake, perhaps you could hold the chain? Thurb, was it?"

"Nothing better to do," the minotaur said.

He lumbered over to grip the crank for the chain holding the gate in place, which Euphoria now noticed was affixed to a counterweight that lowered into a pit a short distance away. She fought with the switch until it released and the gate rumbled open. After a moment, Lattica guided her carriage inside.

"Hey! Who said you could invite in strangers?"

"This is my associate."

"She needs to tell us the password too."

Euphoria turned to Lattica. "Would you do me the favor of telling these gentlemen the password, which is cerulean?"

"Cerulean," Lattica repeated, her eyes dancing back and forth between the pair with the same unblinking intensity of someone who was trying to decide if a stray dog was going to beg for scraps or attack.

"That's more like it. See? That's why they put me back here. I know my job," said the goblin. "You're here for Teya, right? She's the only one anyone comes here for."

"That is correct," Euphoria said, climbing back beside Lattica.

"Thurb'll take you. She's down that way. Sticks closer to the wall than the old people in charge used to."

"Thank you. Though I would suggest he crank the gate until it shuts again."

"Ain't no gate," the goblin corrected.

"Then perhaps crank it until it would have shut."

Thurb lumbered over and did as he was told.

"I don't understand how you are so calm," Lattica whispered.

"I'm not. I'm absolutely terrified," Euphoria said.

"It doesn't show."

"Feeling one way and behaving another has proved to be rather an important skill in both sales and family diplomacy."

"Every time I think I got stuck with the hard job, I find out some weird thing the rest of the family has to be good at, and I wonder if maybe bashing people in the head with a heavy stick is the best job in the clan."

"I wouldn't want to do your job, but I don't much relish doing mine either. Sometimes I wonder what it must be like to be a part of a family that isn't also a career."

They kept such conversation to a minimum once Thurb started guiding them to Teya. It would have been reason enough to silence themselves out of fear that he might overhear something. The much more prevalent reason was the minotaur's tendency to dominate the conversation himself. He was anything but a sparkling conversationalist, and his choices of topics ranged from dull to unsettling, but at least his affable and endless talk, combined with the stiff pace his towering frame afforded, made the time pass quickly.

"... I remember this one bird fellow came in. I think it was a fellow. Hard to tell with birds, but usually it's the fellows who have the bright plumage and this fellow had bright plumage, so I think it was a fellow. Anyway, he died a little bit after he showed up. He was lost in the labyrinth. Took the right at the beginning of that left-right-ladder down-ladder down stairs-right-left section I talked about. That'll put you in a big circle real easy. Really pretty skull though. And pretty feathers too. Still got a few here."

Thurb reached back to his tangled mane of hair and revealed a few long green feathers that produced an iridescent red coloring when the soft light of the evening struck them properly.

He tucked it away again. "And then there was this squishy thing. No skull at all on that one. It got lost in the—"

"I'm terribly sorry," Euphoria said, desperate to avoid yet another story focused on lists of twists and turns and the aesthetic qualities of dislodged anatomy. "But I imagine you are leading us to that camp ahead?"

"That's the place. Teya's usually in the big tent there with the three fires around it," Thurb said.

"We can find our way from here."

"You don't need me to introduce you?"

"I believe my history with Teya will serve as introduction enough."

"Suit yourself. I'll head back, then. The little fellow gets antsy when I leave him alone."

He turned and shifted from an ambling stroll to a trot, shaking the ground and carrying him out of sight in no time at all. They rolled toward the little tent city ahead of them. Lattica waited until the trembling of the ground had completely faded away before she spoke again.

"I never expected to head into anything even resembling the Greater Lands," she said. "But if you'd asked me to guess what it would be like, I would have nailed the 'scary and full of monsters' part on the head. The 'long, boring, one-sided conversations with monsters' is a surprise."

"I agree. But given the alternative, I am hoping the dull conversation remains the primary interaction," Euphoria said.

She raised their torch as they approached the cluster of tents. Its light reflected back to them in a galaxy of large, serpentine eyes.

"Yeah. I'll take a description of a skull over learning what a dozen gnawing creatures would do to mine," Lattica said.

The glowing embers of animal eyes started to cluster together, their vague forms in the dim light gradually showing themselves as they approached the trio of flames and formed a defensive line between them and the large tent behind. It was a collection of kobolds. Maybe forty in total. They didn't look overtly hostile, but they all stared at the newcomers with the sort of calculated intensity that quite effectively delivered the warning that overt hostility was available at a moment's notice if necessary. Hammering home this implied danger was the mound of weapons and armor that Euphoria's and Lattica's adjusting eyes had finally been able to discern in the shadow of one of the tents. The threat was sufficient that when the time came to stop the wagon, the decision was made by the increasingly intimidated horse rather than either of the riders.

"I am a friend of Teya's," Euphoria said. "Euphoria Graves. I come seeking aid, advice, and protection."

The reptilian eyes of the cohort of kobolds narrowed with a sequence of distrusting squints. Something between a grumble and growl boiled from the group. The one nearest to the flap of the large tent slipped inside.

"Friends!?" piped a sudden, excited chatter.

Teya bounded out of the tent so quickly she almost stumbled into the largest of the three fires. She was still rubbing sleep from her eyes but seemed genuinely happy to see Euphoria. "Fora!" she crowed, bounding over, much to the consternation of the horse. "Sister of Fel! Least worst friend kin!" The kobold scrambled up onto the cart and balanced on the crosspiece at their feet. "And you?" she asked, pointing at Lattica.

"Lattica Graves."

"Same name! Family too?" Teya said.

"She's my sister-in-law, to varying degrees of sister and law," Euphoria said.

"Law?" Teya said, dismissing the word. "Family of friend? Friend! Friend of family? Friend! And friend? Just like family. Same. Welcome, always. You need food? You need drink?" She turned. "Food, drink! Cooked food, or fruit. Humans? Don't like raw." She turned back. "This one? Good host."

The defensive edge evaporated from the kobolds in a way that was almost magical. Distrust and threat shifted to gleeful acceptance as quickly as one might snuff out a candle flame.

"Maybe wine instead?" Teya offered. "You like wine? This is good wine. Good strong wine. Head hurts for days."

"That's very kind of you. Water will be fine. And if I may? Right now refreshments are secondary to communication. I don't suppose Wick is present?"

Teya pointed to the fires. "All Wick fire. Dancing, so no Wick. Soon, though. Wick? Talking to Martin. This one? Sleeping until then. Big job tomorrow. Important. You need help?"

"We've made a discovery that has put us at odds with someone far better equipped than we are at the moment. We needed protection and a safe way to send word to others."

"Wick? Send word. Morning. Protection?" She turned and chattered something to the other kobolds. They chattered something in return. "I tell them, protect. Someone come? Mean harm to friends? They will bite. Bite to pieces."

Kobolds started to emerge from the darkness around the fire. Some had pitchers of water. Others, baskets of assorted fruits, vegetables, and grains. Two of them carefully arranged heaps of straw on the ground and draped rough cloth over them to serve as crude but workable beds. A campsite simply materialized before them. Teya gestured to it without even having seen it assemble.

"Food, water. Place for sleep. Place for horse. You sleep. Get rest. Be safe. Tomorrow? We talk. Very very talk. Much to say. Tonight? Sleep. Good night!"

"One moment," Euphoria said. "If I may, why are there piles of weaponry over there?"

"The beacon is lit! Back home, Kazel calls. Needs help. Fel is helping. Soon, we help too. Many battles. Much fighting. Very very fighting. Leather armor, good weapons. We win!"

"Wait... Fel is helping the dragon in the Greater Lands right now?"

"Yes! Good man. And soon? We help too! Wick will say. Maybe before morning? You can wait, maybe. But for this one? Sleep. Good night!"

She hopped down and scampered back into her tent. Just like that, the whirlwind of hospitality relented and the rest of the kobolds went back to other tasks or back to bed. The whole exchange felt oddly like some sort of practiced ritual.

"And that's that?" Lattica said, eying the lingering kobolds with uncertainty. "We just... sleep here. Among these creatures?"

"My brother trusts them. And Teya has never given me reason to doubt her. That's enough for me," Euphoria said, hopping down and fetching a pot of water.

"Yeah, well, it's not enough for me. I'll be sleeping in the carriage and eating provisions. If you need help, give a shout. I'll try to get to you before they bite you to pieces."

Lattica hopped down and climbed into the carriage. Euphoria sat on her bed for the evening and inspected the water. She gave it an experimental sip. It tasted clean enough. She felt a paw at her arm before she could have another mouthful. It was a kobold, ears smooth rather than frilled like Teya's. It pointed to a bowl of wine that had been set down before Euphoria had made her beverage preferences known.

"No wine?" the thing warbled in a deeper and far less expert attempt at the language.

"No. Thank you," Euphoria said.

It pointed next to a hunk of meat that had at some point been propped over one of the flames. "No meat?"

"No. Again, thank you."

The kobold nodded and snatched up the wine, messily draining it. It then bounced over to the meat and pulled it from the flames. The monster gnawed through raw flesh, roasting spit, and bone without an ounce of difficulty.

"I think perhaps I'll join Lattica in the carriage for tonight..."

After supper, Tome handed over the mound of books he'd come here to deliver. While his father had been harsh and cold since his arrival, it hadn't been clear to him just how thoroughly his absence and the nature of his departure had angered the man. Brother Inkbrand had always been cold and harsh. It was almost a requirement for his role in the monastery. But once the time had come to bed down for the night, Tome got his first taste of just what his father really thought of him these days.

"I can't believe this is where we're staying," Tome muttered, fighting with the rusted latch for a shuttered window.

"I don't know. Seems rather nice to me. Spacious. Private," Madge said, dropping her sack of things on an old bed and sending a plume of dust into the air.

Their lodging, at least for the night, was indeed quite large. It was about as large as one of the floors of the Masker household, and thus four times the size of the room they'd rented to him. It also was quite clearly not a room intended for extended residency.

"This is a punishment," Tome grunted, finally dislodging the latch and throwing the shutters open to allow the musty room to air out a bit.

"If this is a punishment, I'd love to see what a reward looks like."

"This isn't a bedroom; it's a storage room that happens to have two beds in it. The lodging for initiates and brothers is a hall of bunks, at least six to a room. Higher-level monks get private rooms. I hadn't expected either of us to be permitted to sleep in either of those. They aren't for outsiders. But we have official guest quarters in the north hall. That father saw fit to stuff us into the storage room above the entryway, where the wind will buffet us endlessly, is his way of specifically telling us that he doesn't consider me worthy of even the distinction of being a guest."

"Seems like it'd be easier to just say that," Madge said.

"Overt aggression? That's beneath a monk of the Gate of the Ancients. Text is for the daily tasks of transcription. Personal matters are relegated to subtext."

"Interesting! It's always fun meeting someone's parents. Gives you some real insight into how they got to be who they are," Madge said.

"That I am a product of my father's parenting is a fact that seems unkind to draw attention to. Like being reminded of one's own mortality."

"Aw, you're not that bad," Madge said.

"I'm not the one I was bemoaning, Madge."

"Look, your dad could have just turned us away. He obviously still cares enough about you to make sure you don't end up out in the cold. That's more than a lot of us have."

"You see it as compassion. I see it as him jumping at the opportunity to spend a few more days grinding away at me for leaving. With a healthy dollop of unwillingness to send me away without first looking into the books I brought. Mark my words. The closest Father will come during this entire trip to seeming to be interested in me and my achievements will be when he finally takes the time to ask how the books in that index might be recovered. When I walked out that door to find my fortune, he discarded the notion that he has any bond of blood with me any longer. I'm just a disobedient wretch who happens to share his name. Everything else is going through the motions and keeping up appearances."

Madge fluffed out the blankets. "I'd suggest you should give him the benefit of the doubt, but I've known plenty of people who didn't deserve that, and you know him better than me. You want me to make your bed too? And check it for creepy-crawlies?"

"If you would," he said, gazing out the window.

Positioned directly over the main entrance as it was, this undesirable room had two benefits. The first was, since very few people looped around from the road to the main entrance, it would be relatively quiet. The second was, since the main entrance faced the ocean, so too did the window. And that made for a gorgeous view. One of the few truly positive experiences he remembered from his days here was his time spent sitting out on the top of the cliffs, reading a book and stealing glances at the sparkling sea. He'd never seen it from this vantage, but a little extra height didn't make that much of a difference. It was still the same beautiful sight, and he'd forgotten how much he missed the peace of the salt air and swishing surf. The view slowly took the edge off his frustration. Even

Madge's sudden appearance beside him to join him in taking in the scenery didn't disturb him much.

"You see any boats out there?" she asked.

"The harbor is up north. Mostly the boats heading south do so during the morning. By now we wouldn't see very much, if I remember correctly."

"Well, if you spot one, maybe tell the people downstairs. Apparently someone stole a boat a couple of days ago, and they haven't been able to find it."

"Where did you hear that?"

"While you were helping your dad load up all the books, I wandered around the monastery grounds and chatted folks up."

"How did you manage that? Women aren't allowed to fraternize with the monks unaccompanied." He paused. "That is to say, they aren't allowed to fraternize at all, and they aren't allowed to walk the grounds unaccompanied."

"You guessed 'she' when you met me. Folks around here guessed 'he.' I didn't correct them either. And that meant I was allowed to wander around and chat folks up. Most of them were annoyed. Seems like you folks don't get much time off, do you? Most of them were writing. But one fellow, Cal, I think his name was, he was quite excited about the stolen boat. According to him, one person just charged up onto it while it was anchored, cut the anchor line, and took off with it."

"What sort of a boat?"

"A big one?" she said, hopeful it would be an adequate clarification.

"Why didn't they just chase him down? There aren't very many boats that a single person can easily pilot. They'd only have to chase him until the first major wind change, and they'd be upon him before he could shift the sails."

"Beats me. According to Cal, he just up and vanished after he got far enough from shore."

Tome shook his head. "Brother Cal isn't going to last long. It takes a certain degree of mental fortitude to spend day after day transcribing books and not get a little harebrained. Cal is clearly slipping if he believes that."

"Makes for good conversation, though."

He sighed and turned back to the sea. When he felt properly calm for the first time in days, he started thinking about the bed. He might actually have gotten some decent sleep that night, if he'd stepped back from the window without first glancing down. But he did glance down, and the moment his eyes fell upon the sculpture in front of the monastery from this angle, his mind seized upon the view.

When viewed from above, the Gate of the Ancients looked precisely like one of the complex locking mechanisms from doors within the Greater Lands Wall. The arches obscured it a bit, but everything from the shape of the tiles to their orientations to the scattered presence of lighter-colored stone was a match for the mechanisms Fel and Martin had been gradually deciphering codes to unlock.

His jaw tightened. This could be a coincidence. It could be simply some sort of allusion to Bygone Era mechanisms by the sculpture's designer. But Tome very much doubted this little discovery was as harmless as that. He didn't know precisely what it did mean, but he knew for certain that it meant something. And because it dealt with the Bygone Era, it probably didn't mean anything good. He turned and grabbed the lantern with its still-smoldering flame lit from Wick. It had been far too long since he'd provided the others with an update. The flame was dancing, and thus he couldn't discuss matters with Wick directly. But a hastily written message burned in the flame would reach him just as surely. Now was no time to do a full investigation of the sculpture, but he could at least have a few moments of privacy to inform the others of what he'd seen.

Chapter 8

For the second day in a row, Lord Katritz was awake at dawn. He had no interest in this becoming a common occurrence, but he was nothing if not willing to deal with a dash of adversity if it meant solidifying and enhancing his position in the world. Finding a way to have a relatively discreet meeting was a bit of a trick, but he'd come up with an appropriately clever method. That it turned out to be unnecessary soured his mood considerably, and he was very much looking forward to venting his frustrations on the individuals to whom he could draw a straight line from the current thorn in his side.

He stepped out of his carriage and gazed up at the monument in the town square. It was a feature common within the major cities of Thayne, a walled garden roughly in the center of town. Beffshire had one called Landmark Square, albeit laughably small compared to this one. Its status as a point of pride for the city notwithstanding, Katritz had always seen it as something of an eyesore in Teskal. The wall was tall, angular, and sturdy. Barely embellished at all. Using this as the centerpiece of town was like commissioning an artist to make a sculpture and receiving the unchiseled slab of marble instead. But then, his taste in art and architecture had always been a bit more refined than the common rabble. He wouldn't begrudge them their reverence. Particularly not when he had been granted one of only five keys to the place. It would be horribly crude to deride something that one has been selected as an honored caretaker for.

Velonia Madritz was waiting for him at the small, heavily fortified entry door. She was alone. He plastered his best false smile onto his face and spread his arms as he approached her.

"Ah! Wonderful. Punctual as always. I hope you are prepared for a truly awe-inspiring sight. Oh, the envy the others of this city will feel for you when they learn that you have joined the elite list of people who have been within the city garden!"

He stepped forward and inserted the key into the lock. It was expertly fitted, but like many of the locking mechanisms built during the Bygone Era, simply turning the key was insufficient. There was an entire sequence of lifts and presses, like navigating a maze blindly. He'd refreshed his memory on the sequence that morning, but it was still wise to take it slowly.

Velonia stepped closer and spoke quietly, her tone far harsher than her neutral expression. "I thought we'd agreed you would be discreet."

"I am a lord. Obvious secrecy draws more attention than pointless bombast. And I am in no mood to be lectured at by you of all people on the subject of discretion." The key clicked. He raised his voice. "Ah! Prepare yourself! A sight seen by precious few beyond the nobility of the land!"

He pushed the door open. She slipped inside. He shut and locked the door behind them.

The "splendor" of the city's walled garden was easily one of the greatest overstatements in the history of a city largely defined by overstatement. Only five keys, four of which were in the hands of the king and lords and the last in the hands of the palace guards, meant there was no one to tend to the so-called garden. It was thus more overgrown than lush. If there had ever been exotic flowers and plants inside, they'd been entirely overtaken and replaced by weeds and local flora. Bees and other insects buzzed merrily about. Thick tufts of grass grew up between the stones of the walkway. And even if none of that had been the case, the garden would still have been underwhelming, as the only feature besides soil bursting with vegetation was a wide path leading from the double doors on the opposite side of the garden to a shelter in the center of it, casting shade over what looked like an unusually wide well with a metal cover atop it.

Velonia marched toward the shelter, waving off the insects that were suddenly very interested in the visitors. Katritz kept pace and let loose the rant he'd been carefully sculpting in his head almost from the moment he'd awoken.

"Let me tell you something, Miss Madritz. My intention for rendering this little meeting less worthy of note involved making a fuss to my servants about my interest in attending one of the blasted pointless and entirely optional 'meetings of the lords' this afternoon. The entirely extraneous and universally valueless meetings happen twice a week, and I've typically sent a scribe to take notes rather than waste my time. But by claiming an interest in attending, I could make the argument that other meetings had to be shifted earlier, and thus this would be explained. But that plan was thwarted, and do you know why?"

"We have more important things to—"

"Because the meeting had already been canceled! And why, you may ask, was this long-running meeting canceled? Because Lord Hundt is taking Donovan Verfessa to see his personal stables. The skinny, inbred dolt hasn't even invited me to see the stables, and I'm one of his closest friends. That Beffshire man is a plague upon my house. He is accumulating favor at an astonishing rate, and favor turns to power very quickly, Velonia. I have acquired a rival, and this is your fault."

"None of that will matter in just a few days. Did you bring the sphere?" Velonia asked, stepping into the shelter and gazing down at the covered well.

"Of course I did. It was the whole blasted reason for this errand."

He pulled the contraband contraption from a bulging vest pocket. Held tight to his body by the relatively snug garment, the strange inertia of the contraption was easier to deal with, and the odd lump in his wardrobe was easy enough to disguise with his overcoat.

Velonia looked it over but seemed reluctant to touch it, then cast her gaze upon the well. With his irritating collaborator clearly unwilling to crumble under the force of his rant, he turned to the well to see what was so interesting about the thing. At this distance, what had seemed to be a simple metal cover was subtly revealed to be something more. Fine lines radiated from the center in a curving sweep, like they'd once been a set of straight lines dividing the plate into wedges, but someone had given the center a quarter turn. Along the edge, where the cover met the well, there was a visible gap. The sharp angle of the morning sun allowed the tiniest glimpse of gleaming metallic details hidden within.

"It looks to be in good repair, but that's no surprise. This is Bygone technology. If the fall of an era couldn't destroy it, why would a few hundred years of the elements?" Velonia said.

"And this is the thing? This is what will revolutionize everything, and through it secure me an unbreakable place of power within Thayne?"

"Thayne and the rest of the world," Velonia said. "Now, help me find some markings. I have been instructed by Lens to work out some identifying aspects of the contraption before we can activate it. He will need to make some determinations about it. It will take some time."

"It is covered in markings," he said. "And just precisely how long will it take to make these determinations?"

"Unclear. At least a few days, I would imagine."

"A few days. It has already been a day since I acquired the sphere. It won't be long before it is discovered to be missing. I do not imagine the clod who I was able to trick into allowing me to take it can be relied upon to keep a secret regarding my actions. I need incontrovertible proof that I was right to take my actions before then."

"I make no promises. These things need to be done delicately. Ah, here. I believe these are the markings he was interested in. Here, take the sphere. I'll make a rubbing."

She handed him the contraption and took out a bit of charcoal and a piece of paper. He clutched the device in his grip and stalked angrily around the perimeter of the well. This whole mess was, in part, due to a single leaked message. The risk of scandal and the uncomfortable questions that would be asked regarding the contents of a message vaguely referencing someone or something name Gem had forced him down a road that led him to this unenviable point. The consequences of a lord abusing his privileges to acquire a piece of forbidden technology that it was, in part, his duty to protect would make the Gem nonsense seem quaint and charming by comparison. He briefly considered working out how to quietly return the sphere to the vault until it was once again needed, but each interaction of that sort compounded the risks rather than lessening them. No. It was better—nay, essential—that it be put to its proper use before its removal was discovered.

He lowered his gaze to the thick stone rim around the well. At the precise opposite side of the rim from where Velonia was taking her rubbing, a metal plate with a hinged round cover was set into the stone. He flipped the cover up to find a hemispherical hollow. Small registration marks around the edge were a match for those engraved on the sphere itself.

"Hah. Child's play," he said.

He pressed the sphere into place. A soft click, deep within the wall of the well, affirmed it had been properly seated. Then came the high-pitched whine of unseen gears and wheels working themselves up to speed. In short order, a deeper rumble joined the whine. While the sound of operating machinery slowly subsided, the rumble grew steadily. Velonia looked up from her work.

"What did you do?" she said.

"The task was to determine the operation of the contraption. I have done so," Katritz said, endeavoring to sound more certain than he felt.

"The task was to determine how to operate the contraption safely and securely!" she snapped.

The lord briefly attempted to pull the sphere from its place, but it was quite firmly affixed. If there was a way to remove it, his fingers were simply not the proper tool. The rumbling continued. From the sound of the raised voices outside, it had not gone unnoticed by the rest of the town. Dust tumbled down from the shelter overhead. The rumble, like the whining machinery, finally reached a steady level, just short of tooth-rattling in its intensity. The lines in the metal cover began to widen, each of the curved wedges they'd traced out retracting into the wall to reveal a deep hole. Before their eyes, it was getting deeper. The soil at the bottom roiled and churned, agitating like sand in a sifter. Someone may as well have pulled a stopper from the bottom of the well. The soil was just draining out of it, revealing stone walls. Blocks on one side started to slide out of the wall. Blocks on the other side receded into the wall, giving the entire well a diagonal pitch. As the angle sharpened, the blocks formed a staircase.

The rumble continued, very slowly reducing in intensity. For a moment, the fear of what was happening, and moreover the fear of being punished for making it happen, was pushed aside by the realization that, at least from this vantage, he'd actually achieved what he'd set out to do.

Far to the north, within the Lesser Greater Lands, the flames were still and Euphoria and Lattica were watching as Teya carefully loaded up a series of engraved plates. The unassuming engravings would, if all went according to plan, allow her to wipe the influence of the clockwork diamond at the center of the Lesser Greater Lands from the minds of her people. When Euphoria and Lattica had awoken and eaten breakfast, Teya was already up and about, deep in her instruction from Wick. She was practically crackling with nervous anticipation now that it had been completed.

"I take plates. Take to center. Long trip. You look at plates. New ones, old ones, both. You say if good. If good? Everyone, go to wall. Close as can get. I fix diamond. It works? Everyone can leave. It doesn't? Everyone must leave. Very fast. Or else dead. Is correct?" she said.

"That is an accurate assessment of the situation at present," Wick said.

"And just so I'm clear, this will mean that the creatures here are free to leave?" Lattica said.

"They will no longer feel compelled to remain here, nor will they fail to perceive places besides this place," Wick said. "Assuming Martin's assessment is as accurate as Teya's."

"And what's to stop them from just running amok in the nearby cities? Ram's Rest isn't all that far away, after all," she said.

"Once they leave these walls, they will fall under the influence of the clockwork diamond at the center of the true Greater Lands. That will restore a similar compulsion that kept them here, but directed instead at the Greater Lands," Wick said.

"So once they leave, they'll lack the capacity to do anything but return home? Will they survive? That's a very long journey to have to make without a proper way to interpret the world around them."

"I know it. Very very well," Teya said. "Went to Clickspring. No earring. Same thing. Hard to do? Very. But with help? Small groups, staying close? Safety. I believe. Very very."

"That's still hundreds of these creatures marching across two kingdoms," Lattica said.

"Not hundreds once," Teya correct. "A few, many times. Unless break, not fix. Then all at once."

"That will take ages. And it will still be very dangerous," Euphoria said.

"Difficult? Yes. Worth doing? Very very yes."

"At least there will be time to discuss it before—" Euphoria began.

Teya shushed her and raised one frilled ear. The kobolds around her did the same.

"What? What's wrong?" Euphoria asked.

One by one, the kobolds dropped low to the ground and placed their ear to it.

"Shaking. Big. Deep," Teya said.

"I don't feel anything," Lattica said.

"You will. Soon." Teya chattered at the other kobolds. They dashed off to the west.

"Follow. Stay close. If bad? Many friends, safer," Teya said.

As Teya bounded off, she grabbed a torch and lit it from one of Wick's flames. A few other kobolds did the same and followed.

"I think we should follow them," Euphoria said. "There are plenty of things here to worry about, and I'd rather stay with the experts. Even if I don't feel... no... no—I do feel it now."

The rumbling finally grew strong enough for their comparatively small human ears to pick up. Not long after, they felt it as well as heard it.

Lattica hastily finished hitching the horse into place, and the humans pursued the scampering kobolds. The journey was a short one. Not far from the little tent city the kobolds had been living in was the work camp that had formerly been their "home." The place was largely deserted, stripped of materials, and left in ruin as a way of exacting some small, petty bit of revenge on their captors. The only things fully intact were a few of the stone foundations of the semipermanent buildings that had become far less permanent once a horde of angry kobolds had found some hammers to play with.

One such foundation was dominated by a near match for the stone ring in Teskal's garden. It only lacked the metal cover. Even the socket for the sphere was present, though vacant. The kobolds were perched around the entire perimeter, staring down inside. Euphoria and Lattica hopped down from the carriage, approaching cautiously as the rumbling slowed.

"What is it? Euphoria said. "What's happened?"

Teya pointed into the stone ring. "This? Was shallow, dry well. Was. Not shallow anymore. And not well. Stairs now. Does this happen? A human thing?"

"I've certainly never heard of such a thing," Euphoria said.

Teya addressed the flame. "Wick? You know this?"

"The rumbling is new. But the ring is familiar. There was one distantly visible from Tellestressa Archives. A much larger one. The conquering forces emerged from it," Wick said. "I do not know its nature beyond that."

"A stone hole that a conquering army emerges from?" Lattica said. "That sounds like an excellent thing to keep away from, just in case—"

"I look and see!" Teya crowed.

Without a moment of hesitation, she hopped over the stone rim and scampered down the crude steps formed from the side, torch firmly in her grip. One by one, the other kobolds followed until only a single one remained. Euphoria crept forward and peered over the edge. The staircase continued farther than the morning sun's rays could shine. Even the bobbing light of the torch was soon swallowed into the darkness.

"You've got to admire their enthusiasm," she said.

"I'm not sure I'd call that enthusiasm, and I don't know that it's to be admired," Lattica said.

By the light of the flame, Teya and her cohort finally reached the bottom of the steps. The same crudely formed bricks that had made up the staircase formed the walls and arched ceiling of the tunnel. Teya held the torch high and inspected the masonry. The stonework had a repeating pattern, but it was subtle. Certainly not the result of design or artistic intent. Any given section of it looked to be a random arrangement of poorly cut stone blocks. But squinting down the wall as far as the light shone revealed a repeating pattern, like the same precise blocks occurring in sequence. She took a moment to do her best to find a unique-looking stone, eventually settling on one that had a particularly poorly smoothed surface. She then counted her way along. After precisely twenty blocks, she found another stone that looked to be a perfect twin of the bad block. Twenty more blocks along, there it was again.

"How can this be?" she asked, in her own language, as she was only in the company of kobolds. "Did they do their best to make a copy of each stone and lay them out like this? Or is it actually a copy of the stone?" She turned. "Come, tell me if I'm correct. Is this…"

She trailed off when she realized she was alone. The other kobolds were visible only as gleaming eyes some distance back along the tunnel. She paced back to them and saw a familiar, distant look in their eyes. They'd reached the limit of distance the wall and diamond would allow them to travel.

"We haven't gone past the wall," she said, waving a hand in front of them and barely receiving a reaction. "The tunnel isn't nearly long enough for that. And it isn't depth. They had you working in the mines, and they ran much deeper than this."

She paced past them, the group shuffling with her until they were near enough to the entrance for the logic and wisdom to return to their eyes.

"Go back. Tell the humans I am going to continue investigating. I will return if I find anything bad. Or good."

The others nodded, a dash of gratitude in their words and expressions as they were given permission to leave this fuzzy, lost feeling behind. When they were safely away, she turned and continued down the tunnel. After about ten copies of the brick pattern had passed, the quality of the echo seemed to change. Not long after, she came to a branching path. The tunnel continued forward, but a second tunnel led off to the right as well. A short hoot and shout sent back two very different echoes from the two paths. The one directly ahead seemed much quicker, much more subdued. The end of that tunnel was near. She took a moment to scratch a mark into the stone to indicate which direction she'd arrived from and continued forward.

Not a dozen paces along, she found the first unique feature of the tunnel. It was a bit of debris. Not from the ceiling or walls; those seemed fairly intact. More to the point, the debris wasn't stone but metal. A twisted bit of bronze or brass, to her eye. It wasn't natural. The thing looked like it had been part of a well-shaped bar before it had been damaged by whatever misadventure had led it here. More bits and pieces sparkled in the distance. Each step forward cast Wick's light upon a tunnel floor increasingly scattered with the broken pieces of metal. Other things mixed in among them before long: high-quality fasteners; jagged, broken pieces of wood. She was wading through the stuff before long, with steadily more variety.

A minute or so later and she was no longer walking on the ground. The floor was completely covered with debris, forcing her to scamper atop it. The level of the debris eventually reached so high that she had to crouch along the top of it to avoid scraping her head on the ceiling.

"Strange," Teya said. "Is this a tunnel made for throwing trash in?"

"Stop. Wait," Wick said suddenly. "Beside your left foot."

She looked down and brushed some bits of broken stone aside. The top half of a wood-plank sign was jutting up from the pile. She pulled it free.

"That is a portion of a street sign that was in False Clickspring," he said.

"I thought False Clickspring was gone. Claimed by the land," Teya said.

"It would seem the land dumped at least some of it here, wherever here is," Wick said. "The location is unclear to me."

Teya crouched and rummaged through the debris some more. As she dug, all the little habits and instincts that kept a beast like her safe and fed continued ticking merrily along. She listened. She sniffed the air. And both of those little habits delivered fragments of a very important message. The air had the merest dash of the scent of blood. And somewhere farther along the tunnel, there was the almost imperceptible wheeze of pained breathing.

"Someone is here," she said quietly. "And they are hurt."

She threw Wick's torch forward into the narrow gap between the debris and the ceiling and scrambled forward. A few minutes of half-digging, half-crawling led her to a place where the ceiling lifted away somewhat. The whole river of broken stone, metal, and timber tilted upward into what she realized was a match for the stairs that had brought her here from the surface. And at the point where the debris mounded up at the bottom of those stairs was a pile of broken scaffolding and a badly battered worker. He was dazed. Barely conscious. He must have ridden the avalanche of debris this far, because if he'd tumbled down that many stairs, he wouldn't have been breathing. Larger chunks of timber and debris fully clogged the stairwell a short distance farther along, and from the slow, quiet crackle of wood bowing under stress, it wouldn't be holding back the next cascade of stone and metal for much longer.

She grabbed him as best he could and started hauling him back, leaving the torch behind.

"Tell them on the surface I'll need help!" she called to Wick.

The little beast grunted and huffed. It probably wasn't doing this man any favors to have his already battered body dragged over a few dozen yards of stone and debris, but a snap and a fresh rush of stone hammered home the fact that another minute or two of delay would have been the end of him. She dragged him until she saw the glow of a torch along the tunnel. The others had come as near as the mental affliction of this place would allow them, but when she reached them, they snapped to attention and helped haul the injured man toward the surface.

Euphoria and Lattica stood by, accompanied by a single kobold, while the scraping of claws and paws gradually approached from within the tunnel. Lattica had bandages ready. Euphoria had water ready to clean wounds. The torch beside them was still, Wick watching and waiting in the tense moment.

Lattica leaned toward Euphoria and whispered, "Are we sure they simply found an injured man?"

"As opposed to what?" Euphoria said. "Crawling through a hole in the ground and savaging the first thing they came across?"

"Yes," Lattica said simply.

"You're here to be my bodyguard, among other things, and as such I respect your caution, but I think these creatures have illustrated their demeanor."

"Maybe so, but if this man ends up looking like there's a bite taken out of him, I'm getting you out of here and we'll take our chances with whoever Lens has sent after us."

"Sensible."

The kobolds emerged from the tunnel and set the man down. Two things were immediately clear. First, this man's injuries were from a fall, not claws and teeth. And second, he was no stranger. The torn and damaged clothes he wore, which Lattica had to cut away to expose the lacerations, were a worker's uniform. The cuffs of his sleeves and the cuffs of his trousers both featured the Graves family crest. More specifically, one specific branch of the family tree.

"This is one of Nevil's men," Euphoria said.

"Certainly looks like it," Lattica said.

"He doesn't seem to be at death's door," Euphoria said.

"No. He'll make it. It might be a few minutes before he comes out of this daze. Just as well. It's keeping him from squirming... or screaming his head off when he realizes he's surrounded by kobolds."

"Teya, you had told me there were workers digging about in the remains of False Clickspring. Is this one of those men?" Euphoria asked.

She shrugged. "Humans are humans. But there were things! Clickspring things. In the tunnel. Broken."

"How far did you walk in that tunnel?"

Teya looked about. "From here? As far as tree. Maybe more. Maybe less. Not much."

"That's not nearly far enough to have reached False Clickspring. Even outside this place, where distances make sense, that's not far enough," Euphoria said.

Euphoria looked over the man as Lattica finished binding the more troublesome wounds. As she did, her mind tugged and twisted at the new knots that had been presented to her.

"I don't feel any broken bones. Maybe a finger or two. I think this is as good as we'll be able to do," Lattica said.

"Good. Teya, if we could move him into the carriage."

"Yes! Sure sure." She chattered something to the others, who helpfully scooped up the weakly shifting man and hauled him to one of the seats within the carriage. "Why the carriage?"

"Because he seems to be coming around, and I think I'll have more luck getting answers out of him if he doesn't have to grapple with being surrounded by kobolds immediately upon awakening. No offense, but you folk are disquieting to the unprepared."

"Yes! This makes sense. Same for you. Humans? To kobolds? Scary. Very very."

"Good. I'm glad we see eye to eye. Lattica, join me?"

"Of course."

The women climbed into the carriage and shut the doors. For the first time since the trip began, three of the four seats inside the carriage were filled. A few minutes of uncomfortable moaning and fluttering of his eyes eventually brought the injured man around. His eyes fixed on Euphoria, and pain was briefly tempered with confusion.

"Mrs. Graves?" he groaned.

"There are quite a few of us. Do you have enough wits about you to recall a first name?" she said.

"Euphoria? Euphoria Graves?"

"Quite so. That is encouraging. You've had a bit of a fall."

"I know." He tried to adjust himself in the seat and, after a wince of pain, thought better of it. "I thought I was done for. What are you doing here?"

"We'll go through that in a moment. Do you need anything? Water? Food?"

"I don't think I could stomach anything right now."

"You should try to drink anyway." She handed him a canteen. "Tell me. Do you remember what happened? And how it happened?"

"I was digging. The job, you know. I had to dig up the... the, uh..." He rubbed his head. "I don't... I don't think I'm supposed to tell anybody."

"A secret? Even from the other Graves family members?"

"It was... my boss was... he was pretty clear."

"Nevil will be pleased to know that even in such a state, you are willing and able to keep his secrets for him."

"He was pretty clear, was the thing, and... I don't... I don't think I was even supposed to say he was the boss."

"Uniforms are rather poorly suited for those trying to keep secrets. Tell me what happened. The accident. That much you can tell me."

"I was digging. Everything started shaking, and then the ground sort of opened up. Like the plug was pulled on a tub. The scaffold buckled and I went right down."

"And what were you digging for?"

"That's... that's one of the things I can't say."

"Perhaps if I guess? There is no harm in telling me if I am incorrect, surely."

"I... I suppose."

"Were you digging for a tunnel?"

"No."

"Were you expecting a tunnel? Perhaps told to watch out for one?"

"No."

"Does the name Mr. Lens mean anything to you?"

"It doesn't."

So far, his answers seemed earnest. They came with the casual dash of relief that comes from not having to lie.

"Were you digging for Bygone contraptions?"

He shifted uncomfortably and did not answer.

"Were you doing a vault dive? Excavating a ruin in search of any random treasure you might find?"

"No. I wasn't doing that."

"So you were looking for specific contraptions. Contraptions you knew you'd find?"

He shifted again. "I think maybe I shouldn't be answering any questions at all. I think you're going to figure it out if I keep answering, and that'll make Mr. Graves cross with me."

"Again, I can certainly appreciate that. It is laudable to have such a dedication to your assignment despite the situation you are in."

"You rescued me. I'm not in a situation anymore."

"Aren't you?" Euphoria opened the carriage door. "Teya? A word?" she said.

The kobold popped her head into view.

"What in the world? What is that?"

"A friend of the family. My family. The Masker family. Teya, I think you could set our friend at ease with a friendly smile."

Teya tipped her head and grinned, revealing twin rows of teeth as cruel as arrowheads.

"Th-the Maskers are friends with a monster?"

"Oh, no, no," Euphoria said. "Not just one. Teya, would you invite your associates over to say hello?"

She turned and chattered. A dozen more heads popped into view, some even dropping down to peer in the door from above. Her grin briefly became a bit of a smirk. Teya squinted one eye at Euphoria in something akin to a wink. She then chittered to the others once more. The kobolds grinned in unison.

"What are you going to do?" the worker asked.

"Me? Well, I had intended to have a nice long conversation with you. But as you seem unwilling to chat, I suppose we are through here, and I'll be asking you to leave."

Teya's grin widened, and she rubbed her paws together. The others followed suit, though this did send the upside-down one tumbling down past the doorway.

"I'll talk! I'll talk! I have loads more to say!"

"Oh! How nice. Thank you, Teya. I appreciate the help," Euphoria said.

The kobold nodded and dropped down from the side of the carriage. The others followed. Five more of them dropped by the door, jumping down from where they'd been perched, unseen, on the roof. She pulled the door shut.

"What were you digging for?" she asked.

"Lots of things. Uh. Not lots. Two things, but a lot of both. The main thing was these… statue things. Wood and metal. Mostly metal. No heads. Weird joints in them. We found dozens of them. A lot of them were broken; a lot of them weren't. And parts of them, too. Lots of those. It took a lot of digging to get down to where they were, but once we did we must have filled six, seven wagons with those things over the last few weeks."

"And the other items?"

"I don't know. He gave us a sketch."

He grimaced, trying and failing to reach for something in his pocket. Lattica fetched it from him and handed it to Euphoria.

There were two drawings. One was a sketch of a small locking chest with a panel labeling it A-8. The other was a reasonably simple-looking contraption that had the general appearance of a small chandelier or a gilded spider.

"Do you know what this is?"

"They didn't tell me that."

"No. I don't suppose they would. And do you know why they didn't want anyone else in the family to know?"

"They didn't tell me that either."

"Again, unsurprising. Well, I believe that is all for now. For your cooperation, reluctant though it may have been, I'll ask you to stay here and stay comfortable. Lattica and I have some business to attend to."

She opened the door and stepped out, Lattica close behind.

"Teya?" Euphoria called.

The kobold trotted over. "It was helpful?" she asked, winking somewhat more obviously.

"Exceedingly. Thank you. Is a torch with Wick's flame about? I have to send a message to my father."

"Of course!"

She scampered away. Lattica cleared her throat.

"Thoughts?" Euphoria said.

"Do you think your method of information extraction is going to be a problem for us?" Lattica asked.

"Lattica, I think we already have problems. The focus now is finding out how many, and how to solve them."

Allie blinked the last bit of sleep from her eyes and trotted out into the cool dawn air. She'd been dead asleep a minute ago, as she'd only been able to chase the last folks out of The Fox and Log a few hours earlier. But there were few things better suited to jar a person from sleep than having the whole house rattle and quake around them without explanation. The streets were flooded with people who had similarly been roused from sleep and were looking for answers. For the most part, they were asking each other what was going on, for lack of a better choice. She had to shrug off several such questions as she navigated the streets. Unlike most people in this part of town, or any part of town, Allie did have someone better to ask. In short, if something unexpected and dangerous was happening in town, chances were very good that the Maskers were involved.

As she hustled through Beffshire, she saw that a little rumbling had a way of causing a lot of chaos. The market district had more than its share of shopkeepers and vendors hauling barrels of damaged or destroyed merchandise. The things that make a pottery display sturdy and pretty don't have much overlap, and since it takes a very cautious shopkeep to suppose that the shelves attached to the wall might shake and tremble, a lot of people had learned just how little vibration it takes to send an entire inventory tumbling to the floor. The same rules applied to handheld lanterns set on shelves. If it had been more firmly at night, and the dawn sun hadn't risen quite so far, half the city might have been ablaze from fallen candles and such. As it was, the scent of smoke and char was in the air, but no out-of-control fires were burning.

When she reached the street with Masker's Antiquities, Allie saw that she wasn't alone in her insight into the Maskers and bizarre happenings. Captain Boltt was in front of the shop, having a highly animated conversation with a bleary-eyed Martin. The lesser harpies were arranged on the roof, watching with interest.

"I assure you, Captain. I would dearly love to say I knew what caused this. A few rather precious statuettes fell from the shelves as a result. But it was not my doing."

"I'm not saying you caused it, Martin," the captain snapped. "I'm asking if it's happening because of you." He pointed at the facade of a nearby store. "You see that patched-up bit of brick? That's from when a hippogriff went mad and tried slicing up your boy. Remember? These things happen around you, and I want to know if there is any reason that this might be one of those things."

"I can't say for certain that it isn't someone trying to do something to me or my family, but I don't have any control over that or insight into it," Martin said.

"You're an expert in antiquities, aren't you? A historian of sorts? Has this ever happened before that you're aware of?"

"Nothing in memory. I could look through some of my books if you like, but it will take some time."

"Rotten chicken rat," remarked Rudy from above.

The captain rubbed his face. "If I wanted research, I'd have asked for it. People are going to be asking questions, and I can't afford to wait for answers. What about contraptions? Are there any contraptions that could shake a whole town like that?"

"In theory one could be made, but I don't have any in my possession, and I don't imagine I'd ever have any need for one."

"Stinky thief," added Moody.

"If a contraption did do this, where would it be located? What would it look like?"

"Obviously I can't know that with any certainty either. But I can reason it out a bit. It would have to be very far away, because to my eye it doesn't seem as though any one part of the city suffered greater damage than the rest. If something in the city was causing this, it would stand to reason that things closer to it would receive greater damage than things farther away. As for size, it would have to be quite large, I suppose, though it may not appear large visually in isolation. I've recently discovered that what appears to be an isolated contraption can in actuality be a component mechanism in a much larger compound contraption that—"

"Masker," he barked.

"I'm sorry. I'm sorry, this is a fascinating conundrum. Er... I would say this is probably a large contraption located either quite distant from the city or buried some distance beneath it. Were I to make a wager, buried beneath it makes the most sense. It would very effectively shake the city, and Bygone contraptions tend to be found some distance belowground. But I'm afraid that's all I can give you."

"Monkey stinking monkey—" Judy interjected.

Boltt shot a furious look at the harpies. In a testament to the raw intensity of his anger and authority, the four of them huddled down a bit.

"…rat," Judy finished, almost meekly.

The captain gritted his teeth and glared at Martin. The remarkable capacity for authority figures to assign fault and blame in whatever way they saw fit was on full display here, as it was crystal clear the captain now considered Martin Masker to be entirely responsible for this unexplained phenomenon remaining unexplained, and potentially for it even happening in the first place.

"Keep me informed if you learn anything more," he snapped before stomping away.

Martin stepped back into the shop. Once Boltt was far enough away that Allie was confident she wouldn't catch any residual ire from him by being in the wrong place at the wrong time, she slipped inside the shop as well. Martin was helping Vivian and Epiphany inspect and reorganize the goods that had been jostled by the rattling.

"Hello, Mr. and Mrs. Masker. Hello, Epiphany. Sorry to intrude. Anything I can do to help?" Allie said.

"Allie! Not at all, no intrusion. Please, come inside. I apologize for the mess," Vivian said.

"Hey, no need to apologize. I heard the whole thing with the Watch. This isn't your fault." She cleared her throat. "Unless you weren't being entirely honest with him."

"I was entirely forthcoming," Martin said. "I would never claim ignorance about something that could do this to a whole city."

"Good to know you're a decent, honest man, but I wouldn't be honest if I didn't say that I wish you had a little more light to shed. Here, let me help."

She picked up one of the fallen music boxes. It was none the worse for wear from the fall. Allie tried to assemble her thoughts in her mind. She honestly hadn't imagined it was possible that she would come here and not leave with at least a notion of what had happened. Once you knew someone in your city was a magnet for disaster, you could plan accordingly. Having a disaster strike the town, even a minor one, that didn't have its roots in Masker's Antiquities cast the situation in a different light, like finally finding an umbrella that could stand up to the rain, only to discover that today the rain had chosen to fall sideways.

As she tried to grapple with the possibility that she'd have to start dealing with being friends with the Maskers, working for Verfessa, and subject to mysterious natural disasters, the flame burning in the lantern on a shelf upstairs came to a stop.

"Ah. All of you are in the same place," Wick said. "That will save time, and presently there seems to be very little to spare."

"What now?" said Allie and Epiphany at the same time.

"There has been an unexplained event in the Lesser Greater Lands. No major danger to Euphoria, Lattica, or Teya, but still a matter of great concern."

"Unless it involved the whole region shaking like there was a stampede, I think we have greater concerns here," Epiphany said.

"Have you received news of this event through alternate means?" Wick asked.

"What? No," she said. "Did... did that happen up there too?"

"Indeed. A short but relatively intense quaking of the ground. The kobolds were able to track it to its source, or at least its area of greatest effect. It was a platform which, according to Teya, they had previously believed to be a well filled with soil. Following the event, the well formed the entrance to a tunnel. Did a tunnel appear in your region as well?"

"Not that we've encountered," Martin said. "But the chaos of the quake has not subsided sufficiently for people to be likely to have investigated such matters if the placement of the tunnel is not obvious."

"Euphoria sent me to inform you, and to inquire if you had any insight into the phenomenon," Wick said.

"It is genuinely flattering that so many people consider me wise enough to be the first point of contact after such a curious event. I'm afraid I don't have any additional information for you off the top of my head... though now knowing that tunnels and... wells, was it?"

"Not a genuine well, but a circular hole approximately the size of the Beffshire city gate, if it was lying down on the ground," Wick clarified.

"Did the stones that formed the ring feature any markings?" Martin asked, snatching a notebook from behind the counter and scribbling some notes.

"There was a small collection of scattered markings. Crudely rendered by Bygone Era standards."

"Yes, well, the Lesser Greater Lands was not created by people of the era. The creation would be an imitation and thus lacking some degree of accuracy. But perfect accuracy is not strictly necessary for functionality." Martin held up the book. "Were any of these runes included?"

"The third, fifth, and ninth runes seem to have been present."

"Interesting, interesting. Fascinating, even."

"Do you just know those cold?" Allie asked. "They're just floating in your head?"

"Normally, no. But I've been working rather hard to help Teya with something, so some runes are fresh in my mind. Those are runes involved in the operation of the clockwork diamond. Do we know any more?"

"The tunnel appeared to lead, with disproportionate speed, to the ruins of False Clickspring. There was more to the tunnel, but Teya was unable to investigate it prior to dispatching me."

"Is there anything else?" Vivian asked.

"They encountered an injured worker in the employ of the Graves family who confessed to digging up a sizable quantity of damaged automatons over the course of the last few weeks, as well as a contraption that was unfamiliar to me but which I have memorized and can sketch for you if you require."

"Yes! Immediately. Downstairs to the workshop."

"Wait!" Allie said quickly.

"What is it?" Martin asked with the tone of a child being kept from his favorite game.

"What about Fel?" she asked.

"Fel is currently astride the neck of an ancient dragon, flying over the sea within the Greater Lands, and will remain so until at least this evening, when the dragon will have to find an island to rest upon. He is dealing with the least uncertainty among those presently under my oversight."

"Sure. Nothing uncertain about flying on a dragon's back," Allie snarked.

Martin dashed down the stairs. The flame began to flicker. While still grappling with the revelations, Allie was jostled from her swirling musings by a touch on the shoulder from Epiphany.

"Allie. I don't suppose you have a moment," she asked.

"A moment? Right now what I'd like to do is go back home and get to sleep, but there's not much hope of that happening. Barring that, I'm a little worried what's become of the bar. Loads of shelves full of glass bottles aren't likely to survive a good shaking particularly well. So if you have something for me, I'll ask that you make it more important than either of those two things."

"That will be a matter of judgment for you, not me. But I'm sure, having heard all that we just heard, that I'm not alone in wondering if all that rattling we endured was due to the presence of one of those tunnels."

"The thought had crossed my mind, but if there is one, it can't be inside the town. Something the size of the gate isn't the kind of thing that'd be hidden inside a building, and I sure haven't seen anything in this town that matches that description."

"My thoughts exactly, which means it's in a part of the town we haven't seen, or a part that's been built up, or built over."

"We've both lived here all our lives. There's not much we haven't seen," Allie said.

"I know, but if there's a tunnel like that nearby, it's worth knowing where it is. Especially considering we don't know where it leads or what it's for. So let's put our heads together."

"The presence of a tunnel means it will have to be fairly isolated," Vivian reasoned, having evidently been eavesdropping on the conversation. "Most of the buildings in this town have very deep basements. So unless the tunnel leads straight down, it will have to be far enough for the slope to avoid popping out into any basements."

"There aren't a whole lot of isolated spots in Beffshire. We're kind of on top of each other around here. Maybe dead center of the livestock district? But that's some awfully muddy ground. I don't think there's a well hiding anywhere there."

"It could run along the streets. The north street out of town and the one in from the west are about as wide as the gate," Epiphany reasoned.

"Even so. The north gate ends in that weird three-way intersection. And the other one..." Allie began.

She trailed off as she and the others came to the same conclusion.

"The big festival place," Allie said.

"Landmark Square," Epiphany agreed.

"It's got that big grandstand. The founders might have been dumb enough to build it over a well or whatever," Allie said.

"It would have been built right after the Bygone Era ended," Vivian said. "Martin is always on about how much of a dedication people had to finding ways to cover up the evidence of contraptions and such in those days. Hence half of the vaults that ended up getting cleaned out by his ancestors."

"All right. So if there's a tunnel, it's under the grandstand in Landmark Square," Allie said. "What good does knowing that do us? It isn't like we can get in there to check it out. They lock up Landmark Square for every day of the year besides Founder's Day, and that's not for months."

"The good it does us is, if we hear something unpleasant happening near Landmark Square, it's probably related. So we should either stay clear of the square or keep an eye on it," Epiphany said.

Allie winced. "Tell me you aren't about to ask me to keep an eye on it."

"No, no, no. You have enough on your plate. Frankly, so do I. I'd suggest we find a place to perch Wick to keep an eye on things, but he's stretched thin as well. And that's all of us fresh out of people we can impose upon."

Allie scratched her chin. "Actually... maybe not. I'll get back to you."

Among a rapidly growing list of lessons Fel had truly never expected to learn, presently he was discovering just how unpleasant it was to travel by dragon-back. He was straddling Kazel's neck, huddled mostly behind the crown of horns blossoming from the top of his head. It shielded him from the worst of the whistling wind, though if he'd been thinking, he would have had the sylphs bring his goggles from his gear as well. At his size, riding Kazel was anything but comfortable. It was less like riding a horse and more like someone had flipped a boat upside down and asked Fel to ride that. He was uncomfortably close to doing a split, thanks to the sheer thickness of the dragon's neck, and the spike-like neck frills meant he had to be very mindful with his position. On the plus side, his proximity to Kazel's head meant he could speak to the dragon without having to scream over the wind. It was a mercy that was owed mostly to Kazel's sharp hearing, but it meant he at least had conversation to keep his mind occupied.

"When I was a boy," Fel shouted, "there were only two times any of the other kids ever talked about dragons."

Kazel released a hissing breath, which Fel decided served as an acknowledgment.

"There were the little kids who were terrified of the very idea of dragons," he said. "And there were the ones who daydreamed about all the exciting tales people made up about dragons. Most of them fancied themselves would-be dragonslayers."

"This is as I would expect," Kazel rumbled.

"If it makes you feel any better, that Duurth character is about as big as they ever imagined dragons get, and I don't think they could take out even him. But there's always one or two kids who dream about riding dragons. Drawing pictures of it. Talking about how majestic it would be. It's nice to know they are just as wrong. I feel like any moment now the wind is going to pluck me off your back and send me smashing into the sea. And I don't want to think about what shape my hips will be in by the time I climb off your back."

"Humans believe the world is made for them," Kazel said.

"Speaking as a contraptioneer, and considering what the Greater Lands Wall achieved, we're pretty good at rebuilding it to suit our purposes."

"You are skilled at building cages. To keep your enemies in or to hide yourselves in. It is the only skill humans truly have. Building cages."

"We're pretty good at weapons, too."

"No. Only cages. You're so good at building cages and choosing new shapes for them, you begin to fool yourselves about their nature. Even the weapons are another form of cage."

"I don't follow."

"You arm yourselves. And when armed, you fancy yourselves equal to the challenge of your foes. So you face your foes. Surround yourselves with your foes. But you know that without your weapons, your foes will overcome you. So you cannot go where you cannot bring a weapon. You wear them like shackles. Suits of armor? Contraption weapons? All artfully crafted and cleverly disguised cages. In the elven language, the name for humans is 'forgers of chains.'"

"I can see how a bunch of creatures who spent their lives locked in cages we built would see the world that way," Fel grumbled.

"You take my words as criticism. A cage is like anything else. Only as good or bad as its use. We all build cages. Those who lead live in a cage of obligation, dedicated to protecting and advancing those they oversee. Those who value familial bonds build a cage of loyalty and concern. Villains build cages to protect themselves from their foes. Heroes build cages to protect the weak from the evil. And legends live in a cage built by destiny, guiding them to their intended fate."

"Don't tell me you're going to be singing the praises of destiny too."

"It does not warrant praise. Destiny will have its way regardless of what we choose to believe or how we worship or deride it. The most important choice a creature has is which cages it chooses to live in. That is as near to freedom as any of us have. But destiny is the cage we do not choose. For even the beasts who choose no cage of their own, destiny is the one cage we can't escape."

"You know, if you people keep talking about destiny and how we can't escape it, you're going to make me want to escape it just to be contrary. I'm like that."

"To seek to escape destiny is to acknowledge it exists. And worse, to show the hubris of claiming to know one's own destiny with certainty."

"Is this what happens when you get locked in a room for hundreds of years? You just sit there, thinking yourself in circles about things you can't ever truly know."

"The alternative is madness."

"I'm not sure I see a difference."

"And how do you view a tiny, flightless creature hurling gentle but unmistakable barbs of mockery toward the creature that is presently carrying it through the sky?"

"Look, I never said I wasn't stupid or crazy. This, what I'm doing right now, is not something a sane, intelligent person does. But just like when you start talking yourself into seeing cages everywhere when you've got chains around your neck, I need to at least acknowledge the mess I'm in, or it'll drive me to despair."

"Then hurl your barbs, Fel Masker. You have earned that." Kazel rumbled a half growl. "For now, at least."

Tome glanced back out the front door of the monastery toward its titular monument. He'd slipped out of bed well before dawn after hours of lying awake, wondering what it could mean that the monument had so close a resemblance to the lock of a Bygone Era vault door. It was a small mercy that he'd not yet reached the monument when the ground began to shake, or he would have easily convinced himself that his investigations had been the cause of the quaking ground. The chaos in the monastery had been fairly short-lived. This was a lifestyle that rewarded calm and reason, so when it was clear there was no immediate danger beyond a small fire caused by a fallen candle that was fortunately handled before it did any lasting damage, the others had settled back down.

"I can't believe they were able to get back to sleep," Tome muttered to himself. "If there is one thing that convinces me I was right to leave this place, it is how thoroughly the others here have squashed their curiosity. Though I do sometimes envy the peace of mind that can come from disregarding things you don't understand rather than investigating them. If nothing else, it would leave me better rested."

He approached the edge of the monument, his lantern in hand. It was a small wonder that he'd been able to keep the flame lit from Wick smoldering in it for this long, particularly with Madge perpetually hanging about, preventing him from engaging with it. At the moment, the flame was dancing. A shame, because this rare bit of solitude would have been an excellent time to receive and provide an update. But right now he was more interested in the lantern's light than the conversation. He stepped closer to the monument and squinted at the shapes. Up close, the resemblance to the complex locking mechanism was much less pronounced. The color variations between blocks of stone were more muted, and the designs etched into them were large and clumsy looking. He had to hold the image of the contraption from above in his mind and try to draw links between features he'd spotted from above and what he was seeing now. And to be frank, what he was seeing now wasn't much. He'd have to climb on top of the thing to get a good look. Before his little discovery, he'd have avoided climbing all over it simply because it was disrespectful to an important aspect of the monastery. Now, he was doubly concerned about getting anywhere near the thing. He'd seen what had happened when Fel had incorrectly entered an unlocking sequence. It stood to reason that a larger lock would have a larger trap.

After nearly three full minutes of consideration, he resigned himself to an idea a child could have thought of. A short search turned up a large rock. He would heave it onto the face of the monument, and if nothing happened, he'd consider it safe enough to inspect at least as far as where the stone had landed. It was silly, both in that there was no real reason to believe if a stone didn't activate it that a human wouldn't and in that Madge had been scampering about on the thing yesterday and hadn't been rendered a smoldering grease stain by some ancient contraptioneer's handiwork. But this was the best balance he could strike between his thirst for knowledge and his quest for safety.

He heaved the stone and, from the moment it struck, he knew something was wrong. There was no flash of light. No clank of battering rams or ring of steel spikes. There was a clack of stone against stone. And more importantly, a long reverberation of echoes. Precisely as though the space beneath it was hollow.

"No. That's not possible," he said.

He cautiously climbed onto the face of the monument, testing each successive block as he moved toward where the stone had landed. And with each step, the sound of his boots striking the stone produced the same echo. He knew the stone had been resting on solid ground yesterday. When Madge climbed out onto it, he hadn't heard the echo. Could the rumbling have been a sinkhole or some sort of underground collapse? If so, what were the odds that only the land beneath the monument would fall away and not disrupt so much as a stone in the process?

Slow searching turned up a place where two rings of stone and the seams between two stone blocks intersected. The rounded edges of the four stones came together to reveal a gap just about large enough to stick a finger into. He dashed to the edge and found a pebble, then hurried back and dropped it through. He heard it click and clack along stone that couldn't have been more than a few yards away. Stone. Not soft earth. This was something man-made. He just knew it. But surely if there was some sort of vault or room beneath the monument, the monks would have said something.

He shut his eyes and tried to recall everything he could about the monument, but his harried mind could only churn up the pointless little facts he'd relayed to Madge. He trudged to the perimeter, looking over the symbols with a fresh eye. Most of them meant nothing to him, though he suspected Martin would have had a great deal to say about them, as it was becoming increasingly clear that this had some sort of connection to contraptions. The only symbol that had a meaning he'd actually been taught about was on the large stone pointed roughly toward the west. The warning to seafarers about the pit of the sea, a stretch of ocean that had claimed dozens of ships over the years. It was a thing that no one truly understood, but all had learned it was better to avoid than to investigate. Too many sailors and too much cargo had been lost already. The cost of curiosity was too high.

The sky behind him was still slowly brightening, and thus the sky on the western horizon was still firmly in the grips of night. He didn't truly expect to see anything when he looked. Even if it was broad daylight, there was nothing to see. Nothing but sea from shore to horizon. Even boats wouldn't be on that stretch of sea, specifically for fear of encountering the pit of the sea. But when he looked, he felt something. Something that would have been meaningless to him until just a few months ago. The very same faint feeling he'd been dreading when he was investigating the so-called plague in Fenfield. It was a faint flutter of his mind, a dart of his eyes that he would have dismissed at any other time. But right now, it may as well have been a slap to the face.

"I need a telescope, my pack, and some blasted daylight..." he said, dashing for the monastery.

CHAPTER 9

Euphoria stood before the flickering flames, waiting for them to go still. Meanwhile, she turned the charred mask that they'd acquired along with Lens's lantern about in her hands.

"Has anyone ever told you that a watched pot never boils?" Lattica said.

"When I was a little girl, when I tried to get Father to teach me how to make the stew that more or less kept the family alive, since it was one of the only things he knew how to prepare, I accidentally let the pot boil over, so there are risks for not watching a pot as well."

Lattica picked up a bottle of wine, still set out for them in a kobold attempt at hospitality. She sniffed it. "What do you think the odds are this'll make me go blind?" she asked. "I don't like to drink so early in the morning, but I don't like anything else about what's going on, and a bit less clarity of thought would be rather nice right about now."

"Frankly, I wish I had a bit more clarity of mind. I inherited a bit of Father's focus, but insight into contraptions isn't quite so hereditary. Now would be a wonderful time for our two places to be swapped, him and me. This mask would potentially solve a lot of problems in his hands."

"The Scholar, right?" Lattica said.

"Right. And a half-functional Diplomat was able to launch the Graves family to new heights of success. One can only imagine what a fully functional Scholar could achieve. Not only does this mask, if it can be repaired, contain huge amounts of information, it was designed to educate. No games aimed at teasing information out of a Student. No attempting to cast general knowledge questions as diplomatic questions. A specific, direct education."

"And you're confident your father can fix it?"

"No. But I'm confident no one else can, and he has the best chance."

The flame went still.

"Euphoria," Wick said.

"What do you have for me, Wick?" she said.

"A great deal. First, he has a theory about the contraption diagram. It appears to be a lock, or more specifically, a secondary lock. He says it is almost certainly a device used to prevent a Bygone Era vault door from being opened, even if one knows the proper code. He found a small passage in one of his texts in which a similar device was used to secure a door after a man learned his brother had been robbing him thanks to knowledge of the code to his door, and thus an additional means to lock it was necessary."

"Curious..."

"Martin also wishes to inform you that the rumbling you experienced was experienced in Beffshire as well, though no similar tunnel has been forthcoming. There has been some minor damage to the city, nothing tragic. The Watch is investigating. Epiphany and Allie are attempting to investigate further as well."

"Wait. Truly? The ground shook in Beffshire? When?"

"To the best of our knowledge, at or about the time it was rumbling here."

"That cannot be a coincidence."

"That seems to be the prevailing feeling among the rest of your family as well."

"Anything else?"

"Only that the symbols around the outside of the tunnel have a similarity to those associated with the clockwork diamond."

Euphoria's mind churned through the possibilities. "Teya. Teya? Where has she gone off to?" She singled out one of the other kobolds. "Where is Teya?"

The kobold she'd asked gave her a stricken look and scrunched its face up in its efforts to reply. "Teya. ... swim... on... rock... bottoms?" he croaked.

"One of my flames is presently some distance away underground. As the one at the bottom of the second exit to the tunnel has burned out, it may be safe to assume it is presently in the possession of Teya. Shall I deliver her the update and ask for one from her regarding her whereabouts?"

"If you would."

The flame fluttered to motion as Wick departed.

"That sounded like you had a pretty specific idea in mind," Lattica said.

"Not so much an idea as a notion. And quite a wild one. But given our present situation, a wild notion doesn't feel quite as farfetched."

"And that notion is?"

The flame went still once more. "Teya is still exploring the branching network of tunnels," Wick said.

"Branching network?" Lattica said. "I thought there was just the one turn."

"One turn led to another, and another. Some have led to locked doors that she has wisely chosen to avoid interacting with. Others led to evidence of other cave-ins."

"But none have led to the surface?" Euphoria asked.

"Not yet," Wick said.

"How quickly can she be back here?"

"As I understand it, she has been moving forward through a very tricky sequence of turns. She's left marks to navigate her way back, but it will take her ten minutes to return, at least."

"Tell her to get back here, as quickly as she can. Oh! And before you go, just how far away is she?"

"That is a very difficult question to answer in a way that makes sense, as there seem to be at least two different scales of distance depending upon whether one is inside or outside the Lesser Greater Lands."

"What city is she nearest to?" Euphoria asked.

"Presently, I would estimate the nearest city to be Flackonelle."

"That's eighty miles away from Fenfield," Lattica said. "And she can be back in ten minutes? Are you sure that's where she is?"

"It is the best estimate I can provide."

"Ask her to come back immediately."

Again the flame flickered and danced. Euphoria paced to the door of the carriage and threw it open. The injured and frightened Graves family worker flinched at her sudden appearance.

"Sir, I apologize, but I require the carriage. I'll have to leave you in the care of the kobolds."

"What!? But I told you what you wanted to know! You can't leave me with those bloodthirsty monsters!" he said.

"I assure you, they are harmless." She paused. "No, I suppose that's not entirely true. They are capable of extreme violence, of that I have no doubt, but I have no reason to suppose they will do so to you, particularly in light of the fact that you are alive and breathing entirely because one of the kobolds saw fit to rescue you. Now if you'll excuse me. Lattica, please help this man down."

Lattica obliged, though it was less "helping someone down" and more "manhandling a terrified, injured man who didn't want to leave the carriage." It didn't take long, and the kobolds gathered around him, grinning pleasantly in a way that left the man at the ragged edge of hysteria.

Once he was dealt with, Euphoria and Lattica climbed to the driver's seats.

"To the gate."

Lattica snapped the reins. When they were far enough from the kobolds to not be overheard, Lattica spoke up.

"If you have a method behind your madness at the moment, I would very much appreciate being given some sort of a clue."

"It seems clear to me, and it would no doubt be similarly clear to you if you put a bit more thought into it, that those tunnels are some sort of a system of shortcuts. I don't know how useful they'll be to us, given the fact that she's run into so many locked doors and caved-in exits. A combination of leftover security from when it was created and general disrepair from hundreds of years without upkeep may well have left it completely unusable. But I very much doubt these tunnels reopened today out of the blue. A new way of traveling from here to what appears to be one of the doors directly beneath a Graves man who had been dispatched to salvage items from a re-creation of an ancient town, one such item being a secondary means of security? This is the culmination of a plan, or something close to it. Those tunnels, mark my words, are about to become very, very important. And as with any method of transportation, mastering navigation is of the utmost importance."

"And that's got something to do with us asking Teya to come back and then immediately heading for the gates?"

"Quite so. Let this be a lesson to you, Lattica. Even when someone is painfully dull, listen to what they have to say. You never know when it will be the difference between stumbling about in the dark and finding the way to daylight."

Tome had been marching back and forth in the hallway near his father's room for nearly an hour. All other preparations had been made, but there were still places within the monastery that one needed special permission to access. Madge was with him, having woken up while he was rummaging through his things.

She yawned. "Why don't you just go up there? Seems like they don't really lock doors around here."

"And how, may I ask, did you learn that?"

"I did some exploring yesterday after supper."

"... You didn't steal anything, did you?"

Madge shrugged. "There wasn't anything worth stealing. I don't have much use for books."

"I would really prefer you have a more moral motivation for not stealing from your hosts."

"You and me both, but food isn't usually free, and who knows how much longer this apprenticeship will last? Gotta keep my eyes on the future."

The door to his father's room opened. The older man marched out with a book under his arm. Notably, it was the third of the volumes that Tome had brought for assessment. He looked up and saw his son, and for the first time since they'd arrived, he seemed genuinely pleased to see Tome.

"Tome! I've been reading through the index you've provided, and I must say, the width and breadth of the knowledge being listed is truly remarkable. I think it will be an excellent exercise for the initiates to take on the task of categorizing the easily interpreted titles. It will also be a very good test of our translator's skills. Tell me, are these books truly available in some form?"

"Not yet, but they will be. Father, much as I'd like to discuss such things, I have a small question I would like to answer for myself, and it requires access to the tower."

"The tower? Why?"

"I need someplace from which I can see a great distance. Are the telescopes still there?"

"I believe there is one kept in ready condition in storage in the tower, but I do not recall you having any interest in such things when you lived here."

"The circumstances of my life have fostered a great many new interests. Do I have your permission?"

"Of course, of course. Tell any who would stop you that you and your apprentice have my blessings. But do return quickly. We have much to discuss."

"Thank you, Father," he said.

He turned and headed for the stairs with the very precisely calibrated gait of someone who had grown up being told not to run in these very halls.

"Your father's mood seems to have changed," Madge said brightly. She was moving at precisely the same speed as Tome but managed to look like she was running recklessly.

"Now he knows I have something that he wants."

"Besides the companionship of his son?"

"Like I said, something he wants."

"If he's such a cold, distant fellow, why did you even bother getting his permission to go up here? I'm not the petty sort, but if I was, this is exactly the kind of pettiness that would appeal to me."

"Because my father values respect. He fancies himself a paragon of dignity and comportment. I know for a fact that he believes I am everything but respectful. Rigidly observing his rules in his presence proves him wrong. And being proved wrong will burn him infinitely more than any petty acts of rebellion I might perform."

"So to irritate your father, you are following his rules?"

"It isn't the only reason I'm following his rules, but it is a pleasant side effect."

"Intellectuals play very foolish games with one another."

"I've been told that focus on academic pursuits deprives us of time others might spend upon social pursuits."

They spiraled their way up the stairs, encountering no fewer than three monks who attempted to prevent them from moving farther. In each case, the mere mention of Brother Inkbrand was enough to get the would-be guards to step aside.

"Do you keep valuables up here?" Madge asked.

"No."

"Then why do you keep all the doors unlocked in the rest of the place, but people carefully prevent access to the tower?"

"I'd like to say that it is an arbitrary rule. We have quite a few rules in this place that are abundantly arbitrary. But the truth is a bit more grim."

"Oh? Sounds like a good story."

"It is a terrible story," Tome said.

"Sure, sure. But terrible stories are the best stories, sometimes."

"Not in this case. I've mentioned that many people don't have the mental fortitude to spend the bulk of a day tediously copying texts. There was a time when the monastery was used as a sort of reformatory for people who had demonstrated a lack of discipline elsewhere. They would not be permitted to leave until they had advanced beyond the level of initiate."

"Like a prison?"

"I'm sure it felt that way from their point of view. Endless tedium, no obvious means to bring that tedium to an end, and ready access to a tower lead to a very predictable outcome."

"Oh? ... Oh."

"It's been years since that happened. Never once in the time I lived here. But precautions remain in place."

"Leaps from towers, strained relationships, illegitimate children. If I'd known life in a monastery was so interesting, I might have considered it an option."

"Why you would seek out sources of potential drama and tragedy is only the most recent question that arises about the deepening riddle of your odd mind, Madge. But we'll set that aside for now. Another potentially more important riddle awaits."

At the top of the steps, a lighthouse that had been dormant ever since a new one had been constructed closer to the harbor served as dusty, damp storage. The old torch was in the center of the room, and large sturdy racks stood around it, formerly home to the firewood that kept it burning. Now those racks were stacked with assorted items the monastery had little use for. It took three tries before he located the crate that contained the telescope.

"Here, Madge. There is a mount on the wall there. It should match the bottom of the telescope. Set it up, would you?"

"Sure thing!" She grabbed the device and fiddled with the mount, trying to get it to slot into place. A crust of sea salt had fouled the brace a bit. She brushed at it. "Wouldn't it be better to wait until the full light of day before trying to sightsee?" she asked.

"I'm a profoundly impatient man in certain circumstances. This is absolutely one such circumstance."

The telescope finally slotted in place. He stepped up and peered over the edge to see where the monument below was pointing. When he started adjusting the stiff brace that held the telescope, he found there were notches, one of which was slightly offset from the others. It was a match for the angle the monument indicated.

"Look. See here? What I'm about to look at is something the lighthouse keepers had to look at frequently. There's an alignment tool."

"And what are you going to be looking at?"

He winced. There it was, the tug of his mind telling him to look away. The precise feeling he'd dreaded in Fenfield and the precise feeling he'd been searching for today. He locked the telescope down and stepped back.

"Do me a favor, Madge. Look through there and tell me what you see?" he said, digging into his pocket as he did.

She stepped forward, and he saw the same dull look come to her face that he'd seen on innumerable mystics and a handful of humans.

"I don't see anything," she said, eyes squinting as if looking into the glare of the sun.

"Nor did I. Now step aside for a moment."

He gripped the earring tight in his hand and looked through the telescope again. The view was hazy at best, but the feeling that he should look away was gone. Then, he saw it. A flash. Like the light of the rising sun twinkling off polished glass. It came again, and again. Blinking at a precise interval. He slowly pieced together what it meant, but the thought was chilling.

He stood and handed the earring to her.

"Take a look again, please."

"Fun!" she said, leaning low and peering inside. "I don't see any... wait... No, I don't see any... wait... Oh! It's something flashing. Did it just start?"

"No. No, I would say that's been going for hundreds of years. Since the end of the Bygone Era at least."

"Then why couldn't I see it?"

"Because it was designed to keep you from seeing it. And me. And anyone like us."

"Then why can I see it now?" she asked.

"Because you're holding an artifact that was enchanted to sweep that effect from the wearer's mind. Stolen from workers serving a demented consciousness residing in a contraption lantern. Built from designs crafted by murderous elves."

She backed away from the telescope and raised an eyebrow. "We spent how long in the cart together and you didn't bother telling that story?"

"It's not the sort of story I relish recalling."

"Well, what is that thing?"

"That is a clockwork diamond. Which means 'the pit in the sea' is nothing more than the island it was built upon, hidden from view by its enchantment." He released a shaky sigh. "And someone just stole a ship and 'vanished' after heading toward it."

"Is that bad?"

"What are the odds it would be good, Madge?" he groaned. "Somehow, I'm guessing the rumbling of the ground is involved as well. Maybe even caused by whoever went rushing out there."

"Are we going to do anything?"

"Someone is going to have to, and I don't foresee anyone else leaping at the opportunity. But first, we need to tell some people."

"Your father?"

"Getting him to believe that he has an ancient contraption of unimaginable size sitting on the horizon right outside his window without his knowledge will take more time and effort than simply dealing with whatever this mess is."

"Couldn't you just show him what you showed me?"

"You underestimate his stubbornness and tendency toward self-delusion. Not everyone shares your gift for credulity."

"It's one of the many things that makes me special," she said proudly. "But if you're not going to talk to him, then who?"

"As it so happens, I have access to a means to communicate with my friends back in Beffshire."

"Is it the lantern?" she asked.

"... Yes. How did you know?"

"Every so often during the trip, you'd sneak off with the lantern and come back looking a lot less anxious."

"And you'd assumed I was communicating across the width of multiple kingdoms using the lantern?"

"No, no. I'd assumed you were doing something else that required privacy. But now that I know there are lanterns with minds, it stands to reason you were chatting with one. And if a lantern can talk, who's to say it can't do other fancy stuff?"

"That my life has aligned with your logic is perhaps the most concerning turn in a long sequence of concerning turns. But yes. You're quite correct. Frankly, I shouldn't be telling you about it, because it really isn't my secret to share, but given the present circumstances, I suspect you and I are about to engage in something that will expose you to a great deal more of the unseen than the existence of sentry lanterns, and so I don't imagine there's any value in holding that information back."

"Hey! Who said I'd be helping you out with whatever this is?"

"I... I'd assumed. You were so game for so many other bizarre things, I—"

She slapped him on the arm. "I'm pulling your leg. Of course I'm going to help. So what do we do?"

"We head back, we get the lantern, and we wait until Wick—that's the name of the entity within—pays us a visit. I need advice. I need instruction, and it is only available from Martin Masker. And if you don't mind, I'll be taking that earring back."

"You don't have a spare?"

"I hadn't anticipated having a partner, and as it so happens, they are a rather rare commodity." He glanced toward the once-again-unseen island. "Though perhaps not quite as rare as I would have hoped."

Lord Katritz had returned with Velonia Madritz to her room at the Green Hedge Inn. At another time, he would have been concerned what others would think about someone as lofty as him going somewhere as lowly as this with a woman who was not his wife. Presently he and the entire city had greater concerns. While everyone coped with the minor damage and major uncertainty that came with the strange rattling of the ground, he had the task of avoiding the consequences of causing the rattling, as well as preserving the reward he'd intended to reap through this scheme. On one hand, it meant he could come here without raising suspicion. On the other, it meant he had to do so without his usual complement of guards. The only semblance of security was Inspector Cartwright at the door. All in all, it wasn't going well.

"You cannot honestly tell me that the fastest means to contact this man is via messenger," Lord Katritz snapped.

"It is the fastest means available to anyone," Velonia replied angrily as she furiously jotted down a message using the codes she'd been provided.

"When operating at this level, surely it would be sensible to have a designated representative in the city."

"I am the designated representative. As is Cartwright. We had all the necessary instructions. Every procedure that could and should be done with the information available."

"I mean someone capable. Someone who can deal with contingencies."

"We wouldn't have to deal with contingencies if you'd been able to control yourself like something other than an overgrown toddler."

"I will remind you who you are talking to. I am a lord."

"Not for much longer if we don't solve this problem," she hissed.

"Well then, why has it taken you more than an hour to compose a simple message?"

"Because it isn't a simple message. Lens requires codes for messages like this, and I need to both include the information he'd requested and explain the damage that's been done. Composing a single message that contains all the information he will require to provide us with the next steps takes time. And you keep interrupting me!"

"And then what? You hand this to a man on a horse and we wait days for him to tell us how to correct this problem?"

"That's the best-case scenario. We may not be able to fix this problem. He was abundantly clear that everything should be done according to his exacting procedures, and that means there may not be an opportunity to correct your mistake."

"I will not have this blame fall on my shoulders. Mark my words, if this cannot be fixed—"

"A messenger is coming," Cartwright said, squinting out the window to the street below.

"I hope you're finished with the message, if the man you've arranged to pick it up has already arrived."

"I didn't order a messenger yet," she said, eyes wide and alert.

She rushed to the window. Lord Katritz peered past her. The messenger approaching the door of the inn was wearing the uniform of a pricey courier service, the fastest messengers not privately maintained by the nobles such as himself. They employed some of the most reliable messengers and owned some of the fastest horses, and their reputation afforded them a few privileges. Not the least of these privileges was permission to make their deliveries directly to the room of their customers rather than leaving their messages with the inn staff.

"I am not here. You will not allow him inside, and I am not here," the lord said.

"I would suggest we don't know for certain that he's even coming to this room, but as it would further complicate matters, I can only assume that this is his precise destination. Get behind the bed."

"I will not lower myself to so undignified a—"

"Get behind the bed or be discovered. At this point I couldn't care less what happens to you."

Lord Katritz seethed for a moment, carefully assigning as heinous a punishment as he could imagine to this woman at the first opportunity. But she was right. He swallowed his pride and dropped to his hands and knees behind the bed. A moment later there was a knock at the door. Velonia silently opened it. There was some sort of jangling exchange, and the door was shut.

"You can stand up now," Velonia said.

He stood and brushed himself off. He'd expected to find her holding a message, likely written in the same absurd code she was pecking her way through. Instead, she held a lit green-enamel lantern.

"Is this some sort of idiotic sign?" Lord Katritz asked.

"I don't know. This has never happened before, nor has it been discussed," she said.

The flame suddenly went still. "Place the lantern on the table and listen closely," announced Lens.

"What in the world?" she squealed, her steady demeanor cracking.

The voice was clearly coming from the lantern.

"That's Lens's voice," Cartwright said.

Velonia shakily placed the lantern on the table.

"Things were already moving at a pace and in a direction that was making success a difficult proposition even before whichever of you fools saw fit to open the tunnel before we had the means to secure it. I would ask which of you is responsible, but I genuinely do not care. The only thing that matters now is that a way is found to ensure the items that I require are not taken from me before I use them. In very short order, what appears to be an attack on this city is going to commence. Lord Katritz, you will order the City Watch to stand down and offer no resistance. You will similarly order those responsible for securing the Contraption Vault to deactivate any traps or locks and stand aside."

"Now listen here. I don't know who you think you are or what you think you are doing, but this—"

"Who I think I am is irrelevant. I am not asking you to do anything. I am instructing you to do what will make my task simpler to achieve. You may choose to do otherwise if you wish, but that simply means a short delay and some quantity of spilled blood. The former, I would prefer to avoid. The latter, I imagine *you* would prefer to avoid."

"You can't threaten me. This is Teskal. It is the best-equipped, best-defended city in Thayne. You would need an army to genuinely threaten it."

"An army is not so rigidly defined as you might imagine. You believe it is a legion of soldiers. I am of the opinion it is merely a force large enough to be undefeatable. And depending on the nature of the soldiers, that number can be quite small."

"Do your worst. I won't be cowed by a coward who hides behind a magic flame."

"As you wish. Your decision has been noted and will be considered when you next choose to attempt negotiation. Which will be occurring sooner than you might realize. As I believe, at present, another more useful associate of mine is arriving to seek instruction as well."

Nevil Graves delicately blotted the corners of his mouth with a handkerchief. Generally he would be up and active at the crack of dawn. Business waits for no one, after all. But thanks to Euphoria's insistence and the astonishing agreement by his fellow family members, business had been doing an awful lot of waiting. No one else was willing to use the Voice of the Flame. The messengers had been disrupted thanks to the concerns she'd sown about poor old Piotor. He'd been able to sleep late ever since she'd gone off on her wild-goose chase. It wasn't entirely unpleasant, but as it came at the cost of the timely and expedient execution of business, it was difficult to enjoy it.

"Will there be anything else, sir?" asked his butler.

"No, no. That will be all. I shall retire to my private study until lunch. As usual, I do not wish to be disturbed."

He stood and paced down the hall, then down the stairs. As was only proper for a serious man of means, Nevil had two studies. There was the one just off his den, where he occasionally conducted business and had meetings. In addition, there was the private study. It was where he could be alone with his thoughts and dig into the serious and occasionally surreptitious business that set true experts apart from pretenders and dilettantes. Lately, it had served another rather crucial role. One which had been allowing him to keep abreast of some very important tasks and, as a pleasant side effect, gain some ground over some of the members of his family who clung too closely to the agreed-upon communications precautions.

When he was certain the door was properly locked, he carefully opened the stove he used for heating the place. It wasn't lit. He was a dyed-in-the-wool Shalian and rather enjoyed the stiff chill that lingered through most of the year. But it did conceal what he supposed was the only Graves family lantern still in use in Ram's Rest. His timing was exquisite, as the flame was stationary.

"Any messages for me?" he asked.

"There is an urgent message from Piotor Graves as well as a request for information from the same."

"As expected," Nevil said with a nod.

He'd initially honored the family's decision that the flame should be avoided. But when, for the first time in memory, his regular correspondence with Piotor had been interrupted due to Euphoria's little crusade, he'd thought better of their decision.

"First, the message," he said.

"Piotor has requested that, at the earliest opportunity, you take the Graves family flame to the storehouse where the excavated automatons are being held and touch the flame to the exposed neck post of each one."

"That's a rather specific and... menial task. Are you certain it wasn't meant for someone else? Perhaps when the moratorium on the flame has officially been lifted?"

"Piotor was quite clear that this was a time-critical task, and it should be performed as soon as possible. In addition, any of the locking mechanisms that have been uncovered should be prepared for deployment and left in proximity to the automatons."

"Curious... And the information request?"

"Piotor requires an update on the secondary excavation occurring in Shingleton Quarry."

"Oh, by the High. And I thought *I* was impatient. The excavation has not yet begun. He ought to know that."

"In the last written message delivered to you, it was made abundantly clear the excavation was of equal importance."

"Yes, Piotor made that point. Perhaps it hasn't been delivered yet, but in my written reply I made the point that there was nothing much to be found in the quarry. It's been stripped of any valuable stone, and the vault has been empty for a generation. I thus prioritized the Fenfield excavation, which has been bearing considerable fruit."

"Piotor provided instructions to excavate both. Your opinion at the time was that neither excavation would be worth your resources and the potential discovery by the family of your circumvention of some of their more forceful decisions and policies. That you have uncovered value in one suggests you will uncover value in both."

"I'm unaccustomed to editorial and supposition from my flame," he grumbled. "But you may tell him that I have only so many workers who are capable of working with sufficient discretion, so I shall maintain the current priority."

"I reiterate that Piotor's instructions and advice placed equal importance on the two sites."

"No need to repeat yourself. What's done is done and will continue to be done while—"

He was interrupted by knock at the door.

"Can no one learn to listen when I speak?" he grumbled before raising his voice in reply. "I thought I'd made it clear that I was not to be disturbed."

"Yes, sir, but Mr. Jonathan has returned from his trip and requests an audience. You'd suggested you were eager to speak with him."

"Wonder of wonders, an interruption that is actually warranted. Tell Jonathan I will be up shortly." He turned back to the flame and lowered his voice. "And inform Piotor that I will reassign the excavation crew as soon as it is prudent, and this... flame anointment business will have to wait until this evening at the earliest."

"Damn it, Nevil," the voice from the flame snapped, dropping its tone of cool subservience. "Things are at a tipping point, and I don't need you placing your weight on the wrong side of the balance because you're too full of yourself to listen to instructions and get your hands dirty. I have carried this family to the very zenith of its wealth on the shoulders of my insight, advice, and instruction, and I will not have it all be for naught because you've chosen to stop listening at the exact moment when time is of the essence."

Nevil scoffed and stammered, unable to coax words from a mind that may as well have just been insulted by a music box or other contraption. The flame continued.

"If you can't be trusted to do as you are told, then I may as well dispense with the charade, as it is all on the verge of revelation regardless. A labyrinthian network of tunnels connecting many of the largest and most important portions of our world has just been restored to usability thanks to the premature application of the activation component. In effect, the world has just become very small as a result. At a surface level, I had instructed you to clear the Shingleton Quarry because that quarry holds the nearest outlet of the network of tunnels and, for the moment, it serves my purpose that Ram's Rest maintain some semblance of its position of power within this world. At a far more fundamental level, the automatons you have been unearthing were intended to be deployed through the Shingleton gate, and because you have failed to clear the way, their deployment will be delayed. Every moment they are not in position is a moment closer to a decades-old plan collapsing. And I assure you, if it collapses, few involved will survive with their status and reputation intact. Indeed, few involved will survive at all. Now take this lantern, go to the automatons, and apply the flame to their necks. Do so immediately, and let nothing threaten the successful completion of this task. Is that clear?"

"I... er..." Nevil stammered.

"I have the means to communicate *with* anyone in this family *as* anyone in this family. I have access to every message you have ever sent. I know all of your secrets, and I have no qualms about sharing them. You've profited under my oversight, and I will see to it you feel the greatest and most immediate brunt of failure if you do not act as you have been instructed."

Nevil, for half an instant, chafed at the implication that he'd done things worthy of extortion. His mind soon flooded with myriad little improprieties, any one of which would cost him the trust of the family, and taken as a whole would entirely justify cutting him off from communally held resources. He snatched the lantern from the oven, nearly burning his hand in the process, and closed the frosted-glass hatch to better conceal the nature of the flame.

His butler was still waiting for him when he left the study. "Oh, I'll take that for you, sir," the servant said.

"No! No, this is—I have need for this. Thank you. I have an errand to run, if you would inform the others. I'll return shortly."

"But Jonathan Graves, sir."

"Later, later. This is really a rather important—"

"Nevil!" came the merry voice of his young associate.

He turned to see Jonathan Graves and struggled to wrestle his mind into some level of composure. Despite being thirty years his junior, Jonathan was something of a golden boy within the family. While he lacked the overall management skill that most of the upper echelon of the family prided themselves on, he was a wunderkind at negotiation. He thus spent the vast majority of his year on the road to distant trading hubs to secure large purchases and sign trade agreements. Spending only a few days in Ram's Rest each month meant business with the family typically couldn't wait. Everyone knew this, and he was thus given tremendous latitude in scheduling meetings. In short, the man came and went as he pleased.

Jonathan gave him a slap on the back. "First, the bit you'll care about. I knocked another twenty percent off the price of tin from that bearded gentleman out east. You know the one. It was a battle for the ages, but in the end I only had to give up ground on the schedule. He wants delivery guarantees. We'll need to invest in a few more cargo wagons and hire a driver or two. We'll be in profit on this deal by the middle of next season."

"Right, yes. Excellent news, my boy. Wonderful. That will be a boon for the bronze and the pewter, eh? Fine, fine. Good work. Knew you could do it. If you'll excuse me—"

"I'd like a word about Euphoria, if you have a moment."

"I really don't, my boy. Terribly sorry. Time is money, as they say."

"Where are you headed? I'll walk with you," Jonathan said.

"It's not something that I—"

Jonathan placed a hand on his back, leading him toward the door as if, despite his actual words, all the younger man had heard was "what an excellent idea." "She really seems to have uncovered something heinous, eh?"

"Rubbed the family raw, though I'm thinking she may be onto something," Nevil said, glancing at the lantern.

"Are you? As I'd heard it, you were one of the more resistant members of the family when she raised concerns about Piotor. Dirty business, if it's true. And Euphoria doesn't speak unless she's certain."

"Right, quite so. Er, the errands, you see."

"Have we had word from her? You're my second stop, after my own home, and as I understand it, she's overdue for sending an update."

"I wouldn't worry yourself too terribly, my boy. The network of messengers is a bit of a mess these days. I've had a few expected messages fail to arrive as well. Probably we'll have news in another day or two. No worries. No worries."

"I'm always worried about Euphoria. She's a Masker after all. They're all a bit touched. Not that I'd say a word against her. Love of my life. But she's always teetering on the edge of doing something better left to servants."

Jonathan grabbed the overcoat offered by Nevil's butler, then snatched the lantern from the older man's hand and gave it to the butler before holding up the coat. Nevil tried to keep the anxiety from his gaze as he slipped his arms into the coat.

"I only hope that I get to see her again before I'm off to talk to the copper merchants down south," Jonathan continued. "It's not fair to her or me that I see random bartenders in forgotten taverns halfway across the world more often than I see my own wife."

The pair stepped outside.

"By the way, what's this errand that's so important the great Nevil Graves himself has to see to it personally?"

"It's… You see, I have to… There's a matter of great—" Nevil stammered.

Jonathan's head snapped aside suddenly. "Ho there! Is that Henrique?" He turned back to Nevil and slapped his back. "We'll talk later. I need to tell him about the wagon he'll need to buy."

Nevil released a shaky breath and rounded his home to the stables. He gave the driver his orders. Not until the man was in motion did he feel a measure of the fear of discovery ease away.

"What, precisely, are we off to do?" he asked.

"You will apply the flame to the neck of the automatons and your task will be complete."

"But to what end? The automatons are incomplete. A great many of them are visibly broken. As I understand it, not a single one had been fully assembled."

"You will apply the flame to the neck of the automatons and your task will be complete."

"I'm not comfortable being left out of the loop, and being denied agency and control."

"You've never been in the loop. And no one has ever had agency or control. Now do as you are told and you may return to your comfortable little life."

Allie stifled a yawn as she marched up the street of upper-class shops on the north end of town. Today would have been a long day even without a disaster to cope with and a mystery to unfold. She'd stopped by The Fox and Log. A few heartbreaking piles of glass on the floor were the only casualties of the quake. All told, five bottles had broken. Because fate was cruel, the cheap stuff was entirely spared, but one of the pricier bottles of whiskey and three wine bottles had fallen and either shattered outright or lost their corks. She cleaned up the mess and pushed the other bottles back into position before heading out again.

The city was more or less settling back into order now that the sun had fully risen. People were a degree more anxious and irritable, and the streets here on the "nice" side of town were a good deal more cluttered than elsewhere. One of the benefits of being in a poor neighborhood: if you hauled damaged this or that out to the street, it didn't stay there long before someone came along and decided they could get a duot or two for it or use it in their own home or business. Around here, furniture and such that, even with their damage, were better than most of what Allie had in her home remained on the road in broad daylight. She'd have to make it a point to tell some of the folks in her own neighborhood about the windfall waiting for them if they could load it up quickly enough to avoid being yelled at. The wealthy were strangely protective of their garbage.

She came to the door of Divinity's Oven and slipped inside. From the looks of it, the bakery had been spared any serious damage. The piles of buns and cakes were a bit smaller than they ought to be so early in the morning, and Mariss was looking a bit more flour-covered and frazzled than usual, but the patrons were still clamoring for their pricey morning meals.

"Allie!" she said brightly as she handed over a basket. "Quite the commotion today. Is everything all right?"

"Could have been worse. Looks like you didn't have much trouble."

"Two stacks of sweet buns, all over the floor. Those little rascals on the Maskers' roof are going to have quite the feast this evening."

"As if they needed any more encouragement. Listen, I know it's your busy time of day, but I seem to remember you talking about Founder's Day. Regarding Landmark Square?"

"Oh, yes!"

"You don't, by chance, know anyone who can help me or someone else get a glimpse of Landmark Square, do you?"

"Oh, I can certainly see to it that Father invites you for the next ceremony! It's a lovely occasion."

"I was hoping sometime sooner. Today, if possible."

"Oh! That's another matter entirely. I don't think so. Certainly not anyone I know. Why so urgent?"

Allie leaned forward so that she could lower her voice. The older woman looking over the pastries didn't seem terribly interested in their conversation, but it still wasn't something that she felt needed to be general knowledge.

"I was talking to the Maskers, and there's a bit of a theory that there might be a big round well or something under the grandstand." She lowered her voice further. "It might have something to do with the quake."

"Might it now..." Mariss said. "One moment. Will that be all, ma'am?"

As Mariss completed a transaction, Allie gazed out the window of the shop. Her lip curled into a half-sneer as she realized that Marcus had appeared in the street outside. He had the distinctive look of a man who had been awake for just a few minutes. She knew he was staying on this side of town, and somehow the knowledge that he was rolling out of bed after dawn just irritated her further. There were plenty of things to criticize Captain Boltt for, but he was at least attentive to the needs of the city. This was a man who wanted his job but had endured the quake and still hadn't hit the street until after Allie herself had done multiple checks of her own. Shameful.

After the irritation had a moment to settle, the more scheming bits of her mind took over. "I'll be back in a moment," she said quickly.

She trotted out the door. When Marcus noticed her, he did an impressively similar half-sneer to her own.

"If you've come to apologize, it won't do you any good," he said.

"Apologize? Hardly," Allie said. "I'm here to give you a warning. With all this madness going on after that quake, you're going to start hearing rumors about Landmark Square. And you're probably stupid enough to search it. Because I don't want there to be any bloodshed, I'll just let you know that there's a reason Captain Boltt doesn't go near that place, and it's the same reason you shouldn't either. They open the square up once per year for a festival, and it's locked down for the rest of the year. It doesn't take a genius to know that makes it a darn good place to hide something. It also doesn't take a genius to know that anyone hiding something valuable anywhere in this city is going to want to check to see it's intact after the quake. So now is the perfect time to look the other way from Landmark Square. Because otherwise you're liable to see someone or something that doesn't want to be seen. Understand?"

"Now you listen to—"

She turned away and dismissed him with her hand. "We're through here. Remember what I said."

She marched back into the bakery, where Mariss was finishing up. Once the old woman left with her sweets, Mariss leaned on the counter.

"Just what was that about? That man you were talking to stomped off like you'd spat in his face."

"Just planting a seed. It should have been the most obvious bit of manipulation that man's heard all year, but when it's exactly what you want to hear, it has a way of slipping past logic. I just hope he does what I tried to get him to do while I'm still free to see it happen."

"Well, if you're still curious about Landmark Square, I can tell you that I don't remember there being any well or anything like you described, but the grandstand did strike me as a bit odd. Fully enclosed. Not an elevated stage. Not even those nice little trellised sides like you see sometimes. Tightly shut, like a huge, low, flat box. I imagine it could be built over something like what you're looking for. Funny. I'd always half remembered that there was some sort of statue there, but for some reason not until this moment did it occur to me that there's nothing in that square that even looks like it used to be a statue. Still, there must be *something* there to qualify it as a landmark in the eyes of our city's founders."

"Sounds like there is. With any luck, we'll know for sure soon."

Nevil arrived at the warehouse north of town where he'd been storing the items retrieved as a result of the excavations in Fenfield. Despite this warehouse playing a key part in several private business ventures over the years, he'd never actually visited it personally. Considering a private business venture was almost always using family resources but only enriching *him*, it was just good sense to keep clear of it. Being seen and connected to this place could only cause him trouble in the future. But presently, direct attendance was the lesser of two evils. More accurately, he was being threatened by the greater of two evils, and thus self-preservation dictated that he dispense with all other precautions.

The warehouse was secluded from the city, but not nearly as isolated as he'd envisioned when he acquired it. A river flowed nearby, and two separate water mills were visible. One seemed to be associated with a lumber camp, considering the heaps of timber around it. The other must have been used for textiles. None of the other buildings were near enough to overhear conversation, and a smattering of trees would have made it difficult to see precisely what was going on in the warehouse, but it lacked the sort of privacy Nevil thought he had paid for. On another day, it would have been an outrage worthy of a furious rant. Right now he had bigger concerns.

He stepped from the carriage with the lantern in hand. "I have some... inspection to do," he explained to the driver. "I am not to be observed. You will wait with the carriage behind the warehouse and come when called."

The driver nodded and snapped the reins to coax the horse and carriage forward. When he was out of view, Nevil turned to the warehouse door. The door was sturdy, secured with a brace to keep the wild animals out but otherwise unlocked. He lifted the brace out of place—the most physical labor he'd done in more than thirty years—and opened the door to reveal a small entryway and a second door. Were a curious thief to come this far, they would discover two very important things. First, there was absolutely something worth stealing hidden within this warehouse; and second, it would be easier to bash through the thick wooden walls than defeat this door. Reinforced with metal plates and sporting something akin to—but not identical to—a Bygone Era contraption lock, it was the closest thing contemporary contraptioneers could muster to something that would protect a Bygone vault.

"If you'll grant me a moment to think," Nevil said. "I've not had to interact with this door personally, and I need to recall what code is necessary to open it."

"The white tile of the outer ring will be moved to the three o'clock position. The blue tile of the inner ring will be moved to the nine o'clock position, the red tile of the middle ring will be turned to the twelve o'clock position. Execute that procedure and I will provide the next."

"... Right. I suppose Piotor oversaw the design and construction of this lock," Nevil said, clicking through the procedure.

Three more rounds of instruction eventually disengaged the lock. Unlike proper contraption locks, this one had a heavy, awkward feel, and did nothing more than withdraw a bolt rather than potentially trigger a mystic punishment for a flawed unlocking procedure. He shoved the door open and held the lantern high.

The treasures within briefly pushed Nevil's concerns aside. He'd been intellectually aware of just how many artifacts and valuables had been pulled from Fenfield, but this was the first time he'd observed it personally. Entries on a ledger failed to do it justice. Glittering treasures, some clearly recently constructed imitations, others exquisitely restored Bygone artifacts. And in the center of the floor, rather haphazardly heaped, was a collection of automatons in various states of disrepair, as well as a collection of spare parts.

"I will remind you, you had been instructed to retrieve only the automatons and some sort of locking contraptions that I've never had adequately explained to me," Lens stated. "If you had focused your efforts thusly, rather than gathering the rest of these items, I suspect far greater progress could have been made."

"I requested advice from Piotor. He gives me guidance, not marching orders. He is the researcher, I am the businessman," Nevil defended.

"Your excuses will do you little good if the delays they caused result in failure. Touch the flame to the neck of the automatons."

He approached and opened the lantern. When he'd located a metallic post in the tangle of mechanisms that seemed a likely candidate for a neck, he paused.

"Just what is going to occur when I do this?"

"The final steps toward a long-awaited return to a golden age will begin. And more importantly, you will be allowed to return to your little corner and resume deluding yourself that your wealth and status are earned rather than inherited. Hesitate or refuse and it all comes crashing down, with you at the center of the collapse."

Nevil shook with a mixture of anger and concern. Some shriveled and neglected sense of duty briefly stayed his hand. But it was swiftly overpowered by the desire to do precisely as the flame had said. Return to the life he'd carved out for himself and pretend none of this had happened. He awkwardly slipped the lantern around the post and touched the wick to it. The post flared and took to flame.

"That's enough. Back away," Lens instructed, voice now emanating from the flame on the automaton.

He scrambled to the doorway. The automaton shuddered and shifted, pulling itself from the mound of others. The one he'd selected was missing an arm and had a badly bent leg.

"A-astounding," Nevil gasped.

The contraption dragged another automaton from the pile, this one more intact, and spread the flame. In a chain reaction, each new automaton sprang to life and found another to activate.

"Go, Nevil. You need not observe this any longer, and it will be best if your driver does not witness it."

He nodded numbly and scurried out the door, uncertain if he'd saved his own hide or condemned it.

Just past midday, Kazel had finally decided it was wise to stop and rest. Fel strongly suspected the dragon was doing him a kindness, as when they spotted a forgotten little blob of sand and grass jutting up out of the sea and landed on it, there was no real sign the massive beast was winded or weary in the least. But if the dragon was willing to bend the truth to preserve Fel's dignity rather than pointing out that the mere act of remaining atop a dragon's neck while it was in flight was taxing to him, then he certainly wouldn't spit in the beast's face by pointing it out.

He paced about in the sand by the sea, slowly easing his hips back into some semblance of pain-free operation. Kazel, for his part, simply paced out into the waves and cut sleekly beneath the surface, as though he was just as much a creature of the sea as of the land, air, and flame. He emerged some minutes later, the carcass of what Fel assumed must have been a whale clutched between his jaws. He dropped it to the sand with a ground-shaking thump and started messily consuming it.

It was the first time Fel had seen the monster's claws and teeth put to their intended purpose, and it hammered home just what a force of nature Kazel truly was. They sliced through hide thick enough to turn away harpoons and made a meal of a beast that probably could have capsized a boat with little effort. After the layers of primal fear finished washing over him, his mind grabbed hold of the one question the display had put into it that didn't center on his own soul-searing fear.

"You've been around since before the Bygone Era ended, right?"

"Since long before that time," Kazel said, licking his chops.

"And you're not the only dragon."

"There are others."

"All right. Now don't get me wrong when I say this. I know more than many the kind of damage that humans do if we put our minds to it. But it takes time and effort to make something potent enough to be a threat to something as big as you. And even when you were locked up in that vault, you seemed to know plenty of what was going on in the world. How can you have let it get to the point that we were able to twist this world into knots?"

"Mystics have long lives, Fel Masker. And with those long lives comes wisdom. But wisdom is simply the accumulation of mistakes and the lessons they taught. And worse, there exist things that masquerade as wisdom. False assumptions which can seem to hold true for ages before their fault is revealed. For me, and those like me, one such false wisdom was that great things happen slowly. A dragon grows to its full might. A mountain is worn away by gale and stream. But a human life is short. For your kind, if things do not happen quickly, they will not happen at all. These things are not as vast or impactful as the forces of nature, but small achievements feed and pile upon each other. Not the wearing of a mountain, but the rush of an avalanche. By the time I and those like me saw that the humans were becoming a threat, they had created things which could hold us at bay. Some of us were content to cede ground to the humans. What more could your kind do beyond what you'd already done? Others resolved to conquer you. Some of them fell.

Others learned that it would take all of us to stop you. Because you were a single race with many threats, it granted you the gift of unity. All of humanity worked as one to defend itself. We lacked that unity. And lacking it, we lacked the strength to be your undoing. Thus, you were *our* undoing."

"What was it that started it all? What was the thing we built that made you realize it was too late to do anything?" Fel asked.

"The honest answer, the accurate one, is the accumulation of many minor pieces. Better armor. Better bows and arrows. But the answer that stands tall in the minds of all who came to fear your people is the Guardians."

"The Guardians. I just found some sculptures with that name. Some sort of troops. Contraption-based."

"So much more than that. It does not surprise me that you do not remember them. No one who had created something such as they could last long as a race without a proper foe to use them against. You would have had to make the decision to destroy the Guardians or destroy yourselves. For that reason, perhaps it is best if I do not tell you. Better to let them be forgotten."

"If you think you telling me about these things is going to lead to me building them again, you've got me all wrong. My dad? Maybe. But not me."

"Perhaps so. The Guardians were great, towering contraptions. It would be charity to say they were built in your image. More accurate to say they were built into the image of what you strove to be, or perhaps what you believed yourselves to be. Armored, such that no weak point showed. Mightier than even their great size would suggest. By the mercy of the High, there were only two of the size we conjure in our dark memories of the days that the balance shifted. There were others. Smaller ones. Those could be destroyed. But the largest would walk the land and stand guard while cities were built. And when the city no longer needed the Guardian, when its walls were raised and its armies built, it would move on. If the Guardians had not arisen, perhaps the cities would not have been built. Perhaps there would be no clouds blotting from my mind the notions of things I know exist but cannot perceive."

"Wow... So those sculptures were to scale..." Fel murmured. "Forgive me for saying this, but it's a little flattering to have something as big and as scary as you talking about how frightening you find people like me."

"No. Not people like you. If there were more like you, people with a heart and a mind with room for views beyond what you are taught, then history would have unfolded differently. You are proof of something that I did not think possible. Proof that there can exist a good man."

"If I qualify as a good man, there's more of us than you might think," Fel said. "The trick is, you sort of have to get us one at a time. Gather enough humans together and we start getting funny ideas and telling each other they're right. If there's one thing we're great at, it's agreeing with whatever makes it easiest for us to keep rolling on the way we want to."

"A flaw shared among many." Kazel raised his head and sniffed the air. "We will rest here for an hour. Then, we will travel until the sun sags in the sky. That will take us as near to the destination as I am able to carry you."

"What happens then? You just dump me in the ocean? I have an awful lot of gear. Swimming isn't an option."

"The elves have entrenched themselves. In doing so, they have cut free some of the boats that occupied sections of the harbor they required for their ships. I will deliver you to one of those. They will have drifted far enough to be beyond their view, though my approach will likely make them suspicious. You will have to find a way to make your way from there to the shore."

"How hard could it be?" he said, making no attempt to conceal his sarcasm.

He turned his eyes to the lantern. The flame was dancing. Wick was absent. It was entirely possible that Wick had checked in on him regularly over the last few hours, but while he clung to the back of a dragon, it was not altogether reasonable to be checking the lantern regularly. Wick had gotten rather savvy to the situations when someone would or would not have useful information, and as such he wouldn't have bothered Fel. None of that changed the fact that, here on an isolated island, behind a contraption wall with mystical effects, half a kingdom from his family and half a world from some of his friends, he was suddenly feeling quite alone and a friendly voice would be very welcome. As Kazel resumed his meal, filling the air with the crunching and snapping of sea creature, he realized any sound but that would be welcome. But without a suitable distraction, he had to manufacture an unsuitable one. The first one to present itself was the old standby—the equipment check.

He tested rope for strength, hefted his weapons, and took inventory of each little item in his pack. The last item was the enchanted silver earring. He picked it up and fiddled with it in his hands, letting the odd mental tingle stir in his head. Slowly, something dawned on him. He experimentally dropped it into his bag, then picked it up, trying to focus on his thoughts and state of mind. And though it was subtle, there was a difference. When he held the silver in his hand, he found himself far more anxious about the mission in which he'd entrenched himself. It didn't make sense to him why an enchantment that, as far as he knew, existed only to remove the influence of the clockwork diamond would rob him of some of his confidence. Then, like a bolt of lightning, the answer became clear to him. The realization must have visibly shaken him, because the moment it struck him, Kazel spoke.

"Is something troubling you?" Kazel asked.

Fel took a breath and tried to put his thoughts to words. "When I came here, I felt like the way forward was obvious. Even before that when I saw the beacon, I felt like the way forward was obvious. You people needed me. I had to come. There was no other choice that made sense. And for all of the time I've been here, that one-way path was the one my mind had been following. But just now, I touched the earring. The one the elves made. And within a few seconds of holding it, for the first time since I looked at the beacon, I legitimately asked myself if I had made the right decision in coming here."

"Doubt is wise in the face of such risk."

"Yeah, but I didn't have doubt. Not until I touched the earring. The earring only protects me from the same thing that keeps you from thinking about precisely where we're going. But there shouldn't be any effect. Not here, not now. The clockwork diamond in False Clickspring was monkeyed with, and that's why it affected me. But this one shouldn't be doing anything, right?"

"I do not know and cannot know."

"Right, I know. I'm asking myself. I'm thinking out loud." He gripped the earring tight in his hand and shut his eyes. "I don't think it really made a difference. It's in my hand, and I'm still pretty sure I'm doing the right thing. Morally, that is. I'm pretty sure I would have come here anyway. But when it isn't in my hand, I can't imagine doing anything else but coming here. And when I was in False Clickspring, that diamond all but rewrote my entire identity. So I know it can be made to do things like that. But again, no one has altered this one... unless the elves have worked that out, and if they did, why would they make it so that I'd come and clash with them?"

He rubbed the ring in his grip. "You and yours are pretty sure that destiny is real. And I was pretty sure it wasn't. Now I'm starting to think it might exist, but not in the form you think it does..."

Chapter 10

"I would say that the nearest location is Karndale," Wick said.

"Astounding. The movement is so swift," Martin said, jotting down a new location. "It is one thing to be aware that distances can be somehow collapsed or condensed by the function of contraptions, but to have a visual indication of it is something quite different—I struggle to imagine anything moving as swiftly as they are."

For the last few hours, Wick had been helping put a plan into action. If these tunnels were truly as extensive as they seemed, Euphoria reasoned the first act should be finding a way through them. So a team had been assembled to explore, and Wick checked back regularly to help track their progress and report it to Martin. The map they'd been marking down had been populated almost as quickly as he could write it. Initially Wick had attempted to draw the map himself, using the articulated bust, but jumping back and forth meant the arms had to go slack every few seconds, threatening to foul the map with stray lines or spilled ink. It was simply faster and easier for Martin to do the notation.

He checked the clock. "The last two landmarks are dozens of miles apart, and they were traversed in mere minutes," he said. "At this rate, they'll arrive here before the hour is up."

Martin looked up to find the flame dancing again. Wick was already gone, off to get another update. He took advantage of the brief respite to wring his sore fingers a bit and observe the form the map had taken. Estimating the distance traveled within the tunnels themselves was impossible to do accurately. If not for Wick's ability to roughly estimate his location, they would never have known where the tunnels were even leading. They'd found two dozen potential exits, and not one of them had been open. Piles of rubble blocked many. Locked doors blocked many more. And sturdy barricades blocked the rest. Whatever the purpose of these tunnels, the people of the various kingdoms had been in agreement that they shouldn't be allowed to serve that purpose anymore. But that much, at least, was a decision made by people *after* the creation of the tunnels. More baffling was the decision that must have been made by the tunnel-makers themselves. The tunnel was a maze. If it was not purposely confounding, the makers at least hadn't done anything to simplify the routes. They doubled back upon one another, led to dead ends without even steps leading back to the surface, and accumulated dozens of pointless turns along the way. It almost felt like a sin to know that these tunnels were faster than any means of travel Martin had ever heard of, yet they were designed such that no two exits were connected by a straight line. They could have been even faster. As it was, Euphoria and her crew had set off with the goal of reaching Beffshire, the one place they could be reasonably certain an exit was waiting for them with people who may be able to open it. It would be a proof of concept, illustrating that the tunnels worked as a shortcut. And even with that direct route in mind, they'd encountered all those other exits, not knowing which paths would lead them toward their intended targets.

He ran his finger along the north and east sections of the map. Plenty of unexplored paths in the tunnel were clustered there. Even more were clustered to the west. As tangled up a rat's nest as the path between Fenfield and Beffshire was, it had been tracing the right general trajectory. No detours led as far as Teskal or deep into the central or western stretches of the continent. More fortunate was the lack of traps. Not only had they not triggered any, there hadn't even been evidence of traps to trigger in the first place. The tunnels weren't just a swift way to travel, they were a safe one.

Again, the flame went still.

"Just call out the sequence of turns," Martin said, pen once again in hand.

"I'm afraid this update is less mundane and more urgent. They are not alone in the tunnel," Wick said.

"A threat?" Martin said seriously.

"Unclear. The sound of heavy metal clanking drew their attention to an as-yet-unexplored intersection, and upon investigating, they saw two or more glimmers of light receding down the tunnel. They've chosen to pursue."

"Tell them to be careful," Martin said.

"They have in fact instructed you to do the same. Whatever the things are, they are moving with purpose and with apparent knowledge of the tunnel layout. Despite taking turns which wouldn't appear to be the most direct ones to lead toward Beffshire, upon their pursuit, it was clear that they were indeed following the shortest path through the maze of tunnels. Euphoria fears they are headed directly to Beffshire, and further fears they may have malicious intent."

"I would suggest that she is being overly concerned, but recent history suggests she is not. I will endeavor to be ready."

"I will provide additional information as it becomes available."

Wick's flame danced once more. Martin opened the dumbwaiter and leaned his head into it, shouting up the shaft.

"Vivian! Epiphany! We may soon have some unwanted company. Take the proper precautions. I shall join you shortly."

Toward the center of Beffshire, Allie snacked on a meat pie and watched the commotion. She'd seen to it that The Fox and Log opened properly, albeit a bit early, then managed to get Oovay to handle the trickle of customers as soon as he'd arrived. It pained her to not be present on a day like this—anything in town that produced a greater-than-average amount of gossip sent people flocking to the taverns to share and invent said gossip. It was going to be a busy, busy day with the quake still fresh in people's minds. But seeing as how what was happening here was her own doing, she felt obliged to be on hand to see how it unfolded.

"I'll give him this," Allie muttered to no one in particular. "The man works fast."

Somehow, in just the few hours since she'd planted the seed in his mind, Marcus had managed to arrange for the opening of Landmark Square. He and a handful of people she imagined must be the folks he intended to replace the City Watch with if he were to take over were the only ones permitted inside. In what must have felt like a knife in the back, Captain Boltt and a few of his Watch were on hand to keep the crowd back while the place was searched. But they'd left the gates open. The view through them showed little more than what Mariss had described and what Allie vaguely remembered from the scattered festivals in the past. The grandstand was strangely large and very solidly built. Entirely enclosed. It did look as much like the top of a giant crate that had been sunk into the ground as it did a proper stage. Yes, it had railings and little additional platforms for speeches to be read from and bands to be situated atop. But they almost looked like an afterthought. Even the steps leading up to the top of the grandstand looked a good deal younger than the grandstand itself.

"That's it, boys. Get it open!" Marcus barked.

The crew he'd brought were working at one of the broad planks along the side, easing it out against the force of the nails holding it in place. It was the act of a man hedging his bets. On the off chance he didn't find a hidden cache of goods that he could use to prove Verfessa was up to no good and thus add a feather to his cap in his attempts to prove himself a better captain of the Watch, the capacity to quickly restore the grandstand without any lasting damage would be quite handy.

A final heave against their pry bars popped the plank free. Marcus called for a torch and ducked through the opening. After a few seconds, he emerged again, face beaming triumphantly. He climbed the steps and raised his voice.

"Ladies and gentlemen of Beffshire, here, right in the heart of your city, hidden beneath the grandstand where so many festivals have been held, is a tunnel. A massive one. I do not know who built it, but the mouth of it yawns open, wide and echoing."

A murmur went through the assembled crowd. Confusion and a dash of excitement. Captain Boltt marched forward to confirm it.

"I put it to you, dear people of Beffshire. What purpose could this tunnel serve but to smuggle goods? Perhaps even smuggle people? And how long must it have existed here, unbeknownst to the venerable Captain Boltt?"

Never before had the word "venerable" been so devoid of actual veneration. He continued carefully casting doubt on the captain's capacity to protect the town, but Allie didn't bother listening. She'd already turned, ready to head to Masker's Antiquities to let them know the tunnel had been found. But something stopped her. Somewhere, far beyond the voice of the bellowing blowhard, she heard a strange rhythm. Something like the rattling of the heavy metal lid of a pot. It became steadily sharper, more akin to hammer blows striking an anvil. All wrapped in the echo of a long tunnel.

She wasn't the only one who noticed it, but whereas the crowd shuffled closer to inspect the source of the sound, Allie stepped back, carefully getting clear of the street. She didn't know for certain something bad was on the way, but she'd been given very little reason to believe anything good would be coming out of that tunnel. In a testament to his dedication to making what was now clearly a prepared speech, Marcus didn't allow the hammering sounds to interrupt him until they were joined by a rattling of the boards of the grandstand.

He should have paid attention a few seconds sooner.

The plank beneath his feet lurched upward like it had been smashed from below with a battering ram. He was hurled aside. Another blow splintered the plank, and a metallic fist burst through. Voices rose in fear, and the people in the street rushed for the safety of the buildings. Allie was forced back into a side street, but the shouting of the Watch and the splintering of wood told the tale of more metallic limbs shattering the wood. She caught a brief glimpse of a humanoid form thundering down the street, a length of wood still trailing from one of its fists. In place of a head, the bulky contraption had a perfectly stationary shaft of flame. A second and third contraption followed. The Watch pursued, with Leonard moving faster and with more purpose than Allie had ever seen. She stumbled back out into the open. The automatons were hammering their way along the middle of the street, spreading the sparse foot traffic like the bow of a ship and knocking aside anything too large to dodge on its own. Allie had no doubt that they were headed for the Maskers' place, and they were moving a good deal faster than anything on two legs ought to.

She looked about. The once shoulder-to-shoulder crowd had completely abandoned the street around her. Most were charging down the other streets surrounding Landmark Square. Some were still shoving and heaving their way through the doors of overcrowded stores lining the street. None had remained behind. And thus, Allie alone was witness to the new sound thundering up from the tunnel. It, too, was a hammering sound. But a little less steady, and a lot less metallic. Again she backed toward a wall, any other means of escape having been clogged by other city folk. A form bounded out of Landmark Square. It whisked by with such speed that the thing was a good distance down the street before her mind was able to make sense of what she'd seen. Though even having grasped it, her mind still resisted logic.

The monster that rattled by was a hulking thing. Huffing great steaming breaths from bovine nostrils. A minotaur. Clinging to its neck, wide-eyed with gleeful excitement and bellowing a righteous "Yaaahaaaa!" was a kobold. Specifically, it was Teya. And cradled in the monster's arms like a bride being carried across a threshold was Euphoria Graves, holding a lit lantern and pointing toward the charging automatons like a general directing her troops.

"I swear, every time I think Fel is the craziest person I've ever met, I'm reminded the rest of his family are constant contenders for the title," Allie grumbled before taking off in pursuit.

She'd made it all of three steps before she heard the sound of hooves behind her. She turned and saw Lattica Graves riding somewhat haplessly on a horse. The beast was bareback, with remnants of gear that suggested it should have been pulling a carriage, and was thundering up out of the tunnel. She hauled back on the reins, bringing the horse to a stop, and looked about. The automatons and the minotaur had already vanished down a side street. Her gaze quickly settled on Allie.

"Did you see, er, a—" Lattica said breathlessly.

"They went that way. Give me a boost and I'll guide you to where they're headed."

"It's too dangerous."

"I'm as deep in this as you are. Now let's get moving."

Vivian, Euphoria, and Martin stood along the back wall of the shop. The fragile items had already been removed or secured after the quake. Heavy shutters, normally deployed automatically via contraption, were already locked down and secure. All three of them were armed with contraptions that any inspector would have taken away and fined them for possessing. The sound of commotion was approaching, including the rising shouts of profanity from the lesser harpies atop their roof.

"Remember to brace yourself before you attack," Martin said. "Those things have a kick."

"And do aim for the windows. They're easier to replace than the inventory," Vivian said.

"Why do I get the feeling Reynard has never had to fortify his shop and arm himself?" Epiphany asked.

"Lesser professions take lesser precautions," Vivian said.

A wave of startled people rushed past the storefront. Then, chaos. The automatons came to a stop in front of the shop one by one. They moved in a strange, slightly offset sort of unison, each one snapping to the position the previous one had held a moment before. They raised their fists and hammered the shutters. Glass broke. Shutters rattled. Two rounds of blows finally dislodged the shutters entirely, taking down the shelves on one side of the shop with them. When the shutters had clattered to the ground, Vivian was the first to fire. Hers was the oft-modified net launcher. Four barbs, twice the size of crossbow bolts, launched from the end of the contraption with a twang that kicked the weapon back like a mule. The darts whistled through the air, a web of wire strung between them. One of the darts lodged in the joint of one of the automatons. The other three whizzed by on either side. When the net ran out of slack, they swung around and clattered against the thing with enough force to produce sparks. Thus entwined, when it attempted to mimic the advance of the other two, it stumbled and fell.

Martin fired next. His contraption sputtered a thick, muddy substance that stuck to the approaching automaton like tar. After a moment of doing little more than mucking up the thing's surface and joints, the surface of the substance turned glassy, fully solidifying to a level of hardness that brought the thing to a complete stop.

Epiphany held her weapon up and fired. It produced no substance, no projectile, but the sound of its activation was so intense that it was actually visible as a wavering distortion in the air. The sound was muted from the point of view of the Maskers, but for the automaton facing it head on, each wave of the rumbling roar struck like a hammer. It rattled and rocked, buffeted by the sound. Epiphany fought to keep her weapon raised and aimed. Wave after wave of the sound thumped against the automaton, each one causing the flame to waver and flare. Finally, the flame was snuffed out through force of the sound alone, and the automaton crumbled to the ground like a puppet with its strings cut.

She tried to shift its blast to the black-encrusted mechanism, but it broke free of the rocky coating. Fragments of the black stuff scattered around the shop with terrifying speed. A bit of it slashed across her fingers. The contraption fell to the ground. Martin tried to apply a fresh coating to the automaton with his own improvised weapon, but it lurched forward and smashed the thing from his grip with a backhand. It reached for him. Vivian pulled a switch behind the counter. The floor in the center of the shop dropped away. The entangled and free automatons both tumbled down, smashing the dining room table below. The drop snapped one of the cords of the net. Both automatons climbed to their feet. One thundered toward the stairs leading lower, barely able to navigate the tight space. The other lurched up and grasped the edge of the floor.

Vivian bashed at the thing's grip with her heel. After trying to get her slashed hand to cooperate, Epiphany tossed the sound contraption to Martin, who trained it on the thing's flaming head. At this range, it took three rattles to extinguish the flame and send the thing tumbling down again, but a component of the hastily weaponized sound-blaster rattled free, and it abruptly ceased functioning. He cast it aside.

"You're hurt," Martin said, once the immediate threat was gone.

"It's fine! What about the third one, where has it gone?" Epiphany said, wrapping her knuckles in a bit of shredded sleeve.

"It's headed downstairs. No telling what it's after. Our full inventory. The contents of the workshop. It has to be stopped."

He picked up the muck-slinger and handed it to Vivian. "Aim for its head. This may not stop it in place, but if you can coat the burning bit, it should extinguish it. And that's enough. I should have anticipated our goal would be to extinguish flame. I have a dozen contraptions that—"

Somewhere far below, a heavy thump shook the house.

"That's the trap on the workshop door," he said quickly.

He rushed down the steps, Vivian close behind. Significant damage had been done to the steps. Many were broken by the weight of the automaton. Some damage elsewhere suggested the thing had passed through other portions of their home. Finally, they came to the final level of the stairs. The automaton was there, entirely filling the stairwell. One arm had been impaled by a spike that had thrust down from above, holding it in place. Martin stepped aside. Vivian aimed and fired. The thing raised its free arm to protect its flame, then lashed back when the stuff solidified, once again sending fragments scattering dangerously about. It lashed its arm, not as an attack, but as a swipe clearly focused on grabbing Martin. If not for the spike driven through its other arm, it would have had him.

"The thing wants you. Stay back," Vivian said.

Martin scrambled free of the stairs. He cast a single look back toward the automaton and realized that he wasn't the only target. Indeed, getting damaged in the doorway may not have even been a mistake. The automaton was its own lure, and the skittering form of Oiler had taken the bait. The repair contraption climbed onto the automaton and started tugging and twisting at the torn ends of metal. The thing pulled away from the spike, shearing its whole arm off. It had no way to hold on to Oiler, but with the feast of broken mechanisms set before it, Oiler had no interest in being anywhere but the remaining section of the arm dangling from the shoulder. The automaton charged up the stairs. Vivian was barely able to get clear before it burst past her. One bounding step later, it was near enough to reach Martin. He tried to scramble free. The vicelike fingers snapped shut, snagging his shirt and holding tight. It effortlessly pulled him off the floor.

A painful blur of cramped motion dragged him up several flights of stairs. Then he was sent flying onto the remnants of the dining room table. He shook his head and tried to regain his wits. The damaged automaton had lifted the extinguished one from the floor and relit its flame. Instantly the second one grasped Martin with one hand and leaped up to haul itself through the open hatch to the main shop. The damaged one followed. Martin dangled by one arm, painfully bashing against the doorway as the thing forced its way out. But something just outside brought it to a standstill.

Martin blinked and shook his head. He looked up. A minotaur had braced its meaty paws on the intact automaton's shoulders. He snorted and huffed, straining to keep the thing in place. Euphoria appeared beside it, smashing and thumping at the automaton with a club to little effect. Teya, still dangling from the minotaur's neck, angrily swatted at the flame with her one free paw.

"Bad thing! Bad fire! Go back!" she chattered.

Hideous sizzles and sputters punctuated each slap and thump against the burning neck, but interrupting the flame did some good. The thing started to shudder and twitch with each blow until the fingers gripping Martin's arm loosened just long enough for him to scramble free.

The damaged automaton smashed into the intact one from behind. Two of the mechanisms were more than a match for the minotaur's strength. The monster's hooves scraped against the ground. It slid back into the street. The broken automaton slipped by and dashed up the street. The intact one delivered a punishing punch to the minotaur, causing it to stumble back.

Martin had barely gotten to his feet when the automaton grabbed for him again. He dodged the first grab, and before a second could come along, a horse charged down the street with two women astride it. The pair of them were able to grab him and drag him to the back of the horse between them. The animal made it only a few strides before the lack of a saddle and two too many riders sent Allie and Martin tumbling to the street again. It had gained them enough distance, and enough time, for the Watch to arrive. Crossbow bolts peppered the automaton, one for each arriving member of the Watch. It was enough to distract the automaton, but only just, and only briefly. While they were drawing their crossbows for a second salvo, Vivian charged out of the shop, armed with a pot of stew from the disheveled dining room. She upended it over the automaton. The flame sputtered out, and it went limp.

For a precious moment, there was silence and stillness. It ended with the click of the first crossbow to be readied for its second shot. Boltt leveled it at the minotaur.

"No! No! Wait! Friend!" Teya squealed. "Very very friend!"

"Don't shoot! I can vouch for the minotaur," Euphoria said.

"So can I," Lattica concurred.

The Watch readied their weapons, one by one, and held them stiffly at the ready. Only when the captain lowered his did the others do so as well.

"Maskers," he rumbled. "By the High, you will tell me what is happening!"

"Did the other one get away?" Martin asked when he was able to pull together enough of his rattled mind to speak properly.

"The broken one? With the other thing clinging to it?" the captain asked. "Yes."

"I can't speak for everything that is happening. But I can tell you that we can be certain that this is not the last we've seen of those things. And next time, there will be more of them."

"Fine," the captain said shakily. "But what about those things?"

He pointed at the minotaur, who flicked an ear and snorted once. Teya, still clinging to his neck and perched on his shoulder, waved.

"I'm not entirely certain. But we'll just get them off the street, shall we?" Martin said.

A few minutes later, the group had gathered in the dining room. The broken shutters had been propped into place to block the broken windows, the shattered remnants of the furniture in the dining room had been swept aside, and the trap door between the shop and the dining room had been shut. Both of the automatons that had been snuffed out were lying in a heap on the side of the shop floor, with a liberal coating of the black contraption-stone on their necks lest they have some capacity to relight. From the point of view of the city, for now at least, that restored a semblance of order. All injuries had been bandaged. Martin was rather badly bruised but otherwise intact, and he'd already busied himself repairing the sound-blaster. Epiphany's hand was slashed badly, but the bleeding was under control. She'd have a new scar, but that was likely the worst of it. For the Maskers, there was still the matter of the damage done to the shop, what to make of this attack, and perhaps most pressing of all, what to do about their visitors.

These days, the dining room normally didn't need to provide room for anyone besides Vivian, Epiphany, and Martin, and rarely were any more than two of them present at the same time. Presently it hosted all three of them, plus Euphoria, Lattica, Allie, Teya, and Thurb the minotaur. It was rather cramped, to say the very least. Thurb couldn't stand, but he seemed strangely comfortable crouching. If anything, he seemed to feel more discomfort from the company, and from the effect on his mind caused by his presence beyond the walled-off sections of the world that the clockwork diamond considered suitable for a beast such as him. For the journey here, his state of mind had been maintained by Teya keeping the earring pressed to his skin. Now he was at the mercy of the clockwork diamond's influence. This had translated to a distant, dazed look in his eyes whenever he wasn't focusing on Teya or one of the humans. In this way, it was fortunate the room was so crowded. It gave Thurb a rather disarming appearance, as he sat with his arms wrapped around his knees, looking uncertain. Teya had taken it upon herself to keep him focused; and thus, keep him calm and not fidgeting. The smell was another matter entirely, but polite company kept quiet about it.

Martin had some books piled around him and Wick's lantern set beside him. He glanced at them frequently between the final touches he was putting on the blaster. All were sipping tea. Even Thurb, albeit out of a bowl that still seemed comically small in his grip. Epiphany glanced between Thurb and Euphoria.

"You just had to one-up Fel on his little problem with bringing pets home, didn't you?" Epiphany mumbled.

"Hush," Vivian said. "Martin, anything?"

Martin shook his head and rubbed his eyes. "At this point I'm beginning to lose track of the things I'm supposed to be working on. For those automatons upstairs, it seems as though any sentry flame, or mask... I suppose anything that could broadly be considered a thinking contraption should be able to control it if placed in contact with the neck. Flames can simply be applied; the masks would have to be clamped in some way. How precisely the Graves flame, which I suppose we are now calling Lens, is able to control them all at once is a bit curious. I'd built the coupler for that purpose, but these don't seem to need them. The automaton matches what Fel described in False Clickspring, and thus we have to assume it is spreading its control over many of them by rapidly shifting from one to the next and controlling them for an instant each. It boggles the mind to suppose how such a thing is achievable. Lens's intellect must be staggering. But that's beside the point. At the speed the automaton seemed capable of, and assuming the tunnels aren't any more or less complex between here and wherever the other automatons are being kept, Oiler will be delivered to them within a few minutes from now. From there, based on what Fel said, it will be able to repair one in no more than ten minutes each. I don't know how many there are total, but in very short order, we will have far more than we can handle."

"But the flame is the weakness. All we have to do is extinguish it," Epiphany said.

"And make sure the others don't reignite them. No small task," Martin said.

"What about the locking devices?" Euphoria asked. "There were locking devices being acquired along with the automatons. What do we know about them?"

"They're a bit of a curse and a blessing. If the device is applied to the far side of a door, even knowing the proper code, we won't be able to open it. But the mere fact that Lens felt the need to build or otherwise acquire them suggests that he imagines we would be capable of unlocking them, which means the codes must be available in some capacity that he knows we have access to. Though if we have them, I don't know about it. And Wick doesn't seem to either."

"What about the mask?" Euphoria asked.

"The Scholar? The damage is fairly evident. I think I can repair it, but thinking something and knowing something are very different things. We have the Warrior mask available to us to compare, and I am quite certain that every mask we have has the same etchings in the same location. I could burn away the damage with acid and re-etch it, but if I'm wrong and that isn't the issue, I might permanently destroy or irreparably damage one of the most important Bygone artifacts available to us. Beyond that there's the issue of working out how Lens came to be and what's to be done about him. There is the lingering issue of reworking the clockwork diamond in the Lesser Greater Lands..."

"And least worst friend?" Teya said. "What about him? Fel? No words for long."

The rest of the family blinked.

"When is the last time any of us heard from Fel?" Vivian added.

"And Tome?" Teya said.

"I will check on them now," Wick said.

The flame danced away.

"When this is through, we all have to collectively agree not to let the family get so spread out again for a long time," Epiphany said.

Euphoria squinted. "A thought," she said. "Regarding the codes for the doors that block off most of the exits for the tunnels. Do you recall the page that was passed to you to be translated, ages ago, when you first gained access to the Greater Lands Wall?"

"I do," Martin said.

"It contained the codes to some of the doors in the wall. And you never gained access to the rest of the book it came from."

"Quite so," Martin said.

"We haven't translated most of the rest of that book. At least, not to my knowledge. Or I suppose it would be more accurate to say no one has shared the complete translation with me. The book containing those codes is a precious artifact. But back home, the family refers to it as simply 'the codebook.' Lens would obviously know that I have access to it, since he's served as the family flame for decades and knows anything we've ever said through him. I would wager any amount that it has the codes to the doors."

"Not that it matters," Epiphany said. "Because he can lock them separately."

"Not all of them. The excavation wasn't complete. And even if it was, I doubt he would have enough equipment to lock more than a small subset of doors. Given how many doors there are, we might not be able to use the tunnels to get right on top of him if he locks the nearest door, but we can get close by opening the next nearest door."

She turned. "Thurb. Do you think you can help us find our way to Ram's Rest, or the nearest door to it?"

The minotaur gazed vaguely into the distance. Teya thumped him on the flank.

"Hmm? Oh. Oh. Sure. Yes. It's an easy maze. Nothing like the labyrinth back home. I can get you through it fast."

"That'll kill a few birds with one stone," Euphoria said. "It'll get him out of your hair, and it'll possibly get us access to the rest of the tunnels and doors."

"And if the doors closest to Ram's Rest are locked rather than just blocked like this one was?" Epiphany asked.

"Worst case, I can get back to Fenfield, which is six hours away from Ram's Rest, more or less."

"I hate to send you on your way while there is so much danger afoot," Martin said.

"There was plenty of danger afoot before we came here," Euphoria said. "We just didn't know how much. Come on. Let's go. We should buy some proper gear and perhaps a second horse."

"Take this," Martin said, holding up the repaired blaster. "It should be sturdier now."

Epiphany stood. "I'll see if I can figure out how to help keep the city from losing its mind when Thurb here makes the trek back to Landmark Square."

"Don't forget to keep a flame lit from Wick's lantern," Martin said, standing to give each of his daughters a hug. "And Teya, again our family owes you a debt."

"Yep!" she said brightly.

"Ya owe me one, too," Thurb said.

"I'll need to start a second ledger for life debts," Vivian remarked.

They said their goodbyes, and Epiphany, Euphoria, Teya, Thurb, and Lattica made their way upstairs. When they were gone, Martin looked to Allie.

"Not that I'm not grateful for your help as well, but do you and I still have business?" he asked.

"I've got my own problems. Not sure if this has made them specifically better or worse, but I'm sure I won't have to wait very long to find out. Tell me, before I go. Are we sure those man-shaped contraptions are going to come back here?"

"They tried, and failed, to kidnap me," Martin said simply. "If I have a place in Lens's plan, he'll be back to collect me."

"Well all right," she said with a nod. "I'll be expecting them, then. And if you need anything from me at all, you let me know. I'm not as good with accounting as Vivian. I've lost track of who owes who when it comes to me and the Maskers."

"We appreciate it," Vivian said. "And though I hate to burden you, I'm not naive enough to suspect we'll be getting through this safely without every drop of help we can get."

"Stay safe until then," Allie said.

She climbed the broken steps. Martin and Vivian were alone. They gave each other a meaningful gaze. Vivian grasped Martin's hand and squeezed it. The moment of calm passed when Wick's flame became still once more.

"Fel is safe. Presently still en route to Clickspring astride a dragon's back. It seemed unwise to interrupt him in that state. I do not want to startle him in so compromising a position."

"He's a steady boy. He'll manage. It's important he know what's happening," Martin said.

"Then I will return to him shortly. Tome has discovered what is almost certainly a large, locked tunnel entrance at the Gate of the Ancients. He has further discovered that there is an island near the horizon that was hidden from him in much the same way that the wider world was hidden from those in the Greater Lands. He believes it contains its own clockwork diamond, and he further theorizes someone who passed through the area recently stole a boat specifically with the goal of accessing it."

Martin blinked. "That is a substantial sequence of discoveries."

"Agreed," Wick said. "He wishes to know how he should proceed."

"Don't we all," Martin muttered. "You can tell him we may be on the trail of something that will allow us to unlock that tunnel. And there is almost certainly value in investigating the island. It's possible, I might even say likely, that the island is accessible via the tunnel, but there's no telling how long it will take to get the code, or even if we truly have access to it. Anything to add, Vivian?"

"I suggest we leave it to his judgment," she said. "He's a sound thinker, and our plates are quite full."

Martin nodded. "Pass it along, and get word to Fel as quickly as you can."

Hours later, Fel had his eyes set on the island ahead. In any other circumstance, he would have been tearing himself apart that he wasn't home with his family when the attack had happened. No doubt, when his mind had time to settle, that would loom out of the depths of his memory and burn at him. But things one hears while riding a dragon have a strange way of seeming unreal. He embraced that, for now, his family was safe, and that gave him permission to treat the present situation with his full attention.

This was the second time he'd approached Clickspring, though last time it was by sea. Thus, this was the first time he'd properly seen the clockwork diamond behind courtyard walls at the island's highest point. At first glance, one might have supposed it was nearly the same size as the one in False Clickspring. But first glances tended to lack context. The thing was double, if not triple the height of the one he'd dealt with before. And since it had both depth and width, that meant the moving, glittering assembly of crystal panels and metal struts was easily ten times the complexity. As they spiraled closer, the details of the city resolved themselves.

His last visit had revealed this place to be devoid of any life aside from a very grumpy dragon. That had changed. The dragon had been chased away, as he already knew, and those responsible were present in force. Elves. A cluster of seven elven ships had moored at the harbor. The elves had set adrift the boats that had previously been anchored there. That they were still floating after centuries of neglect suggested why the elves hadn't scuttled them. They probably couldn't. The Bygone technology was simply too sturdy to be worth the effort.

The elves clearly had built up a foothold in the harbor, which was just beyond the influence that kept Greater Mystics clear of Clickspring. It looked like a floating city, but not every elf had kept clear of Clickspring itself. At this distance, it was difficult to tell how many elves were in the Bygone city. They were visible mostly as vague notions of motion. But it was clear some sort of life had returned to Clickspring. Wildlife seemed to be scurrying across roofs and through courtyards. Not until Kazel started to swoop down toward the largest of the drifting ships did Fel spot the detail that made the rest of the clues click into place. In one of the main streets, an elf was pacing behind a lesser dragon strapped to a harness as it tugged and yanked toward the center of the city.

"That's how they're staying here," he shouted to Kazel. "They're using the Lesser Mystics as guides. Teya did the same thing when she came to help us. She tied herself to Parch and stayed focused on him. With effort she could see the immediate surroundings of other creatures. Now I just need to figure out what they're doing, how to stop them, where Parch is, how to get him back, and how to escape without dying."

"I wish you luck, Fel Masker. I will watch for you. I am too far to focus on these creatures as you do. When next you become visible to me, I will retrieve you. I entreat you to have achieved your goals and mine by that time."

"I'll do my best. But just so you know, I'll probably be in a hurry on my way out."

"My eyes are sharp and my wings are swift."

"And I may find my own way off the island, if my dad is right about the tunnels."

"I will seek you elsewhere if you haven't shown yourself by midnight."

"All right, then. Let's get this done."

Kazel wheeled closer to the ship. Fel's mind chewed on the puzzle of how to get from the ship to the shore. He was no sailor. But a dinghy dangled from the rear of the ship, the sort meant to be rowed ashore when there was no proper harbor. That much he could manage. Of course, moving at the speed of a rowboat when other ships lingered nearby, each populated by a race celebrated for the skill of its archers, seemed like a death sentence, but an ancient dragon soaring overhead was another element to the equation. It made certain there was nothing even approaching stealth to his approach, but it also meant the threat of his reprisal was ever-present.

When he was close enough that he was confident a fall wouldn't break anything, he leaped from Kazel's neck. He remembered halfway through the fall that his hips were still coping with the discomfort of riding a dragon. A moment later his landing reinforced that fact in the form of searing bolts of pain from thigh to spine. He rolled, staggered to his feet, and jumped down to the dinghy. In proper Bygone Era fashion, the dinghy was lowered via contraption. A lever attached to a winch on the rowboat itself produced a whirring sound when pulled, quickly reeling the ship down. He slapped the water with jarring force, and the winch finished reeling out the rope and slipped free.

He worked the oars. The winch continued its whirring, but he didn't bother shutting it off. That could wait. The boat bobbed on the waves. Every few moments he spared a glimpse over his shoulder, then at the ships in the distance. The shore didn't seem to be getting any closer. There was a long way to go. Meanwhile, elves were beginning to assemble on the deck of the nearest ship. They were too distant, and he was bobbing too much, to be sure if they were raising weapons, but it served as motivation to work the oars a lot harder. Minutes ticked by. His muscles and lungs burned with the exertion, but he was approaching a stretch of harbor that the elves hadn't reached. He cursed whatever ancestor thought a powered winch was called for on this little boat but not some sort of automatic rower. Regardless, the sweeping shadow of the dragon overhead kept the elves from firing their arrows long enough for him to ram the dinghy into the dock, hastily tie it with a dangling rope to ensure he had some means of escape, and dash along the planks toward the city. Only when he felt the cobblestones of the Clickspring streets beneath his feet did he take moment to catch his breath.

A lot had changed in the time since he'd first come to this place. Back then, the ghost city was a heady mix of eerie stillness and ancient wonder. Now it was anything but still. Little bat-like dragons flocked and roosted there. He didn't know if they'd escaped or if they were purposely released into the city to give the elves a fighting chance of finding something to focus on no matter where they were. The presence of dozens of fire-breathing reptiles, even if they weren't much larger than the lesser harpies, was a source of concern, but at the moment they seemed more frightened of him than he was of them, so he could set that fear aside. The source of terror on the heap was how perfectly Lens had duplicated this place when he'd made the false version that had imprisoned Fel not so long ago. Vivid memories of that time assaulted his senses. Tiny flickering residues of what it had felt like to be controlled prompted him to check that the earring was still secure in his ear after donning it midflight. That he'd been fooled once meant there was still the chance that somehow this place was false, a facade built to once again ensnare him. It didn't make any sense, but if he'd limited his fears to those that made sense to him, he'd have been dead years ago.

When his breathing returned to something tolerable, he began slinking through the city. Not until this moment had he thought to tackle the question of precisely what he intended to do in the city. Yes, he had to find out what the elves were up to. And yes, he needed to find Parch. But those were "what" questions. "How" was another matter entirely, and presently it was a genuine riddle. With no obvious answer, he went with the clearest choice: head toward the denser portion of town. More buildings meant more cover and more materials to salvage.

Progress was slow. Though he still spotted Kazel doing his lazy loops around the island, he knew he was hidden from the beast's view. If Teya's recollection of her time in this place was accurate, in her mind the world around her faded into nonexistence after just a few feet if there was nothing "real" like an animal or human to focus on. And even those things vanished into the haze after ten or twelve feet. So long as he kept well clear of that range from any elves, he should be as good as invisible. It should have been easy.

Nothing was ever easy.

He'd made it as far as the ring of taller, more closely clustered buildings a few streets farther into the city when he encountered the first scouting party. The elf himself moved in near silence. But he was led by a tethered lesser dragon. This was not a beast capable of tracking, or if it was, it had not been trained. The elf directed the thing's motion through fear, stepping behind it and startling it in the direction he wished to travel. It was a noisy and halting way of moving. But Fel realized there was one massive benefit. The dragon would be just as scared of Fel as it was of the elf, and if it noticed him and tried to escape, that would be a sure sign to the scout that Fel had been found.

He crept low and spent as little time in the open as possible. These were the homes of the less wealthy residents. The risk of Bygone Era traps was low. But as he moved deeper, the buildings became more extravagant, and the risk of springing a trap became at least equal to the increasing density of elven scouts. The flit of wings and skitter of claws alerted him of a fresh search, and he slipped into what had been the kitchen of a cozy little home. It was too dangerous to glance out from his hiding place, so he strained his ears and tried to envision the location of the scout. Soon it became clear that there were in fact two scouts. He heard them approach one another and whisper in a language he couldn't understand.

Out of the corner of his eye, he spotted the flame in the lantern going still.

"Are you safe?" Wick asked, his voice low.

Fel shook his head.

"Are you hurt?"

Fel shook his head again.

"Your sister Euphoria has nearly reached Fenfield again. We will soon learn if there is a swifter way to reach Ram's Rest. Your family is recovering nicely, though the Watch, the aspiring replacement for the Watch captain, and assorted city-goers are beginning to question their role in an assault on the city by what were clearly contraptions."

Fel tightened his jaw. It was only a matter of time before that would happen. People liked to have someone to blame, and contraptioneers always found their way to the top of that list.

"Tome's situation is unchanged. Teya will be back in the Lesser Greater Lands with Thurb as soon as Euphoria is safely on the surface again. Is there anything I can do to help you?"

Fel held up a finger to indicate Wick should wait, then listened once more. The scouts continued down their routes. When they were far enough, he spoke.

"I am going to hold you up to the window," he said. "You tell me if the coast is clear."

He moved as slowly as he could, hoisting the lantern and sliding it onto the windowsill.

"Two elves, each with lesser dragons, are moving away. Kazel was briefly visible in the sky. He has vanished off to the left. No other elves are visible."

"Do you see anyplace that's a good hiding spot, farther toward the center of town?"

"I am not equipped to make that determination."

Fel sighed. He pulled himself up and scanned the city ahead. The estates farther along were a bit more sprawling, with plenty of open land between them. Using them for cover wasn't a pleasant option. They'd have more traps, too. And he still didn't know precisely where he was headed. He needed a better lay of the land. That meant height. After taking the risk of leaning out the window to check farther along the side streets, he spotted a tower of some kind rising up above the roof lines. It stuck up at least three stories higher than anything else and had a flagpole on the top, reaching another two stories higher. Getting there would take him along the edge of the fancier neighborhood. Mediocre cover the whole way. But it was a destination. He was about to scramble out the window and make a dash for the next bit of cover when the flutter of a fleeing lesser dragon froze his heart in his chest. He dropped back down and pressed his back against the wall. He realized he'd left Wick on the sill, but he dared not move him.

"What do you see?" he whispered.

"The fleeing dragon is not tethered. It appears to have been startled by another scout that is approaching."

"Does he have a dragon too?" Fel asked.

"She, it would appear. And no. This one is being led by a leashed lesser sphinx."

Fel shut his eyes tight. A lesser sphinx. He'd dealt with them before. Deadly to fight. Worse, they more or less followed orders. This wouldn't be an awkward instance of trying to spook a terrified animal into heading in the direction a scout wanted to go. This was a beast that could almost certainly be ordered forward with all the nuance and precision of a scent hound.

A scent hound...

"Wick, can lesser sphinxes track things by scent?" he whispered urgently.

"I do not know."

"One way or another, today we're going to find out. Have you been spotted? Are they looking this way?"

"No, and no."

He snatched the lantern down. "Check in again in a few minutes. I'll be either running for my life or in the base of that tower."

Two automatons stood stock-still at the opening of a tunnel. The flames that served as their heads cast light into the tunnel, each flame flickering briefly to some unheard, rapid rhythm. They stood at attention as the clattering of hooves echoed up the tunnel. Heavy metal legs widened their stance. Gleaming metal gauntlets shifted into defensive positions. Whoever hoped to emerge would face their wrath.

The clattering of hooves grew louder, but they stopped just short of where the glow of the flame would illuminate them.

"You didn't think I would allow you to leave these tunnels, did you?" came Lens's voice from the flames, flicking back and forth between them in a bizarre and unnatural perversion of proper speech.

Now boots thumped against the ground.

"If you are wise, you will surrender. There may still be a place in the world for someone with good sense and a history linked to the contraptioneers of old. But that place, whatever it may be, is not a vital one. My plans will progress flawlessly if I am forced to shatter your bones."

A boot became faintly visible in the glow. Then, the gleam of a metallic component. One of the automatons burst forward, ready to attack. A rattling thump of raw sound erupted from the bit of metal in the darkness, and the automaton's flame fluttered, fouling its motion. Lattica stomped from the darkness, the booming contraption in her hands held steady. Both automatons attempted to retreat. The one held in the cone of intense sound lost its footing and tumbled forward. Lattica vaulted two steps forward and managed to fully extinguish the flame. She raised the weapon to target the second automaton, but it was far enough away to avoid the wrath of the weapon.

"Teya? Thurb?" Lattica shouted.

The minotaur surged from the darkness, kobold astride its neck. Teya's gleeful battle cry was absent, as she had raised a canteen to her lips. The automaton was steadily accelerating. At its top speed, it was faster than Thurb. But that wouldn't matter if he acted quickly. The journey from Beffshire was far shorter than it should have been but quite long enough for plans to be made. Thurb reached up. Teya shifted her cunning little paws from his shoulder to his palm, just barely able to fit them in his broad grip. He thrust his hand forward, and she leaped from it, launched like a dart through the air. She struck the automaton square in the back and scrambled up to spit a mouthful of water onto the flaming post, extinguishing it and sending the contraption and its rider tumbling to the ground.

"Breathe fire and breathe water!" Teya crowed, scrambling up and dashing to Thurb.

Briefly separated from the silver earring she'd been holding against him, the minotaur was visibly struggling to hold his place. The veil of mental haziness lifted from his eyes when she finished scrambling to his shoulders. She was busily scanning the surroundings as Lattica and Euphoria approached, riding their freshly purchased horses.

"No sign of any more?" Euphoria said.

"None," Teya said.

"He only left two to defend this place. He had either very little faith in us, very few automatons to spare, or more important things elsewhere," Euphoria said.

"Or there's an ambush somewhere down the line," Lattica theorized.

"That's a chance we're going to have to take." Euphoria pointed to the sign nearby. "If we're at the quarry, then we can be to Ram's Rest in a bit more than an hour if we hurry. Which means automatons can reach it from here even more quickly. I'm not wasting another moment."

"Very well then," Lattica said. "But you're making it very difficult to be your body-guard."

"Anybody easy to guard doesn't need a bodyguard to begin with. Teya, Thurb. We thank you for your help, but without the chaos of an attack to dull the effect, I think your company in Ram's Rest will do more harm than good."

Teya gave a crisp salute. "We go to place. Fake Greater Lands. You need help? You call."

"I assure you, I shan't hesitate."

The kobold and the minotaur thundered back into the tunnel. Euphoria snapped her reins and galloped toward Ram's Rest.

Martin finished hammering home the last of the planks of wood that served to both fortify the front of the shop and replace the front windows until the expensive glass could be repaired.

"No more window-shopping. Not for a while," Martin said, wiping his forehead.

"I suspect we shouldn't expect any sales of contraptions for quite some time," Vivian said. "The overall attitude regarding them isn't likely to recover in the next few days. We'll get by on silver polishing and jewelry. You should get back downstairs. Surely you have something more important you could be doing."

"There are a thousand things I should be doing. None of them seem achievable. I needed a moment to see to something simple. If only all problems were as solvable as hammering a nail."

He sighed and looked around the shop. Shelves still broken. Floor planks that would need to be replaced. Working alone, or even with his children, it was the sort of work that would take days to repair, and that didn't even touch the rest of his home.

"Is it worth it, Vivian?" Martin asked.

"It's worth it, darling," she said, flipping through one of her endless ledgers.

"I dig through the dirt to find fragments of the past. I wring my mind for every last drop of insight, trying to find ways to build the future out of them. We weave back and forth across the lines drawn by law and society. But it seems like everything I do, every line I draw, flirts with ruin. Maybe the past should stay buried."

"Nonsense," Vivian said simply. "It doesn't matter if it's buried or not. It doesn't matter if you dig it up or not. The past is still there. It's the one thing we can never truly be rid of. Because every day is built on the day that came before. The future is already made from the past. It's the only thing there is to make it from. The people who say the past is buried and should stay buried are fooling themselves. At least people like us have the good sense to learn where we came from and see if maybe we can make some better decisions about where we're headed as a result. It's worth honoring our history. It's worth using it, mixed with a bit of the ingenuity of today, to build tomorrow. We won't do everything right. No one does. But we can do our best and try our hardest and the world can make of us what it chooses. When all is said and done, we will have spent our lives trying to understand, and to build. And I can think of nothing more worthwhile for a human to do.”

“But the children. Fel is out there fighting elves. Epiphany’s bandaged up and off to the tavern to get her nerves back. Euphoria is traipsing about in underground tunnels...”

“We are who we are, we’ve done what we’ve done. If you feel as though you’ve done wrong by them, that’s your sign that you need to do better by them. You have a lifetime of skills. You can do things no one else can do. Yes. Things are a terrible mess now. There is a long road ahead. A difficult one. And we’re not going to make it to the other side by having you doubt your strengths.”

He took a breath. “You have a very clear mind, Viv.”

“You’ve always got a ready riddle to put your mind to. My mind has a broader field to wander in. I’ve asked myself an awful lot of questions, sitting behind this counter. I was bound to find a few answers to go along with them.”

“It makes me wonder, if I’d been behind the counter and you’d been tinkering with contraptions, would we have ended up in the same place?”

“I should say not. I’d at least have the sense to go downstairs and solve some problems rather than marching about in the shop and moping,” she said with a hint of a grin.

“I suppose I’d best get back to it, then,” he said.

“In a moment,” she said.

She stepped forward and hugged him tightly. He hugged her back and the pair stood in one another’s arms for a few precious moments. When they slipped from the embrace, she kissed him lightly on the lips, then patted him on the cheek.

“There. Now you can get back to it.”

A grin briefly found its way to his lips as he headed for the steps. His heart was still heavy, but his mind was at least clearer than it had been. He walked past the mess his dining room had become, carefully navigated damaged stairs, and stepped over the half-deployed trap in the shop doorway with the remains of the automaton’s arm. Sitting on his workbench, inert and unassuming, was the Scholar mask.

“Best get back to it...” he repeated, opening a drawer and setting out some tools.

Chapter 11

At the Gate of the Ancients, it had reached midday. Madge was eagerly stuffing herself with the beans and cabbage that had been set out. Tome's plate was full and untouched. He'd set the lantern lit from Wick's flame on the table, something that earned a few curious looks. The monks were quite willing to keep their curiosities to themselves. Madge, on the other hand, continued to give voice to every passing thought in her mind.

"With all these beans, I guess it's lucky you're not one of those monasteries that takes a vow of silence," Madge said with a snort.

Brother Inkbrand didn't even give her the satisfaction of a withering look. His expression was utterly blank as he acknowledged the comment.

"So, Tome. I've assigned some of those books to the initiates. And I must say, the sheer volume of it is difficult to believe. At the same time, there is a verisimilitude to the information. If it is false, it was falsified by someone with a deep understanding of what would have been kept in the archives."

"It isn't false," Tome said flatly, eyes fixed on the far wall of the dining hall as if he could see the ocean beyond it and the twinkling gem of a contraption beyond that.

"I have no doubt you believe it is genuine, but there is no harm in verification. Regardless of the availability of these titles, I've decided that the translation and categorization task shall be performed. As it happens we have a gap in our schedule. We will of course ask for a contribution before we turn over this information. To cover the cost of the many books that will need to be filled and to further fund our efforts."

"Of course," Tome said, little sign that he'd actually processed what had been said.

"The timing of the payment is negotiable of course. Any time after completion."

Tome nodded.

"But, again, the issue of verification. On the off chance these books are genuine, we'll be quite interested in acquiring copies of some of the titles. To that end, I have searched our 'fragile and damaged' shelf and discovered a badly water-damaged copy of a book that the index you have provided has listed as available and complete. When you return to the source, please request a partial transcript of the first five pages. I will compare them with the copy we have, and if it appears to be accurate, then perhaps the price can be reduced appropriately for each missing book that is provided."

He handed over the page, which contained only the title of a book. Tome nodded dully and pocketed it. Brother Inkbrand nodded in satisfaction and resumed eating. Madge leaned forward and glanced back and forth between the two.

"That's it?" she said.

"What more should there be?" Brother Inkbrand asked.

"Your son is sitting there, staring out at nothing like a scarecrow. He's not eating his food, answering questions like you asked them in a dream, and you're not going to ask what's wrong?"

"The boy is entitled to the privacy of his own thoughts."

Madge shook her head. "And to think I'd wondered why he would leave a place like this, with free room and board and plenty to do. He was looking for something he couldn't get here."

"Yes. It has been well established that he fell victim to the twin siren calls of greed and the forbidden. But he has returned, a sign he has some sense left."

Madge snorted again. "You know, he actually met a siren? Or half of one. I forget. It took some doing, but I pried the story out of him last night. You're interested in books. You ought to take a look at what's going on in his head. He could fill a few. And there's so much you don't know about this world."

"Yes. The forbidden," Inkbrand said.

"Not just that." She elbowed Tome in the side. "Tell him about the sparkly thing. And what's been going on with the sea hole."

"The pit in the sea," Tome corrected.

"I'm not interested in fanciful tales," Inkbrand said.

"But it's not fanciful. It's just true. You can go look! Or go look at the monument out front. It's hollow underneath now. It's because of that shaking. There're tunnels or something under there."

Tome turned to her and raised his eyebrows. "You know, some of this was meant to be kept secret."

"I'm only saying the stuff that he can go out and look at," Madge said. "Go out and look at the monument. It's hollow and it wasn't before. I know, because I walked on it."

Brother Inkbrand stirred at his food. "If your friend continues to spread this sort of lunacy, I may need to rethink the generous lodging I have been providing."

Tome's eyes narrowed, and he shuddered with irritation. "Father, at some point you might consider learning something rather than simply collecting knowledge."

"I am one of the most learned men in the kingdom, and I'll thank you to treat me with the respect I deserve. A wise man is a skeptical one."

"There's a difference between skepticism and stubborn ignorance," Tome grumbled.

"What did you say to me?" Brother Inkbrand thundered.

The flame on the lantern became still. Tome grabbed it and stood. "I have more important things to do," he said.

"You will not insult your father and the senior brother of this monastery and simply walk away!" Brother Inkbrand boomed.

The echo of his voice died away to utter silence. Every eye in the place was turned to them. Tome gritted his teeth. He turned to the lantern and retrieved the page.

"This book is accessible within the indexed collection," he said, addressing Wick.

"That is so," Wick said, the lantern's voice audible only to Tome.

"It can be accessed at will."

"With a moment to recollect it," Wick confirmed.

"So you say, but you've given me even more reason to avoid blindly believing your claims," Brother Inkbrand said, believing Tome was addressing him.

Tome stomped back to his chair and shoved his plate aside. He thumped the lantern down and slapped the page beside it, then dug a quill and sealed bottle of ink from his robes.

"Shall I begin dictating?" Wick asked.

"The first two pages," Tome said.

The lantern read out the contents of the book word by word in a clear, steady tone. Tome wrote the words as they were spoken. In eerie silence, the page filled while the others watched. When he was through, he slapped it in front of his father.

"There. Go. See for yourself. And while you're at it, go outside and look at the monument. There are things going on around you. You can become a part of them or become a victim to them. Right now, I don't care which. I have work to do."

He grabbed the lantern again and stalked toward the door. Madge scurried after him with her plate and spoon in hand.

"I hope there was nothing too urgent," Tome said under his breath as he emerged from the sea-facing entrance and stood before the monument.

"Nothing that required your immediate action, and presently there is nothing elsewhere that will immediately benefit from my presence. I merely came to update you that Euphoria has reached Shalia and will soon be entering Ram's Rest, and that Fel is actively infiltrating Clickspring. I shall have to check on him soon. Nonetheless, did I check on you at a bad time?"

"As good a time as any," Tome said, rubbing his eyes. "Nothing to report from me, save that Father has formally agreed to have the index fully translated and categorized. The price could well be zero, depending on how many of the books he requests copies of. Though that may all have changed after that little demonstration."

"A fortunate update on a difficult task, albeit one that doesn't solve the immediate problems we are facing."

"It's hard to believe that when I left Beffshire I expected the biggest challenge of this trip to be talking my father into helping me," Tome said.

"What do you intend to do now?"

"One way or another, I intend to reach that island. The only way that seems achievable right now is via boat. I'll try to acquire one."

"Then I shall leave you to it," Wick said. "Good luck."

"Someday I would dearly love to do something that doesn't require good luck..." Tome grumbled.

Fel panted and wiped sweat from his brow as he climbed the ladder leading to the top of the tower he'd spotted from afar. Getting here had been done relatively without mishap, though "without mishap" was somewhat generously defined at this point. He had a bloody tear in his pants after he skinned his knee diving for cover to avoid being spotted by a scout. A plume of smoke was also curling up from one of the larger estates he passed through along the way, after he discovered almost too late that someone hundreds of years ago had been far too concerned about people potentially stealing their roses and had set a trap that knocked the lantern from his grip and spread Wick's flame to the descendants of those roses. Wick's ability to extinguish himself was enough to keep it from getting out of control, but it had brought easily half of the scouts in the city to that one spot, which was unsettlingly nearby. But he'd survived, and he was only slightly bloody. In the present context, that may as well have been a walk in the park.

He peered over the edge of the tower and took in his best view of the city since he was on Kazel's back. Better, in fact. The most he'd seen of the island from Kazel's back was the half of it nearest to the mainland. He might have gotten a better look at the far side if he'd thought to take it in, but his focus had been the ships full of people who would be trying to kill him once he landed, so the far side of the island may as well have been hidden by fog. Now, he could see more like a quarter or a third of the city. Still no glimpse of the far side, but what he could see, he could see with enough clarity to pick out specific threats and points of interest. Not so far away, the cathedral that had formerly served as Duurth's lair had an awful lot of activity around it. That stood to reason. It was reasonably central, not very hard to reach since the main streets that led up to it reached almost to the harbor, and it was relatively free of functional traps, or else Duurth wouldn't have been able to call it home. It was also loaded with heaps of precious metals, but somehow he doubted the elves particularly cared about that. A thin haze of smoke rose from one section of the building. A cooking fire, perhaps?

Scanning along the huge, ornate building revealed a courtyard mostly blocked by a wall, but what he could see beyond it was stacked with cages. The Lesser Mystics. If he had any chance of finding Parch at all, it was there.

He squinted, optimistically hoping that perhaps he would be able to spot the creature, but the residents of cages and the things tied to stakes were just hazy blurs at this distance. The light seemed to be fading. It didn't feel late enough in the day for that, but considering the perversions of space that the Greater Lands represented, he saw no reason why it shouldn't also pervert time.

The flame in his lantern went still. "Ah. I am pleased you have reached your destination intact," Wick said.

"You and me both. Anything new from back home?"

"Nothing relevant to your present tasks."

"That beats bad news. How well can you see from up here?"

"Not very well at all."

Fel pointed. "That thing you can't see down there is the bad dragon's old lair. The elves have moved in. The smart thing to do would be to avoid it. But since I'm here to find Parch and find out what these people are up to, that's where I'll have to go. I wish I'd known I'd have to do this, because if I had, I would have brought one of those invisibility bracers. It would be worth the headache and upset stomach to have a chance at slipping in and out without alerting anyone."

He scratched his chin. "All right. Here's the plan. I head back down. If I'm fast, the scouting parties I see now are the only ones I'll need to worry about. So I wait for those two to pass, then head along—"

A terrible sound split the air, something between an old crone and a screeching cat. He turned to the source of the sound and saw the lesser sphinx, its eyes fixed on him. While the elves had no chance of seeing him from so far away, he'd forgotten to watch for the one lesser beast he'd seen so far that might be both wise and sharp-eyed enough to spot him.

"Whatever," he said. "I'm lousy at making plans anyway."

The lesser sphinx guided the elf to the base of the tower at a near run. By the time Fel reached the bottom of the tower, he'd be trapped in a stairwell with an elf that was close enough to fight him directly and a sphinx who would be a handful even without the elf. He needed a better way down. Or at least a faster one. Half a thought forced its way into his head, and he latched onto it. Strapping Wick's lantern to its dedicated strap on his belt, he planted a boot on the railing and heaved himself up to its sloped roof.

"Two stories of flagpole," he muttered, grabbing a tool he'd scavenged along the way. "Top to bottom twice to raise the flag. That's four stories of rope. This is a five-story building..."

With all but one fastener removed, he tied a double knot in one end of the rope and hauled it up to lodge it in the loop at the top of the flagpole. A few sharp tugs at the rope would be all the assurance of its strength that he had time for. He'd have to hope the people of the Bygone Era made their rope with the same absurd quality they made everything else... and that the fasteners were exactly as strong as he needed them to be.

He was beginning to second guess the wisdom of this idea halfway through the stride that sent him vaulting off the roof. He held the rope tight. It pulled taut.

"Bend, don't break, bend, don't break, bend, don't break," Fel chanted quickly and desperately as the weakened flagpole started to tip.

The remaining fastener creaked and deformed, the flagpole yanking aside under the force of his leap. It teetered horizontal, then continued to dangle down at an angle as the return swing sent Fel past the side of the tower. He slowed his slide down the rope to something he hoped would be survivable. The friction was hissing at his sliding gloves until they smoked. The end of the rope was getting close, and he was getting close to the ground, but this speed was still easily in the range of bone-breaking. He'd have to wait for another swing.

Alas, the flagpole was not so obliging. Just as he was approaching the apex of the second swing, the pole snapped free, and he continued forward rather than swinging back. What might have been a relatively graceful tumble to the street on the return swing became an arc through the air that was quite a bit higher than he'd hoped for. He cleared the side of a house across the street and struck its sloped roof feet first. His boots slid up along the roof, his back and head struck it hard, and he started to slide down. A wild, desperate grab caught the edge of the roof just as he slipped past it. His bulky frame pivoted around his grip, much to his wrist's chagrin, and his fingers slipped free to send him plummeting the remaining ten feet to the ground. His feet touched the ground first, but it wasn't fair to say he landed on them, because the actual force of the landing was absorbed by his rear end when he stumbled back and went sprawling across the ground.

Somewhere down the street, the flagpole clattered down. He clambered upright and ignored the half-dozen sharp pains assaulting his body as he took off at a sprint. Nothing important seemed to be broken badly enough for him to pay it any mind, the bulk of the scouting parties were rushing toward the much louder sound of a fallen flagpole, and the only scout with the means to visually track him was somewhere inside the tower. So long as he wasn't near a window, there was the chance he'd lost them.

The horrible screech of the lesser sphinx, followed by the unrecognizable shout of its handler, let him know that at least one link of that chain of good fortune had broken. He continued his sprint.

"Wick, you there?" he huffed.

"I am," came the voice by his side.

"How close are they?"

"There are presently no elves visible directly trailing you. No. Correction, there is one, led by a lesser sphinx. It will catch up to you in ten strides."

He leaped, caught the top and side of a window for the house he was passing, and pivoted through. The maneuver sent him sliding across a table within. He tumbled to the floor and got to his feet again just in time for the sphinx to arrive at the window. It spread its wings to fly through, but the decidedly flightless elf failed to achieve the same speed of entry. The leash snapped tight, and Fel was able to escape the room. He barreled through the house. The front door was open. His journey through the city had taught him that the switches beside the door were there to activate or deactivate traps. They seemed to be in the active position. He took the chance that the trap was triggered by a pressure plate just outside the door and vaulted as far as he could down the walkway to the door. The elf probably would have had the sense to do the same. The sphinx did not. What he heard next was a metallic ringing and a heavy blow to something meaty. It wasn't enough to kill the sphinx, judging by the continuing screech, but it was either unwilling or unable to give chase any longer.

Fel didn't slow. He knew the moment he let the rush of exhilaration fade, his steadily accumulating injuries would make further running much more difficult. He turned and dashed down a street that, if he was correct, would take him past the cathedral rather than directly to it. He could hear elves and lesser dragons flooding out to the street, drawn to the commotion he'd left behind. He circled around to a wall. He could hear the cacophony of animals on the other side. A leap just barely caught the top of the low wall. He hauled himself over and dropped onto the top of a pile of cages, which promptly fell, releasing their contents.

These must have been the beasts that the elves had found less useful for acting as guides, because there were many, many more types of beasts here than he'd seen in the streets. He didn't know what half of them were, but as the shuffle of feet approached, he decided if the elves wanted them locked up, he wanted them free.

It was impressive how many cages could be opened in a few seconds when desperation was a factor. By the time the first elves stumbled out from within the cathedral, two dozen creatures were unleashed. Most were just looking for a way out. Some were looking for revenge. Fel shouldered his way past the guards before they were able to make sense of the chaos he had wrought. By the time they realized the nature of the threat, they'd been mobbed by all manner of beasts with claws, teeth, and a grudge.

For the first time since he'd left the tower, a proper plan started to assemble in his head. The cathedral was almost empty, but not entirely. He could hear voices shouting in Elven. Orders being delivered. It had to be the leader. Fel dashed into the main hall of the cathedral. At the edge of his mind, he took note of the carefully sorted remnants of the dragon's hoard. It didn't appear as though they'd taken much of it, but they'd quite clearly searched it. The stink of smoke, more like a foundry or furnace than a cooking fire, poured from one of the adjoining rooms, and he saw motion within.

He slid the dagger from his belt and swept a handful of gold coins from the top of a pile as he rushed for the door. Now he saw that there were three elves within. One was heavily armed. Another was gathering something from a chest. The last was the one shouting orders. The guard spotted Fel and drew a sword. Fel hurled the fistful of coins at the man's face and heaved a shoulder into his chest, shoving him through the doorway to collide with the one clutching a small, closed chest. Both of them tumbled to the floor. The leader spat three syllables. Even without a knowledge of their meaning, Fel could tell they were most certainly the beginning of a spell. He got his filthy hand over the leader's mouth to silence him before the rest of the spell could be spoken. The others tried to stop him, but he wrenched the leader's neck aside to put a blade to it.

"All right!" he barked, gasping for breath. "I've got your boss! I've got a knife to his neck! And I am in no mood for any more trouble! So you're all going to drop your weapons and start answering questions. Got that?"

The others climbed to their feet but didn't heed the warning. The guard still held his weapon.

"Drop the weapons!" Fel growled.

"It is likely they cannot understand your words," Wick said.

"Do you speak their language?" he said.

"Sufficiently, I believe."

"Then tell them. I don't like the look in that guard's eye."

Wick did so. After a moment, the guard's weapons rattled to the ground. With the immediate threat to his life briefly set aside, Fel took the time to properly observe the room. Sure enough, the smoke and heat were coming from a furnace that had been assembled in the corner of the room. The bellows were manual, and presently stationary, but the heat was quite intense. Tools he recognized from his father's workshop, crucibles and molds for jewelry, were scattered about. A small mound of silver jewelry lay on the corner of a table, too old to have been the result of their efforts. They must have been raw material. And just beside them were four lanterns. All extinguished. All charred as though they'd been immersed in flames recently. And all quite similar to Wick's lantern.

"Are those what I think they are?" Fel said.

"Sentry lanterns," Wick said. "And they are... depleted. Weakened possibly past the point of recovery."

Fel gestured at the elf with the chest. "Open it," he ordered.

Wick translated. The frightened assistant glanced to his master. Fel pressed the knife a little more firmly to his neck. The hostage nodded. The assistant opened the chest. Inside were silver earrings. Not many. Two dozen, perhaps a few more.

"So that's what you came here for," Fel said. "You've been digging through the remnants of Clickspring for months, searching for sentry lanterns to make more rings. So you could give this place the slip and send a whole squad out like Mevrelle. I gotta hand it to you. Clever. But why are you out there bumbling around blindly, following sphinxes and dragons instead of wearing the damn things and being able to see properly?"

Wick translated. The assistant stammered something in reply.

"He says that is known only by the wizard," said Wick.

"Oh. So I have to ask the man who can fight me just by saying words. Isn't that convenient."

He took a few breaths. His body was really starting to throb as the fear of death ceased to dull the aftermath of his accumulating injuries. A thought came to mind. He pulled the wizard's head painfully aside, a visual indication to those looking on that a snapped neck was as bad as a slit throat. He then sheathed the blade and rummaged in his gear until he unearthed the sparker.

"Here's what you're going to tell them. And really sell it. This is Clickspring. Capital of an empire built by contraptioneers. And I am one of the greatest living contraptioneers. This city was built to serve my whims. And in my hand is a contraption handed down through the ages. A contraption that was built right here. With a roll of this little wheel, this contraption will trigger the final trap. The clockwork diamond will blot out the minds of any nonhuman in the city. All it will take is a few clicks and I'll be the only creature on this island who still remembers how to breathe."

Wick translated. It was clear the lantern was doing a fine job of matching Fel's emphatic tone, as the elves became increasingly uneasy as the complex words flowed. When Wick stopped speaking, Fel started again.

"I don't want to wipe you out. Contrary to what you've seen here, I'm not a violent monster. But you and yours have given me very good reason to believe I shouldn't hesitate to act against you. So when I take my hand away, I don't want to hear anything that even sounds like a spell, or that's it for all of you. Got that?"

The number of half-truths and outright lies in the threat was staggering, but Fel had gotten a lot of practice bluffing on poor runs of tiles. And Wick, to his credit, delivered the threat with close to the same level of intensity as Fel had.

"Are you going to behave?" Fel asked.

Wick translated. After a delay long enough to preserve some level of dignity, all nodded. He took his hand away.

"Answers. Fast. Start with why you aren't wearing those earrings you've been making." Wick translated the reply.

"The enchantment draws upon the contraptioneer's art. To utilize such an artifact for more than a few moments at a time is to be tainted by it, to be rendered unfit to continue as a part of elf society." Wick clarified. "The words they are using have a religious connotation. They view using the artifacts as a form of sacrilege or blasphemy."

"Then why make them at all?"

"Some are willing to sacrifice their place in exchange for... and then he hesitated," Wick eventually relayed.

"You see, now, you pause because you're afraid the truth will make you look bad. But believe me, you don't want me trying to figure out what you think is worth keeping a secret even at the cost of dozens of your people."

The answer came slowly.

"We are at war, your people and mine. In war, lives are lost. Those willing to lose their lives have nothing to fear from exile," Wick relayed.

"Kind of a one-sided war."

"You believe this only because you are too young to remember a time before your people made prisoners of ours."

"Don't pick a fight with me and pretend it's my fault. In fact, don't pick a fight with me at all. Now here's another question. And you had better hope I like the answer. You kidnapped a lesser unicorn from me. Where is it?"

"We acquired seven lesser unicorns."

"This one had a chipped horn, a cute harness and leash, and was definitely a pain in the neck."

"I know nothing of this beast."

Fel turned. Visible outside the doorway of the room were at least a half-dozen other elves waiting for their opportunity to act.

"What about them?" he said. "And do me a favor and remind them what's at stake."

An exchange swept through the assembled elves. One of them spoke up.

"Your beast was more stubborn than most. It is affixed to a salvaged chain attached to a wall at the edge of a section of the city deemed too dangerous to search, as a warning."

"Keeping him alive was the smartest thing you ever did. Now listen closely. Here's what's going to happen. I'm going to take those earrings. You're going to lead me to Parch, and then we're all going to walk back to the harbor. You get back on your boats, you go back home, and you never try coming here again."

"You won't be able to hold us prisoner here forever."

He held up the sparker. "There's always the alternative."

A tense silence followed. Finally, words were exchanged among the others and they cleared the doorway. With the sparker held firmly, Fel marched out.

"I think you can go and give the others an update. But don't take long. This could go very wrong very quickly."

Something unidentifiable, one of the things he'd released, screeched and scurried out one of the windows after lurking on the ceiling.

"Very, very quickly," he added, keeping his eyes peeled for other escaped beasts.

Euphoria's and Lattica's horses thundered into Ram's Rest. If Euphoria had taken a moment to consider what it must have looked like for one of the city's most respected businesswomen to come galloping through town, disheveled by a long and eventful trip, it would have brought her some pride. After spending years taking care to fit in, it felt good to stick out. But she had a job to do.

Along the way, they'd allowed the Wick-lit lantern to go out. It was a calculated risk, but keeping a mundane lantern safely lit while at a full gallop was nontrivial, and a far more reliable and actively tended-to lantern was waiting for them in her own home. A part of her wanted to return home, if only to check in with Wick that they'd arrived safely. So close to her target, it was better to wait until she had more than her arrival to report on. She set her gaze on the Graves family compound.

The thinking had already been done. If there was a codebook, that Lens was trying to lock the doors suggested either the Graves or the Masker family still had access to it. And considering the impressively comprehensive removal of information in the family archives that had led to this journey to begin with, it certainly wouldn't be there. That left only two other places either she or Lattica could conceive of that might be beyond Lens's reach. The first was her own library, and she very much doubted she was in possession of something without her knowledge. That meant it could only be one place. Gunther's study.

The pair of women brought their horses to a stop in front of the old man's home. One of his servants rushed out.

"Mrs. Euphoria? Mrs. Lattica? What are you doing here? This is most—" the man began.

Euphoria tossed him the reins. "See to the horses, please. A recent purchase and we've ridden them quite hard. They need to be fed and watered, generally cared for. You know what to do."

"But you weren't expected, ma'am. There is protocol," he sputtered.

"Right, yes. Absolutely. Protocol. I assure you, I'm an expert at protocol. It just so happens I'm in something of a hurry. Won't be a moment." She climbed the steps toward the front door.

"But, ma'am," he insisted.

She stopped and turned, flipping a switch in her mind and assuming the role of authority figure, a position her fellow Graves family members reveled in and one she tried to make sparing use of.

"Protocol, Luke? Is it your place to lecture me on protocol? Or is it your place to tend to the horses? Something, I note, you have yet to do."

"Right! Sorry, ma'am!" he said suddenly, scurrying away, leading both horses along behind.

She shook her head and wrangled her hair as Lattica joined her at the door.

"It is depressing how many people are willing to seek the refuge of future admonishments in order to escape the admonishments of the present," Euphoria said.

"It certainly did the trick."

"Just because I rely upon something doesn't mean I have to like it," she said, rattling the door knocker.

With the best expedience money can buy, the butler of the patriarch's home answered the door.

"Madam Euphoria. You were not expected," he said.

"So I've repeatedly been told," she said in a kinder tone than the words would suggest. "If you wouldn't mind. There's been a bit of a ruckus out here. Two women riding wildly through the streets on horseback. I'd just as soon be inside and wait for Mr. Graves in his study."

"Is that what that sound was? Gracious, come inside. We mustn't have you out there while wild women are charging about."

Euphoria stepped inside. When Lattica followed, the butler tried to stop her.

"I'm afraid I—" he began.

"She will be joining me," Euphoria said simply.

"Er. As you wish, ma'am."

It was staggering how much one could get away with when one possessed both a dash of privilege and the willingness to abuse it. The butler led them directly to Gunther's study and left them alone to fetch him. Lattica and Euphoria immediately went to work.

"You're sure it had a blue spine," Lattica said, standing back to scan the multiple bookshelves flanking the massive desk that dominated the room.

"Not as sure as I'd like. I only saw the book once," she said. "It's smallish. If we're going to find it, it'll be because it's a good deal shorter than the books around it."

She could feel the pressure ramping up in the back of her mind. Gunther guarded his private things quite jealously, and this book in particular had already been established as something not meant for public consumption. Euphoria was family, but her role was a few steps closer to public than most other family members, and crossing this line would put her solidly in that realm from this point forward.

"Unless he sorts by height," Lattica reasoned, crouching to more closely investigate the lower shelves.

"Right... Right. Here, this is it," Euphoria said, reaching to the top shelf of the adjoining bookcase. "More gray than blue. A trick of the light, I suppose."

She slipped the book from its place and opened it on the desk. A few desperate flips took her to the page that had been so carefully copied to rope her father and brother into the mess at the Greater Lands Wall. It, like the rest of the book, was written mostly in a code that Martin was able to break and the Graves family wasn't. But having seen the page in both translated and untranslated states, she at least was able to determine that the complex codes meant to unlock Bygone Era doors were present on several other pages.

"Euphoria."

The voice came from the doorway. She looked to its source and found Gunther in the doorway of his study. His expression was even. Unreadable. Trained by a lifetime of negotiating and deal-making.

"I do not recall inviting you to my home. And I certainly do not recall inviting you to rifle through my library."

"I can explain, but I assure you, this is necessary."

He raised a shriveled finger. "In a moment. Jonathan? This way, my boy."

Jonathan Graves arrived in the doorway beside Gunther. His expression lit up at the sight of Euphoria.

"Darling! You're home early!" he said, marching up to her and taking her hands in his. Displays of affection were another of those things carefully moderated by the less official aspects of the protocol that the other servant was so worried about, but Jonathan scandalously gave her a kiss on the cheek.

"So good to see you again. It feels like it's been ages. I was afraid I would be gone again before you returned." He noticed the book on the desk. "What's this?"

"Yes, Euphoria. What is it?" Gunther asked.

Euphoria looked back and forth between Jonathan and Gunther. A few half-constructed fabrications bobbed to the surface of her thoughts, candidates for a yarn to spin to try to justify this in a way that would be easy for them to swallow. She dismissed them.

"We found Piotor, or rather the source of the messages that Piotor has been sending. The Graves flame is currently inhabited by an entity that calls itself Lens. This entity is, or has replaced, Piotor, who was killed in the fire that moved him to his more secure lodgings. He has been manipulating our family for years toward a sinister purpose. Those manipulations most certainly extended to the Bolivan family through their 'theft' of our flame, and at this very moment are coming to a crescendo. The rumbling that shook our homes was felt the world over and is due to ancient tunnels that permit travel from one side of the world to the other in hours. Lens has sought precautions to lock the exits to the tunnels, which we have reasoned means he knows or suspects we have access to the codes to unlock those doors. I believe this book contains those codes, and I deemed the time necessary to negotiate access to this book to be greater than the amount of time we have left to act before some unknown tragedy befalls us through the culmination of Lens's machinations."

"That is... a staggering sequence of claims, dear," Jonathan said.

"Quite staggering," Gunther said.

"I agree. A lie would have been easier, but I respect you too much to attempt to manipulate you as Lens has."

The patriarch paced to the desk and sat stiffly in his chair. He slid the book in front of him and casually turned the pages. As he reviewed the contents of the book, he spoke.

"Piotor," he remarked. "I have known Piotor Graves for longer than anyone else in this room has been alive. The amount of trust I have placed in him cannot be measured and cannot be matched by anyone in this family or beyond it. Not even my own wife has earned such reverence from me. And yet. I looked upon the evidence that you set forth as justification for the journey that has sent you off to make these supposed discoveries and found it sufficiently compelling to allow the journey. Because I learned through hard and painful lessons of the past that no trust should ever be unbreakable. But nonetheless, when I received a message from him not long before your departure that I should keep one of the family flames burning and consult with it directly on occasion, I did so. And it was thus that I came to be warned of your arrival. And that I was warned that you were no longer to be trusted."

"Gunther, I—" Euphoria attempted.

He silenced her with a raised finger. "The words that reached my ears ostensibly came from the lips of Piotor, with only the flame as an intermediary. As I said, I've known Piotor a long time. He is measured. Uncouth, at times. Awkward. More interested in the present focus of his studies than decorum or tact. But always, always measured. The words that reached my ears did not reflect the tone of the man I know. Either they did not come from the man I know, a worrying thought, or they were altered by the flame. Equally worrying. You make extraordinary claims. But they align with my own concerns. If they came from almost anyone else, I would be inclined to believe them without reservation. But you are a newcomer to the family and represent a famously unstable rival that only recently has been made an ally."

"Newcomer or not," Jonathan said. "She is family. And more to the point, she is my wife."

The young man made the remark with calculated intensity. He wanted to be firm but not disrespectful. From Gunther's expression, his aim wasn't quite true.

"I was your age once," he said sharply. "There are many forces that shape the mind of a young man."

"This isn't a matter of where I'm doing my thinking. This is a matter of where I chose to place my trust and whether you trust my judgment. Euphoria has given the Maskers more reason to doubt her devotion to them than she's given us reason to doubt her devotion to us."

The patriarch tightened his lips and shut his eyes.

"What, may I ask, do you suppose I stand to gain by deceiving you now? And while you consider that, ask yourself what you stand to lose by placing your trust in the Voice of the Lantern," Euphoria said.

The old man's eyes remained shut. He took two slow breaths.

"Tunnels. Codes." He shut the book and pushed it forward. "This is not the book you are looking for."

With effort, he stood again and steadied himself on the back of the chair as he stood behind it. "When the Ambassador was found, a great many other items were with it. One was this book. The codebook. Another was the atlas. There were, in fact, two copies of it. Piotor kept one. He gave the other to me. There was little indication to what the pages referred. But there were maps of things that seemed to cover an area barely larger than a city. The descriptions were coded. The only things we were ever able to decode ourselves were vague references to places associated with the exits to those streets or paths. And the places they referred to were impossibly distant. There *were* locked doors in some of the places, but the locks led to dead ends or were otherwise completely inoperable. We disregarded the value of the book, but it was still in excellent condition, and still a remnant of the Bygone Era. Precious. I kept it with the maps."

He made his way to the opposite side of the room and opened a cabinet. Many rolled maps were inside. A large leather-bound book awaited him there as well. Jonathan carried it to the desk for the patriarch. Once there, he opened the cover. Euphoria unfurled the hand-drawn map that she had been producing along with her father through Wick. She held it down to the network traced out on the page. It matched a large swath of the one in the book. And more blocks of text that could only be the encoded sequences to unlock the doors in the tunnel accompanied small sections of text.

"The book remains here," the patriarch said. "But you may bring in the Masker flame. I trust it will be able to relay the information appropriately?"

"He will. Thank you, sir, for your trust," Euphoria said.

"Thank you, ma'am, for having patience with an old, cautious man."

Donovan Verfessa marched through the halls of Lord Katritz's house, a few steps behind one of the man's many servants. He was led all the way to Katritz's study. The lord sat in a bear-hide chair adorned with antlers. One shaky hand held a snifter of brandy. The other held the bottle. His eyes were fixed vaguely on the window facing the center of the city.

"Katritz!" Verfessa said. "I was surprised to get the invitation. From your behavior over the last few days, it seemed like I wasn't welcome here anymore."

"You aren't. But I wanted you here because I wanted the pleasure of telling you this personally," he said, slurring slightly from too much drink. "The quake, and the events soon to transpire, are on your head, not mine."

"The quake? You're blaming me for the earth beneath our feet getting antsy?"

"No cuteness. No turns of phrase. Sit down and listen to what I have to say. You came to my home and quickly illustrated that I had something to lose and you had everything to gain. I don't like losing. And more than that, I don't like seeing a pointless, lowborn cretin such as yourself winning. I hold a lofty position in this world, and I don't need ogres like you bringing your rancid fumes and giggling grunts. So I was pushed to the brink of poor judgment. And mistakes were made. You are the reason those mistakes were made. And when their consequences fall upon this city and this world, I will not be blamed for what you forced me to do."

"I think you've been doing a little too much drinking. It's impressive how much a man can inflate his self-worth but deflate his sense of responsibility. You're talking like you've done something to bring down the whole city. That's the sort of thing it takes a war to do, and even if you could start a war all by your lonesome, I don't think you could do it in just a few days."

Katritz laughed dryly. "A final barb." He tipped his head up slightly and eyed something outside the window. "And I do mean final."

Verfessa turned. Something deeper into the city was causing a commotion. A large wooden door in a walled off area toward the center of the city had been broken and splintered. Nine automatons marched through. If he'd seen the originals, he would have had cause to remark how different these looked. They were more complete, most notably in their heads. Rather than having exposed posts where a head should be, a full helmet with a perforated faceplate had been installed. They marched relentlessly forward. Guards assembled in the streets before them. Longbows and crossbows peppered them. Even at this distance, the sound of the bolts impacting metal could be heard. Some of the braver guards attempted to clash with sword and club. Their blows were no more effective.

"What did you do, Katritz?" Verfessa rumbled.

"I did what you forced me to do," Katritz said. "They are here to harvest some goods from the Contraband Vault and quash any resistance. I was able to contact the man responsible and assure him of my cooperation. I instructed the guards not to resist, but it seems the word of a lord is insufficient for the idiots to act in their own best interest."

"Do you have any idea what sort of damage soldiers will be able to do with the kind of contraptions that end up in that vault?"

"I know perfectly well. I know better than anyone. But look what they are capable of now. How much worse could it get?" Katritz asked.

"I don't mean to find out," he said, marching for the door.

"Oh! By all means. Get yourself killed. That will be the silver lining on a bloody great, big, dark cloud," Katritz called from behind him.

Verfessa stomped out to the street and climbed into the little carriage that had been loaned to him by one of the other nobles. "Get us down toward where those things are," he barked.

"I'll give it a shot, boss, but this isn't my usual area," came the voice of someone who was certainly not his driver.

Verfessa leaned forward through the hatch to where the driver sat and found, rather than the man who had been carting him around town for the last few days, his surreptitious bodyguard Davie was waiting for him. If the little fellow wasn't fully a gnome, he was more gnome than most and thus wasn't the proper size for driving horses. Verfessa scrambled to the front driver's seat and took the reins himself.

"Where did the driver go?"

"Too little fortitude or too much sense to stick around. And I'm thinking he had the right idea."

"We're doing something about this," Verfessa said, snapping the reins and guiding the carriage against the traffic of people rushing away from the attackers.

"I'm a blade man, boss. Looks to me if I drag this across a throat or two, it'll do nothing but dull my knife. Sometimes cowards got the right ideas. What's any of this got to do with us?"

"You know how I feel about someone else letting their dogs loose in my yard."

"This ain't your yard, boss."

"Gimme a couple more weeks and see if it is," he said. "And besides. Seems like they left the gate open, so if they know where the power and money is for Thayne, the next stop is Beffshire. And that's if they haven't been down there already. So we fight them where we find them until there's no more of them to fight. Now let's get in there and see what we can do."

Martin tapped the handle of an engraving tool, teasing a tiny curl of metal from the inside of the Scholar mask. It was the narrowest, thinnest filament of metal, but he had to hammer at the salvaged Bygone Era tool like he was chipping through a quarry stone wall. The contraptions from that era were so impressively resilient, he couldn't dream of how this one had been damaged so badly. But, if he was correct, the job was done. All he needed to do was place it on the bust and it should wake up. For the sake of safety, he decided the original, armless bust would be best. When testing something, it is usually best to prevent it from being able to physically assault you.

He hesitated briefly. It wasn't that he was afraid something would go wrong. It wasn't even that he was afraid nothing would happen at all. Mostly, after so much sizzling acid, careful rinsing, and endless hammering, this moment of peace was precious. But it wasn't truly peaceful at all. Yes, he was free of his own racket, but without that distraction, he was made aware of the complete stillness of his own home. He was many levels below the surface, but somewhere in the back of his mind he could always hear the sound of activity elsewhere in his home. Fel thumping about in his room. Epiphany sorting through books or inventory. And if he listened hard enough, sometimes he could even hear the hint of people in the shop. But right now, nothing. Silence. And yet nothing had ever felt so loud.

He slipped the mask into place on the complex head of the original bust they'd salvaged. It was very slightly warped, barely enough to open a gap the size of a sheet of paper, but that was enough to keep it from properly seating and activating. A few turns of the fasteners finally brought the disks of irises flashing up into the holes in the mask.

"What lesson shall we have today?" said the mask in a clear, if somewhat soft, voice.

Martin picked up a rag and wiped his hands. "I certainly have questions. A thousand of them."

"Ah. You speak clearly and confidently. A pleasant departure from the muddled mess of communication I've been forced to endure for these many years."

"I've had questions that have plagued my mind for my whole life, and I've dreamed of getting the opportunity to ask them. But right now, I'm afraid they will have to wait. There are more pressing concerns."

"The wisdom to prioritize is an important lesson in and of itself."

"What are the limits to your role? What can and can't you do?"

"I can, and must, work with any student who asks me to do so. I can, and must, render my lessons with clarity in the pursuit of bringing understanding to my student. I can, and must, share any and all information that I know to be incontrovertible and true. I can, and must, help my student extrapolate intelligently and logically from that information, provided I am clear in my guidance that such lessons may change if firmer grounding becomes available."

"Fine. Excellent. I'll begin, then, with Lens. Your previous student was an entity that calls itself Lens, is this correct?"

"This is so."

"Lens claims to be the result of a union of intellect between a sentry lantern and a human, when the human was consumed in the flames of the lantern. Is this correct?"

"All evidence indicates that this is so."

"What was his goal in his interactions with you?"

"Lens sought knowledge of the Bygone Era. Specifically, he sought the means to adapt and, if I interpreted his words correctly, correct the effects of certain Bygone contraptions."

"Which contraptions?"

"He had a specific interest in a subassembly of the clockwork diamond that defines the nature of its influence."

"And did you provide that information?"

"I provided as much of it as I was able, but that is a subject that I lack comprehensive knowledge in. More accurately, that is a subject for which no single answer is necessarily definitive. It is an art, as much as anything else. And thus a full expertise depends upon the insight and point of view of the artist. He appeared to lack the proper insight to produce effects with the level of nuance and the depth of control that he required. I instructed him to locate someone else to render aid, as we had reached my limits. It is, again, refreshing to be able to speak so articulately on the subject. The nature of our connection was such that it took many months to properly communicate this information."

"Did you have a specific person in mind when you sent him to find aid?"

"I did not. My absence from the world had deprived me of up-to-date knowledge of its inhabitants. But I advised that someone with a great degree of insight in contraptions in general would be a good candidate."

"So, in effect, you sent him after me."

"If you are Martin Masker, then such is the case, as he stated his intent to find you."

"What precise effect did he wish to produce?"

"He wished to force the world back into the mold of the Bygone Era at its peak; restore the knowledge of the Bygone Era; take direct control over any minds that would be necessary to rebuild, relearn, and reinforce that era. He furthermore sought to remove any threat that might allow that era to fall once more. In particular, he wished to quash any sentiment critical to contraptions, and to remove freedom, or life, from the Greater Mystics. I advised that their capacities were the only things capable of rivaling contraptions as a force of domination for the world."

"He sought world domination. And you helped him."

"He sought knowledge, and I am obligated to provide what lessons I can. Additionally, domination was not his goal but a step along the path toward his goal. What he sought was world restoration."

"And what of everything that the world has achieved between then and now? What of the people who live in this world?"

"This was not relevant to his way of thinking and thus was not a part of the lesson which he sought to pursue."

"Well it is quite relevant to mine. So I ask you now. What can be done to stop him?"

"He has had years to discuss contingencies with me. I will gladly, and freely, provide you with options. But please be aware that any option that will come from me is one that he has prepared for. My advice eventually settled upon arming himself with automatons as well as finding and activating the Guardians."

"The Guardians?" Martin said.

"Large, manually controlled defensive contraptions in the shape of a soldier. If either or both of those contraptions have been brought to bear on the present problem, there is no tactic I can determine which will allow you to defeat him."

"What if we acquire the aid of said contraptions?"

"If you are the first to access and activate both Guardians, then there is the possibility. If even one of the Guardians is activated and brought into position, defeating Lens will become impossible through means within my consideration. The Guardians' armor is stronger than their operating mechanisms. That is to say, a Guardian will destroy itself before it will cause enough damage to an entrenched, defending Guardian to disable it. The contraptions have warding against magic and will permit nothing to enter once the operator has taken its place and activated the contraption."

"And you say he has a place for me in these plans. What if I can be kept from him?"

"He has contingencies for your absence as well. They are bloodier than his primary goals."

The workshop trembled lightly. It was subtle and might have been missed if he'd not been dreading such a thing ever since the arrival of the first automatons. They were back. He knew it.

"Tell me what those contingencies are," he said urgently.

Elsewhere in the city, Epiphany emerged from a shop to the sound of anxious clamor from the others in the city. The streets were trembling with the tension of people simultaneously desperate to find safety and desperate to learn the nature of the new threat. She caught a man by the arm as he rushed by.

"What is it?" she asked. "What's happening?"

"They're back! Those metal things are back! And there are six of them instead of two."

Epiphany cursed under her breath. "I'd hoped we'd have more time."

She hurried toward the shop. Fortunately for her, most of the route back to Masker's Antiquities was with the flow of panic. She was in greater danger of being trampled for traveling too slowly than having to shoulder her way through people to get to where she was going. She reached the shop to find her mother at the door.

"Inside. Inside quickly," Vivian said hurriedly, a rare break in her cool and measured demeanor.

When Epiphany was safely through the door, Vivian slammed it and braced it. Buckets of water lined the floor of the shop, and the contraption that fired the black gunk was slung behind Vivian's back, ready to be deployed.

"Where's Dad?"

"Downstairs, working."

"Should we get him up here?"

"He knows what's happened. If he hasn't come up yet, he's deep in something more important. What do you know about what's happening?"

"I've been told there are six of those things."

"It could be worse," Vivian said. "I'd expected more."

Epiphany pulled a bucket from the ground and held it ready. With the wooden slats replacing the windows, both she and her mother had to lean close and stare out between them to see what was going on. The chaos settled more quickly than anticipated, replaced instead by an eerie calm. After what felt like an eternity, a new sound came. Footsteps, both natural and metallic, were approaching from down the street. There were raised voices as well, like someone was having a heated argument. The source of the sounds became visible between the slats. There were not six of the things, there were eight. And they were surrounded by members of the Watch. Fresh gold gashes across the things' chests showed where attempts had been made to stop the automatons, but the damage was superficial. Scarcely more than a scrape in the layer of patina. Epiphany's heart dropped as she got her first look at their heads. No longer exposed posts so easy to douse, now they were full helmets, the glow of their flame gleaming through the grid of holes that replaced a face. Water would just splash over those masks. And unless the whole mask could be sealed airtight, the black gunk from the contraption wouldn't do much good either. This was bad.

They came to a stop, and the voice of Lens boomed out from the automatons.

"I have come for Martin Masker," they said, the voice flickering between them. "Give him to me and the city will be spared. Keep him from me and I will destroy everything and kill everyone I can reach until the city itself tears him from the bowels of his shop and delivers him to me."

Vivian and Epiphany braced themselves. Slowly, the City Watch assembled themselves in front of the shop, their backs turned to the boarded-up windows.

"Hold your ground," Captain Boltt instructed.

"You see?" shouted Marcus. "You see the sort of flawed instinct and impaired reasoning that will bring this city to ruin if this man remains in control of the Watch?" He stepped forward. "It is one man! You've seen what just two of these things can do to a city. Now there are eight. You give up the one man, you protect the rest of the city."

"We are the Watch. We protect the city from those from beyond the walls who would see it come to harm. Martin Masker is a part of this city. He will not be taken against his will."

"Your dedication is admirable. Foolish, but admirable," Lens said. "I will give you two minutes. And then you will be shown the error in your ways."

Marcus charged toward the captain. "Get down there and get him, or I will do it myself. Do you hear me? I'll show you that I'm the man for this job. I'm the man to protect this city."

Boltt held his ground. Marcus tried to elbow his way past him. Leonard delivered a punishing blow to the abdomen that sent him crumpling to the ground, coughing.

A sound behind them drew Vivian's and Epiphany's attention to the stairs. Martin was there. He had a bag over his shoulder, and a look of resolve on his face.

"Get back downstairs," Vivian hissed. "They're here for you."

"I'm going."

"Martin, no," Vivian said.

"Viv, I've heard the alternative. The Scholar is awake. Lens has been planning this. If I don't go... trust me. It's better this way."

The two shared an intense look. Vivian trembled with something between fear and frustration.

"You realize if you go, we'll have to find a way to get you back," she said.

"I'm doing what I have to do. You'll do what you have to do." He gave her a hug, then turned to Epiphany and gave her one as well. "Hopefully you two have some better ideas. It seems mine haven't been doing us much good."

"Dad, there are other ways to be a hero besides sacrificing yourself."

"Oh. I intend to survive. But... may the High help me, I only hope when I come back, it's to a world worth living in. Talk to the Scholar. Spread the word to the others. The end of this madness is near. The only question is what follows it."

He unbraced the door and stepped into the street. The Watch turned to him. He nodded. They stepped aside. He stepped face to mask with the automaton at the front of the line.

"I knew if ever there were a Masker would make the right decision, it would be you," Lens said.

"We're just letting him go?" Epiphany said, shaking with anger.

"What your father knows, he knows better than anyone else. We have to trust him," Vivian said.

The first of the automatons picked Martin up and threw him over its shoulder. They then turned and, true to their word, left the city in peace. Those near enough to witness the selfless act gave Vivian and Epiphany some knowing and empathetic looks. Epiphany slammed the door and braced it again.

"We have to trust Dad. Dad throws himself to the wolves and we have to trust him," she fumed.

"Yes. Now go downstairs and see to the Scholar, and inform Wick of what's happened when he next pays his visit. We're putting our minds to the task of getting Martin back.

Because part of trusting his judgment is knowing that he trusts us to do what we can with whatever time he's bought us."

It had taken Verfessa longer than he would have liked to force his way through the capital. By the time he passed the Contraband Vault, the automatons had harvested their fill. That must have been the main reason for their visit, because according to the bystanders, once they'd done so, most of them had carried their crates of stolen artifacts back to the hole in the ground from whence they'd come. But not all of them. Two of the things stood stock-still in front of the main doors of the palace. Everyone else had fled the area, save the row of soldiers visible through the arrow slits above and around the doors. Countless bolts and broken arrows littered the ground around the attackers in such quantities it may as well have been hailing arrows. But they still stood, fully intact.

Verfessa's carriage lurked in the shadow of the nearest of the little buildings that served the palace but were too dirty or lowly to actually be a part of it. Namely, they were beside the blacksmith's shop and across from the royal stables.

"Remind me again what you thought you'd be able to do to those things?" Davie asked from his perch atop the carriage.

"Why do you suppose they're standing still?" Verfessa said, ignoring the jab.

"They're not standing still. They're swaying a little. In a sort of a rhythm. But I don't know how or why they're doing that."

"One more minute. Give up the king, give up the lords, or the city will be razed," bellowed the automatons.

"That'll do it," Davie said. "They're waiting on an ultimatum to run out."

"Makes sense the lords would hole up with the king if something like this went down. Probably they'd have hauled me in there with them if Katritz hadn't called me over. Probably why he did. Didn't want me somewhere safe."

"I'm not so sure that palace is safe, boss."

"No. I don't think it is." Verfessa glanced about. "Tell you one thing. If I want to get myself in the good graces of the king and the upper crust, saving their lives is a good way to do it."

He scanned the surroundings and took stock of what might do good. The door was sturdy, but not sturdy enough to turn those things away, he'd wager. Plenty of good sturdy things to clobber someone with in the blacksmith's shop, but if point-blank crossbow bolts didn't punch any holes, he didn't like his luck with a ten-pound hammer. The palace had a moat, but they'd failed to raise the gate in time, if it could even be raised at all. He had a feeling the water was more for show these days. Across the way, a few horses, a few bales of hay, and the hay wagon were waiting for him. A thought came to mind.

"How heavy do you figure those things are?"

"Too heavy to lift," Davie said.

"Sure. But I'm not looking to lift them. Head over and borrow us that hay wagon. Bring it around back of the palace, and as soon as you can, come by the front here moving as fast as you can get those horses moving."

"I already said I'm not the best with horses."

"You want to be the one having a word with those things, then?"

"... I'll manage."

Davie scampered across the street and, with a bit of shouting and cursing, managed to motivate the horses to move. The rattling rumble of the wagon careening off down the street that wrapped around the palace was enough to get the attention of the automatons. Verfessa grabbed two stout ropes from the stable and four hay hooks. As the automatons marched toward him, he tied a hook to either end of each rope. While he worked, he spoke.

"Haven't seen your kind around here before."

"No," Lens said. "But I know you."

"Two fellows speaking as one. That's an odd affectation. Give you credit for originality."

"You have complicated my schemes, Verfessa."

"You've got me at a disadvantage."

"Yes."

"What I mean was, I don't know your name."

"My name is Lens. And in very short order, it won't matter. Turn around, Verfessa. Walk away. As frustrating as you are, you at least seem to have negotiable morals, and considerable resources. If things do not go as I intend, you could be useful. But if you don't have the wisdom to retreat, I may as well kill you now."

Verfessa trotted toward them, ropes trailing from each hand. "You'd kill a man before even talking to him? What's the matter? Haven't got the confidence in your plan to gloat about it?"

The automatons stopped just forward of the center of the drawbridge over the moat. He stepped up, near enough to be just clear of the range of a grab. At this range, he could see the flames through the mask.

"That's quite a face you have there. So what are you? Some sort of demon?"

"What I am is a long-overdue return to form for humanity."

"I don't recall humanity ever having fire for a face."

"If your intention is to talk me out of this, or to gain some sort of valuable knowledge, you are wasting your time. And even *you* couldn't be foolish enough to think you could pierce me with one of those hooks."

Verfessa let the hooks slide toward the ground and started to swing them, speeding the rotation until they were whistling. "Not wasting my time. Just biding it. And I'm really not interested in piercing you."

The rattling wagon appeared, streaking along the road perpendicular to the drawbridge.

"The king's time is up," Lens said. "But since you fancy yourself his protector, you may be the first to meet his fate."

The first of the automatons advanced, ready to grab him. He dropped back and let the first hook whistle forward, wrapping around the thing's arm. The second one remained behind, but not far enough to avoid the hurled second hook. It wrapped around its neck. With both of them, for the moment, snared, Verfessa turned and dashed. He snatched the trailing hooks from the ground, each affixed to the opposite end of a rope. Davie's out-of-control hay wagon streaked by. Verfessa tossed the hooks. One bit into the plank of the wagon's bed. The other wrapped around one of the supports for the side of the wagon. The rope snapped up from the ground and drew tight.

The automatons may have been strong, but it didn't matter how strong you were once you were yanked off your feet and sent sliding. Both of them ground a deep furrow into the wood of the bridge. The rope struck the chains meant to raise the bridge, suddenly turning a lateral drag into a forward yank. One of them tumbled over the side, breaking free of the hook and plunking into the water. The other managed to dig its gauntlet into the plank of the bridge. Wood splintered. The heavy automaton dangled over the edge but held firm with a single hand.

Verfessa dashed toward it. Badly damaged wood was creaking under the grip of the gauntlet. The other arm, responsible for dragging it over the edge, was still hooked, and the other side of the rope was entangled in the chain. For the moment, the contraption couldn't sort it out well enough to grab the drawbridge with the other mitt. Verfessa jumped. He didn't so much kick the grasping fingers as hurl his entire body at them feet first. His heels struck the metal mitt. The ailing wood shredded between its fingers, and a second massive thing plummeted into the moat.

He lay on the ground, huffing and puffing. Throwing himself across a splintered wooden bridge wasn't the brightest choice he'd made that day. An unhealthy number of wooden shards had punched through his pants to gouge at him. When he was able to climb to his feet, Davie had trotted over to him. Both of them peered over the side. Barely visible through the murky water were the gleaming heaps of the automatons.

"How'd you know that'd work?" Davie said.

"Seemed to me, if a thing can talk, it can breathe. And if a thing can breathe, it usually has to. And armor and a moat combine to make that sort of thing tricky."

"Good thinking, boss."

"I got good at thinking so I wouldn't have to put my flesh on the line quite so often. Might be the first time I've had to do both in quite a while. Here's hoping it's the last."

The palace doors opened, and soldiers started to pour out. Davie started to trot away.

"No, no," Verfessa said. "There's a whole lot of glory about to come splashing out of that palace. May as well stick around for your share."

"That went better than I thought!" Madge said, marching along beside Tome, eating an apple.

"We failed to get a boat," Tome said. "It was the entire reason we went to the city, to see if we could get a boat and see if we could reach the island."

"Right, but we were offering a pathetic amount of money. In my experience, when you offer a pathetic amount of money to someone with a very valuable object like a boat, even just to borrow it, sometimes they can be very cruel. They just sent us back empty-handed! I think it's a great sign. I think it means things are looking up!"

Tome was still attempting to formulate a suitable retort when he noticed the flame in the lantern suddenly become still. "Time to see if your optimism is warranted," he said, raising the lantern.

"Tome. Madge. There have been developments," Wick said.

"I bet they were good," Madge said through a mouthful of apple.

"Automatons have attacked Beffshire for a second time. They issued an ultimatum that the city would be relentlessly attacked or Martin would be handed over, and Martin went willingly."

"Oh…" Madge said.

"Fel has managed to, for the moment, bring the elven invaders of Clickspring to their knees through bluster and false threat. Euphoria was able to locate and acquire something called 'the atlas,' which contains a full map of the tunnels and a nearly complete set of codes for the locked exits of those tunnels. The Gate of the Ancients is among those listed."

"Do you have the full atlas available to you?" Tome asked.

"I do."

"Is there a route connecting the Gate of the Ancients to an island off the coast?"

"It is an unbranching path heading due west," Wick said.

"There!" Madge said, clapping Tome on the back. "You see? Things are looking up. Just when we failed to get a way to reach the island, a new way pops up."

"Stunningly convenient, if you ask me," Tome said. "Rarely does convenience come without a significant price."

"Oh, you worry too much," Madge said.

"I've rarely had a concern that fell short of what reality chose to serve up."

He thrust the lantern into her hands and tugged out a slip of paper and a quill. He awkwardly dipped the quill in his hastily unscrewed ink bottle. Madge helpfully turned to offer her back as a writing surface.

"Wick, tell me the code to open the Gate of the Ancients. And any other doors between us and the exit on the island."

There were only two, and Wick helpfully provided each one with slow precision. "That is all," Wick concluded. "Have there been any developments on your side?"

"I angered my father," Tome said.

"And we failed to get a boat!" Madge added.

"We're going to open the gateway and head for the island. You can go to the others. They probably need you more than we do."

"I concur. Be safe."

"Impossible," Tome said.

The flame flickered away. They quickened to a sprint. The timing was such that it took barely five minutes of swift motion to reach the Gate of the Ancients again. Considering the actions he was about to take, it would have been polite, and some would say manda-tory, to receive permission to attempt to enter the code in the gate. Tome chose to forego that courtesy. If he survived, he could seek forgiveness. If he didn't, this was hardly the worst of his sins.

Tome looked at the page of instructions and eyed the monument that had lurked outside his home for his entire childhood. He'd seen what happened if an incorrect sequence was entered into the doors in the Greater Lands Wall, and those mechanisms were barely the size of a dartboard. This was closer to the size of a courtyard. He would very much like to avoid a wrong entry. As luck—or design—would have it, the code was quite simple. Not so simple that one would stumble upon it in a single try, but far less complex than the codes at the wall. He knelt at the edge of the first ring and grasped the edge of an upraised block. With surprisingly little force, he was able to raise it an inch or two and start rotating the entire ring. When it reached the proper position, he stood and found the indicated block and clicked it down. Onward to the next ring.

"What is this? What are you doing?" shouted Brother Inkbrand from the doorway of the monastery. "You are desecrating the monument!"

"Are we telling him what we're doing?" Madge called to Tome.

"If I manage this code properly, we won't very well be able to keep it a secret," Tome said, stepping onto the now-secure ring and beginning work on the next one toward the center.

Madge trotted forward to intercept the head of the monastery. "Your son is entering a sequence that will cause this whole thing to slide open. It'll reveal a tunnel that leads to the island we can't see right now, among other places. Probably the person who stole that boat a while back is over there, and we don't know what they're doing, but it's probably bad. Oh! And maybe some mechanical men will come marching through at some point? Not so clear on that, but they seem to show up everywhere something important is happening, and this feels pretty important."

"I don't understand! The monument is entirely immobile. We would have known if it wasn't," Brother Inkbrand said.

Madge shrugged. "Things change."

"We need to stop him. This isn't right," Inkbrand said.

Madge stepped in front of him as he attempted to get around her. "You didn't think this could move. He knew it could. You didn't know what was under it, he does. Did you go check if he was right about the content of that book you tested him on?"

"... It matched."

"Seems to me like this is an excellent time to trust that your son knows what he's doing. Or at least knows better than you do about this right now. Also, I think maybe something big and bad will happen if you interrupt him."

"It will," Tome shouted. He worked his way forward to the next ring. Only three more rings and the sequence would be complete.

"Why would all of this be happening now, right when he came home, if he wasn't somehow the cause?" Inkbrand snapped.

"Fate, coincidence, dumb luck? Does it matter?" Madge said. "We'll have an answer soon enough."

Another ring clicked into place. Inkbrand stepped forward. Madge physically stopped him.

"Why not give him a chance?" she asked.

"Because... there is the weight of history. There is reverence for antiquity. The entire purpose of this monastery is to pay honor to that which came before."

"Right. Yeah. That's fine," Madge said. "But what about now? And while we're at it, what about tomorrow? Seems silly to spend all your time thinking about yesterday if something might come along and keep tomorrow from even happening."

Brother Inkbrand seemed frozen with indecision. For now, that was as good as acceptance. The smaller rings had fewer tiles and thus clicked into place faster than the outer ones. By the time Brother Inkbrand was gathering himself for an answer, Tome had depressed the center tile and dashed for the far edge.

For a heart-stopping moment, nothing happened. Then the rings began to recede. They dropped down and pulled back, one after the other, revealing a yawning emptiness beneath. The farther the stone surface pulled back, the more of the void below was revealed, soon uncovering a stone stairwell filling a large section of the slope.

"Wow..." Madge muttered. "That's enough to twist a brain up into knots."

The monastery and monument were atop a seaside cliff. The edge of the cliff was only a dozen yards or so beyond the edge of the monument. The slope within the opening that had been uncovered should have exited the cliffside at that point, but it continued on into pitch darkness.

"How is this possible?" Inkbrand murmured.

"Doesn't matter how. It just is. Are we going inside?" Madge said.

Tome checked his tunic. "I have enough spells to ward off most anything that would try to kill us at least long enough to get back through. I hope."

Madge slapped Inkbrand on the back. "We'll see you soon, Brother!"

The pair dashed down the stairs into the darkness, the flickering light of Wick's lantern barely cutting deep enough for them to see the way.

"Do we know what we're running toward?" Madge asked.

"Only that there's likely a clockwork diamond."

"And someone who stole a boat."

"Probably."

They reached the bottom of the steps. If distance still held sway, it would have been at least a dozen feet above the surface of the water. Instead, smooth stone continued downward in a smooth slope while the ceiling remained level, raising the space overhead more and more. Finally the ground leveled. They rushed a few dozen more strides. A huge tunnel led off to one side, much, much larger than the one they'd used to get this far. At the precise moment they passed it, both of them lost a step. It was a familiar feeling, like a pressure in their minds.

"The earring," Tome said, fishing it from his pocket. "We only have one. You'll have to either stay behind or stay close. You'll have a very hard time resisting the urge to return to the tunnel and head back to the mainland."

Madge grabbed him by the hand. "What are we waiting for? Put that earring on and let's go!"

Marching through Clickspring, now that it was swarming with Lesser Mystics, was a curious experience. Marching through it with a cluster of elves who desperately wanted him dead pushed the experience far past curious. It was impressive how far into the city they'd managed to get, and how deeply entrenched. He wasn't so small as to withhold credit where credit was deserved. They'd developed a baffling but effective system for exploring a place their mind insisted didn't exist. The most insane aspect of it was the usage of the less useful Lesser Mystics as beacons along the edges of dangerous areas. All sorts of particularly hostile or particular dimwitted creatures were chained or caged around the edge of an area just northeast of the central wall. Spritzes of blood and the fresh remains of fallen creatures were a regular feature of the streets beyond their improvised safety perimeter. The traps set beyond it must have been particularly heinous. And there, attached to the wall at the edge of the danger zone with a heavy harness and Bygone chain, was Parch. When the little creature spotted him, he trotted toward him, hooves scraping at the deep furrows he'd managed to dig into the stone through his endless attempts to pull free.

"I don't want to think about what I would have had to do to you elves if Parch wasn't alive and well when I found him," Fel said, working at the harness as best he could without setting down the sparker that was holding the elves at bay. "Now, it's a straight shot from here to the harbor. We're heading down there, getting on the boats, and giving up on this whole earring business, understand?"

The elves blinked at him.

"No, of course you don't. I need Wick back here to translate. So we wait until then, and..."

Fel trailed off as he realized there were sounds within the dangerous portion of the town that didn't seem like they were coming from Lesser Mystics. He squinted down one of the avenues. A flash of brassy metal confirmed his fears.

"You all stay put. Don't follow," he said, accompanying the words with exaggerated motions that he hoped would transcend language. "I have something to deal with."

They seemed to understand his intention; and more to the point, seemed a little too pleased to know he was planning to enter the part of the city that had nearly taken so many of their lives. He made it all of three strides past their perimeter when the first pressure plate in the street informed him he'd be taking it slow, and more to the point, that he'd be spending much of his time persuading Parch not to charge too far ahead.

He'd never been in this part of Clickspring. The city formed a ring about the wall in the center that protected the clockwork diamond. In his mind, the whole town was roughly the same. But this was plainly more military than the rest. Buildings stopped looking like homes and started looking like fortresses. Multiple streets were blocked off by gated walls, though the gates were mostly open.

And when he crossed the last of them, he began to see past the edge of the large, ornate dome that dominated the center of the area. It wasn't a full dome. More of a clamshell sheltering something akin to an amphitheater, with tiers of stone steps surrounding an enormous stairwell leading down into the ground. As awesome as the sight was, two other things captured Fel's mind far more powerfully. First was the towering, building-sized mechanism huddled in the back of the clamshell. It looked like a somewhat lankier version of the automatons but dozens of times the size. It could only be the Guardian he'd been hearing about. The other was the cluster of man-sized automatons at its feet, and the man who was with them.

"Dad…" Fel murmured.

He started moving closer, if only to see the condition of his father. From here, Martin seemed to be unhurt, and he seemed to be cooperating with them. He'd been told Martin had given himself up, but Fel had convinced himself his father had a plan. That he wouldn't actually allow himself to come this far. Fel peeked out of an alley, his eye sneaking past the edge of the building a fraction of an inch. The moment he did, all the distant automatons stopped what they were doing and turned toward him.

"Fel Masker. Quite the world traveler."

The voice came from a short distance away, where a lit torch's flame remained stationary. Fel cursed himself. Of course a sentry flame would be keeping watch.

"What are you doing with my father?"

"Commencing the final stage of a long and arduous task," Lens said.

"Not if I can help it."

A flame flared somewhere within the head of the massive Guardian. Then that flame became still. The behemoth turned slowly to him. A mesh cage obscured the view of what was controlling the thing. It looked like nothing more than a larger, cruder version of the coupler his father had made a few weeks earlier.

"You cannot help it," boomed the voice from within.

The voice returned to the nearest flame.

"How frustrating it must be for you to be so close to this place and fail to see that you were already too late. As we speak, I am guiding other automatons to the other side of the world. They will awaken the Guardian there, and I will be free to bring about the long-awaited return of the Bygone Era."

Fel marched from his hiding place and approached. The automatons and the Guardian looked on. The threat they represented was such that even Parch knew to huddle behind Fel and keep close.

"You are a Masker, and though it is an indication of the sorry state of contraptioneering in this world, you are quite high on the list of experts in the field. I would hate to have to destroy you. I hope you aren't planning to do something foolish, Fel."

"I never plan to do anything foolish," Fel said. "Those things just seem to happen."

As he descended the tiers of steps, the automatons assembled shoulder to shoulder between him and his father, but otherwise made no motion against him. When he was near enough to be heard, Martin spoke.

"Listen, Fel. I have heard his plan. Both what he hopes to do, and what he plans to do if things do not go as desired. By far the greatest tragedy would be an incomplete victory," Martin said.

"You've already lost," Lens said. "I have a Guardian. Soon I will have two. From this point forward, the actions of you and the others who would call themselves heroes decide how many must lose their freedom and their lives. My way is simple. You've felt its influence. Revise the clockwork diamonds. For humans? The knowledge and civility of the Bygone Era return in full. Hands will turn back to the fashioning of contraptions. Hands will rewrite what was lost when the Tellestressa Archives fell. The greatest tragedy of history, the loss of its most complete record, will be undone. The creatures of this land? The Greater Mystics? Their lives need not change at all. They will remain here, hidden away, and the rest of the world hidden from them. Some will be brought to bear on the task of preparing the materials that will rebuild the world. But when that task is through, peace."

"You're talking about robbing the whole world of its freedom. That's not peace. That's servitude," Martin said.

"Call it what you want. It will be a time of no war. A time of ease. An end of scarcity. But if you seek to stop me, there is an alternative. If you and the others somehow keep me from the other clockwork diamond, then I will be forced to change the role of the Lesser Mystics. Rather than laborers for a time and free denizens of their world ever after, they will be my army. I will strike away their ignorance of your world and take control of their minds. Those who are able to resist will be wiped out by those who are not. And I shall unleash them across the outer world to snuff out resistance until I am able to achieve my goals. There will be blood. So much blood. And in the end, the same outcome."

"You could at least have the decency to sound ashamed of being so utterly evil," Fel said.

"Moral judgments become pointless when complete control over the thoughts and minds of the populace is possible."

"Dad..."

"Fel, if they will allow you to go, go. They have shared with me what they know of the clockwork diamond. I've chosen to help. It's the best option. By this time tomorrow, what will be done will be done."

"Dad, this isn't right."

"This time tomorrow, Fel. It all ends this time tomorrow. Do what you need to do to prepare," Martin said.

"Obey your father, boy," Lens said. "He knows best."

"This time tomorrow," Fel repeated. "So be it, Dad."

He stepped down into the tunnel. As he paced down into the darkness, Parch clippy-clopping behind, the flame went still.

"Fel. Your father. Have you encountered him?" Wick began.

"I have."

"Were you able to free him?"

"They'd already woken up the Guardian. What could I do? Any attempts to set him free would just as likely have killed him. What kept you?"

"I had to fully observe the atlas depicting the layout of the tunnels and the codes for the doors. I also had to deliver some of that information to Tome and Madge. There was also the matter of the Scholar, which is now awake and active in Martin's workshop. Epiphany collected and relayed some information to me from him as well. I apologize. If I had been here earlier..."

"Wouldn't have done any good. Those things are nearly as formidable as that body the Warrior was controlling, and it took a whole crew of us to take one of them out. I'd have gotten myself or Dad killed trying to beat them, like I said."

"So what happens now?" Wick asked.

He shut his eyes. "The world is in bad shape when someone is asking *me* that. Do we know if Lens has control of the other Guardian?"

"I do not know."

"From what he just said, he doesn't yet. But with these tunnels and his little army of automatons, that can change in seconds." He tightened his fist. "You say you have a map of these tunnels?"

"I do."

"Is it accurate?"

"Accurate, but perhaps not comprehensive. There are at least two additional exits to the tunnels than were listed in the atlas, but—"

"Fine. Are there any other tunnel exits on this island?"

"There is one additional exit near the harbor on the opposite side of the island. The path leading to it should be a short distance ahead and to the left. Why?"

"Because I have to have a word with a dragon," he said. "Dad was very, very clear that whatever they're having him do won't happen until tomorrow. He wouldn't have said it if he didn't want us to know. That means we have until then to stop it."

He clicked open the chest he'd stolen from the elves. "There are plans to be made."

Tome and Madge marched up the steps of the tunnel toward the daylight ahead. For lack of a better option to keep Madge able to move toward a place that her mind desperately wanted to reject, they'd been walking hand in hand.

"I can't believe there is no lock on the exit on the island," Tome said as they neared the surface.

"Do you suppose they assumed it would be enough that most of the world wouldn't even be able to see this place?" Madge said.

"That we've reached it is a sign that if they did believe that, they were mistaken," Tome said. "Here. Hold the lantern. And I need my hand back if I'm going to have spells ready."

Madge took the lantern and shifted her grip to the back of his shirt. Slowly, the pair stalked out into the light. Having only Clickspring as an example of what to expect in the place surrounding a clockwork diamond, Tome had anticipated some sort of a deserted city awaiting him. It was most certainly not that. The island was quite small. Three things asserted themselves above all else. The first was the sea around the island. It was a ship's graveyard. Every ship that had "fallen into the pit in the sea" lay half-submerged or mostly rotten in the shallow waters around it. Only one seemed fairly intact and recent, no doubt the one that had been stolen not long ago. The second major feature was the clockwork diamond, surrounded by a wall that made it clear in no uncertain terms that it was never to be crossed. Spikes lined the top, and it looked sturdy enough to turn away a dozen battering rams. But dwarfing them all in terms of provoking awe and fear was the Guardian. It huddled against the wall like it was cold and trying to keep out of the wind. A milky-green patina colored the thing, the sea doing its very best to corrode it to nothingness, but it had held up well over the centuries. The rest of the island was sparsely covered with trees, coarse grass, and shrubs.

"The Guardian. No wonder the thing could turn away armies," Tome said.

"Can I borrow the earring?" Madge asked. "I'm in a mystical, hidden place, and all I can see are some trees. It's very disappointing."

"We're not here for sightseeing."

"Good, because I'm not seeing any sights."

"The Guardian still sleeps. It hasn't been taken," Tome said. "How is that possible?"

An unexpected voice provided the reply. "Even now, you ask that question?"

Tome snapped around and readied the first spell in his packet to be torn. Even though he scarcely would have needed a moment to activate it, he didn't have that moment. The tip of a drawn arrow was so close to his face, he'd slashed his own cheek when he turned. It was, of course, Mevrelle. He wore a silver earring in his ear and a defeated look on his face.

"It is possible because it was preordained," Mevrelle said.

"Now you have to give me the earring," Madge said. "You're the one who's supposed to be able to see, and you missed a whole elf!"

"What are you doing here?" Tome said.

"My mission. But I should have known it would come down to me and one of you blasted humans... It was preordained."

"You're going to blame fate for this?"

"No. No... Fate is fair. Fate is balanced. Are you really so blind, even with an earring of our own enchantment, that you cannot see what I mean? That you cannot see how all of this has come to be?"

"I am that blind!" Madge said.

"I came here because it was my mission. My purpose was to leave the Greater Lands and find what we knew must exist. The match to the clockwork diamond within our own lands. I was assigned the task of finding some way to use it to punish you as you have used it to punish us. If it took me years, it would have been worth it. I crossed kingdoms, braved the sea. But there is no crossing the wall. I've tried. It nearly cost me my life a dozen times over. And that abomination of a weapon, crouched and sleeping. I have no doubt there is a way to awaken it. But I've yet to find it. What I did find was something else. Something that makes it all so clear."

"Get to the point!" Madge said. "I'm using every ounce of my willpower just to be aware of you. You could at least be interesting."

"It must have been the enchantment placed upon me. The one that allowed me to use the masks as a means of leaving the Greater Lands. But I can hear it. Hear it whispering. Not words. Not real ones. More like notions. Thoughts. Things that slide beneath petty things like language and logic. Repeating. Over and over again, day after day. No mind behind it. No intelligence. Just an impossibly complex sequence of commands. Again, and again. Over and over. Relentless..."

Madge leaned aside. "I think he's lost his mind."

"We thought you humans had built this horror and spared yourselves of its influence. But we were wrong. You are influenced. In subtle ways. Ways that hide it from you. Ways that blot out the memories of why it was built or why those who built it are no more. But there are so many more commands than that." He pointed. "That is not a thing of nature. It did not grow. It was built. And things that can be made can be unmade. The people who created it knew that all it would take was a single savvy mind free of its control and the diamond could be defeated. Someone like me. Someone like Lens. So it needed to defend itself. Traps, walls, even the Guardian? Things that were made and can be unmade. So it threads its control out into the world. Tipping this way and that. When something moves toward its destruction, it pushes on other minds. Maneuvers them into place, moving in a preordained dance. You, here. Masker, wherever he is. No coincidence. No luck. All the pieces guided into place so that when the clock strikes midnight, the bell can still chime."

He motioned with his head toward the diamond. "That thing exists to keep you as you are, just as ours exists to keep us as we are. We are all prisoners to the minds of the past."

Behind them, the rhythmic hammering of metallic feet started to echo up from the tunnel.

"Listen to me, Mevrelle," Tome said. "Regardless of why you think we're here or what you think that thing is for, Lens has sent contraptions to lay claim to the Guardian and start making changes to the clockwork diamond. Now tell me this. Do you think he has anything good in store for the elves and other mystics?"

Mevrelle took a slow breath. "Lens serves humanity. If he comes to make a change, he comes jangling the keys of your cell. And I will not allow him to release you before we can be released."

"Then believe it or not, right now, you and I are on the same side. We stop whatever comes through that tunnel, no matter the cost."

"We are not on the same side. You think you are fighting to retain your freedom. I know I am fighting to retain your confinement."

"Fine! Believe what you want to believe. But if you can extinguish their flames, they'll drop until another of them can relight the flame from their own. At least, such is the claim of the others." Tome turned to Madge. "Stay close. I don't know how much help you'll be without an earring, but don't be a hero. If you start to lose the fight against the diamond pushing you away, let it take you to the tunnel and get clear."

He and Madge hurried to the shelter of a tree near the tunnel. Mevrelle vanished among the trees to the other side. Tome ran his finger over the marked ends of the spells he had left. The nine ice spells seemed like the only ones that would do any good. He peeled off three of them and slipped them to Madge.

"Tear from the notched end and toss toward the automatons. Make sure there is no one in the path of the spell but automatons."

"Sure thing," Madge said, the first tremor of nerves in her voice.

The hammering footsteps approached. Tome held his ground. Victory could only come when they were all down. The best chance was to act quickly and aggressively. The very moment he saw gleaming metal emerge from the tunnel, he tore the first spell and tossed it. Blue mystic flame consumed the page, and the air ahead of him swirled with frost. The curls of white engulfed two of the automatons. Their motions became halting and labored before finally they dropped to the ground. Two more emerged from the tunnel. They each hoisted a fallen one from the ground. Madge tore and tossed her first spell. A second icy swath sent one of the new automatons tumbling to the ground atop the one it carried. Tome blasted the other, but it raised its frozen duplicate as a shield and thundered toward him. By now, four more had emerged from the tunnel, for a total of eight.

Tome retreated. There wasn't time to activate another spell before the things reached him. He needed to buy some time. Madge followed. As he dashed, a single voice dancing between the still-functioning automatons addressed him. There was no anger or effort in the voice, as though speaking and acting were two wholly different acts for these contraptions.

"Tome. A paper mage. Magic is a fascinating but ultimately pointless enterprise. It has very little place in the world I am planning. And thus, neither do you."

A dozen witty retorts flooded Tome's mind, but he didn't take the bait. Survival was very slightly more important to him than scoring rhetorical points. He squeezed through a gap between two trees that would be too small for the automatons to follow through and pivoted. Madge's tiny form followed with no effort, and she took her place behind him, clearing the view of the contraptions approaching. Six of them were functional, one having already been relit. As he watched and prepared his next spell, the faceplate of one of the automatons split open. The plate of a frozen one was wrenched open, and a brief touch to the coupler within brought it back to life. Madge was the first to act, tossing a spell at the pair to freeze both the rescued and rescuer. Tome tossed a spell that took out another pair. But the remaining four were well out of range. They were uninterested in Madge and Tome, seeking instead to reach the Guardian.

When he was sure the near ones were motionless, he dashed for the others. Instantly, he saw that he was doomed to fail. They were far faster than him. But they were the only remaining threat. He had to try.

Tome pushed himself hard and cursed himself for not keeping any speed spells prepared for this moment. He was still twenty strides away when the four automatons reached the sleeping giant and began to scale it. He redoubled his efforts, his mind working at the puzzle of what sort of range would retain the effectiveness of an ice spell. They were slower at climbing than running, but they were already outside the range of a spell before he was even halfway to them.

The things were climbing in a perfect line. Tome could only assume it was to make it easier for a single mind to control them. One of them reached the faceplate of the Guardian. It grasped the plate. An arrow burst from nowhere. It struck squarely in the back of the automaton's hand. As good as the modern approximation of Bygone technology was, the elven arrow was better. The hand shattered. The automaton fell and knocked each one below it free. The timing was perfect. All four clattered to the ground just as Tome and Madge arrived. Madge's final spell and the next of Tome's thoroughly extinguished the flames.

Frozen metal creaked. Madge and Tome huffed and puffed. But all else was still.

"That's it?" Madge said. "I expected a bigger battle for my first one."

They heard the twang of a bolt. Tome turned. Two more of the automatons had emerged from the tunnel. One of them had an arrow through its head. The other was crouched to light the flames of the fallen. Another arrow blasted through its head, but it continued to function, and quickly the others began to rise. Tome readied another ice spell, but already the machines were far too spread out for him to hope to get them in a single casting. They rushed toward him. He managed one ice spell, knocking three of them down again, but before he could activate the next, a metal fist closed around the bundle of spells, and his hand as well. He was able to wrench his hand free from the grip, gashing the back of it on its jagged metal. The thing tore all the spells and backhanded him, sending him to the ground with the horrid snap of two ribs.

Destroying the spells came at a cost. Three of the ice spells activated. The attacking mechanism went still and collapsed. But it meant little. The damage was done.

Tome coughed a glob of blood. His hearing filled with a terrible hiss. His vision started to blur. He could hear Madge call out. Somewhere the twang of a bow came once more before the snap of wood. He blinked his eyes. They were scaling the Guardian again. No one could stop them now... unless.

He coughed into his hand and dragged himself to the nearest fallen automaton. With shaky motions, he smeared two runes onto its chestplate.

Freeze. All.

The pain and dizziness amplified. But great swirls of frost coiled up from beneath each of the automatons. He didn't have to aim. He didn't have to direct. The spell sought out all that matched the entity he'd cast it upon, within as wide a range as his blood had the potency to empower it. In a single blow, the others were silenced. He collapsed, his strength spent.

The hissing reduced to a soft throbbing. The pain began to dull as well. His consciousness was fading. He dully wondered if it would return. Then, darkness. Peace.

He felt the distant sensation of warmth. Then a massive shock of pain. His eyes shot open, vision rushing in and mind suddenly and unmercifully sharp. He held his chest and gasped. The pain eased away steadily. When it dropped to the point that he could breathe again, he gasped and looked about. Madge was beside him.

"Blood magic isn't so bad," she said, with a drunken sort of smile.

He took his hands away and saw that his chest had been smeared with, simply, "heal." It was one of the few runes he'd taught her, and it was drawn as poorly as it could possibly be drawn without failing entirely. Madge blinked and shook her head. Blood was running down her cheek, the source of the writing material. The already half-focused eyes suffering from the influence of the diamond were looking increasingly addled. She slumped forward. He caught her.

"Madge. Try to focus."

"Wow..." she murmured. "I can't... lift my head."

"You are a novice and you used blood magic. You're lucky you aren't so drained you can't breathe."

"Yeah. And you're lucky I didn't care and did it anyway. Saved your life."

He took a painful breath. "That's... quite possible. So long as nothing else comes along."

The last of the hissing in his ears faded away, and with impending death no longer there to occupy his mind, he slowly became aware of a familiar voice. He realized it had been talking to him almost from the moment he'd cast the blood spell, but he hadn't been able to spare the mind to address it.

"Please respond, either of you. Are you safe?" said Wick.

Tome fumbled beside him where the lantern had fallen. He picked it up. "Alive," he said. "I don't know if we're safe. But presently the automatons are still. But we're badly hurt. Neither of us can so much as crawl. I seem to have lost track of Mevrelle."

"I do not see him. Mevrelle was present?"

"Indeed."

"The Guardian appears to be inert. You protected it."

"So it seems. So long as nothing more threatening than a rabbit comes along to try to claim it."

"Stay where you are. Fel is presently en route to Beffshire. He has explained a plan, and if the Guardian remains free, there may be a chance. He'll come to you as quickly as possible, and he will have friends with him. He estimates three hours."

"Three hours? Seems like these tunnels could get him here in half that time."

"There are preparations to be made. The inert automaton immediately to your left appears to have a damaged faceplate. Are you able to touch my flame to its neck?"

"I... I hadn't thought of that."

He fought with his body, and burned his hands twice, but managed to put flame to the frost-covered post. The thing shuddered, and slowly it arose.

"I should be able to protect you," Wick said, now from the automaton. "I will return momentarily to inform Fel he can delay slightly."

"I'd rather he didn't," Tome said.

"For the sake of our world, I believe it is for the best. Fel has to learn how to activate and operate a very complex contraption as part of his plan."

"What contraption?" He sluggish mind sputtered. He glanced toward the wall behind him. "Oh..."

Chapter 12

Spread across the world, Fel and the others did their work. Lens had taken years to make his plans. Fel and his friends had only a few hours. But they had many friends, and thanks to the tunnels, they had access to them all. Working without rest, and without sleep, they charged from one end of the world to the other. No idea was too outlandish, no source of aid too great or small. The knowledge of the Adept and Kazel were combined with the ingenuity of the Maskers and Graves families. It would require expertise in language and diplomacy, something the Greater Mystics and Wick could provide. It would require things scavenged from the north, the west, and the east. Artifacts and weapons new and old. Things found by Euphoria, things found by Tome, and everything in between. Most of all, it would require recklessness. That, they had in abundance, supplied dutifully by Fel and gleefully by Teya.

After every drop of repair, preparation, and training they could manage, the time had come. Lens may well have made himself unstoppable, but they refused to succumb to his schemes without a fight.

Eighteen hours had passed. Martin gazed up at the rotating crystal plates and down at the arrangement of small, etched brass panels before him. Oiler sat beside him, pleasantly clacking its claws and awaiting some sort of task. In the first few hours, Oiler had been busy repairing and restoring a handful of additional automatons. Their numbers had dwindled significantly. With the ones that had failed to return from the other clockwork diamond, and others destroyed along the way, there were only five fully functional mechanisms left. But the presence of the Guardian made that something of a moot point. Presently, two of the remaining automatons stood guard over Martin as he worked, with the Guardian standing on the far side of the wall, peering over it like some terrible overseer. Sweeping arms at the base of the clockwork diamond clacked across the ancient plates of old. Martin was previously familiar with the clockwork diamonds in Fenfield, and even those, only through detailed description. But it was clear that the one he worked on now was much, much larger and more complex. The arcs of plates had a diameter three or four times larger, and there were multiple arms moving at multiple speeds. Though there had been plenty of work for Martin to do, the primary delay had been the motion of the arms. The plates needed to be replaced in between sweeps, and they needed to be placed in a proper order. The periods of rotation on the sweeping arms only aligned properly once per day. That moment was approaching. The rhythm of the clockwork diamond's clicking and clacking felt uncannily like the ticking of a great clock, counting off the moments before midnight on the final day.

"You have done fine work, Martin," Lens said.

"I have condemned untold creatures to death," Martin said.

"That was not your doing. If Tome had failed, or if he'd had the wisdom not to resist, then we would have had a bloodless revolution and a utopia. We shall still have a utopia. It will merely cost a bit more."

A thousand potential schemes had passed through Martin's head, but Lens's time to prepare had been well used. The entity may not have had the insight to complete the etchings himself, but he was able to confirm that the ones Martin had done would serve the purpose. Full crates of contraband had been brought in from Beffshire. There was no end of things he could try to use them for, but he was never given sufficient time to utilize them to build something to defend himself. A sentry lantern first and a sentry lantern foremost, Lens's gaze was unblinking and vigilant. He could only make use of the tools and materials brought from the vault to do as he was asked. Now that job was done. There was nothing to do but wait until the time came to slot the plates into place and turn every last mystic into an enslaved army to unleash upon the world beyond the Greater Lands.

Everything Martin could have done, Lens had predicted. But there was still a chance. Fel and the others were still out there. And there was no one in this world less predictable than Fel Masker.

The thought must have put a glimmer of hope on his face, because Lens chose that moment to take stock of his own victories.

"The dragon ceased its circling. If it had gone off to eat, or to rest, it would have returned by now. Your son no doubt sent it on its way. The elves did not heed his warnings.

They linger. But they remain as blinded by the diamond as they ever were. No real threat, despite their efforts to the contrary. The world has put up a significant defense against its salvation, but greater minds and better preparation prevailed."

There was a pause. Each of the automatons shifted slightly.

"Ah. As expected, a final attempt. Be ready to place the plates. I do not anticipate this will take very long."

Outside the walls, the Guardian gazed down as a glow approached from the steps in the yawning tunnel. A slow, plodding metallic thump echoed out of the darkness every few seconds. When it was near enough, a single automaton became visible. Its flame was still and steady, in complete and direct control of a single sentry flame. And it was not Lens.

"So. Wick. I suspected you would try something like this. When one's own tactics fail, the weak always attempt to steal the tactics of the strong."

"Your tactics are far from ideal," Wick said.

"For you, certainly. As I recall, you were quite inferior when last you tried to control an automaton. And I have had considerable practice since that day."

"Indeed. Even now, I find myself completely incapable of controlling even two of the automatons left behind. It is just as well. Most of those elsewhere are in some state of disrepair, and without Martin or Oiler, only Fel had anything near the expertise to mend them. This was the best that could be managed."

"So what shall it be? Did they send you to speak to me as an equal?" Lens said. "You do, after all, have access to the Ambassador and the Warrior."

"As well as the Scholar," Wick said.

"Martin was able to repair him, was he? Impressive."

"But on this point, all three masks we asked were in agreement. The only way to end what you have begun is through destruction."

"And you believe you can achieve this?"

"We have devised a number of potential methods. My favorite was to utilize sylphs to simply extinguish all flames within Clickspring. But evidently there was no clear way to lend them the protection of a silver earring. Still, I am here to offer my services in the execution of the first and most likely scheme."

"You are here to help to destroy me?"

"I am."

The Guardian stood, effortlessly smashing through the ornate stone shelter above it.

"And how, may I ask. Do you propose such a thing?"

"You shall see."

"No. I shall not."

The Guardian raised its metal fists, ready to smash Wick's automaton to fragments. Wick snapped into motion, dashing at full speed up the tiered steps. Strong and powerful as the Guardian was, it took time and force to get something that size up to speed. By the time the fists came down, Wick was bounding into the city. Huge strides brought the Guardian swiftly to where Wick was running, but the smaller mechanism was nimbler. Ancient buildings crumbled beneath the feet of the lumbering giant. Hidden traps activated with flashes and crackles, useless against the massive thing. Two additional automatons were dispatched to corner Wick for destruction, but even they couldn't keep up with him. Wick must have spent what little time he had with the automaton learning strictly how to run. Furthermore, because he was controlling only one body, there was no flicker away to control another one to rob it of some measure of speed and reaction. For nearly a minute, Lens continued his pursuit and allowed other automatons to fall limp so that additional time could be spent guiding the Guardian and those seeking Wick. Then, realization, almost too late.

"This is a distraction," Lens rumbled.

He didn't need to look back to the tunnel entrance. Other automatons were still there. And what they beheld when he took the time to observe what their light fell upon was infuriating.

A green monster, the second Guardian, was emerging from the tunnel. Its motions lacked the fluidity of Lens's own, and the reason was clear. Visible behind the mesh visor of the thing was Fel Masker, inexpertly controlling the Guardian with levers and wheels rather than directly as Lens was. The thing had been modified, as well. The armor plating of one arm had been removed and instead was lashed to the other forearm, with the edges of the plates aligned roughly as the head of an ax.

"I am disappointed, Masker," Lens boomed from his Guardian. "Surely you spoke to the Scholar. Surely you know to attack one Guardian with another is a fool's errand."

"Maybe you haven't heard," Fel said, his voice blaring from a tinny trumpet of some kind somewhere within the twitching, barely upright mechanism. "All I seem to do is run errands. And I'm a fool. Ask anybody."

"Plainly so," Lens said, stepping face to face with the poorly piloted Guardian. "Just what did you imagine you would do?"

"I figured I'd destroy that Guardian you stole, get my dad out of here, and find a way to make sure you never cause any more harm."

"Lofty goals. And you imagined you would do so alone?"

"No, no, no. Unlike you. I have friends."

"Oh? And just what friends could possibly help you?"

"You're the sentry lantern. You tell me."

Lens flicked rapidly through the other vantage points and quickly discovered another supposed threat. Once again, Kazel was circling the island.

"The dragon? Have you forgotten this place is inaccessible by Greater Mystics?"

"Have you forgotten how much dragons love jewelry?" Fel asked.

Fel awkwardly raised the ax arm of the Guardian, ready to attack. Lens gave the huge contraption a shove that knocked it off balance. A moment later, the shadow of Kazel swept overhead. Somewhere nestled among those scales was a silver earring.

If the Guardian had been a man, then compared to him Kazel would have been the size of a horse. Far from the staggering size difference that made the dragon so fearsome a foe for a normal human, but nothing to sneeze at. A curling torrent of fire poured down on the Guardian. By the time the dragon had swept over, the chest armor had been charred black. A second pass was lower, the fire more focused. It left the Guardian's chestplate glowing cherry red. Kazel returned for a third pass, closer still.

Too close.

Lens reached out and clutched the monster by the neck. The momentum dragged Lens's Guardian aside, nearly sending it tumbling down into the open mouth of the tunnel. But it held firm. Kazel slashed and clawed and kept his fiery breath rushing over the hulking contraption. Nearly a full minute of flame breath came to an end only when Lens was able to grasp the dragon's maw in his other mitt and clamp it shut. A ferocious throw sent the dragon tumbling aside to smash through buildings that had survived the pursuit of Wick.

Not one to be fooled twice, Lens quickly surveyed the other automatons to see if any other plans were afoot. Sure enough. Wick's automaton had just dropped down inside the wall, having scaled it and, it would appear, having taken the brunt of a trap or two, as it was missing an arm. He used the two guard automatons to grapple and subdue Wick, then returned his attentions to the Guardian just in time to see the ax arm coming down.

Fel had put all the power of the Guardian behind the swing. Combined with the still-radiant heat of the metal, and the re-purposing of the Guardian's own armor plate as a weapon, the edge of the makeshift ax bit into the chestplate. Grinding and shattering sounds signaled the complete failure of the ax arm, destroyed by the power of the impact. The blade fell away, showing a gap a yard wide. He raised the unarmored arm, fingers curved into a claw, ready to rake at the damage. Lens caught the arm with one hand. Kazel had gotten back to his feet and charged. Lens caught him by the neck as well, holding the beast's head upright to keep the fiery breath curling skyward.

"That was your plan? The full force of a dragon, sacrificing a Guardian, and you managed barely more than superficial damage."

Fel spun a wheel. The mechanical hand in Lens's grip curled down to grasp his wrist. Behind the face visor of the thing, Fel only grinned.

"Yah-haaaaa!" crowed a shrill voice.

Teya emerged from beneath the remaining armor plate on the arm that was grappling with Lens. She was wrapped in leather armor and brandishing salvaged Bygone tools like weapons of war. In her frilled ear, her silver earring. And behind her?

Friends.

Every last earring stolen from the elves had been given to another kobold. They swarmed down the arm and dove to the chest. Leather armor sizzled against the cooling metal, and they scrambled in through the hole in the armor. Lens tried to release Kazel to slap at the attackers, but Kazel held tight to the arm and just barely managed to restrain it long enough for the last of the kobolds to wriggle inside the Guardian.

"Had a chat with Tome, and he said an elf had a great point. The Guardians were made. And what can be made can be unmade," Fel taunted. "I'm lousy at building and fixing things, but world-class at breaking stuff. And kobolds are quick learners."

"You fool. You fool! All you're doing is destroying the precious gifts of antiquity," Lens growled as the tiny blows and twists of dozens of tools started working at the internal components. "I still have the other automatons. I am a sentry flame. I cannot be extinguished. I cannot be defeated!"

One of the Lens Guardian's arms shuddered and fell limp, the kobold tampering making steady progress.

"You are a lousy sentry lantern," Fel said. "Watching everything and still missing the real threats."

"Empty claims. What could truly threaten me? I am eternal," Lens growled.

"Oh, don't worry. You'll find out."

Lens scrutinized the city around him, cataloging everything of the slightest interest and concern. There was nothing. He knew the city far better than anyone. He'd scoured it with the light of his perception. The elves in the city had retreated to their place in the cathedral. Martin had made no move. Wick's automaton was subdued. He flicked from flame to flame, every vantage available to him, to confirm it. There was nothing. *Nothing.* He even danced to those lingering flames around the world. The ones in Ram's Rest. The ones spirited away to hidden places to deliver messages to forgotten agents. No threat. Nothing anywhere. But there was a flame out of place. An old lantern. The first lantern. The one taken from its hiding place in the mountains of Shalia and extinguished. He had thrust it from his mind. It was no longer necessary. But now it burned again. And it was not in the outer world. It was here in the Greater Lands. He cast his consciousness to it.

Around him, he saw elven mystics. He was in their village. Below him he saw the smoldering of coals. And perching on a branch just outside the twisted tree that served as this little laboratory, a greater harpy flanked by two more blasted kobolds. The Adept. She nodded, as though she knew she'd been seen, and spoke in the elves' own language.

"He is present. Begin."

Arcane words flowed from the elves. Lens felt a terrible tug at his very essence. The same spells that leached the power of a lantern to make the earrings were being spoken. And they had an artifact lantern. One that he was bound to. One that could be relit. That he couldn't escape.

He snapped back to the Guardian. He needed to reach the lantern, to reclaim it from the elves. With the tunnels and with the speed the automatons could reach, it was possible. But it would mean abandoning this place, leaving the meddlers to finish their meddling. One of the Guardian's legs no longer responded to him. If not for Kazel's grip immobilizing the other arm as a counterbalance, he would have crumbled. One of his hands dropped away, kobolds briefly peeking out before climbing deeper to pick apart the next joint.

"You can't do this. You can't do this! I contain half of the wisdom of Tellestressa Archives. Destroy me and it is gone forever!"

"Considering what it drove you to, I think we're better off without it," Fel said. "But if you back off and let us fix what you did, maybe the Adept can talk the elves out of playing with their new toy."

"No... No..." Lens shrieked.

A panel in the head of Lens's Guardian dropped away. Teya wriggled through the new gap into the space where the flame blazed, controlling the contraption.

"Bad fire! Bad!" she chattered, unfurling a leather hide and using it to beat at the flaming coupler affixed to the controls.

"If I cannot have victory, then *you* shall have defeat."

With his control over the massive contraption faltering, Lens lurched away from Kazel. The arm separated at the elbow. The failing Guardian tumbled back against the wall protecting the clockwork diamond's courtyard. The top of the wall crumbled and slumped under the force of the fall. The disassembly efforts of the kobolds had weakened the torso of the Guardian so greatly that, without the weight to hold it in place, the handful of struts and mechanisms that hadn't been knocked out of place by the kobolds wrenched free. The top half of the Guardian tumbled over the wall. With a final violent flail of what remained of its functional arm, exposed struts screeched across the outer ring of plates that the clockwork diamond's components were rolling along. The sweeping arm knocked the flailing limb out of the way, and the world around them rattled and groaned as the huge crystal contraption swept across the damaged plates.

The diamond's rotation rolled past the plates and the rattling ceased. The shaken-up but still feisty Teya managed to extinguish the flame within the Guardian's head, and the hulking mechanism went still.

Fel awkwardly brought the damaged Guardian into a crouch and cranked the wheel that would open the face cage to release him. He scrambled toward the broken wall and scaled the rubble. All around him, the remaining automatons were rattling and coming to a rest. Lens plainly couldn't keep flicking through all the different flames while enduring the torture the elves were inflicting. Fel struggled to feel empathy for the experience. Considering Lens's plans, and his disregard for the people of the world, this was well-earned.

Kobolds crawled out of the wreckage of Lens's Guardian. The tumble and crash had taken its toll, but they were sturdy little creatures, and for the most part they were rattled but not injured. The same, he was relieved to find, could be said of his father. The older man was rushing about, recovering plates that had been jostled and spilled by the battle.

"Dad! You're all right!" Fel said, rushing to him.

"I am. For now," Martin said quickly. "And though I am endlessly grateful for the rescue, I do wish it hadn't come at the cost of two of the greatest creations of the Bygone Era."

"More like one and a half. Now come on. Let's get out of here before we discover some final, final, final contingency plan Lens might have left."

"We can't go," Martin pointed. "Seven plates were damaged."

"What does that mean for the Greater Lands?"

"I don't know. Certainly tremors each time the diamond sweeps its arm past the damaged section. I very much suspect that won't be the end of it." He sorted a stack of plates. "Based on what happened in False Clickspring, it could lead to the complete destruction of the Greater Lands. Steadily increasing severity of the tremors. Slow failure of the influence over the land. If we are very fortunate, the damage will be contained by the Greater Lands Wall, but there's an equal chance the failure of the Greater Lands' diamond will have effects that spread well beyond the walls."

"No!" Teya said, scampering up and throwing off the charred leather armor. "Fix it! Martin is smart. Very very."

"I don't know if I have the time," Martin said. "It took me most of the last eighteen hours to prepare for the change Lens had intended to make. And that was with things working properly. Each sweep of those arms across the damaged plates will change the amount of repair that's needed. It will be irreparable, or at least beyond my capacity for repair, within just a few rotations."

"So work fast, Dad," Fel said.

"It isn't a matter of mere speed, Fel. Lens had to rob the vault in Teskal to get the materials necessary to make the plates we have. It might take months to find enough of those materials to make the right replacement plates to put things back as they were. And again, it could all become pointless after just a few rotations."

"So don't put it back the way it was. Make it something new."

"The only complete set of replacement plates are those I was forced to prepare for Lens. You aren't suggesting we do as Lens desired," Martin said.

"I... Slavery is better than death, right?" Fel said, agonized to even hear the words leave his mouth.

"Not very," Teya said firmly.

"Is there... I don't know, a compromise?" Fel said.

"Take these plates. All of them. Everyone help me get them to where the damage is done. And Fel, wrangle Oiler. We don't need it making the decision of what repair is to be done before we select it."

Fel found and shouldered Oiler, who was already eying up the fallen Guardian like a child given full run of a candy store. The kobolds scrambled to help Martin get the plates into position just outside the damaged portion of the ring. The master contraptioneer stood in silence, eyes dancing across the array of plates. The click and rattle of the clockwork diamond counted off the precious seconds remaining.

"I hate to rush you, Dad, but—"

Martin held up a hand to silence him. "This needs to be done properly or it may as well not be done at all."

Fel glanced around. Kazel gazed in stoic intensity over the wall. Nearly thirty kobolds watched, vibrating with anxiety. And still, Martin stood. Silent. Thinking. After the longest minute of their collective lives, he folded his arms and nodded.

"With the parts we have and the time we have, there are three choices. We can do as Lens required. Not an option. But picking through his parts and picking from those that are undamaged, we may be able to render something similar to what we have now. The damaged portion deals with the precise mechanism of keeping the Greater Mystics separate from the rest of us. Our options are to wipe it entirely away. To render every Greater Mystic equivalent to those present here today, freely capable of crossing the wall. Or we can make the effect symmetrical. The Greater Lands and all within it will be snuffed from our minds beyond the wall just as the world beyond is snuffed from theirs. Lesser Mystics as well. And quite likely anything with a mixed ancestry. The world beyond the wall will be entirely, for lack of a better word, mundane, and all who are mystic in the slightest will find themselves drawn here, never to return."

"So we can either conquer, come together, or go our separate ways," Fel said.

"Subjugation, separation, or integration," Martin said with a nod.

Fel turned to the kobolds, and to Kazel. "We are about to make a choice that changes the world. I'm sure not making it alone."

"I worry that our world will suffer greatly if the more potent Greater Mystics are freely able to access it," Martin said. "It may be better for all of us if we forget each other."

"So long as those of my world may live their lives without rule by yours, I am satisfied," Kazel said.

The kobolds nodded, as though Kazel's words were their own.

"More friends, more better," Teya decreed, poking Fel in the chest. "Least worst friend. No goodbye."

"Wick?" Tome asked.

"I will serve faithfully regardless."

"Go ask the others," Fel said.

"No. We don't have time," Martin said.

"But it's one vote for isolation, one vote for integration, and two votes for basically either. That leaves the decision to me! I just said—"

"Time is running out," Martin said as the sound of the swinging arms grew louder with their approach.

Fel tightened his fists. At times like this, he'd learned that thinking would only make things worse. He let his heart and his impulses have their way with the riddle, and the winner was his inner contrarian. Lens had wanted to conquer them. The creators of the diamond wanted it to separate them. And one option stood as the furthest thing from either of those.

"I hope the world is ready for a little more excitement. Integration it is."

"So be it," Martin said. "Oiler, down. Teya, we're pulling all the plates that look like this. They'll be in threes. Have your friends line up these three plates, in any order, in front of each gap you create like that. There should be enough to fill them all with nine spares. Fel, set Oiler at the right end of this ring. Watch how it replaces the missing plates with the new ones. Then all of us, as quickly as possible, match that same order in each gap. Go. Now."

They rushed into action. The diamond rattled and clicked relentlessly. Kobolds received chattered orders from Teya and swarmed over the plates. Oiler inspected the parts presented and selected them one by one. Cunning paws and shaking hands clicked plates into place in the same order, hastily filling gaps from right to left. The arms rattled around, sweeping over the plates as they were replaced. Five gaps remained. Now three. The arm clicked closer. Martin knelt at the final gap and pressed the plates into place. He pulled his fingers clear a heartbeat before the arm swept over. There was no rumble, no rattle. Nothing seemed different at all.

"Is that it?" Fel asked. "Did we do it?"

"I believe so. The old way had centuries of momentum behind it. The effects will linger for a few weeks. Perhaps a month. Then, the wall will merely be a wall."

"All right. All right... Now, let's say in a month or two, we decide we made a big, big mistake just now. Can we fix it?"

"If we can find the right materials, and we can once again return to this place, then it is possible. But it will take time."

"Let's get to work on that. Just in case." Fel turned to Kazel. "Any chance you and yours can convince any would-be rabble-rousers not to rouse any rabble?"

"I shall endeavor to encourage peace, provided you can do the same."

Fel nodded and rubbed his face. "I guess we're all going to find out. But for now, I think it's time to go home."

EPILOGUE

Six Weeks Later...

Fel and Tem sat at the grum table. The Fox and Log had never been so packed. After a long delay that most of the people in the room would never fully understand, the final game of the tournament was underway. Fel had almost forfeit. The first issue had been the mere fact that the tournament was supposed to be completed two weeks from the previous game, not six. But threatening to drop out had convinced Tem to allow things to be rescheduled. Then there was the cost. The family shop had needed extensive repairs, and even with the heaps of artifacts he'd brought back from Clickspring and the Greater Lands Wall, dumping a few thousand duots on the table for the purpose of a stupid game hardly seemed appropriate. Having the gratitude of a dragon who now had access to the horde of *another* dragon was a highly desirable position to be in. A handful of very old coins had convinced Fel and the family that some foolish expenditure might be acceptable.

"I don't care how much you want to see what's going on, no standing on the bar! What are you, apes?" Allie shouted, slapping an overeager spectator with a rag. "Fel, Tem, if you're toying with each other, cut it out. The extra business is welcome, but enough's enough."

Everyone had expected it to be a single game. Tem and Fel were aggressive players, and the extra delay had provided ample time for additional trash talk to build tension. But they were deep into the fifth run, with the pile of chips sliding back and forth across the table seemingly with each game. Presently, Fel was behind, considering the tiles up for bid.

"No shame in giving it up, you know," Tem jabbed. "You're just prolonging the inevitable."

"Seven hundred duots," Fel said. "For the black milkmaid."

Tome, leaning heavily on a cane as he lurked behind Fel, shook his head.

"You're making a mistake," he warned.

"You already failed out of this tournament. No advice from losers," Fel grumbled.

"Yeah," said Madge from her seat at the bar, crumbs of a meat pie sprinkling those around her as she spoke. "Let the man play!"

"You're certainly paying a *lot* of money for a very poor tile," Tem said. "Which means you've got a trash hand and you're trying to salvage it. And we can't have that, can we? Eight hundred."

"Nine hundred," Fel said quickly.

"Good heavens. Desperation, eh? A thousand."

"Take it," Fel said.

A stack of coins joined the pot.

The final tile turned over.

"Hah. Blue milkmaid," Tem said. "Eager for that one too?"

"Pass," Fel said with a resigned air.

"Ooh... That's the face of a man who knows he's lost. Much as this would go nicely with the rather pricey black milkmaid I've *just* acquired, I think it's long past time to put this one out to pasture. Shall we show our runs?"

"Let's get it over with," Fel said.

He didn't wait for Tem to flop his tile down before flopping his own. The spectators rumbled. It wasn't a good run, but it was a solid one. All three queens. All three black-smiths. The eyes turned to Tem. He cleared his throat and brushed at his tiles, rearranging them. From his face, he knew he didn't have it. He flipped the tiles down. Three kings. Two milkmaids, and one queen. It wasn't enough.

"Fel takes the pot!" crowed Epiphany. "And if Tem had actually bought the third milkmaid, it would have gone the other way!"

"That's seven thousand eight hundred fifty for him now. A healthy lead," Euphoria said.

"Fine, fine. Let's get the next run dealt," Tem said.

Fel piled his winnings into neat stacks. "I think I'll call it here," he said.

"Call it... *Call it?* I still have money for the ante. What if I'd decided to call it after that last run?" Tem said.

"Then you'd have been the winner."

"It's winner take all!" Tem said.

Fel shook his head. "Nope. It was a five-thousand-duot buy-in. No one said anything about this last game being winner take all."

"But I... But you... What's the point of playing if you can't have the whole pot!?"

"The point? The point is I'm up over two thousand, and I just showed this whole room I can play you like a fiddle. Squeezed the difference out of you by getting you to buy a tile you didn't need, then got you to pass on the one that could have got you the win," Fel said. "I'm the better player, and I don't need to break you to prove it."

Tem stood. "If you walk away with that money now, when I still had a chance to beat you, you're admitting you're afraid of me. You're admitting that *I'm* the better player."

Fel shrugged. "Fair enough." He turned to the crowd. "Folks! That man, who just got played out of coughing up the majority of the pot in a losing hand of grum, is the better player and I'm too scared to face him. I'll just have to live with winning the tournament and a pile of money. Tem can have the trophy, though."

"You heard the man. We have a winner! Settle up your bets, settle up your tabs, and make room for some proper drinkers," Allie proclaimed.

The tavern erupted. By the time Fel made it out the door, his back was sore from congratulatory slaps and he'd turned down several gallons worth of victory drinks.

"Ladies, gentlemen! I appreciate it, but I have a heap of money and I'd rather get home with it. Not that I don't trust you all, but I don't trust you all."

He stumbled out the door. A moment later, Mariss sidled out.

"Congratulations!" she said with a hug. "I never thought a silly little game of pushing tiles around could be so exciting!"

"Thanks! Yeah. Turns out it's more about who has the steadier nerves."

"It's getting late. I should get home. Don't forget! Tomorrow is our supper together. Allie is picking the place this time. It's *sure* to be a place I've never been. Exciting!"

"I wouldn't miss it," Fel said. "Oh. And do you have the stuff?"

She giggled. "Always."

She passed him a hefty sack that still smelled faintly of yeast and sugar despite spending a very rowdy hour in a crowded tavern. "See you soon!" she said brightly.

"Until then. You sure you don't need me to walk you?"

A flap on the bottom of the tavern door swung open, and Parch trotted out.

"See you soon too, cutie!" Mariss said, crouching to tousle the unicorn's ears. "And no, Fel. I found a very nice fellow just a few doors down to watch my cart. I'll be riding home. Be safe!"

"You too!"

As Mariss headed off, Fel glared at Parch. "I still can't believe Allie installed that for you."

He paced toward the shop. Six weeks had been time enough for Beffshire to lick its wounds. Most of the damage done by the automatons and the quake had been patched up, now visible mostly as a bit of new wood or stone here and there.

"Fel!" called Allie from behind him.

He turned to find her trotting toward him. "What are you doing outside of that tavern while it's packed?"

"Giving Oovay a taste of the medicine he's been giving me for too long. Figured I'd walk you home after that little performance," she said.

"You can trust him to handle that?"

"Believe it or not, he's actually shaping up to be something resembling a reliable bartender. I guess he finally realized how much money you can make by actually doing the job well."

"Having a good boss will do that."

She punched him in the arm. "Don't you ever call me that again."

"You run the tavern! What else am I going to call you?"

"I'm still tending the bar. I'm still a bartender. Just because Verfessa's too busy in the capital to handle the purse strings of the place doesn't mean I have to take on a filthy title like 'boss.'"

"So are they going to make him a lord or what?"

"You didn't hear? They made a whole new title. 'Vanguard.'"

"What's that give him?"

"The obligation to 'safely utilize' the tunnels."

"Oof. I can't wait to see what form *that* takes."

"And in the meantime, I'm on the deed as the operator of The Fox and Log so he doesn't have to deal with the day-to-day stuff. At least it gives me the opportunity to step away and know I'm still making *some* money, so long as the place doesn't fall apart. So how has the shop been?"

"Finally got the windows replaced. Back to business in full."

"Right. Sure. But how has the *shop* been."

"We're getting there. Not as good as we were before but better than I expected. A couple of out-of-control contraptions running amok through town has a way of putting a bad taste in people's mouths when it comes to having a place that sells them right next door.

But Dad volunteering to be taken away to protect the others goes a long way toward earning back that goodwill. Plus, you know, coming back alive. You'd be amazed how much 'those things couldn't kill him' counterbalances 'I'm worried he'll make things that'll kill me.'"

She stepped a little closer. "Any news from the Greater Lands?"

"No news is good news. Seems like Kazel's as good as his word. He's been keeping the peace down there. A couple of centuries is a long time to get cozy. Maybe we'll get lucky and they'll just stay put."

She gave him a look.

"Yeah, I know," he said. "So far the only side effect is Teya's been using those tunnels like her own personal highway to bring her kobold friends to visit. Gotta say. They're growing on me. Turns out a bunch of them are carving out their own little kingdom in the place in Fenfield, selling ore and such to Euphoria and Dad. But otherwise, the calm before the storm."

"We should appreciate the peace while we can get it."

"Speak for yourself. Tome's old man got the index translated, and we have a list of the first seven hundred books or so that need to be transcribed. So now Wick is writing morning, noon, and night."

"Writing doesn't sound like a very noisy pursuit."

"It is when it's an automaton doing it, with my dad ooh-ing and aah-ing at every new word like it was a performance."

"You can always stop by my place," she said.

"Why? Having trouble sleeping?" he said with a snort.

She punched him in the arm again, then threw her arm around him. "Seriously. Stop by."

"When are you through at the tavern?"

"Whenever I like."

"So, closing then."

"... Yes."

"See you then."

She craned her neck to give him a kiss and hurried back to the tavern.

Fel's heart was still fluttering as he approached the shop.

"Rotten *stinking* family," croaked the welcoming committee.

"Good to see you too," Fel said, opening the sack. "Courtesy of Mariss, naturally."

They politely selected one each, then gulped it down, then squabbled for the rest. He watched the show for a bit, then slipped inside.

"How did the game go?" Vivian asked.

Fel sighed and looked over the freshly rebuilt store, then set the sack of winnings down. "This was it. The big win, Mom. The big win."

FROM JOSEPH R. LALLO

Thank you for reading! If you liked this story, or perhaps if you found it lacking, I'd love to hear from you. For free stories and important updates, join my newsletter at: www.bookofdeacon.com

Discover other titles by Joseph R. Lallo:

The Book of Deacon Series

An epic fantasy series spanning six main novels and assorted spin-offs and prequels. Follow the journey of Myranda Celeste and the rest of the Chosen as they fight to save their world from a terrible war and its aftermath.

The Big Sigma Series

A sci-fi action adventure series with six novels. Trevor "Lex" Alexander is a former hover-racer who finds his world turned upside down when he becomes embroiled in the schemes of mega-corporations, criminal syndicates, and a mad engineer with a quirky AI.

The Free-Wrench Series

Take to the skies in this six novel steampunk series about airships in an era of steam, brass, and excitement. Nita Graus joins the Wind Breaker crew, a group of smugglers in a constant clash with the twisted and nefarious fug folk who run the world from their place in the toxic mists that blanket the land.

The Shards of Shadow Series

An ongoing Urban Fantasy series following the trials and tribulations of a photographer named Alan who unwittingly becomes entangled in the dark machinations of the shadowy shades thanks to Blot, one of their weakest agents. These exciting stories take place in modern day Philadelphia and shed light on the supernatural invasion that could tip the balance of power for the entire world.

The Greater Lands Saga

An epic fantasy adventure in a world where magic and supernatural contraptions coexist. Fel Masker is an explorer and adventurer, tasked with securing mysterious, arcane devices for his family to repair and sell. Rivalries with other contraptioneering families are heating up, and soon the lost history of the world may return with a vengeance.